SALBINE'S EMBRACE

Sarah Ettritch

Norn Publishing
Kingston, Canada

ISBN: 978-1-927369-59-3

This is a work of fiction. Names, characters, places, and incidents are the product of the author's imagination and are used fictitiously, and any resemblance to actual persons, living or dead, business establishments, events, or locales is entirely coincidental.

Published by Norn Publishing
Kingston, Ontario, Canada
www.nornpublishing.com

V1.0

1

Emmey set her quill on the writing podium so she could scrutinize the page she was scribing without smudging her copy of it. Was the first letter in the word an *e* or an *o*? An *e* would be *ear*, and an *o* would be *oar*. She couldn't decide from the context and wished the original scribe's script wasn't so tiny. Mistress Averill insisted that all her scribes write their letters "a little larger than feels natural." One of the former head scribes at the—Emmey flipped to the first page in the slim book—Redworth monastery hadn't directed her scribes to do the same. How had the book ended up in Merrin's library? Perhaps a visiting sister had forgotten it.

Returning to the last page in the book, Emmey squinted at the letter again, then picked up her quill and scribed a larger-than-natural *o*. The original letter had a faint mark inside the *o* near its top, but it didn't extend all the way to the other side of the letter. It would have helped if the poems Emmey was copying had lines that rhymed, or at least sounded coherent. This poem made no sense to her, making her wonder if some of the original wording had changed with each copy. Either that, or Sister Annora, the poet, had been addled.

She scribed the last line in the poem, and then the last line in the book, a familiar line that she instantly recognized, even though some of the letters were ambiguous. *Thanks be to Salbine.*

Satisfied, Emmey set down her quill again. Her surroundings came into focus. She lost track of everything when she scribed. Her sense of time, the stale air she breathed in Mistress Averill's office, the dust particles that danced in the sunlight shafting in through the window, the scratching of Mistress Averill's quill as she scribed next to Emmey, though Emmey could hear it now and turned to her.

"I'm finished," she said proudly. But then she remembered, and her shoulders sagged.

Mistress Averill lifted her quill and surveyed Emmey's work. "Excellent," she murmured.

Despite her sadness, Emmey's chest swelled. She had one last step to complete before Mistress Averill could bind all the pages into a proper book. "What should I scribe on the title page?"

"What do you mean?"

Emmey returned to the first page in the original book and tapped the scribe's name, the one whose tiny script had made her want to scream at times. "I scribed this whole book myself, so should I scribe my name at the front?" She'd never scribed an entire book before. She'd always done a page here and there, when Sister Clara or Sister Elouise was ill or taking too long to finish a book. When Mistress Averill had handed her the poetry book and told her to scribe it from front to back, Emmey had seen it as an acknowledgement of her skill, but now she wondered if it was something of a going away present. Either way, she'd enjoyed every minute of it, despite her frustration. "Should I scribe, 'Emmey, of the Merrin monastery'?"

"Oh." Mistress Averill put down her quill and twisted on her stool to face Emmey. "I don't know. If you were a sister, you'd scribe your name, but that's because we have a tome for every sister who's ever belonged to the Order." She swept her arm toward the door that led to the library's second floor. "If a scribe or scholar wants to learn more about the sister who scribed a book, she merely has to read the sister's tome. It can be important, you see. Some scribes allow their biases to influence the letters they see on the page."

"You mean they don't write the word that's there? They write something they know is wrong?"

"They don't deliberately make a mistake. But when a word isn't clear, their interpretation can be clouded by who they are."

Emmey was sure she'd never changed a letter or word on purpose. But with the book of poetry she'd just finished, how would she tell? None of it had made sense.

"Of course, you can always add notes to the back of any book you scribe, explaining your choices. But sometimes a scribe doesn't do so, or doesn't even realize she made a choice, and that's when her tome can be useful. We don't have a tome for you."

"And so I can't scribe my name, even though I was the scribe?" Emmey swallowed. "It will be as if I was never here."

The mistress's brow puckered. "That doesn't feel right to me. Let me speak to the abbess."

The chapel bells struck five. Emmey wiped her fingers with a damp rag and slid off her stool. "I have to go. I'm having supper with the abbess." And Maddy and Lillian and Elizabeth. She couldn't wait to tell them she'd scribed a book all by herself. Hopefully they wouldn't ask her to recite any of the poems. She doubted she could do it without giggling.

"The scribes from Hedgerow arrive tomorrow," Mistress Averill reminded her. "It means we won't be able to scribe together for a while."

The mistress meant never again. The visiting scribes planned to stay for a month. Emmey would turn fourteen in three weeks, so she'd be gone by the time the scribes left. She'd no longer climb the stone steps to the top of the Mistresses 'Tower and gaze out at the stars, and if she squinted hard enough, see the bobbing of torches and the pinprick lights of burning candles in Merrin. She'd no longer sit in front of the fire with Maddy and Lillian, listen to their muffled voices as she lay in bed, help Maddy—

Her fingernails dug into her palms. Stupid rules! Why did she have to leave when she turned fourteen? She'd lived here for almost six years. Six bloody years. The monastery hadn't fallen into chaos. Salbine hadn't struck Sophia down for allowing her to stay. So why? Why would she be torn away from the people she loved more than she could express? Why would she have to leave the women who'd saved her life? Emmey couldn't bear the thought of life without Maddy and Lillian, but stupid rules were stupid rules.

Mistress Averill's voice broke into her thoughts. "It's bad timing, I know."

Emmey avoided the mistress's eyes, worried that her own would tear up. "I have to go, or I'll be late." She hitched up the plain brown robe she wore and hurried from the office.

~

MADDY LEANED BACK IN her chair and nodded when Sophia offered to pour her a mug of warm cider. At this table, sitting between Lillian and Emmey and across from Sophia and Elizabeth, she could almost forget the crushing loss bearing down on her. Her belly was full, the roaring fire in Sophia and Elizabeth's sitting room cast a comforting glow, and she had a busy day ahead of her tomorrow, one that would see her serving the Order and her goddess. But a dark cloud hung over everything she did, especially with Emmey. Everything would soon be a "last": the last time they went to the market together, the last time they ate breakfast together, the last time they prayed together, the last time they laughed together. Maddy's stomach felt permanently clenched. She thanked Salbine for the three women at the table with her. She'd cry a river of tears on their shoulders.

For now, she'd try to enjoy herself. She wanted to put her hand on Lillian's leg while drinking her cider, but having only one hand, that would be difficult. She'd grown used to doing things sequentially. She sipped the cider, letting the warm liquid linger on her tongue before swallowing, then she put the mug down and rested her hand on Lillian's leg. She almost smiled when Lillian's hand covered hers.

"Can I have some cider?" Emmey asked.

Sophia gave her a pointed look. "No."

"Can I leave, then? I want to water one of my gardens before evening prayers."

Everyone looked to Maddy. "If you get dirt on your robe, make sure you change it," Maddy said, remembering the time Emmey had arrived at the chapel looking as if she'd crawled through muck to get there.

"I will."

"See you at prayers," Sophia said. Everyone murmured a good-bye.

When Emmey was almost at the door, Maddy called, "Wait!" She went to her and gave her a quick hug. "Don't be late."

Emmey nodded and left. Too restless to sit again, Maddy collected her cider and stood by the fire. "She'll miss her garden."

"They have gardens outside the monastery," Lillian said.

"I know they do, but it won't be the same." Emmey wouldn't be here, surrounded by the monastery's walls and those who loved her. She'd be out there, in Merrin, unless she married a traveller and went home with him or wanted to get as far away from the monastery as she could.

Tears prickled at Maddy's eyelashes, a regular occurrence lately. Hoping nobody had noticed, she set her cider on the mantel and quickly brushed her tears away. If she thought it would make a difference, she'd beg Sophia to let Emmey stay, but Sophia had already stretched the rules so Emmey could be here in the first place and would be almost as devastated as Maddy when Emmey left.

As if reading her mind, Sophia said, "I didn't realize what we were getting ourselves into when I negotiated the agreement with that horrid duke."

Elizabeth's brows rose. "You thought you'd remain detached."

"Rather naïve of me, wasn't it? And now, here we are."

Lillian shifted in her chair. "You weren't naïve. I thought the same thing—at first." Her voice grew soft, wistful. "By the time we arrived at the monastery with her, I'd somehow grown fond of her."

And, Maddy knew, had come to dearly love her. They all had to find a way to let go of the girl who'd stolen their hearts and enriched their lives.

Sophia heaved a sigh. "I was going to ask to meet with you tomorrow, but now that Emmey's gone, I might as well tell you now. I've narrowed it down to three families."

Maddy sat back down at the table, then inwardly groaned. She'd left her cider on the mantel. "I hope one isn't the Carmichaels. They're decent folk, but Emmey would only be one of many workers."

"She's a bit old for the Carmichaels now, and we've already disappointed them once," Sophia said with a chuckle.

Normally Maddy would have felt some guilt over breaking an arrangement, but not the one Sophia had made with the Carmichaels before Duke Bradford had arrived at the monastery with the intention of throwing Emmey into prison again. Instead, Emmey had served her sentence here, at the monastery. She'd complete her penance in three weeks. Three short weeks.

"The three families are the Abernathys, the McMillans, and the Stephensons," Sophia said. "They're all open to taking Emmey on."

Mr. Abernathy ran a bakery, the McMillans, a tailor and a seamstress, sold clothes, and Maddy believed the Stephensons were cleaners. "I don't think she'll want to clean."

"I'll ask her when I speak to her about it, which I intend to do tomorrow. I wanted to tell you first."

"She loves scribing."

"Only men scribe outside the walls."

"I'm just saying that's her first love." Scribing and reading. Emmey had taken to both like a duck to water. She spent hours in the library, and Mistress Averill indulged Emmey's love of reading by allowing her to borrow some of the stories sisters had written. Emmey always promised to care for the tomes, and she always did, treating them as the precious treasures they were to her. If she took the robe, she'd be a scribe, and perhaps head scribe one day. But to join the Order, she had to be marked by Salbine and dedicate her life to the goddess. Emmey had never said anything that suggested she was marked. Surely if she were, she'd shout it from the rooftops. It would mean she could stay, assuming Sophia allowed her to remain here until she turned sixteen and became a novice. Maddy was sure she would. What purpose would it serve to force Emmey to live outside the walls for two years?

"What about gardening, then?" she said to Sophia. "That's her second love."

Sophia gazed at Lillian. "I know she grows herbs, but I thought you were making her do it."

"Me?" Lillian shook her head. "She does it because she wants to."

"For you."

"I don't know, Sophia. I haven't asked her."

Maddy wasn't sure either, but Emmey seemed to enjoy planting and harvesting herbs and flowers. She'd never shown any interest in baking and always had to be reminded to tidy her chamber, though when Maddy had been Emmey's age, she'd been the same. Emmey was a competent sewer and often patched their clothes, something Maddy couldn't do with one hand. "Out of the three you've suggested, she'd like sewing the best."

"But you think gardening might suit her even better," Sophia stated.

"Yes."

"I'll ask her about it. I want to do the best for her."

Normally Maddy would thank her, but the words wouldn't come. She would try to feel a speck of gratitude toward the family who offered Emmey a home and vocation, but despite praying about it every morning and night, and every time she was on her knees in the chapel, all she felt was resentment and sorrow.

Under the table, Lillian gripped Maddy's fingers. "When will she have to go?"

Sophia lifted her mug but didn't drink from it. "Not too long after she turns fourteen. Within a week, I think." She gripped the mug, her knuckles white. "We don't want to prolong the inevitable, do we?"

A mere month and Emmey would be gone. The thought took Maddy's breath away. She wanted to rest her head on the table and pretend it wasn't happening.

Elizabeth rubbed Sophia's back. "Our suppers certainly won't be the same."

A gloomy silence settled over them. Maddy couldn't see them ever getting past Emmey's absence.

"I'd imagine the novices are excited," Lillian said.

Maddy wanted to hug her. Lillian didn't care one bit about how the novices were feeling about taking their vows and having the backs of their hands tattooed with red branches, a visible representation of Salbine's mark.

Seizing the opportunity to think and talk about something else, Maddy did her best to sound enthusiastic. "It's a big step, and I'm pleased to say that nobody is thinking about backing out and leaving. They're looking forward to moving to the Initiates Tower."

Maddy was a mentor to the novices, someone they could talk to, share their triumphs and fears and questions with, and pray with when they were going through a rough patch. She would continue to mentor them until it was time for them to take the next step on their journey to becoming mages: learning how to draw elemental fire, air, water, and earth.

When Maddy had discovered that she couldn't draw the elements, the only Salbine sister alive who hadn't received Salbine's gifts, she'd struggled not to feel resentful of her fellow initiates. To research her malflowed condition, she'd set out for another monastery that held the journals of a long-dead sister who'd also been denied the gifts.

She hadn't reached the monastery. She'd ended up in prison and lost her right hand and part of her right arm. But she'd returned with Emmey and a new purpose. After that, her chest had stopped tightening when her friends dashed off to a training room or talked about their progress with one of the elements.

Maddy had built a new life for herself in the Order. In addition to caring for Emmey, she worked in the adepts' Monday clinic, embroidered using the special frame one of the carpenters had built for her, and regularly went to the market. The townsfolk trusted the sister who couldn't draw the elements. Maddy had worried they'd pity her, but they'd embraced and respected her. She was like them.

Word had gotten around that the kind sister who always stopped to listen when she was in town also read the petitions folk rolled, sealed, and inserted into the petition box that stood outside the monastery's main gate. In recent years, the number of missives had jumped almost twofold. Maddy occasionally unrolled a parchment and discovered a letter that read and appeared as if a child had scribed it, though she knew the letters had been composed by an adult hand. Most people recognized a word or three, like *tax*, and *road*, and *Salbine*. They drew pictures for the words they didn't know, and so the petitions usually consisted of numerous tiny sketches interspersed with the odd word. She quite enjoyed reading them; she usually had to puzzle out what they were trying to say. She suspected such letters were scribed with great effort, and in private.

Anyone watching her from the outside would see a busy and contented sister who contributed in important ways to her community. Maddy wouldn't disagree with them. But now that Emmey would soon turn fourteen and leave the monastery, her malflowness was taunting her again. She'd accepted her condition and no longer resented it, but she still wondered what she'd done to earn Salbine's wrath. She must have done *something*, but try as she might, she couldn't figure out what had angered her goddess, despite recalling every bad thing she'd ever said and done.

She squared her shoulders. "I'm going to speak to Mistress Averill about the material we received from the other monasteries."

Everyone blinked at her, confused by the abrupt change of subject. "What material?" Elizabeth asked.

"About malflowed sisters." Before Maddy had left on her ill-fated journey, Sophia had written to the other monasteries, asking whether their libraries held anything that would shed light on the malflowed condition. Several monasteries had replied in the affirmative, Heath chief among them. While Maddy was away, scribes at monasteries other than Heath had copied the material and sent it to Merrin.

When Mistress Averill had told her about the documents, Maddy had said she wasn't ready to see them. Having returned to the monastery only a couple of weeks earlier, she'd wanted to focus on Emmey and learning to live with only one hand. She'd expected to read the material a few months later, but the longer she'd left it, the more she'd dreaded it. The documents would only consist of dry after dry passage and were unlikely to tell Maddy anything she didn't already know. She'd tucked the material's existence away in the back of her mind, until now, when it was at the forefront again, along with questions about her condition.

"It's time I read it," she said to the others. "I wasn't expecting to wait almost six years, but I've been busy." If any of them thought she might have had another reason for waiting, they didn't say so.

Sophia grimaced. "Is that wise, reading it now, when . . . "

"When I feel like throwing myself off the top of one of the towers? It's the best time. I won't be able to feel any worse."

"It might help you."

Maddy doubted it. "Will you read it with me?" she asked Lillian.

"Do you want me to?"

"Yes, I do."

"Then I will. I'm curious about the condition myself."

Maddy knew Lillian meant it in the best possible way. Lillian's eyes always burned with curiosity, one of the reasons Maddy loved her.

Poor Lillian. Her usually cheerful consort was about to become someone who moped around with red-rimmed eyes and gazed wistfully at Emmey's bedchamber door. Only it wouldn't be her door anymore, would it? It would be the door to an empty chamber, one where the stones had grown cold and candles never burned. It would feel dead, as Maddy would.

2

EMMEY'S FINGERS GRAZED THE stone wall as she followed Maddy along the hall. "You're dreaming!" a voice—her voice— shouted in her head. Yet it felt so real, just as it had all the other times. Shadows cast from the flickering torches danced along the walls, and when she glanced at her knuckles, she could see where the stone had scratched them.

Dreading what was coming, she drew a deep breath. When they turned a corner into the hall that led to the chamber, she wanted to cry, scream, grab Maddy's robe and beg her to stop. But she was trapped, forced to enact the same horrible events once again.

They approached the chamber. Flames flickered inside it. "Don't, Maddy, please," Emmey hissed. Why did she have to suffer through this over and over again?

Suddenly they stood only several paces away from the chamber doorway. Despite the raging fire, Emmey's hands and face felt like ice. Maddy fell to her knees. Her mouth moved, her words coming too quickly for Emmey to make them out.

Emmey silently said her own prayer. *Please, Salbine. If you have any influence in the world of dreams, please stop her. I know it's only a dream, but I can't bear to see her do this. I can't.*

Maddy lifted her head and stood, the glow from the fire silhouetting her profile. "I'll be fine," she said flatly.

No! No, she wouldn't. Maddy walked toward the chamber. Emmey grabbed the back of Maddy's robe with both hands, tugged as hard as she could, but Maddy shook her away as if she were a flea.

"Maddy, don't!"

Maddy stepped across the threshold. Emmey did what she always did at this point. Turned away. Squeezed her eyes shut. Chided herself for not plunging into the fire to rescue her. Hadn't Maddy saved her all those years ago? She'd lost her hand as thanks. Yet here Emmey stood, shaking and mumbling a prayer and clapping her hands over her ears so she wouldn't have to listen to Maddy's screams.

Light and colour assaulted Emmey's eyes. The smoke from cooking fires wrinkled her nose, and the faint strains of a lute floated above the peddlers' shouted invitations to examine their wares. Disoriented, Emmey took a moment to get her bearings. She was in the market, but none of the merchants were familiar. Duncan's stall should be to her left, and Evie's stall should be next to it. "This isn't right," she said.

"What do you mean?" someone shouted.

Emmey jumped and whirled to Rose in surprise. Rose never shouted.

"Have you come to see her burn?" Rose asked.

"What?"

"Have you come to see Maddy burn?"

"What?"

Rose pointed.

Dread enveloped Emmey, crushing her chest and making her gasp for air. She didn't want to look but did so anyway, then wished she hadn't. Maddy was enveloped in flame, jerking and jumping like a puppet controlled by a novice puppeteer.

"Maddy!" Emmey ran to her.

The heat from the flames prevented her from getting too close, but now she could hear Maddy, hear her screams of anguish. "I'm on fire! I'm on fire! I'm on fire!"

"Stop it!"

"I'm on fire!"

"Stop! I'm dreaming," Emmey sobbed. "It's a dream."

But the heat of the fire warmed her skin, and now the rancid smell of burning flesh clogged her nose. Emmey fell to her knees and gagged. "Stop it. Please."

A cool breeze washed over her. She lifted her head. Maddy lay on the cobblestones, blackened and charred. Tears welled in Emmey's eyes. She scrambled over to Maddy on her hands and knees and—

Maddy rolled over and grabbed Emmey with her right hand, her grip surprisingly firm. "You're not listening to me, girl," she rasped.

Emmey screamed—and sat up. Blood pounded in her ears. As her eyes adjusted to the surrounding darkness, she gulped down air and waited for her heart to stop racing. *It was just a dream.* Listening for sounds of movement, she gripped her familiar woolen blanket, twisted it in her hands. Nobody was stirring, which meant she hadn't actually screamed. Lillian slept through everything, but Maddy sometimes came into her chamber carrying a lamp and stayed until Emmey fell asleep again. She always asked what the bad dream was about, and Emmey always made something up.

The beginning of this dream had been familiar, but the part about the market . . . Emmey swallowed. Maddy burning to death once had been terrifying enough. Now she was dying twice. Emmey lay back and drew the blanket up to her chin, but her eyes were still open when the morning light filtered in through the shutters.

~

IN THE CHAMBERS SHE shared with Maddy and Emmey, Lillian sat in front of the fire, her fingers and toes waking up in its warmth. She'd just returned from early morning prayers, which she attended by herself. When she and Maddy had first pledged, Maddy and Emmey had accompanied her. Lillian chuckled to herself at the memory. Waking up so early hadn't suited either of them. Maddy had sat next to Lillian yawning up a storm, and Emmey had sometimes dozed off.

Eventually Lillian had gone on her own, assuring Maddy that she didn't mind. She couldn't suffer a woman who wanted to be with her every waking moment, but that didn't mean she didn't want to spend time with Maddy. They always saw each other when Lillian returned from early morning prayers, in the communal dining hall for supper, and most evenings. If they could, they squeezed time in during the afternoons too, even if it was just ten minutes in a hallway.

Maddy strode from their bedchamber and stood near the fire. After she finished buttoning the colourful robe she wore, she'd be off to the dining hall for breakfast with Emmey, who sat waiting for her in Maddy's chair, her shoulders slumped. Nobody her age should have dark circles under her eyes and lack energy in the morning.

"You look tired," Lillian said to her.

"You're not sleeping well," Maddy added.

Lillian winced at the catch in Maddy's voice. Not wanting to make things more difficult for Emmey, Maddy was bending over backwards to appear strong, but her sorrow was difficult to mask. Emmey was doing better at appearing stoic. When the horrible day arrived, she'd walk out the gate with a smile on her face and tears in her eyes. She and Lillian were alike in that respect, though Lillian would allow herself one moment of weakness on the day Emmey left. She'd weep with Maddy once, but then she'd need to be strong for her.

To think there was a time when she would have sat in her dreary chambers alone after early morning prayers, listening to the footsteps of the other mistresses as they passed by her door on their way to the chapel or dining hall. Of course, she hadn't thought of her chambers as dreary at the time. They'd been perfectly acceptable to her, but she couldn't have known what she was missing when she didn't have it. Now Maddy's touch was everywhere, in the bright cushions on the chairs, the patterned tapestries hanging on the walls, and the bit of colour Maddy had insisted the seamstresses add to Lillian's newer robes—just a band of red at the sleeves.

But the most valuable additions to Lillian's chambers were Maddy herself, and Emmey. Lillian had never dreamed she'd be sitting here talking to the woman she dearly loved and a girl they deeply cared for, one who'd sneaked into Lillian's heart and nestled within it.

Bloody Salbine Order and its rules, rules Sophia had already bent to keep Emmey here until she turned fourteen. Unless Emmey took the robe, she had to go.

With a sigh, she forced herself to listen to the conversation taking place next to her.

" . . . wants to see you today." Maddy was saying.

"When?"

"She said eleven o'clock."

"Do you know what it's about?"

Maddy hesitated. "She wants to talk to you about what you want to do. It will help her find a family for you."

Emmey grunted and gazed into the fire.

Lillian patted Emmey's leg. "Will you come to the laboratory after breakfast? I need your help this morning."

Emmey perked up. "You need my help?"

Guilt snaked through Lillian. At early morning prayers, Sophia had asked her to come up with a reason for Emmey to gulp down her porridge and leave the dining hall quickly. She wanted to make an announcement when Emmey wasn't there. Lillian had whispered the ruse to Maddy when she'd returned from the prayer service. She always crept into their bedchamber, crouched next to the bed, and roused Maddy with a few gentle kisses.

She wasn't sure what she'd have Emmey do, but she'd come up with something. "I do need your help, and as soon as you can come."

"I can't miss prayers."

"You'll still be able to go to morning prayers. I won't need you for long."

"We'd better get to the dining hall, then." Emmey leaped from the chair. "Are you coming?" she said to Maddy.

Maddy's mouth turned up at the corners. "Can I finish buttoning my robe first, please?"

Emmey tutted and pushed Maddy's hand aside so she could fasten the last three buttons. If it had been anyone else, Maddy's shoulders would have stiffened and she'd bat the other person's hands away. But it was Emmey. Spending time together in a dank prison cell had bonded Maddy to Emmey in a way Maddy would never bond with anyone else. Lillian had been jealous of their closeness at first, but she'd quickly realized how immature it was. Maddy's love wasn't finite, and her and Maddy's bond was unique in a different way.

Emmey stood back and patted the three buttons. "There."

"What would I do without you?" Maddy said.

They stared at each other, each holding her breath, the air between them thick with unsaid words. Then Emmey pulled open the door. "We have to go."

"See you later," Maddy said to Lillian over her shoulder.

When the door had closed behind them, Lillian stared into the fire for a minute, then doused it and set off for her laboratory. She'd soon be more grateful than usual for her work area tucked away in the catacombs, where few sisters ventured. She would have a private place to cry.

3

CARRYING A BOWL OF porridge, and with an empty mug for her milk hooked to her index finger, Maddy approached her habitual table in the communal dining hall. She carefully lowered the bowl and mug so that the mug touched the table first. Maddy made sure it was upright before unhooking her finger from it. As sometimes happened, the tip of her thumb dipped into her porridge. She set the bowl down between Rose and Emmey and licked the porridge away, then sat down and filled her mug using one of the milk pitchers on the table.

When Emmey had been just eight years old, she'd offered to carry Maddy's empty mug to the table. So had Rose, and Nora, and Abigail, and numerous other sisters. But Maddy had refused their kind offers. It wasn't difficult to carry and set down the mug and porridge, just time consuming.

Rose's lips curved. "Morning."

"Good morning." Maddy leaned forward to say good morning to Nora, who was naturally on Rose's other side. The two sisters had pledged to each other several years ago.

Emmey's porridge bowl was already half empty and at the rate the spoon was moving from her porridge to her mouth, she'd be rushing off to Lillian's laboratory in no time. Maddy picked up her spoon and dug into her breakfast.

Abigail plunked down across from Nora. Gwendolyn arrived soon after, followed by Grace. "Does anyone know anything about the visiting sisters?" Graced asked.

Abigail reached for the milk pitcher. "Just that they're from Hedgerow."

"*You* might see them today," Rose said to Emmey. "They're scribes."

Emmey shook her head. "I won't be scribing while they're here."

"She completed a book yesterday," Maddy said proudly. "Scribed the whole book by herself."

Rose's brows shot up. "Really? That's quite the accomplishment. Which book?"

"A poetry book by Sister Annora, of the Redworth monastery," Emmey said.

"Perhaps I'll read it."

"I wouldn't. The poems don't make sense."

"There's a lot of symbolism and metaphor and such in poems," Grace said. "You have to look beyond the words."

Gwendolyn rolled her eyes. "If you ask me, they're too much work. When I read, I want to relax, not solve puzzles."

"Yes, well, there are picture books in the library."

Everyone laughed—except Gwendolyn.

"Done!" Emmey snatched her empty bowl and mug from the table. "I'll see you all later. I have to go help Lillian." She rushed off.

"What's Lillian working on?" Rose asked Maddy.

"Nothing unusual. The abbess wants to talk to everyone and doesn't want Emmey here."

A chorus of voices rose around her. "Oh."

"Do tell."

"Is it about her leaving?"

Maddy sipped her milk. Even if she wanted to tell them, she couldn't. She had no idea what Sophia would say. "The abbess will be here soon."

Five minutes later, Sophia arrived. She sometimes ate breakfast in the dining hall, but more often than not, she ate after early morning prayers and was working in her study by the time most sisters yawned their way here. Maddy rose and bobbed along with everyone else.

Sophia stepped onto the raised platform where she and invited guests ate their meals. Because she was rarely in the dining hall for breakfast, the chairs at the head table were usually empty at this hour. "Good morning, Sisters."

"Good morning," everyone replied in unison.

"Please, continue your breakfasts. I'll speak while you eat."

Sophia waited for the rustling of robes and the hiss of curious whispers to subside. "As you all know, Emmey will be leaving us soon."

Dismayed groans filled the dining hall. Rose glanced at Maddy, her eyes sorrowful. Maddy's cheeks burned, even though she was certain nobody felt sorry for her. They felt sad for themselves. Some sisters held Emmey at arm's length, but as far as Maddy knew, nobody resented her presence at the monastery and most sisters had grown close to her.

"I'd like to send her on her way with something to remember us by. Mistress Averill has an idea. If you would, Mistress."

Mistress Averill rose from her usual place and stepped onto the platform. "Good morning. Yesterday, Emmey finished scribing a book from beginning to end."

Now delighted sounds escaped everyone's lips, and when a couple of sisters clapped, everyone else soon joined in, including Maddy, who slapped her leg several times. Mistress Averill grinned and motioned for everyone to settle down. "She asked me if she should scribe her name at the front, as is usually done. I didn't know if she should, because we don't have a tome for her. And she said to me, 'It will be as if I was never here.'"

"Oh, no," several sisters cried. Others shook their heads.

"We don't want that, do we?"

"No," many voices replied.

"She should have a tome, and the abbess agrees. I thought it would be delightful if we all contributed to it, a memory of Emmey, or an observation, or an experience you shared with her."

"Yes," several sisters said. Others whispered excitely to their neighbours.

"Now, limit yourselves to one page. And please scribe two copies. One will go into a tome we'll preserve here at the library, and the other one will go into a tome we'll present to Emmey when she leaves us."

"I know what I'm going to write," Mistress Meredith bellowed. "I'm going to write about the time I found her clomping down the hall in a pair of my shoes."

Gales of laughter echoed around the dining hall. Maddy joined in, especially because Mistress Meredith was laughing too.

Mistress Averill's eyes danced. "That would be perfect. Now, I need time to bind the tomes, so if you would all bring me your pages within three weeks, that would be wonderful." She returned to her place.

"Thank you, Sisters," Sophia said. "We won't keep you from your breakfast any longer."

The moment Sophia left the dining hall, a cacophony of voices replaced the silence. Maddy caught snatches of the conversations around her. Everyone seemed excited about contributing to the tome, which warmed Maddy immensely and brought a lump to her throat.

Rose's brow furrowed. "What a difficult request! How will I manage only one page? There are so many memories and stories I'd love to record. I'll have to think very carefully about what I'll say." Nora, Abigail, and Grace murmured their agreement.

Gwendolyn sipped her milk and eyed those across the table from her over the rim of her mug. "My contribution will be easy. A blank page with my name at the bottom."

Grace and Abigail groaned.

"Salbine give me strength," Nora murmured.

Rose's mouth pinched. "You can be really horrible, you know that?"

Maddy was used to Gwendolyn's abrasive form of teasing; it usually rolled right off her back. But this time, Gwendolyn had gone too far. "Emmey will read the tome." Her voice sounded deceptively calm. "You can be as much of a cow as you like to me, but don't be that way with Emmey."

Gwendolyn huffed an exasperated sigh. "Do none of you have a sense of humour?"

Nora tutted. "Every time I hear someone say that, it's because they know whatever they just said was hurtful."

Rose turned to Nora. "Exactly." Maddy couldn't see her face, but she was sure Rose's expression showed her agreement with Nora's sentiment.

"What *are* you going to write, then, Gwendolyn?" Abigail asked.

"Oh, I don't know," Gwendolyn said. "I'm sure I'll think of something."

"Perhaps you should write about how you helped Emmey when she was struggling with her lute lessons," Grace suggested. "Or how you helped her mend one of her robes when she fell down because she was running where she wasn't supposed to, and she ripped it."

"When did that happen?" Maddy asked.

"A couple of years ago. She didn't want to tell you and get into trouble." Grace turned back to Gwendolyn. "Or you could write about—"

"Yes, yes, all right." Gwendolyn spooned porridge into her mouth. Everyone stared at her for a moment, then raised their brows at each other and continued eating their own breakfasts.

Maddy would have to decide what she'd write for Emmey's tome. She could scribe an entire—no, several tomes herself. She wanted to send Emmey off with many keepsakes, but she'd already decided to let Emmey choose what she'd like to take. Maddy would limit herself to packing a few letters in Emmey's bag, to be opened when Emmey turned a certain age, or before a significant event in her life, such as marrying, or having a babe. What to do with the letters would be up to Emmey. She could ignore the instructions written on the outside of the sealed parchments and open them all at once, save them for the appropriate times, or throw them into a fire. If she kept them and honoured Maddy's instructions, she might not care by the time she broke the seals and read them, the six years she'd spent at the monastery a distant memory, or an interesting story she shared with those she loved about those who no longer lived in her heart.

~

SITTING IN ONE OF the guest chairs in the warm study, Emmey fidgeted while Sophia poured her a cup of tea, using the silver teapot she'd filled with hot water from the kettle that always hung over the fire. The woman tipping the teapot was the abbess to everyone else, but to Emmey, she was Sophia, sister to one of the women who'd taken Emmey in and cared for her. Loved her. Rescued her from a dank cell and given her life. Well, Maddy had rescued her, though Maddy would say they'd saved each other. Emmey knew better. Maddy had been the one doing the rescuing, and so here Emmey was, watching the woman she called Sophia, but only in private. In public, Emmey addressed her as Abbess and bobbed a curtsey along with everyone else.

"There you are." Sophia rose from her chair.

Emmey leaped to her feet. "That's all right, I'll get it." She transferred the teacup from Sophia's desk to the small round table next to the guest chair and sat down again. "I know what you're going to say."

Sophia leaned forward. "Do you?"

"You want me to decide what I want to do, so you can decide where I'll live. If I want to learn to bake, the Abernathys have agreed to take me in. If I want to be a seamstress, the McMillans will have me. If I'm going to be a cleaner, the Stephensons will be my new home."

Amusement brightened Sophia's face. "Did they tell you, or have you been naughty?"

There was no point lying to Sophia. Somehow she always found out. "They talk when they think I'm asleep. They don't notice when I open my chamber door a crack."

"They will when I tell them."

"It won't matter, will it? I won't be here much longer. You're making me leave." As soon as the words were out of her mouth, she regretted them. Sophia blinked rapidly and picked up her teacup. "I'm sorry, but it's true," Emmey said. "You stretched the rules to keep me here. Can't you do it again? I don't want to be a baker, or a seamstress, or a cleaner."

Sophia returned her cup to its saucer and studied Emmey through her spectacles. "You love scribing."

"Very much."

"Only men scribe out there."

Another stupid rule.

"Maddy said you enjoy gardening."

Emmey gulped down some tea, even though it burned her tongue and throat. "I do."

"Are you sure? It seems a bit tame for you."

"I wanted to be a blacksmith, until Mr. Joseph let me pick up the hammer and try to swing it. I almost fell over." She didn't mind being small for her age, but it meant smithing wouldn't be her vocation.

"A blacksmith? I only know of one woman who smiths."

"The only other thing I'd want to do is help with the horses, but I could do both, couldn't I? Grow herbs and help in the stables."

Sophia gazed into her teacup. "Not here."

Her quiet voice threatened to bring tears to Emmey's eyes. She loved it here. The thought of leaving Maddy and Lillian . . . she couldn't think about it, or she'd scream, fall to the ground, cover her head with her hands and weep forever. She'd try to be in the market whenever Maddy would be there, and she hoped Lillian would be there too, but it wouldn't be enough. She wanted to hear Lillian light the fire in the morning and Maddy humming as she dressed, see Lillian hunched over in her chair as she carved, read with Maddy at night using the light of a candle and stroll the grounds with her when the sun was shining. Snatched time at the market would *not* be enough.

"Why can't it be here? Not everyone who works here is a sister. Why can't I stay and scribe?"

"Workers toil here, and they know their place. They certainly don't have access to the library, and only those who've pledged their lives to the Order have free reign inside the towers."

"I could work here, grow herbs."

"We already have all the tradesmen we need. I could make a place for you, but it wouldn't suit you. You'd have to live in the trade area. You wouldn't be allowed inside the towers unless invited, and invitations are only issued for work reasons."

"I don't suppose I can be a defender." Emmey didn't wait for a reply. "I could be marked by Salbine."

Sophia's gaze sharpened. "You've not said anything."

No, she hadn't. She'd had crushes on both boys and girls in town. None had lasted very long, and Susie Blackson had said it wasn't uncommon for both sexes to catch one's eye, but most people settled on one as they got older.

Emmey sipped her tea as she thought back to the breathless conversation she'd had with Susie not long after she'd turned thirteen.

"Do we get to choose?" Emmey had asked her.

Susie had giggled. "No, silly. It'll just happen. When you're older."

Perhaps Emmey was old for her age—like Maddy sometimes said—because she believed she already knew the answer to whether she was marked. It made leaving so much more heart wrenching. A few months ago, she hadn't been sure. But then it had happened. *The crush.* The one that had put all sorts of fantasies into her head and almost made her forget that she'd be pushed outside the gates when she turned fourteen. Which would be doubly horrible, because the crush lived inside the gates. Inside the Novices Tower, to be exact. Every time Emmey crossed paths with Sister Dolores, her mouth stopped working properly and she couldn't meet the sister's eyes. Emmey wasn't so addled by the crush that she believed anything would ever happen between them. Sister Dolores was involved with another novice, and she was too old for Emmey anyway. Nineteen! But Emmey knew one thing for sure. She'd never feel the same way about a boy.

She was marked by Salbine and should be ecstatic. She didn't have to leave! But there was one catch. As much as she wanted to stay and would give almost anything to do so, she wasn't called to be a sister. More than anything she'd ever hoped for, she wished she was. She wouldn't be sitting here talking to Sophia about what she wanted to do outside the monastery. She'd be declaring that she wanted to take the robe.

But she wasn't like Lillian, who hadn't felt called to service but had entered the Order anyway. Emmey believed it all. Everything. Her prayers to Salbine were heartfelt and genuine. The chapel was sacred. The Order was a community for those Salbine had summoned to serve. Emmey didn't fault sisters like Lillian. Whether a sister belonged here was between each sister and Salbine. But Maddy was Emmey's role model. Maddy had taught her about Salbine, about serving, about honesty and respect. Emmey couldn't—wouldn't—take the robe because she wanted to stay with Maddy and Lillian and everyone else she loved here. That wasn't an acceptable reason. It would be disrespectful to Salbine and every sister here to dare to wear a robe when Salbine had not called her to service.

And so she could never, ever tell Maddy and Lillian and Sophia and Elizabeth and Mistress Averill and anyone else who asked that she was marked by Salbine, because they'd want her to stay, and Emmey might give in to temptation and agree. Perhaps Maddy would understand why Emmey still had to leave, but would she truly accept it? Would she be angry and hurt, or believe that Emmey had insisted on leaving anyway because she didn't want to stay with her? Nothing could be more untrue! She would leave because she wanted Maddy to be proud of her. If she stayed, she would never be able to kneel next to Maddy in the chapel again and feel the fellowship with her that she did now. Every time she saw Maddy in her robe, she'd feel as if she were betraying her. No, she might be young, but because of Maddy, she understood service, and integrity, and commitment. It was because she honoured Salbine and loved Maddy so much that she had to leave.

Her devotion to Salbine didn't mean she couldn't question the Order's rules, which were woman made. Some of those rules were bloody stupid, like the one that would arbitrarily push her out the gates because she was fourteen. Well, there wasn't a rule specifically about leaving at fourteen, because normally the rules forbade someone like her from living at the monastery in the first place. But she was here, because compassion and kindness had taken precedence over a rule. Why couldn't it happen again?

"Emmey?" Sophia was still staring at her, waiting for her to say whether she was marked by Salbine.

Emmey set her cup on its saucer. What should she say? She could stretch the truth, say that she was marked and let Sophia assume she'd become a novice, but what would that do? In addition to being an outright lie and terribly disrespectful, it would gain her another year or two—if Sophia agreed to let her stay until she turned sixteen. Then she'd bitterly disappoint everyone and feel worse than she did now, if that were possible. "I don't know yet," she answered, feeling awful for lying. Stupid bloody rules!

Sophia sighed. "Pity."

You could test me, Emmey almost said. Fortunately she bit her tongue in time.

Sophia pursed her lips. "If you truly want to garden—"

"I do."

"I'll try to find you a place where you can do that. But I might not be able to, so think about the other families I've mentioned and decide which one would suit you best."

"Are you sure I can't stay and grow herbs. I'm not just anybody. I know the rules."

"I wish I could stretch the rules again, truly I do. But suppose I did let you stay beyond your fourteenth birthday? When would you leave? You can't live out your life here. When you were younger, you needed our care. But now that you'll be old enough to earn your own keep, you have to leave us. I'm sorry."

So was Emmey. Desperately so. She clenched her hands on her lap. "I'll be gone within a month, then."

Sophia's lips trembled. "Yes." She snatched up her teacup. Tea dribbled over its sides, but she didn't notice. She drank some tea, then set the cup down and gazed into it again.

Emmey couldn't stand it any longer. She went to Sophia and put her arms around her. "You saved me, you know," she said into Sophia's shoulder. Her robe was smoother than Lillian's rough ones, but familiar all the same, in a way that made Emmey's chest hurt.

Sophia pressed her wet cheek to Emmey's and hugged her back.

Emmey didn't want to let go, but she forced herself to. A lump in her throat, she returned to her chair and composed herself. She was supposed to appear stoic about this, to make things easier for everyone she loved. "Can I ask you something?"

"Of course," Sophia said, putting down the handkerchief she'd used to wipe her eyes.

"Have you ever had a dream that's so real, it frightened you?"

Sophia was silent for a moment. "Are you having nightmares?"

Maddy or Lillian must have told her. Emmey lifted her chin. "Sometimes."

"What about?"

Now it was Emmey's turn to hesitate. She'd never wanted to tell Maddy or Lillian because . . . well, why worry them. Even if she didn't name names, they were good guessers. But she needed to tell someone. "Someone gets hurt," she blurted.

"Who?"

"Just someone. You know how in a dream you see people you don't know? We're in a hall together, and it feels so real. I can feel my knuckles grazing the stone." Emmey balled her hands into fists and thrust them in front of her. "And I can smell the smoke rising from the torches. There's a chamber, and all I can see inside are flames. And the person I'm with, she . . . " Emmey's throat tightened. Could she not bloody-well talk about it without the horror gripping her? She cleared her throat. "She walks straight into the fire. I think . . . I think she dies." She stared at her lap.

"It feels real to you."

Emmey lifted her head. "As real as you sitting there now."

"Dreams can feel real, but they're not."

"I keep having the same one!"

"It's a recurring dream. Perhaps you're having it because you'll have to leave the person in your dream."

Emmey almost tutted. She should have known she couldn't get it past Sophia.

"It will be a big change for you. It's natural for you to feel frightened about it. Perhaps the person dies because when you leave here, it will feel as if she's died."

"Do you think that could be it?" Emmey asked, desperate to accept Sophia's interpretation. "I hadn't thought about it being symbolic."

"Symbolic?" Sophia's mouth turned up at the corners. "I'm impressed."

"Mistress Averill talks about symbolism all the time. You're right. The dream could be symbolism." Maddy walked into the flames and died because Emmey was worried their relationship would die, that over time, they'd drift apart until Maddy no longer cared if Emmey showed up at the market. Suddenly it felt as if someone had thrown open the window shutters and let the sun stream in to chase away the shadows. Emmey still had to leave, but Maddy wasn't going to burn to death.

"That's a wonderful sight to see," Sophia said.

"What?"

"That smile."

Emmey's smile broadened, even though things still weren't all right. She still had to go. She'd still leave behind everyone she loved. "Thank you, Sophia." She drained her teacup. "Can I go now?"

Sophia barked a laugh. "I've served my purpose, have I? No matter. You can go."

Someone rapped at the door. Sophia straightened. "Come in."

The door opened. Barnabus stepped into the study and bowed. "Pardon the intrusion, Abbess, but the sisters from Hedgerow have arrived."

"Give me five minutes and then bring them up."

"Yes, Abbess." He nodded to Emmey. "Good morning, Emmey."

"Morning, Barnabus."

He retreated, shutting the door again.

Sophia plucked a loose thread from the shawl she usually wore. "I wish they'd chosen another time to pass by our doors."

So did Emmey. She'd miss scribing with Mistress Averill. She rose and bobbed a curtsey, even though she didn't have to. "I'll get out of your way."

"You're never in my way, Emmey." Sophia lifted her index finger. "Don't worry about your dream. It's not real."

"Talking to you about it has helped." Maddy wasn't going to die in front of her eyes, not for real. But Emmey still had to leave her because of rules. Stupid bloody rules.

4

Sophia dabbed at her eyes one more time and slipped the handkerchief back into her drawer. She rarely wished she wasn't the abbess, but she seemed to be doing so quite a lot lately. Finding a new home for Emmey was one of the most excruciating tasks she'd ever had to perform. She wasn't used to feeling conflicted about acting in accordance with the Order's rules. The last time she'd struggled with them was when Emmey had surprisingly landed on her doorstep, and she hadn't loved her back then. Still, only someone with a heart of stone wouldn't have been moved by the girl's cruel treatment and neglect, and Sophia had wanted to support Maddy, to show her that not all was lost. Now she wondered if it would have been better to have sent Emmey away immediately. Sophia wanted to hide away from everyone while she nursed her grief, but abbesses weren't permitted such luxuries.

When someone knocked on the study door, she consciously relaxed her shoulders, hoping to appear friendly and calm. "Come in."

The door swung open. Five sisters filed into the study, lined up in front of her, and bobbed one by one. "Mistress Margery," barked the first, clearly the older of the five, with her silver hair and the mottled skin on her hands.

"Mistress Olivia," said the second. Her dark brown hair was

speckled with gray and her eyes were bright, but it was the pitted scars marring her cheeks that drew Sophia's attention.

"Sister Cecily." She appeared to be in her late twenties, the youngest of the five.

"Sister Lorelle," murmured the fourth. She was perhaps in her mid-thirties.

"Sister Felicia," said the fifth, her voice strong. Also appearing to be in her thirties, she clasped her hands in front of her and waited.

Sophia surveyed the Hedgerow sisters and almost wrinkled her nose. A faint scent had arrived along with the sisters. Ale? She wasn't sure. She clasped her hands on her desk. "I am the Abbess Sophia, and I welcome you to the Merrin monastery." In preparation for the sisters' arrival, Barnabus had brought in extra chairs earlier. Sophia gestured at them. "Would you like to sit down?"

"No, thank you, Abbess," Mistress Margery shouted. Sophia wondered if she always spoke that loudly, perhaps because she was half deaf. "We'd like to begin scribing. We have a lot to do."

Mistress Olivia nodded. "At least nine books, and if we have time, we'll scribe more."

"Mistress Averill will help you in any way she can." The letter Sophia had received telling her about the sisters' desire to copy books in Merrin's library that contained information about the founding of the Hedgerow monastery had been signed *Mistress Margery, head scribe, Hedgerow Monastery.* "You're Hedgerow's head scribe, aren't you?" she said to her.

Mistress Margery's chin came up. "I am. For almost thirty years."

"That's quite the achievement."

"Thank you. Mistress Olivia has been my assistant for many years. Her letters are exquisite. Sister Lorelle and Sister Cecily's scripts are also a wonder to behold. Sister Lorelle has dedicated herself to scribing for the past ten years. Sister Cecily became a junior scribe last year. This is her first journey to other monasteries."

Expecting to hear about Sister Felicia's role, Sophia waited. An awkward silence stretched out.

"I'm Sister Lorelle's consort," Sister Felicia finally said. "I'm not a scribe."

That was all the explanation Sophia needed. Consorts would naturally travel together on long journeys, but she sensed tension between Mistress Margery and Sister Felicia. Well, no monastery was without its drama, and long journeys often brought out irritations that usually remained beneath the surface.

"Felicia's skill with the lute is unquestioned, and she teaches embroidery and knitting," Sister Lorelle said.

"I also collect and read the petitions left at the gate," Sister Felicia added.

"Sister Maddy does that for us," Sophia said.

"Does she need any help?"

"I don't know. I'll introduce you and you can ask her."

"I'd be most grateful. I want to make myself useful while I'm here."

Someone muttered under her breath. Sophia sharpened her gaze. It hadn't been Sister Lorelle. Mistress Margery's face was impassive, and Mistress Olivia's expression hadn't changed. She must have imagined it.

"With your permission, we'd like to go to the library and get ourselves settled in," Mistress Margery said.

"Of course." Sophia paused. "I didn't know two of you were consorts. I asked that each of you be assigned chambers."

"Not to worry," Mistress Olivia said. "We explained the situation to, Barnabus, is it?"

"Yes."

"He said he'd have Sister Lorelle's bags moved to Sister Felicia's chambers."

"Good."

"Originally Sister Agnes was going to come," Mistress Margery said. "Sister Lorelle was a last-minute replacement when Sister Agnes came down with a terrible cold the day before our departure."

"I see." Sophia couldn't think of anything more to say at the moment. "It's a pleasure to meet you and to have you here. I'll let you get to the library so you can begin your work."

"We're not sure where the library is."

"Oh. I'll take you there myself."

"What will you do?" Mistress Margery said to Sister Felicia.

Sister Felicia grinned. "I wouldn't mind seeing the library."

"Let's all go, then." Sophia pushed back her chair. "And before I forget, my consort and I would like you all to have supper with us in our chambers. Once you've established a schedule, do let me know which night would suit you best."

Mistress Margery nodded. "We will. Thank you for the kind invitation."

The visiting sisters moved aside to allow Sophia to take the lead. On the way to the library, Sophia asked them the expected questions, such as whether their journey had been pleasant and what books they planned to copy, but uncharacteristically, she only half-listened to the answers. She hoped to feel herself again after Emmey had been gone for a time, but she expected to gaze in the direction of Merrin from her study window more frequently than she did now.

~

MADDY TRIED NOT TO look up from her book too quickly when Emmey stepped into their chambers, but she couldn't help herself. "How did it go?" she asked from her chair in front of the fire.

Emmey shrugged. "We talked about where I might go. I told her what I'd prefer."

"Does it have anything to do with planting seeds?"

Emmey almost smiled. Maddy loved to see Emmey smile, though lately, the sight evoked almost as much pain as pleasure. "It might," Emmey said.

Maddy swallowed. "You could get a good little business going, selling herbs and flowers. You should talk to Evie in the market. I bet she'd buy from you."

"Maybe I'll live with Evie."

Maddy doubted it. Sophia had only approached families with spare coin, though the Order would pay Emmey's expenses until she was earning a living wage or married. Like most merchants who peddled their wares in the market, Evie hardly had two coins to rub together. Maddy liked her, though. When she visited the market, she always visited Evie's stall and had Jonathan trade for herbs for Lillian.

"I said I could grow herbs here, but she wouldn't hear of it," Emmey said lightly. "The only way I could stay is if I were marked and took the robe."

The compulsion to ask tightened Maddy's fist, but she resisted the urge. Surely Emmey would say if she thought she was marked. It would be the answer to all their prayers.

Emmey plunked into Lillian's chair, rather than her own. "We'll be fine, you know," she said briskly. "I'll make sure to be in the market whenever you go."

Maddy pretended not to see the tears glistening in Emmey's eyes. "I'll look forward to it."

When Emmey grasped her hand, Maddy understood why she'd chosen Lillian's chair. They sat silently, watching the flames flicker and trying not to think about when they'd no longer be able to sit in front of this fire together, as they'd done hundreds of times before.

~

AT HER WRITING PODIUM, Averill lifted her head when Sophia's voice drifted into her office, followed by a voice Averill didn't recognize. She slid off her stool and went out into the library.

"Ah, there you are." Sophia turned to the group behind her as Averill bobbed a curtsey. "This is Mistress Averill, our head scribe. And these are the sisters from Hedgerow."

Five sisters gazed at Averill. Three of them bobbed.

Sophia introduced them left to right. "Mistress Margery, Mistress Olivia, Sister Cecily, Sister Lorelle, and Sister Felicia."

"Pleased to meet you." Averill acknowledged their murmured greetings with a nod.

"I'll let you get on. Do come see me if you need anything." Sophia bustled away.

"Time to get cracking." Mistress Margery barked. "Only four of us are scribes. You can go now, Sister Felicia."

Sister Felicia patted Sister Lorelle's arm and strode toward the doorway that led to a stairwell.

"I can see three vacant writing podiums. We'll need a fourth," Mistress Margery said gruffly.

"There's one in my cubbyhole," Averill said.

"You take that one, Mistress Olivia. I'll stay out here, keep my eye on things. Do you have the books we want to scribe?"

"I've pulled them all for you." Averill led them to a nearby table and swept her arm over the books she'd gathered. "I pulled a few related ones as well, just in case you find yourselves with time on your hands."

Mistress Margery grunted. "You never know. We won't if we don't get cracking. Come on, Sisters. Take a tome and follow me."

The two sisters who'd scribe near Mistress Margery did as they were told and trailed after her, leaving Averill alone with Mistress Olivia. They eyed each other. Averill couldn't help but notice the scarring on the mistress's cheeks. A childhood illness, perhaps.

Mistress Olivia blinked at Averill through her spectacles, then selected a book from the table. "Can you show me where I'll be scribing?"

"Of course. You'll be stuck next to me, I'm afraid." On the way, they passed the three Hedgerow scribes already hunched over their writing podiums, dipping their quills into ink.

"Here we are," Averill said. "You can scribe here." She patted the podium Emmey had frequently occupied over the past year.

"Thank you." The mistress opened the book to the title page and placed it on the nearby holder, then glanced around. Her eyes settled on the piles of books on Averill's desk. "Oh! Is that a copy of Musings on the Nature of Trees by Sister Fina?"

"It is."

Mistress Olivia's face lit up. "Do you mind?"

"No, not at all."

The mistress carefully pulled the book from the pile it occupied and thumbed through it. "I've read her musings on stones and want to read this one, but we don't have a copy of it in our library. Are you reading it?"

"I just finished it but haven't shelved it yet." Mistress Olivia didn't need to know that Averill had finished it last month and added it to the pile, where it would stay until all the piles on her desk threatened to topple over and injure someone, though the mistress was now eyeing those piles, so perhaps she'd guessed.

"I recognize quite a few of the titles," Mistress Olivia said.

Averill moved closer to her. "Most of them are waiting to be shelved. Not one of my priorities, you see."

"You've read all of them?"

"Oh, no. Some of them were returned by sisters, but I've read most of them. Not recently, but at one time."

"Which ones have you read?"

Averill wanted to do a cartwheel. She couldn't remember the last time someone had asked her about her reading habits. Of course, sisters asked her about books all the time, but their questions usually began with, "Do we have a book about," or something along those lines.

Feeling a bit flustered, she cleared her throat. "Well, Musings on the Nature of Trees, as I just mentioned. A delightful, whimsical tome that I'd recommend."

"Can I borrow it while I'm here?"

"Of course."

"What else?"

Averill tugged at her robe's collar. "Lina's Gift."

"A classic," the mistress murmured.

Averill agreed. "I read it years ago, probably during my first year here." She lightly touched another book's spine. "The History of Merrin. This one won't be of much interest to you."

"If I was here for longer, I might read it. I enjoy learning about the past. The geography doesn't matter."

"Me too. Oh, Sister Estrilda's travel diary. A bit slow at times, but on balance, an entertaining read."

Averill continued to point out titles and answer any questions Mistress Olivia had about them. When the chapel bells announced that it was half past twelve, she couldn't believe it and almost gaped at the mistress. The sisters from Hedgerow had arrived at the library at about half past eleven. The bells must have chimed on the hour and quarter hours, but Averill hadn't noticed. "Have we been talking for that long?"

"I believe we have." Mistress Olivia grimaced and lowered her voice. "Mistress Margery won't be very pleased. I'd better start scribing."

"I'm so sorry."

"Don't apologize. I never pass on a conversation about books. I enjoyed our chat immensely."

"So did I," Averill said, genuinely meaning it. "Lunch is served at one o'clock. When it's time, I'll show you to the dining hall."

"I would appreciate that very much. To scribing, then."

"Yes, to scribing."

They sat at their writing podiums and dipped their quills into ink. Averill couldn't resist stealing a glance at Mistress Olivia. She almost jumped when she caught the mistress doing the same to her. Hoping the mistress hadn't noticed her burning cheeks, she quickly focused on the half-completed parchment on her podium, but her usual level of concentration eluded her.

5

L ATER THAT AFTERNOON, EMMEY sat slumped underneath the oak tree near the catacombs, angry with herself. She was trying her best not to get all teary-eyed and maudlin around Maddy, but as her departure approached, it was becoming more difficult to appear unfazed. It was easier with Lillian, who was so good at hiding her feelings. Maddy wore them on her sleeve. Emmey couldn't bear the pain and loss she glimpsed on Maddy's face when she was too slow to mask them. She wanted to rush to her, hug her tightly and never let go, tell her it would be all right. But Emmey couldn't lie to Maddy and tell her something she herself didn't believe. So she pretended. And it hurt so much it made her want to cry all over again.

She straightened and craned her neck when a sister she didn't recognize walked past. She must be from Hedgerow, the bloody reason Emmey couldn't scribe with Mistress Averill anymore, which deepened her sadness. Her life here was slowly slipping away. Soon she'd bake bloody bread or mend bloody clothes or clean bloody homes or plant bloody herbs, in a garden far away from Lillian's laboratory.

Oh, there went another sister she didn't recognize. Where were they going? Nothing was in that direction except one of the stables, but it was a ten-minute walk away, and why would two sisters from Hedgerow need to walk all the way to the farthest stables from the gate, where horses undergoing training were kept? Maybe they were lost.

Emmey scrambled to her feet and brushed off the back of her robe. She hurried after the last sister as quickly as she could without running, which wasn't permitted. The sister in front of her must be doing the same, because Emmey wasn't gaining any ground on her. When only trees and unlit torches lined the path, Emmey hitched up her robe, deciding to chance it. She ran around a curve in the path—and stopped. Nobody was there, and the path continued in a straight line as far as her eye could see. Then she heard women talking off to her right.

She threaded through the trees in the direction of the voices. When someone laughed not too far away, she ducked behind a tree, certain now that the sisters weren't lost. They must have deliberately left the path. She shouldn't risk interrupting a private conversation. She should creep back to the path and go visit Lillian, but curiosity propelled her to duck behind the next closest tree, and then the next one.

More laughter. It abruptly cut off, but it had sounded close enough that Emmey expected to see the two sisters when she peered around this tree. She inched her head out—oh. Blood rushed to her face. She jerked back behind the tree, turned around, and flattened her back against it. The sisters were kissing, and judging by how one's robe was half unbuttoned, they were about to do something Emmey didn't want to see or hear.

Hoping they were too preoccupied with each other to notice her, she sneaked back toward the path, watching where she placed her feet. One snapped twig and she'd have two angry sisters chasing after her. She hadn't meant to intrude on what was obviously a private moment, but she'd honestly thought they were lost and needed help—until she'd realized they weren't lost. According to Lillian, curiosity was to be nurtured. That was exactly what she'd been doing. Nurturing her curiosity.

One more step and she was safely on the path. After furtively glancing back into the trees, she walked as casually as she could to the catacombs, her mind filled with questions. Why were the sisters in the trees? Why hadn't they gone to their chambers? Did other sisters lie with each other in the middle of the day? Emmey had thought it only happened at night. Had Maddy and Lillian ever—no, she didn't want to think about that. Though if she was feeling brave, she might ask Maddy. They'd shared a dank cell for months, with a hole in the floor to do their business. There wasn't much they could say or do that would embarrass each other, but that didn't mean Maddy would appreciate Emmey prying into that part of her relationship with Lillian.

Emmey had never stumbled across sisters lying with each other outdoors—or indoors, for that matter. She knew not to barge into Maddy and Lillian's bedchamber. Sometimes she heard them, but it had never upset her. It meant they loved and cared about each other, and she didn't hear them very often. She'd gathered they always tried to wait until she was asleep. Now that she'd learned it could happen at any time during the day, she wondered if they'd ever stolen into their bedchamber when she was at a lesson, or scribing, or tending to a garden. She'd never entered their chambers to discover their bedchamber door closed and those types of muffled sounds emanating from behind it, but that didn't mean it had never happened.

Emmey changed her mind about seeing Lillian. She wasn't sure she could face her right now, not without wondering about all this. She'd go see how the valerian garden was doing and try to forget the two sisters and what they were doing in the trees, so she could go for supper with Maddy and Lillian without wondering about things she'd rather not know.

~

THE NEXT MORNING, EMMEY sagged into Maddy as they walked to the chapel together. "I'm tired this morning."

Maddy slipped her arm around Emmey's shoulders and kissed the top of her head. Emmey was small for her age, perhaps because of the poor start she'd received in life. Her ma certainly hadn't provided well for her, and the slop Emmey had eaten while imprisoned hadn't been an improvement. "If you fall asleep in front of the fire later, I'll leave you there." She felt Emmey's answering nod.

"I need to go to the privy."

Maddy unwrapped her arm. "I'll wait for you outside the chapel."

"All right." Emmey strode away.

A wave of sorrow washed over Maddy. Rather than wallowing in it, she pushed it away, and as she strolled to the chapel, she forced herself to focus on what she'd do that day.

Sophia and a sister Maddy didn't recognize were standing outside the chapels' entrance. Maddy smiled at them and bobbed.

"Sister Maddy, this is Sister Felicia, from the Hedgerow Monastery."

"Pleased to meet you, Sister Maddy." Sister Felicia's eyes flicked to Maddy's shorter right sleeve.

"Sister Felicia is responsible for reading the gate petitions at Hedgerow," Sophia said.

"I'm at a bit of a loose end," Sister Felicia explained. "I'm not a scribe. I'm here with my consort. I was wondering if you need any help reading your petitions."

Maddy didn't, and she quite enjoyed the activity, but the Hedgerow sisters were only here for a month, and Maddy checked the petition box once a week. Not wanting to share the task with the sister a few times would be selfish. "I'd welcome your company. I'll pick up the next batch tomorrow morning. Do you want to meet me here after morning prayers?"

"I certainly would." The sister shifted her attention to Sophia. "I'll go join the others. Thank you."

Sophia acknowledged Sister Felicia with a nod. She waited until the sister was out of earshot, then said, "Thank you for agreeing to let her help. I don't understand why she can't scribe with the others. It might not be her role at Hedgerow, but I'm sure she can write."

"Perhaps her letters aren't very good."

"Perhaps."

Sophia's expression was bland, but Maddy suspected she was keeping something to herself that could explain why Sister Felicia wouldn't spend her days in the library. But she wouldn't dare pry.

She'd grown much closer to Sophia over the past six years, but Maddy never forgot that she was the abbess and would never divulge sensitive information or betray a sister's confidence.

"Where's Emmey?"

"At the privy." Maddy squinted into the distance. "Though I think that's her coming now."

Sophia turned to look. "Yes, I see her too. I'll leave you, then. Salbine keep you."

"And you," she murmured, not surprised that Sophia would return to her study, rather than enter the chapel. She attended early morning prayers with Elizabeth and Lillian, and while she sometimes attended morning prayers too, she was usually in her study.

Emmey stopped walking so she could bob to Sophia. They exchanged a few words and carried on their separate ways.

When Emmey reached Maddy, she met her eyes for a moment, then lowered her head and went into the chapel. Maddy silently followed her. As usual, she'd pray that Emmey would be safe, and loved, and happy, but what she really wanted was for Emmey to stay.

~

THE FOLLOWING DAY, MADDY strolled up the dirt path that led to the training stables, her cheeks warmed by the early afternoon sun. Up ahead, rain pounded the field adjacent to the stables and lightning arced through the sky. Maddy stopped walking when she spotted soggy ground. She shielded her eyes so she could watch the horse and its soaked rider. Lillian thundered by on a chestnut horse, water dripping from her riding robe and her hair plastered to her head. Maddy groaned. Had she forgotten about their plans? Now Lillian would have to change first.

Her eyes followed Lillian as she circled the field again. Even though rain laced through the sky, Maddy didn't have a drop of water on her. At the same time Lillian was drawing water to make it rain and air to whip the rain with wind, she was maintaining a domed shield over the field. Maddy could tell where it ended by where the ground was soaked. If she weren't malflowed, she'd be able to feel the edges of the shield, but she was as adept at sensing the elements—or should it be inept—as the stable hands watching Lillian train the horse.

Lillian, the strongest and most skilled mage alive, always performed a horse's final test. If the horse demonstrated that it could carry Lillian on its back while she drew several elements simultaneously, and it could do so without rearing or bolting, it could be trusted to safely carry any mage drawing the elements.

At the same time the storm inside the shield abruptly ended, Lillian slowed the horse to a trot. Knowing what was coming, Maddy backed away a few steps. Watching this part always made her hold her breath. Poor horse.

Suddenly she could no longer see Lillian or the horse through the fire that almost encircled them. Lillian always left an opening in front of the horse in case it bolted. Maddy slowly exhaled and stared in wonder as the horse continued to trot around the field, not only because it was still calm, but at the skill it must take to draw fire so precisely that it moved with horse and rider, surrounding but not touching them.

The fire stopped moving, then winked out. Lillian dismounted, patted the horse's muzzle, and said a few words to it. She handed the reins to one of the stable hands who'd hurried over to her, then strode to Maddy.

"Did you forget—" Maddy's question died on her lips. Lillian was perfectly dry! Of course. The fire.

"Did I forget what?" Lillian said.

"Nothing." Maddy looped her arm through Lillian's. They strolled along the path that led past the catacombs and to a path that would take them to the courtyard. "I don't know how you can stand to be so close to the fire, and on a horse. What if it threw you into the flames?"

"I'd stop drawing. Elemental fire isn't like a natural fire. If the flow isn't maintained, it goes out."

Maddy thought back to the fire lessons she'd had, when she'd expected to become a mage. "Then there's never any danger of a fire raging out of control in the training rooms."

Lillian snorted. "From what I've heard, when an initiate loses control of a fire, what usually happens is that she shouts for water and tries to stamp the fire out. She never thinks to merely break her connection to fire, not the first time it happens."

"I suppose her tutor could draw water and deal with it."

"Of course she could, but that would ruin the fun," Lillian said, making Maddy chuckle. She understood why Lillian didn't have any first-hand experience with trainees bungling fire. She didn't tutor initiates in the elements. She preferred to work with horses, because she preferred animals to people. Only once had she agreed to take on a human student. If she hadn't, Maddy wouldn't be strolling next to the woman she loved.

"I'd say it was bad luck that the only student you ever had turned out to be malflowed, but it certainly wasn't bad luck for me."

"Or me," Lillian said firmly. "Agreeing to tutor an initiate was one of the best decisions I've ever made. Because I ended up with you."

Maddy leaned into her. "What are the other ones?"

Lillian was silent while she pondered the question. "I can only think of two. One was coming here with Sophia, and the other one was leaving here to find out what had happened to you in Garryglen."

"I can't express how grateful I am that you did."

They strolled in companionable silence until they'd crossed the courtyard. They were almost at the entrance to the library when Lillian stopped walking, pulling Maddy to a standstill. She freed her arm from Maddy's and peered at her. "Are you sure you're ready for this?"

Maddy looked up at her. "Emmey asked me once, 'If Salbine came to you and said she'd grant you one request, would you want your hand, or the gifts?' I didn't have to think about it, not for a second. I'd want the gifts. I'd want to draw the elements."

Lillian nodded. "I'd probably say the same."

Always grateful for Lillian's honesty and refusal to coddle, Maddy squeezed her hand. "You do know how much I love you."

Lillian's face flushed. "I thank Salbine for your love every day," she said without a hint of teasing in her voice. Quite the declaration from someone who wasn't, shall we say, devout. Yet Salbine had blessed Lillian with the gifts, to the degree that Lillian was the most powerful mage in the Order, something that had caused Maddy some consternation when she'd been denied the gifts, despite attending all the prayer services and happily dedicating her life to Salbine's service.

"Come on, then," Maddy said, pulling Lillian toward the library. But as she climbed the stone steps to the library's second floor, her apprehension grew, tempering her excitement. She was trying not to get her hopes up and failing miserably at it. Would the material from the other monasteries offer answers to the questions that gnawed at her about her condition?

The library's second floor was also known as the scribing floor. On their way to Mistress Averill's office, tucked away at the north end of the floor, they passed sisters hunched over writing podiums. Maddy didn't recognize a couple of them and assumed they must be from Hedgerow.

The moment Lillian tapped on Mistress Averill's open office door, the mistress looked up from her podium. Maddy bobbed to her. Another unfamiliar sister occupied the stool Emmey often used.

Mistress Averill gestured toward the stranger. "This is Mistress Olivia, from the Hedgerow monastery. And this is Mistress Lillian and Sister Maddy."

"Pleased to meet you," Maddy said, bobbing again. "Welcome."

Mistress Averill motioned for Maddy and Lillian to move aside so she could step out of her office. "Come with me."

Maddy and Lillian followed her up to the third floor, also known as the quiet floor. Unlike the scribing floor, talking was frowned upon here. Sisters came to this floor to study and didn't appreciate anything that broke their concentration.

Mistress Averill opened the door to one of the study rooms and ushered Maddy and Lillian inside. A pile of documents sat on the square wooden table. The stone walls were bare.

"This is all of it," Mistress Averill said, her voice hushed even though she'd closed the door.

It didn't look like much, but every page would contain information about the malflowed condition. "Have you read it?" Maddy asked.

"I had a peek at the material from each monastery when it arrived, to make sure it pertained to the subject." The mistress grimaced. "It struck me as quite dry, I'm afraid."

Maddy's heart sank. She wanted to take Lillian's hand, but she was standing on the wrong side of her.

"But you might find a gem in there somewhere. Take your time. You don't have to read it all in one go. Just make sure you close the door when you leave, so sisters will know not to use this room."

"Thank you." Maddy expected Mistress Averill to leave, but the mistress remained, her eyes on Maddy.

"I have a project in mind for you," the mistress said. "Have you recorded any of your thoughts about being malflowed?"

"No."

"I think you should, for others who come after you."

Maddy felt as if she'd been struck by lightning. Of course she should! It was blazingly obvious that she should. But she'd been so wrapped up in herself that it had never occurred to her. "I'm embarrassed to admit that I haven't given one whit of thought to malflowed sisters who haven't been born yet."

If Mistress Averill thought any less of her, she didn't show it. "Recounting how you discovered your condition, what's befallen you so far because of it, and how you feel about it all, would be a worthy addition to our library. You can add to it over time."

"I should have started on it long ago." That she hadn't was shameful. She'd pray about it later.

"I'd like you to dedicate some time to it each week, here in the library, but you'll have to wait until the sisters from Hedgerow are gone. There isn't a podium available at the moment."

That would suit Maddy just fine. She welcomed anything that would occupy her once Emmey had left. "I'll try not to write a tragedy."

Mistress Averill's mouth twitched. "Be as honest as you can,

Sister. Nobody will judge, and the more honest you are, the more it will help a sister who's searching, as you are."

Maddy had been half joking. She agreed with Mistress Averill. If she ever had the opportunity to read the thoughts of another malflowed sister, she'd be crushed if the sister hadn't expressed any anger, or doubt, or resentment. At the same time, she didn't want to make it sound as if her life was one of sorrow and anguish. Somehow she'd have to convey that despite her bitter disappointment at being denied Salbine's gifts, despite the nagging thought that she must have done something to earn her condition, her life was filled with love, and she believed she truly was a Salbine Sister, that she could still serve the Order and the goddess who was upset with her for reasons unknown.

"I'll leave you to it, then." Mistress Averill left, closing the door quietly behind her.

Maddy blinked at the documents, almost afraid to touch them. Sensing her hesitation, Lillian pulled out a chair and sat, then pulled out the chair next to her and patted its seat. Grateful for her presence, Maddy sank into the chair and accepted the document Lillian handed to her.

"My spectacles," Lillian said.

"Right." Maddy fumbled in her pocket for them and handed them to Lillian, who'd given them to her before she'd left for the stables, not wanting to risk breaking them while she was testing the horse.

Bracing herself, Maddy began to read. Twenty minutes and three documents later, she leaned back in her chair and rubbed her eyes. Dry didn't begin to describe it, and she'd previously read one of the documents. She nudged Lillian. "Some of what I've read is a copy of passages I'd already read in books we have here."

"That's not surprising. When Sophia wrote to the other monasteries, she couldn't tell them what we already have. Most of it consists of a passage here and there in different books. We don't have any books dedicated to the malflowed condition."

"I know. I'm just disappointed." And she wanted to weep. But the swirling emotions within her also steeled her resolve to ask

Sophia for something she'd pushed to the back of her mind while caring for Emmey. She wanted to go to Heath. She wanted to read the malflowed sister's journals. She'd accepted that it would have to wait until Emmey was gone, and she knew that Lillian would prefer that she gave up on the idea, given what had happened the last time she'd tried to journey to Heath.

But the next time, she'd have documents that explained her condition, and a sister who could more than adequately draw the elements would travel with her, because she wouldn't go unless Lillian agreed to go with her. Which was selfish, because Lillian would rather do anything than leave the monastery for months on end on what could turn out to be a fruitless journey. So Maddy hadn't raised the subject yet and wouldn't unless Sophia agreed to let her embark on a journey to Heath again. Maddy would ask her before Emmey left, to give herself something to look forward to. She wouldn't want to leave for Heath until Emmey stopped coming to the market—because Emmey would stop coming, likely when she married, and since most girls were married by the time they were sixteen or seventeen, Maddy would only have to wait a few years.

"I've had enough for today." She moved the documents she'd read to a corner of the table, away from the others. "I don't suppose you've read anything interesting." Lillian would have said, if she had.

"No. Do you want to read what I've read?"

Maddy shook her head. "If there's anything, you would have told me. And I'll read it all myself, not that I don't trust you."

"I understand why you need to read it all."

"You don't have to read any of it, if you don't want to," Maddy said, wanting to explain it anyway. "I wanted you here because you make me feel safe. And in some strange way, I want to share this with you. I feel so alone in this."

Lillian took Maddy's hand with both of hers. "Because you *are* alone. Nobody else knows what it's like. We can try to imagine, but we can't possibly know." She brought Maddy's hand to her lips and kissed it.

"We'll come back tomorrow—no, after market day."

"That's the spirit. If there's an answer in these documents, we'll find it."

Maddy hoped Lillian would be as enthusiastic about finding answers when she asked her to go to Heath.

6

E MMEY THRUST HER ARM out to steady herself against the stone wall. "I can't watch this," she whispered, even though it was a dream. Symbolism. Yes, symbolism. Leaving Maddy and never seeing her again would feel as if Maddy had died. Still, she squeezed her eyes shut. She would not watch Maddy stroll into the raging room. She clamped her hands over her ears to block out Maddy's anguished screams.

She opened her eyes when the smoke from cooking fires wrinkled her nose. They were in the market, but the stalls weren't where they usually were.

"What are you doing?" a voice bellowed, making Emmey jump. She stared at Rose.

"Have you come to see her burn?"

"No."

"You've come to see Maddy burn." Rose pointed.

Not again. Maddy dying the once had been enough. Emmey turned to look. Maddy was enveloped in flame, jerking and jumping like a puppet.

"Maddy!" she shouted, running to her.

The heat from the flames prevented her from getting too close, but now she could hear Maddy shouting. "I'm on fire! I'm on fire! I'm on fire!"

"Stop it!"

"I'm on fire!"

"It's a dream. It's a bloody dream."

But the heat of the fire warmed her skin, and now the rancid smell of burning flesh clogged her nose. Emmey gagged. "I don't want to see this! I need to wake up. Wake up!"

A breeze tickled Emmey's cheeks and piercing light assaulted her eyes. She shielded them with her right hand, then realized she was holding something in her left, a basket of herbs she'd picked for Lillian. She was standing near the road that led to the monastery's gate. A man strode down it, carrying a bulging sack on his shoulder.

He spotted her and stopped walking. "Morning, Miss Emmey," he shouted, waving.

"Morning, Malcolm. What's in the sack?"

"What?"

She always forgot Malcolm was hard of hearing. She raised her voice. "What's in the sack?"

"Oh. Tinctures, from the mistress."

"Mistress Lillian?"

"Aye."

Not wanting to shout again, Emmey walked toward him. "I didn't know she—" Movement, in the corner of her eye. Her breath caught in her throat. Her mouth opened, but nothing came out.

A horse galloped down the road. Malcolm turned—Emmey lost sight of him for a second under the horse's hooves, then he was lying on the road, twisted and bloody. The basket slipped from her hand. "Malcolm!" She ran as fast as her legs would go, dropped to her knees when she reached him.

But it wasn't him.

Maddy rolled over and grabbed Emmey with her right hand, her grip firm. "You're not listening to me, girl," she rasped.

Emmey screamed and bolted upright, then leaped off her bed, dragging the blanket with her. She stood still and listened, her body shaking. Why was she still having these terrible dreams when she'd figured out it was symbolism? Symbolism! Why did she have to see Maddy kill herself, hear her screaming and screaming? The burning chamber, the market, and now when Emmey was taking herbs to Lillian. What next? Maddy dying in the dining hall, or at the stables, or right here in their chambers? And why did Maddy always say, "You're not listening to me?" She always listened to Maddy.

At least she wouldn't lie awake until the sun rose and the birds sang. Light was already filtering through the shutters, and a muffled thump told her that Lillian was rising for early morning prayers. Emmey scrambled back into bed. A good thing too, because Lillian tapped on her door and swung it open. Emmey lay still. The door closed.

Emmey would stay here until Lillian left their chambers, then get up and fetch water for the kettle. With a shiver, she drew the blanket right up to her chin. Her dreams were symbolism, nothing more. Maddy wasn't going to die. It would be as if she had, but she'd be very much alive. Very much so, Emmey repeated to herself, as she clutched the blanket tighter, her beating heart pounding in her ears.

~

MADDY AND SISTER FELICIA strolled to the monastery's main gate, the empty sack Maddy used to collect petitions tucked under her arm. "How are the others getting along with their scribing?" she asked.

"I think they've finished the first book. Sister Lorelle is binding it while the rest start another."

They were making good progress, then. "You stopped at Redworth before coming here, didn't you?"

Sister Felicia nodded. "We've been away for months. I'm looking forward to sleeping in my own chambers—not that the ones here aren't comfortable," she quickly added. "Thank you for letting me help with the petitions. I'd feel at a loose end, otherwise. I've done a bit of embroidery and practiced my lute, but I want to be useful."

"I'd feel the same."

Sister Felicia glanced at Maddy's right arm, the one she'd tucked the sack under. "Do you mind if I ask you about your arm? Were you born missing part of it—and your hand, of course?"

Folk weren't usually so straightforward. Maddy appreciated her bluntness. "I burned it. Gangrene set in, and the only way to save my life was to amputate my hand and part of my arm."

"Did you do it while you were drawing fire?"

"No." Maddy could tell Sister Felicia about being malflowed, but it had been some time since a sister had assumed she was capable of drawing, and there was no reason for her to know. "I was burned by a piece of flaming wood."

"How?"

Maddy had hoped to leave it at that. At the same time, she admired Sister Felicia's curiosity. It reminded her of Lillian. "A man wanted to harm a child with it. I got between them and grabbed the wood where it burned. Not the brightest move, I'll admit, especially since the wood had oil on it, but he was burly, and violent, and I had to react quickly."

"That was very brave of you. Some wouldn't have done anything at all."

"I don't believe that. Most would have done what I did. Perhaps not grabbed it with their hand," Maddy said wryly. "But they would have done something."

"Do you mind if I ask you another question?" As before, Sister Felicia didn't wait to hear whether Maddy would mind. "I've seen a girl in a robe—not a Salbine robe, but a robe, nonetheless. Mistress Averill told me her name's Emmey. I didn't want to ask how she came to be here. Do you know?"

Maddy wanted to laugh and cry, but neither would be kind to Sister Felicia. She'd provide the same explanation she always did when asked this question. Nobody needed to know that Emmey had been imprisoned for pickpocketing the wrong duke, not that there was a right duke to steal from. But Duke Bradford hadn't believed in forgiveness, or in giving a seven-year-old disadvantaged child a second chance. If Maddy hadn't ended up sharing a cell with her, Emmey would still be rotting away in Dunmurk Prison. "That's quite a long story. I met her while I was travelling. She was living alone, under terrible conditions. Mistress Lillian and I tried to return her to her family, but her ma was nowhere to be found.

A duke asked us—the monastery—to care for her until she's old enough to make a life for herself."

"A duke?"

"Yes."

"So she isn't marked? She's not waiting to take the robe?"

Maddy's stomach knotted. "No. She's leaving soon, when she turns fourteen."

"I see." Sister Felicia moistened her lips. "So you and Mistress Lillian travelled together?"

"Yes."

"Are you consorts, then?"

The sister's curiosity was starting to try Maddy's patience. "Yes. Do you have a consort?"

"Sister Lorelle."

"She must be one of the scribes with you."

"She's about my height, has reddish-brown hair."

"Oh, yes, I think I've seen her."

Thankfully, they'd reached the gate. One of the defenders standing guard opened it for them. Maddy led Sister Felicia to the wooden box by the road and lifted the lid that protected the petitions from inclement weather. Inside the box were rolled and folded parchments and two freshly baked loaves of bread that someone must have dropped off earlier that morning.

She took a moment to inhale their aroma, then unfurled the sack. Filling it could be awkward. She could do it if she set the sack on the ground, flattened it so she could pile the petitions and any gifts on its bottom, and then carefully draw the sack's sides up around the items. But it took forever, and some of the items usually toppled over. She'd cursed under her breath more times than she'd care to admit. Now one of the defenders usually helped, but today she handed the sack to Sister Felicia, who held it open while Maddy placed everything into the sack and closed the box's lid again.

They walked to the study hall in silence and found an empty room. Several inkwells and quills, and a pile of empty parchment, sat in the middle of the rectangular wooden table. A striking tapestry illustrating a defender protecting a sister who stood perilously close to a tornado hung on one of the walls. Maddy and Sister Felicia each claimed parchment and quill, then Sister Felicia emptied the sack's contents onto the table. They'd take the bread to the kitchen later.

Not wanting Sister Felicia to hoard the petitions, Maddy quickly grabbed some. Most would be supplications, especially for prayer. A few would be responses to letters she'd replied to, mainly from the nobility or those whose professions required them to know how to read and write. The odd letter arrived wishing the sisters well. She appreciated those very much. Nobody addressed the petitions to her personally. She signed all her responses with "The Merrin monastery, of the Salbine Order," but she'd made the mistake once of discussing a petition with its writer at the market, and word had gotten around that Sister Maddy read the petitions.

She settled in to read the batch of letters she'd claimed. Occasionally she'd put one down, so she could pick up the quill at her left elbow and add a name to the list of those who'd requested prayer, along with the reason for their request. Sisters would pray for them in an upcoming prayer service, though the prevailing belief was that Salbine paid little attention to supplications. That didn't stop the sisters, including Maddy, from praying to Her. Nor did it stop the people, even though they had other gods and goddesses they could appeal to. They rarely did, because Salbine was the only one who demonstrated Her existence and power through those who belonged to the Order. It was natural for everyone to turn to Her.

Maddy added a name to the prayer list, set down the quill, and unrolled the next letter by pinning one edge of the parchment underneath her stump, and using her left hand to do the unrolling.

"I can't make head nor tails of this one," Sister Felicia said.

"Let me see."

Sister Felicia held the scroll open under Maddy's nose. The petition began with a sketch of a heart and several stick figures in dresses—Dear Sisters. Then a sketch of a flower, followed by a scrawled *V.* Under that, another sketch of a heart and a scrawled *E.* Maddy understood why Sister Felicia was mystified, but its meaning was clear to her.

She lifted her head. "It's from the herb merchant we trade with.

She's saying she's running low on valerian root and she'd be grateful if we could bring her some when we go to the market tomorrow."

Sister Felicia set the letter on the table. "Why would we do that? Doesn't she sell her own herbs?"

"She does, but if she's running low on something, which doesn't happen often, we help her when we can. And we get some of the herbs we use from her, those that don't grow natively. But we also trade for herbs we grow here, even though we don't need them."

"Why?"

"As a good will gesture, and to do something practical for her. When we're at the market, we trade for many items we don't need. It makes the merchants happy and contributes to Merrin in a tangible way. The abbess believes it important that we maintain good relations with the townsfolk."

"I see."

"You don't have a similar philosophy at Hedgerow?"

"We pray for folk, of course. But Hedgerow's economy is Hedgerow's affair."

"I suppose it depends on the philosophy of the abbess," Maddy said. "I don't know whether the previous abbess thought the same as Abbess Sophia does." Maddy had entered the Order two years after Sophia had taken the cassock.

"I suppose that's true." Sister Felicia added Evie's letter to the parchments she'd already read.

"Do you want to come to the market with us? We're going tomorrow afternoon."

Sister Felicia's lips pressed together. "I can't. Mistress Margery wouldn't allow it. She wants us to stay on monastery grounds." The sister lowered her voice, even though the door was shut. "She's quite strict."

"Oh. Well, if you decide to ask her, we meet at the gate right after lunch."

"Thank you for inviting me anyway." Sister Felicia unrolled another letter.

Maddy mentally made a note to ask Emmey to bring some valerian root to the market with her. The thought dampened her mood. Soon the market would be the only place Maddy would see Emmey, and that was only if Emmey was able to be there. With a sigh, she forced her attention to the scroll she'd unrolled and deciphered the sketches on the parchment.

7

ON THE WAY TO the market, Maddy walked next to Rose and Nora, listening to them chattering away about which stalls they'd visit. When they'd joined Maddy and the others who regularly went into town, Maddy had been thrilled. Depending on who came along, the walk down the hill could feel like ten minutes, or ten hours. Rose was her best friend, and Maddy had come to love Nora too.

Rose glanced over her shoulder at Sister Dolores. "You must be excited. Soon you'll be living in the Initiates Tower and will begin your training."

Sister Dolores's voice lifted. "I can't wait. I'll finally be a true sister and—" Her face reddened, at the same time Rose scowled. "My apologies, Sister Maddy. I didn't mean—"

"It's fine." Maddy kept her eyes forward. When Emmey took her arm and hung on to it, she wished she had her other hand, so she could reach over and pat Emmey's in thanks. Instead, she smiled at her, inwardly wincing at the dark half-moons under Emmey's eyes. She wasn't sleeping well. Maddy would have been hurt if Emmey waltzed through the gates to her new home without a backward glance, but she didn't like to see her suffer—assuming Emmey wasn't sleeping because their time together was rapidly coming to a close, a thought Maddy pushed from her mind. She needed to talk to folk and listen to their concerns, not sob on their shoulders.

When they strode into the market square, the brightly coloured awnings covering the stalls lifted Maddy's spirits. Jonathan was suddenly at Emmey's other side. "To the herb stall, Sister?" he asked. Maddy could hardly hear him over the merchants shouting invitations for townsfolk to stop at their stalls.

"Yes." She turned to Emmey. "What are you going to do?"

Emmey shrugged. "See who's here."

"That's a good idea." Maddy had first brought Emmey to the market when Emmey was eight, hoping she'd make some friends among the children who played while their parents traded. She'd worried the children might avoid the girl who lived with the sisters, but Emmey had easily made what Maddy thought of as market friends. "Give Jonathan the valerian root, then."

Emmey handed him the basket she carried.

Sister Dolores patted Emmey's shoulder. "Before you rush off to find your friends, can you take me to the merchant who offers candles?"

Emmey's cheeks reddened. "You-you want me to take you?"

"Yes, please."

Emmey stared at her, then stammered that she would. Maddy didn't understand why Emmey was always tongue-tied around Sister Dolores. The woman wasn't intimidating and always spoke politely to her. She watched Emmey and the sister stroll away, pleased that Sister Dolores was getting into the spirit of a market visit, in that she'd have a defender trade for candles she didn't need while she talked to the merchant and other folk. The sister wasn't a regular market visitor.

Rose nudged Maddy's arm. "I'm going to wander around and see if anyone wants to talk to me. Nora's going to trade for wool. We'll see you in a bit." She, Nora, and a defender headed in the same direction Emmey and Sister Dolores had walked. Maddy set off for Evie's herb stall.

On the way, a girl ran by, then backtracked and bobbed a quick curtsey. "Sister," she said in her high voice.

Maddy grinned at her. "Good morning, Sally." She wasn't surprised when Sally darted away. The girl never stood still for more than a second.

Farther along, a merchant called out to her. "How are you today, Sister Maddy?"

"I'm doing very well, thank you. It's a beautiful day." Maddy surveyed the wooden carvings displayed on the table. They always reminded her of the carvings inside the chambers she shared with Lillian, who'd just completed a beautiful horse. A tribute to Baxter, who'd sadly passed away a few months earlier. Henry carved people, something Lillian didn't do. People weren't her strength. "How's trade?" she asked him.

"Not too bad, Sister. Someone nipped a carving from me a few days ago, though. I hope the guard catches the bastard." He froze. "Begging your pardon, Sister."

"Not to worry, Henry." She lived with Lillian, who wasn't afraid to curse. She chatted with him for a few more minutes, then continued on. Reaching the herb stall wasn't easy, with everyone wanting to talk to her, but Maddy didn't mind. She patiently listened to the concerns the merchants and shoppers shared with her. There wasn't much she could do for most of them, but occasionally the Order could help. She'd tell someone to go to the Monday clinic, or that she'd ask the abbess to have one of the defenders whisper a word into the right ear. She never made any promises, and she believed that listening helped ease the burden. But sometimes she wished the Order could do more.

"Almost there," she said to Jonathan when the herb stall was only two stalls away. Evie always looked out for Maddy. If she'd overheard any juicy gossip, she'd share it with the sister who always arrived with coin to spend.

Maddy pulled the list Lillian had given her from her pocket and handed it to Jonathan. "This is what we need." The defenders did all the haggling. That way, a merchant wouldn't be upset because a sister had driven a hard bargain. Most sisters wouldn't know how to haggle anyway. The skill wasn't taught at the monastery.

Another merchant called to her. Maddy stepped in that direction and— She sniffed the air. Adrenaline shot through her. "Is that smoke?" she said to Jonathan.

Heat washed over her left cheek and arm. The merchant who'd summoned her opened his mouth, but nothing came out. He pointed toward the herb stall, horror widening his eyes.

~

EMMEY LEANED BACK ON her haunches and took in the wide-eyed faces with glee. She had them. The Smithson twins gripped each other's hands. Timmy's mouth hung open. Dina's lip trembled. Emmey drew out the silence a few seconds more, then continued her story. "As I crept down the hall, the chanting grew louder, and then it seemed to be inside my head, tugging at my mind." She jabbed her finger against her temple. "And before I knew it, I was at the training room door. It was ajar. I peeked through the crack." She widened her eyes. "The sisters were—"

Dina screamed. Timmy scrambled to his feet, his mouth agape. One of the Smithson twins grabbed Dina's hand and pulled her upright. The children tripped over each other in their haste to get away, more screams piercing the air.

Confused, Emmey stared after them. "Wait!" she shouted. "I'm just getting to the good part."

A shadow fell over her. She glanced over her shoulder. "Rose!"

"That's Sister Rose to you," Rose said primly. "We're in the markct."

Emmey pointed at the fleeing children. "You ruined my story."

"How many times have you been told? We want them to trust us. You have them running away at the sight of me."

"A scary story never hurt anyone." Emmey stood and brushed the dust off her backside, then took the opportunity to look in the direction of where she'd last seen Maddy. There she was, across the square, at the stall next to the herb stall. Safe and sound, but that didn't stop Emmey from worrying.

Today she was also keeping an eye on Sister Dolores. Emmey searched for her, then relaxed. Sister Dolores wasn't that far from

Maddy, but where was she going? Emmey needed to politely disentangle herself from Rose so she could follow her. "I'm only giving them a bit of free entertainment."

Rose folded her arms and tapped her fingers against them. "What were you going to tell them this time? That when you peered inside the room, we were hurling fire and lightning at some poor child in a cage suspended from the ceiling?"

No, but Emmey would work that into the next story she told. She twisted to look behind her. Sister Dolores had stopped two stalls away from Evie's herb stall and was talking to the merchant. Two stalls down . . . that was Duncan's stall. He sold hunting gear. Why would Sister Dolores talk to him?

She gazed at Rose again, her frustration mounting. She needed to get away! "They know I'm embellishing."

"I don't think they do. They're young, impressionable. And they'll grow up to be the next baker, or physician or—"

Emmey barked a laugh. "Physician? The Smithson twins? Timmy? You must be joking. They'll—"

Something foul and acrid filled her nostrils. A shout rose above the din coming from the market. "Fire!"

Emmey whipped around. Smoke billowed into the sky from a stall—the herb stall. Where was Maddy? Emmey couldn't see her through the people filling the square, rushing to help. "Maddy?"

She ran toward the stall, shoving aside anyone who hindered her. "Maddy!" No, no, no. Don't let her dream come true. "Oy!" a man shouted when she jostled him. She squeezed between two burly men and burst into the clearing around the burning stall, her heart pounding. "Maddy!"

Her eyes stung. She peered through the smoke at the shadowy figures braving the heat. One made a tossing motion. Water splashed onto the stall. "Maddy!"

Someone grabbed her arm and pulled her back into the crowd. Struggling to pull free, Emmey wheeled to face her captor. "Over there," Sister Dolores said, pointing.

Relief washed over Emmey. Maddy was crouched next to someone sitting on the cobblestones a safe distance away from the fire. She leaned into Sister Dolores. "Someone must be hurt," she breathed. "Who is it? It's not Evie, is it?" She couldn't tell through the hazed air. Maddy wasn't entirely visible either, but Emmey had instantly recognized Maddy's silhouette and the curve of her shoulders.

"It might be Evie, but I'm not sure." Sister Dolores's hushed voice was difficult to hear with all the shouting.

The fire was making fast work of the wooden stall and its striped fabric awning, and flames already licked at the stall to the left of the herb stall. Merchants frantically gathered up their stock, stuffing everything into leather bags and burlap sacks. Men, including the defenders who'd accompanied the sisters to the market, were forming a line to the nearest well, but it would take some time to douse the flames.

"Let us through," someone commanded loudly.

Emmey recognized the voice. Nora stepped into the clearing, followed by Rose and Mistress Bertha. The three sisters raised their hands. Water streamed from their fingertips, and rain pounded the burning stall. The fire hissed as it fought extinction, but it was no match for the onslaught. Steam rose from the charred wood, but the fire burned no more. The sisters dropped their hands. Cheers broke out, men doffed their caps, women curtsied. The crowd dispersed.

Maddy strode toward Emmey and Sister Dolores. Her throat tight, Emmey threw her arms around Maddy and clung to her.

"I'm glad to see you're all right," Maddy murmured into Emmey's hair. "Poor Evie. She's lost everything." She shook her head.

Emmey willed herself to let Maddy go and stepped back. "Who were you kneeling with?"

"Evie. She has burns on her hands and arms."

"Burns?" Emmey shrieked. "But . . . "

Maddy placed a calming hand on Emmey's arm. "Nowhere near as bad as mine were, but I said I'd bring her something tomorrow. I'll ask Lillian for a poultice."

"Did you manage to get everything on Lillian's list?"

Maddy tutted. "Is that all you care about?"

It was all Lillian would care about.

"I hadn't reached the stall before it went up in flames. Lillian will have to wait for her herbs. It will take some time for Evie to replenish her stock."

"And build a stall," Emmey pointed out.

"The townsfolk will build her a new one." Maddy's gaze sharpened. "You're shaking."

"It's the shock," Emmey said. "I didn't know . . . " Didn't know if her dream was coming true and Maddy was dancing in flame, her flesh melting off her. She wanted to hug herself, grip herself in horror, but Maddy was safe. Her dream hadn't come true—not that part anyway. But there *had* been a fire at the market, something that hadn't happened in the six years Emmey had been coming here. Was it coincidence that she'd had a recurring dream about a fire here, or had her dream been some type of omen?

Emmey shuddered. No, it was merely coincidence, because if it was anything more, then the other part of the dream—the part where Maddy willingly walked into a room raging with fire and burned herself to death—that part would have to be an omen too. What would it mean? Would one of the monastery's towers go up in flames? Would Maddy be nearby, as she had been here? Maddy would never kill herself, but if someone was trapped inside a burning chamber, she'd try to save them, even if the chances of doing so were slim.

"Are you sure you're all right?"

Maddy's voice brought Emmey back to her surroundings. She realized that she was clutching Maddy's arm. "I'm fine."

"Why don't we see if anyone needs help?"

"May I come along with you?" a familiar voice piped up from behind them.

"Of course."

Sister Dolores fell into step with them. Any other time, Emmey would be thrilled, but not when she couldn't stop wondering if her otherworldly dreams were a harbinger of terrible things to come.

8

MADDY STRODE THROUGH THE catacomb's narrow passage-ways to Lillian's laboratory and sat in her habitual chair in the corner so she wouldn't be hovering.

Lillian stood at her worktable, pulverizing an herb in a mortar. "Just let me finish this."

"Don't rush." Maddy enjoyed watching her work, not that there was much room to do so. Empty jars, herbs and flowers—some whole, some cut—rags, several knives, several crucibles, and an alembic littered the table. And that was just the one table.

Lillian rested the pestle inside the mortar and wiped her hands with a rag. She came over to Maddy, who lifted her chin so she could give Lillian a kiss, and then another one.

"I need a poultice for burns," she said when their lips parted.

Lillian's brows drew together. "For who?"

"Evie. The herb stall merchant," Maddy added when Lillian frowned at her. "Her stall went up in flames today."

"Is Emmey all right?"

"A bit shaken up, but otherwise, she's fine. We talked to quite a few folk after. Only Evie got burned, when she tried to save some stock."

"Silly woman," Lillian muttered. "Stock can be replaced."

"True, but some travelling merchants won't pass through for a while."

"I suppose that means you didn't get my herbs."

"No."

Lillian grunted. "How did it start?"

"Apparently the merchant on one side of her had his oil in a bucket, and it tipped over. He didn't notice, and when the breeze carried a spark from a cooking fire . . . "

"Of course, his stall didn't go up."

"The wind wasn't blowing that way."

"Idiot." Lillian rolled her eyes, then went back to her table and carefully poured the contents of the mortar into a jar. She filled the mortar with another herb and lifted the pestle. Maddy wasn't offended. Lillian rarely remained still in her laboratory for longer than a few minutes and didn't mind chatting while she worked.

"When do you need the poultice?" Lillian asked.

"I told Evie I'd see her tomorrow. We'll meet at the market."

"You're taking defenders with you?"

"Jonathan will go with me."

Lillian's lips thinned, but she didn't protest. They'd argued about Jonathan many times, only calling a truce when Sophia had told them to stop. "Does it have to be you? Anyone can take her a poultice."

"I said I'd do it. And I'd like to. It will distract me for a few hours, keep my mind off Emmey."

Lillian blew out a sigh, but she didn't appear exasperated. She looked . . . troubled.

"What?" Maddy said.

"I have to admit . . . " Lillian gulped, then gripped the pestle and lowered her head. "I have to admit that I wonder if you'll feel your life lacking, when Emmey leaves. When it's just me again."

Astonishment made Maddy's mouth fall open. She wanted to go to Lillian and hug her, but she'd learned that Lillian didn't like to be touched when she felt vulnerable. "No! My life certainly will not be lacking. Will I miss Emmey terribly? Yes. Will I mope around for a bit? Yes. But don't for a second believe that I'll be unhappy because it will only be me and you." She lifted her finger, even though Lillian wasn't looking at her. "Listen to me. When we went to my chambers after my fire lessons, I didn't understand it at first. I didn't understand why I was so drawn to you, and why I felt so at ease. But it didn't take me long to see that we were meant for each other. I believe Salbine must have brought us together."

As Maddy had expected, Lillian snorted. "Salbine doesn't involve Herself in such matters."

"What were the chances you'd agree to train someone? And that it would be me?"

"Mistress Clarissa was away. Sophia asked me to do it, and she paired you with me. I asked her about it while you were on your way to Heath, and she said she hadn't had any particular reason, though I believe she chose you because she knew you were kind and wouldn't make fun of me. But it could just have easily been someone else."

"What were the chances we'd end up in my bedchamber?"

Lillian shifted her weight. "All right, about the chances that Salbine Herself will walk in here and say hello to us. But that doesn't mean She had anything to do with us. You can believe it if you like. I don't, but that doesn't mean it was any less of a miracle to me."

Maddy beamed at her. "I'll say this, then. I love Emmey dearly. Dearly, Lillian. But I love you too, deeply and utterly, in a way that I could never love anyone else. You're as close to my heart as anyone can be. You're the one I always think of when I need to feel safe, and loved, and to remind myself of what a wonderful life I have. When Emmey leaves, there will be dark clouds, but they'll eventually part and the sun will shine again." She didn't say that she feared the storm would last for months, perhaps years, because it had nothing to do with how much she loved Lillian. Every word she'd said about her feelings for her consort was true.

Lillian stood as still as a statue. "You know I'm not as good with words, especially romantic ones."

"You show by doing."

Lillian finally lifted her head and set the pestle down. "It's easy with you," she said, her eyes bright.

Now that Lillian seemed reassured, Maddy left the chair and embraced her. "You have nothing to worry about," she murmured into Lillian's shoulder. When Lillian's arms tightened around her, Maddy believed that she didn't have anything to worry about, either. She'd overcome the despair she'd feel when Emmey was gone, not drown in a bottomless well where she questioned her purpose again and wondered why Salbine had denied her what She granted to every other sister. Lillian's love would be enough. It had to be.

~

SOPHIA SIPPED HER AFTER-SUPPER cider and listened politely as Sister Lorelle told everyone about when she'd discovered her love of scribing. The five Hedgerow sisters had joined Sophia and Elizabeth in their chambers for a scrumptious supper, and now the fire and the cider were making Sophia a bit dozy. The conversation didn't help. They'd made small talk over supper, and the topics of discussion weren't improving afterwards.

Oh, that was unkind of her. Normally she wouldn't be so surly, especially when entertaining visiting sisters. But everything irritated her these days. She dreaded what the atmosphere at the monastery would be like in the weeks following Emmey's departure.

"It was before Felicia and I pledged." Sister Lorelle smiled at Sister Felicia. "I was only eighteen."

Next to Sophia, Elizabeth stirred. "Only eighteen? Were you novices or initiates?"

"I was a novice. Felicia was an initiate. You were twenty-one."

Sister Felicia's head bobbed. Pledging so young wasn't common, nor was it rare.

Mistress Margery reached for the cider jug and filled her mug. Sophia resisted the urge to give Elizabeth a sidelong glance. That was the fourth mug for the mistress, and her voice grew louder with each refill.

"Perhaps you should have waited," Mistress Margery bellowed, her eyes on Sister Felicia. "You might have more respect for what it means to pledge."

Sophia struggled not to raise her brows. Sister Cecily stared down at her lap. Sister Felicia's face tightened, and Sister Lorelle went scarlet. As she had in her study, Sophia sensed tension in the air. There was clearly no love lost between Mistress Margery and Sister Felicia.

Mistress Margery stabbed her finger onto the table. "My Joan was the most exquisite woman ever to walk the land. Oh, I miss her. Oh, how I wish she were here." Down went half the mug of cider. "I miss her every minute of every day, I do. Why'd she go so young? Oh, I miss her."

Sophia was afraid to ask what had happened to poor Joan.

"I never would have hurt her. I meant it when I pledged to her. Oh, why'd she have to go? I miss her so much." Mistress Margery stared into her mug.

Mistress Olivia cleared her throat. "Do you mind if I ask how long it's been since you and Mistress Elizabeth pledged?" she asked Sophia.

"Oh, dear." Sophia mentally calculated the number of years, hoping Elizabeth would do the same and if they spoke at once, their answers would match. "I was older than twenty-five."

Elizabeth gave her an indulgent look. "You were thirty, which means we pledged over twenty-five years ago."

Twenty-five years? It felt like yesterday that she'd knelt in the chapel next to Elizabeth, then kissed her on both cheeks and hugged her. She remembered feeling surreal, and how she'd wanted to pinch herself to make sure she wasn't dreaming. The first woman she'd searched for when she and Elizabeth had turned to face the community was Lillian. She'd wanted to go to her sister and embrace her, and tell her how much she hoped the same for her, that Lillian would find someone who'd make her heart sing. Thankfully she hadn't known it would be years before that special woman came along for Lillian, or a shadow would have hung over that glorious day.

"We didn't like each other when we first met," Elizabeth said.

"Really?" Sister Lorelle breathed, but she was too polite to ask.

Elizabeth answered the question anyway. "She thought I was too flighty, and I thought her too serious."

Sophia wanted to protest. She hadn't thought Elizabeth flighty, not really. They simply approached life differently. Sophia had come to accept, and sometimes envy, Elizabeth's carefree attitude. She refused to worry about things that hadn't happened. Sophia, on the other hand, always tried to anticipate problems that could arise in the future.

"How did you come to like each other?" Mistress Olivia asked.

"The abbess made us work together on a panel that hangs in one of the study rooms," Elizabeth said.

"Made you?"

"I think she knew we'd be well matched."

Sophia agreed. It wasn't unusual for an abbess to nudge two women together when those two women weren't seeing what was obvious to everyone else.

"The panel shows a defender guarding a sister as she draws air."

"The one with the tornado?" Sister Felicia said. "It's in the room where Sister Maddy and I read the petitions."

"That's the one." Elizabeth's hand found Sophia's under the table. "We naturally had to talk as we worked, and we discovered that we enjoyed each other's company."

"Twenty-five years," Mistress Margery wailed. "I wish me and my Joan had had twenty-five years." She drained her mug but didn't reach for the jug. "I'm not sure my Joan would have liked this monastery."

"Mistress!" Mistress Olivia hissed, but Mistress Margery wasn't deterred.

"My Joan was devout. She followed every rule laid down by Salbine. Things here are more lax."

Sophia straightened in her chair. Elizabeth squeezed her hand—a warning squeeze. But Sophia couldn't let it pass unchallenged. "What do you mean?"

"I almost tripped over a girl this afternoon. Got right under my feet, she did. A girl!"

"You must mean Emmey." Only Elizabeth would know that her calm, level voice meant Sophia was anything but calm. "For reasons too long to go into, she's our responsibility. She—"

"This is no place for a girl," Mistress Margery said. "There are rules. We have rules." She reached for the jug.

With a pained expression, Mistress Olivia moved the jug out of Mistress Margery's reach. "It's been a lovely supper, but I think it's time we returned to our chambers."

"Yes," Sister Lorelle quickly said. She pushed back her chair. Sisters Felicia and Cecily followed suit.

Mistress Olivia grasped Mistress Margery's elbow, encouraging her to rise to her feet. Mistress Margery didn't sway. She shook off Mistress Olivia and walked to the door without so much as a wobble.

"Thank you so much for the supper," Mistress Olivia said, bobbing. Sisters Felicia, Lorelle, and Cecily echoed the mistress's words and demonstration of respect. Mistress Margery was already out in the hall. Her Joan might have been a stickler for the rules, but she certainly wasn't. Not that Mistress Margery would remember, Sophia suspected.

Elizabeth shut the door behind the departing sisters. "That ended rather abruptly, didn't it?"

"I hope Mistress Margery isn't in too much pain in the morning."

Elizabeth chuckled, then crossed the distance between them and took Sophia's hands. "I hadn't thought about working on that panel for a while."

"Me, either."

They gazed at each other, remembering their younger selves. Sophia's love for Elizabeth had deepened over the years, grown into a mature love that didn't worry about wrinkles and messy hair, didn't keep a tally of offenses, didn't expect perfection, appreciated the other's strengths, and understood that differences weren't weaknesses or things that should change. Sophia trusted Elizabeth completely, and now, gazing into her eyes, she thanked Abbess Margaret for pushing them together, for seeing what she'd been too young and immature to see.

Elizabeth broke the trance first and eyed the dirty dishes on the table. "I expect someone will be up to collect those soon." Her eyes met Sophia's again, a glint in them.

Sophia lifted Elizabeth's hands and kissed them, then let them go so she could gently pull Elizabeth's face to hers. They kissed, a lingering kiss that made Sophia's cheeks burn and heat rush to all the right places.

"You'd better bolt the door," she said, the moment their lips parted.

With a grin, Elizabeth whirled and went to the door, a bounce in her step.

9

Emmey climbed the steps to the library's second floor and headed for the chamber tucked away behind shelves of dusty scrolls. She peered into Mistress Averill's office and frowned. The mistress wasn't alone. One of the visiting sisters was scribing with her. Oh, well, it couldn't be helped. Emmey needed to speak with Mistress Averill right now. She rapped at the open door.

Both women twisted toward her. "Oh, hello," the visiting sister said. "How are you today?"

"I'm fine, thank you." She bobbed to Mistress Averill. "Mistress."

Mistress Averill smiled. "Emmey, this is Mistress Olivia."

Emmey immediately bobbed to her. "Pleased to meet you."

"And you, Emmey."

"I'm helping the mistress scribe one of the books about the founding of the Hedgerow monastery." Mistress Averill tilted her head toward Mistress Olivia. "Mistress Olivia is an excellent scribe."

"Thank you, Mistress," Mistress Olivia murmured, colour dotting her cheeks. She hunched over the parchment in front of her and dipped her quill into the inkpot.

Mistress Averill's eyes lingered on the mistress's back. Emmey had seen that look before and had to restrain herself from chortling. Mistress Averill liked Mistress Olivia like *that*. But the mistresses had only met a few days ago!

Hoping her thoughts weren't plain on her face, she shook herself. "I need to speak to you." She glanced at the other mistress. "In private."

Mistress Olivia turned to Mistress Averill. "I'll leave you two alone. I wouldn't mind some fresh air."

"Are you sure?"

Mistress Olivia set down her quill. She didn't wipe the ink from her fingers, probably because she'd soon be scribing again. Most scribes' fingers were stained with ink anyway. Emmey's certainly were. But everyone still wiped any fresh ink away, not wanting to stain their fingers further, or leave inky fingerprints on their robes and the other things they touched.

Mistress Averill smiled at Mistress Olivia. "If you haven't strolled through the southern gardens, you should. There are some lovely flowerbeds there."

"Thank you for the suggestion." Mistress Olivia nodded at Emmey on her way out.

Emmey stepped into the office. "She seems nice."

"She is. I like her very much."

Emmey bit her tongue, wound her way through several neat piles of books, and sat on one of the chairs meant for visitors. She inhaled the musty air. It felt funny sitting here, rather than on the stool Mistress Olivia had just vacated.

"Just let me finish this passage." Mistress Averill scratched away on a piece of parchment.

Emmey clasped her hands on her lap and watched the mistress scribe. The mistress's hunched shoulders and the way she pressed her lips together while she wrote were a familiar sight. After Maddy, Lillian, Sophia, and Elizabeth, Emmey was closest to the mistress. She loved all the sisters, especially Rose and Nora, but she spent more time with Mistress Averill.

The mistress was in her early sixties, and more lines creased her face than when Emmey had first met her. But despite their age difference, Emmey considered her a friend and had spent many an hour sitting on this very floor reading or drawing, and later, when she was older, on the stool next to her, scribing.

Emmey would miss her terribly and think of her every time someone commented on how she formed lovely letters, though from what she'd gathered, she'd have no reason to write anything, a notion that sometimes brought tears to her eyes. She'd continue to read! She'd find every book in Merrin and gobble them up. But she'd also spend more time than she should gazing wistfully at the monastery on the hill, wishing she was here, in Mistress Averill's dusty office, scribing.

"Almost finished," the mistress said. The moment she set down her quill and raised her head, Emmey blurted the question that had kept her awake last night. "Can dreams be real?"

The mistress's bright eyes shined with interest. She always looked that way, one of the many things Emmey loved about her. "They can certainly feel real."

"Have you ever had a dream that came true?"

"I've had dreams when I'm worried about something, and that very thing happens in the dream."

No, that was backwards. That was something in the waking world happening in the dream. "I had a dream that sort of came true. I wasn't worried about anything. I dreamed something happening, and later, it did."

Mistress Averill studied her, then pushed away from the writing podium and went to her desk. She pulled open the top drawer. "Do you want an apple?"

"Yes, please." She always said yes, even when she didn't want one.

The mistress handed her an apple and sat back down. "Tell me about this dream."

"Do you think I'm mad?"

Mistress Averill chuckled. "I don't know yet. I haven't heard enough."

Now Emmey chuckled. "I saw someone burning at the market. And it happened. There was a fire at the market, and Evie got burned."

The mistress's brows drew together. "And that's what happened in your dream?"

"Well, not exactly. In my dream, it was another person on fire."
Emmey gulped. "She died."

"Oh."

"I've had dreams like it before. They feel different to my other
dreams. They feel real. Sometimes I have them more than once."
Emmey rolled the apple from one hand to the other, and back again.
"In one, Malcolm is on the gate road, and he's trampled by a horse.
I ran over to him, but it wasn't him." She hesitated. "It was Maddy.
And when I got to her, she was lying on the road all bloody, and
she reached out and said—" Emmey lowered her voice and made
it sound raspy, "—you're not listening to me, girl." She returned to
using her normal voice. "And then I woke up."

Mistress Averill tapped her chin in thought. "In your dream,
who was it that burned in the market?"

Once again, Emmey hesitated. Mistress Averill would say the
same thing about her dreams as Sophia had. "Maddy."

"Have any of your other dreams come true?"

"No, but—" Emmey stopped herself. She wasn't sure she wanted
to talk about her other dream about Maddy. She'd been so eager to
accept the explanation that it represented her upcoming separation
from Maddy, but then her other dream had come true. "I've had
another dream about Maddy," she admitted.

"And it came true?"

"Not yet. But it felt like the dream about Malcolm. It's so realistic,
I believe I'm actually there."

The mistress leaned forward. "What happens in the dream?"

Emmey had to will herself to say it out loud. "I'm somewhere in
one of the towers with Maddy, but it's one of those times when you
think you're somewhere but it isn't like it is for real. The hall ends
at a chamber, and the door is open, and I can see the chamber's on
fire. And Maddy . . . she . . . " Tears sprang to Emmey's eyes. "She
burns to death."

"Oh, dear." Mistress Averill squeezed Emmey's free hand. Emmey
still held the apple in her other one.

"Can you understand now why I'm worried the dream might
come true?"

"I do. I'll tell you what. I'll do some research, see what I can find."

Emmey wanted to hug her. "Please do. And if you find anything, don't tell anyone except me. I haven't told anyone else except the abbess, and I only told her about one dream. I didn't tell her about the one about Malcolm because I hadn't had it yet."

"You mean you haven't told Sister Maddy or Mistress Lillian?"

"No."

"Hmph."

"They'll only worry." Emmey dropped her voice. "And they have enough to worry about right now, with me leaving."

As she'd expected, Mistress Averill's eyes grew sympathetic.

"And I don't want to tell Maddy that something awful happens to her in my dream."

Mistress Averill's brows shot up. "Ah!"

"Ah?" Emmey echoed.

"I just remembered something. Do you want to know what I think about your dream about Malcolm? I think it's a coincidence. You probably don't remember this because it happened not long after you first came here. One of the stable boys—Eddie—was run down by a horse, not on the gate road, but on one of the monastery's roads, nonetheless. He wasn't killed, but badly crippled." Mistress Averill sucked in her breath. "Somehow he managed to hang himself."

"What do you mean, somehow?"

"Well, he couldn't move his legs, you see, and one of his arms didn't work properly. But there he was, swinging from a beam in a barn on his parents' farm."

Emmey gasped. "How awful for them."

"The guard believed he had help, but it could never prove anything. Not that it tried very hard to find out who helped him."

"Why not? Someone murdered him."

"The sentiment at the time was that they helped him."

"If they hanged him, it was still murder."

The mistress's voice softened. "It wasn't that clear, Emmey. Things aren't always good or bad, black or white. The poor lad was morose. He sat in his bedchamber day in, day out. He had no prospects. Nobody would give him work, and nobody was going to marry him. He was also in terrible pain. He'd spoken about dying, but of course he wasn't able to do it himself. Someone took pity on him, perhaps his parents, or his friends. They did what he wanted, you see."

Emmey couldn't imagine how bad the pain must have been for him to want someone to put a noose around his neck and kick away the stool or barrel. She couldn't imagine wanting to die, but then, she led a wonderful life. That would change soon, but she'd still be better off than poor Eddie.

Mistress Averill always included all the sordid details when she recounted a past event. If Maddy or Lillian were telling her about it, they'd leave out the part about Eddie taking his own life and what everyone suspected about it. Well, Lillian might tell her, but only when Maddy wasn't within earshot.

"It's hard for me to imagine it," she said.

"You're young, and your life is filled with possibilities. He didn't think his was, and the pain . . ." The mistress winced. "The physician didn't have anything that could help him, and neither did we." Mistress Averill paused. "When he was run down, it was the topic of conversation for days. Everyone liked Eddie. You didn't witness it, but it's highly likely you heard about it. I know how big those ears of yours are."

Emmey blinked at her innocently.

"You had the dream about Malcolm because you have some memory of what happened to Eddie. We often dream about past events, or memories that are still there, but we think are forgotten. Perhaps, at the time, you wondered why nobody saved him. Perhaps you wondered if someone could have warned him."

If that were true, she could explain the dream about Malcolm away, and the one about Maddy could go back to being symbolism. Emmey would love to accept the mistress's explanation, but . . . "What about the dream I had about the market, though? I know it didn't come true in exactly the same way, but there *was* a fire at the market. If I'd just dreamed it, maybe your explanation would make sense, but then my dream came true."

Mistress Averill didn't take offense, and she never had trouble admitting that she might be wrong, something Emmey admired about her. "You have a point there."

They sat in silence. "Let me see if I can find anything about dreams that come true," the mistress finally said.

Emmey knew where the mistress would start looking. There were records of every book and scroll in the library, roughly grouped together by subject. In one of the fifteen tall cabinets that housed the directory, the scrolls in the bottom drawer listed books about the Order and Salbine Herself. The second-to-bottom drawer contained the scrolls that listed the books about Salbine's gifts. Emmey didn't know what the rest of the huge cabinet held, or the other fourteen cabinets. She wasn't supposed to touch the catalogue, so she'd only managed to look at what was inside the two bottom drawers before she'd been caught.

"I'll let you know if I find anything," Mistress Averill said.

Emmey grinned.

The mistress's eyes crinkled at the corners. "That's what I like to see." But then she frowned.

"What's wrong?"

"I'll miss seeing that grin. I'll miss you."

"I'll miss you too." Emmey swallowed the lump in her throat. "Talking to you always helps, just like it has today. And we're friends, aren't we?"

She hadn't meant to upset the mistress, so she was dismayed when Mistress Averill blinked rapidly and clenched her hands in her lap. "Yes, we're friends," she said hoarsely. "Now you'd better go, so I can begin my research. I'll start right away."

Emmey had no doubt that she would. The mistress never passed up an opportunity to spend time with her beloved books.

~

CARRYING A BASKET OF herbs Emmey had harvested, Maddy strolled along the gate road on her way to meet Lillian, wondering why she couldn't have picked up the poultice from Lillian's laboratory.

"Nice day today, Sister," Jonathan said to her. "Not a cloud in the sky."

She squinted upward and murmured agreement. The gate came into view. There was Lillian, waiting. "I could have gone to your laboratory," she said to her.

"I've decided to go with you," Lillian replied, unable to mask her forced cheerfulness.

Maddy hardened her gaze. Lillian never showed any interest in going into town, especially when folk were involved. She wanted to say, "I know why you want to come. You don't bloody-well trust Jonathan." But she didn't want to argue in front of the defender, so she smiled as sweetly as she could and fumed inside. "I was wondering why you told me to meet you here."

"It's a beautiful day, isn't it? A glorious day for a walk into town."

Maddy resisted the urge to roll her eyes. She walked through the gate, trusting Lillian to follow her. When Lillian reached her side, Maddy glanced at the travel bag slung over Lillian's shoulder. "You have the poultice?"

"Of course I have the poultice," Lillian bellowed.

Maddy inwardly sighed and wondered if Jonathan could sense the tension between them. He always accompanied her into town. He'd apologized so many times for leaving her in Garryglen when she'd been on trial, that she'd lost count. Jonathan had asked Sophia to allow him to be Maddy's personal defender, so to speak. Hoping to show that she truly bore him no grudge, Maddy had agreed to the arrangement. She trusted him. Lillian didn't and hadn't been pleased, despite knowing that Jonathan had likely saved Maddy's life. He'd done right by running away. If only Lillian would see it and let go of her grudge against him.

Maddy's temples pulsed, then she chuckled at herself for arguing with Lillian in her head. They'd settled it, albeit not to Lillian's satisfaction. She'd talk to her later about gracefully accepting defeat and remembering that Jonathan had been escorting her into town for almost six years and no harm had ever come to her. For now, she let go of her irritation and focused on the positive. It *was* a beautiful day, and Lillian was accompanying her into town, an event as rare as some of the bird sightings those in Merrin's birdwatching guild lived to see.

She handed the basket of herbs to Jonathan and slipped her arm through Lillian's. "I'm glad you're here."

Lillian scowled and looked across her to Jonathan. Maddy snickered and held on to her arm.

They walked in companionable silence until they reached the market. Maddy's eyes immediately went to the location of Evie's burned stall. She smiled at the stack of freshly cut wood standing on the empty patch of ground. Evie would want to rebuild as quickly as possible, and Merrin's folk were decent. A beggar who usually called out to her as she made her way along the dusty road into town had mentioned that the merchants had donated coin and tradesmen their labour. Jonathan had dropped a coin into the beggar's hand.

She slipped her arm from Lillian's and pointed. "There's Evie." They strode over to her.

Evie was sitting next to an overturned washtub, the few herbs she'd salvaged laid out on its top. She beckoned to them when they approached her.

"I've brought you some more stock," Maddy said, taking the basket from Jonathan and handing it to Evie. "It's not much."

Evie eagerly accepted it. "Thank you so much, Sister. I'll take any charity I can. I have mouths to feed."

"This is Mistress Lillian."

Evie squinted up at Lillian. "You're the one she wants all the herbs for."

"Yes, I am," Lillian said stiffly.

"She's brought the poultice for your arm too." Maddy turned to Lillian. "Why don't you apply it while we chat?"

She wanted to chuckle at Lillian's horrified face and knew she was being awful, but since Lillian was here, it made sense for her to do it. Maddy would have required Jonathan's help to apply the paste without making a mess of it. "You can use the cooking fire over there to warm it up." She jutted her chin to Lillian's right.

"Can I have a look at your burns first?" Lillian said.

Evie held out her arms and hands. Lillian crouched and examined them. "They're not too bad. The poultice I've brought will help."

"That's kind of you, Mistress."

"I'll be back in a minute," Lillian muttered.

Maddy watched her go, then returned her attention to Evie. "I see the land is cleared and ready for a new stall."

"They've gone to have something to eat and then there'll be the sound of sawing and hammering. Music to my ears, Sister. And travelling merchants have already brought me some herbs, and folk aren't haggling as hard as usual. If it weren't so much trouble, I'd burn me stall down every few years."

Maddy laughed along with her. She admired Evie's resilience, and she enjoyed coming into town and chatting with folk, listening to their concerns, laughing and crying with them. She felt as comfortable here as she did in the Mistresses Tower and the chapel. Lillian was different. She rarely ventured outside the monastery's walls. A burst of warmth spread through Maddy's chest at the memory of how Lillian had ridden to the prison and saved her life. Whenever they had a disagreement or were getting on each other's nerves, Maddy reminded herself of that time, because it showed how much Lillian loved her. She hoped Lillian had a similar memory that reminded her of the depth of Maddy's love. One day, Maddy would ask her.

"If you need more herbs from us, put a letter in the petition box. I'll send someone down with them."

"That's kind of you, Sister. I usually send one of me kids with the letters."

"Do you? How many do you have?"

"Six, Sister."

"Six?"

"I'm lucky. My neighbour, she had ten but only three made it past five."

"I'm sorry to hear that."

They continued chatting until Lillian returned. She kneeled next to Evie, spread the poultice on clean cloths, and wrapped them around Evie's arms and hands.

"I'll leave the poultice with you." Lillian set the bowl and extra cloths next to Evie. "If you can, change the poultice tonight, and then every morning and night until you've run out. Warm it, but not too warm. You don't want to burn yourself again."

"I'll get me Cherry to help me," Evie said. "Thank you ever so much."

"My pleasure." Lillian slipped the travel bag over her shoulder.

Maddy patted Evie's arm, avoiding the poultice. "We won't keep you, then. Don't forget, if you need herbs, let us know."

"I will. Thank you so much, sisters." Evie started to rise, but Maddy motioned for her to remain sitting.

"I'll see you soon." She slipped her arm through Lillian's again and they left the market. "See, that wasn't so bad, was it?"

"What?"

"Helping Evie."

"I prefer to do it in my laboratory."

Maddy leaned into Lillian. "I know you do. And I love that you do."

~

STROLLING NEXT TO MADDY on one of Merrin's insufferable dusty and smelly roads, Lillian couldn't wait to get back to the monastery. Next time she wanted to make a point, she'd just say it, rather than acting like a child. She didn't understand what Maddy loved about the market and talking to folk, but she and Maddy were different, and they accepted each other's differences. Applying the poultice to the woman's arms hadn't been horrible, but Lillian wouldn't be volunteering for the Monday clinic. She'd continue to supply it with tinctures and poultices, and let the adepts deal with the sick.

They hadn't travelled too far from the market when a shout made Lillian look over her shoulder.

"Help!" someone cried. "Someone help me!"

Maddy backtracked a few steps to the alley they'd just passed, pulling Lillian with her. Jonathan quickly darted in front of them and peered down it. "Someone's being robbed," he said.

Maddy's eyes widened. "We have to help him."

"I can see four men around him." Jonathan's expression told Lillian he was calculating the odds that he wouldn't end up dead.

"Help me! They're going to kill me!"

Salbine Defenders were skilled at arms, but Lillian didn't expect one to take on four men. As much as she'd prefer that Maddy stay away from the mess, she needed Jonathan with her, and that meant Maddy would have to come too. "Maddy, stay close to me. Jonathan, unless I'm threatened or faltering, protect Sister Maddy." By threatened, she meant in danger of being overcome by her foes while she was focused on drawing. Though Jonathan had said four men. She wasn't worried. "Wait until I say the word."

She strode into the alley. Four men crowded a man against the side of a stone building. The victim had a dagger at his throat, and the three men not holding the dagger had swords in their hands.

The ground was cobbled, which eliminated earth. She could use fire, but she'd have to carefully control it so that any nearby thatched rooves weren't in danger, and she didn't want to inadvertently slay the thieves. As she knew too well, burns could eventually kill. Air or water it was, then. Lillian threw up an air shield, ensuring the dome was large enough to protect herself, Maddy, and Jonathan. "Now," she said to the defender.

He moved in front of her. "Oy!" he shouted.

The men swung around.

"Be on your way!"

One of the men glanced at the others and sneered. "Stay with him, Ralph." The three with the swords charged toward them.

Sensing Maddy behind her and trusting her to stay there, Lillian set the shield into motion. Leaves and dust and rubbish that had collected in the alley whipped around them. As long as Jonathan remained inside the shield, his drawn sword wouldn't be ripped away from him. Not so for those outside. Their swords flew from their hands and clattered along the cobbles away from Lillian. The thief who'd made it the closest to the shield was lifted off his feet—only a few inches, but it was enough to frighten him. A burst of air sent him flying backwards.

Another thief clung to a stone that jutted from the stone wall on the left side of the alley, his long hair blowing into his face, blinding him. He couldn't hang on and skidded away, arms flailing.

The third thief doggedly pushed against the wind and inched toward Jonathan, his teeth gritted and his clothes pasted against him. Lillian unleashed a focused burst of air. The thief doubled over as if someone had punched him in the stomach, but this punch packed quite the momentum. He hurtled away from her, his feet no longer touching the cobbles, and crashed down on his arse some distance away.

Lillian quickly focused her attention on the man with the dagger. He suddenly spun away from the victim and lost his footing. The dagger flew from his fingers and disappeared down the alley.

"I'm going to kill you all!" Lillian roared. She threw her arms into the air—for show. Two fireballs burst into life and hovered above her hands. Now drawing two elements, she could feel the tension in her neck and shoulders. She stared at the thief she believed to be the leader and drew back her arm.

He scrambled to his feet. "Run!"

His fellow thieves didn't need any further encouragement. They raced down the alley, a few bursts of air helping them along. When Lillian could no longer see them or hear their wailing, the fireballs winked out. She released the shield. The debris it had collected fell to the ground around them.

Lillian drew Maddy into a hug. "Are you all right?"

"I'm fine."

"Should we alert the guard?" Jonathan asked.

Lillian's face flushed and she quickly released Maddy. "No. We're returning to the monastery." She'd had enough of this town and jutted her chin toward the man they'd saved. "He can alert them, if he wants to."

The poor fellow had sunk to his knees. Maddy rushed over to him. "Are you hurt?"

"Oh, thank you, Sister," he cried. "Oh, thank you. Thank you."

"Thank her," Maddy said, smiling at Lillian, whose heart swelled. She'd given up on chiding herself over how one smile from Maddy could make her feel like a lovesick girl.

"Oh, thank you. Thank Salbine. I bow to Her. I bow to Her!"

Townsfolk were warily entering the alley. Jonathan parted a path through them. Lillian dearly wanted to take Maddy's hand, but that would have to wait until they were back in their chambers, when Lillian could draw her close, and hold her, and wish Maddy didn't care so much about helping folk, but at the same time, love her for it.

10

THE NEXT AFTERNOON, MADDY tightened her grip on Lillian's hand when Sophia leaned forward and folded her hands on her desk. Maddy had been embroidering yet another present for Emmey when Lillian had peered into the embroidery room and told her Sophia wanted to see them. On the way to Sophia's study, a rising sense of dread had made her chest hurt, and the words Sophia had just spoken had taken Maddy's breath away. She'd found a family for Emmey.

"I wish I didn't have to do this," Sophia said.

Her words hung in the air, along with the tension.

"We know you have to," Lillian finally said. "We know it's difficult for you too."

"You're her mas. You—" Sophia's breath caught in her throat. She grimaced. "Let's get on with it. You were right, Maddy. When I met with Emmey, she said she wanted to garden more than anything. Except scribing, of course. I thought she enjoyed sewing."

"She does," Maddy whispered. "But over the past year, she's spent more time gardening." She risked a glance at Lillian. "She likes growing herbs and flowers for you. And it suits her."

"She told me she thought she might want to be a smith." Sophia's chuckle sounded forced. "The hammer was too heavy for her."

Lillian stared down at her lap. "The poor mite had a bad start in life. That's why she's small for her age."

"I'm sure Cassy did her best," Maddy said charitably. Emmey's ma had disappeared after Emmey had been thrown into prison. Emmey never mentioned her.

"She's had a good six years with us, and I'm trying to do the best for her now." Sophia rubbed her brow. "I've managed to find a family. The Bennetts."

"The Bennetts," Maddy echoed. "Their youngest married last summer, I think. They live on Grange Road."

"Yes, on the southern outskirts of Merrin. They tend to numerous vegetable patches. From all reports, they're kind. They were good parents to their children and haven't grown used to living on their own yet. They know who Emmey is. They've seen her a few times at the market."

"They're good folk." It would have been easier if there were rumours about the family Sophia had chosen, whispers that they shouted too much at their children, or slapped them harder than they deserved, or were rude to the merchants. Then, when Maddy thought of Emmey, she could imagine her wishing she was back in the Mistresses Tower in her cozy bed, with the two women who loved her dearly and would do anything for her. But Emmey was going to a decent home, with decent people. *And I'm a selfish cow.*

"I'll tell her," Sophia said. "It's my responsibility."

Maddy silently thanked her. She wouldn't be able to get through the conversation. Her voice would fail her. She'd weep, perhaps wail. Emmey needed her to be strong. By the time they spoke about it, Maddy would have had time to cry herself dry and could focus on any questions Emmey might have.

Sophia's head dropped. "I am sorry. For everyone."

Maddy released Lillian's hand and edged forward so she could pat Sophia's. "You managed to keep her here. You have nothing to feel sorry about."

Sophia lifted her head, her eyes glistening. Lillian pushed back her chair and went to her. Maddy fought tears as the sisters embraced. Lillian's eyes appeared dry, but she didn't normally hug

Sophia so tightly, or for so long. When the sisters finally parted, Lillian strode to the door and left.

Maddy knew not to go after her, and she didn't feel slighted that Lillian had hugged Sophia but not her. They'd been consorts for almost six years and knew what each other needed, and when. Lillian wouldn't be ready to talk about it until she'd had some time alone, while Maddy would go to the chapel, say a prayer, pick herself up, and continue on with her day. Because she didn't know what else to do. The rhythm of monastery life would sustain her now, carry her along, not let her curl up into a ball, close her eyes, and waste away. Life must go on. Somehow, her life must go on.

Sophia frowned. "Will you be all right?"

Maddy couldn't see how she'd ever look at the door to what had been Emmey's bedchamber without drowning in grief. How would she walk past a garden Emmey had tended, or get used to two chairs in front of the fire, or visit the library without wandering the stacks of parchment and tomes to see if Emmey was there?

She forced herself to meet Sophia's eyes. "I was thinking that after she's gone, it might be a good time for me to go to Heath."

The corners of Sophia's mouth drooped further. "Heath? I thought you'd given up on the idea."

"The journals are still there. I suppose we could have asked for some of them to be scribed." Now Maddy wondered why they hadn't. Over six years had passed since she'd discovered her condition.

"You've seemed content."

Emmey had masked the ache and filled the void.

"You'd want to leave Lillian?" Sophia asked.

No. A hundred times no. "I'd only go if she agreed to go with me. I haven't asked her yet."

Sophia's forehead creased with sympathy. "Do you want my advice?"

"Always."

"Let some time pass after Emmey leaves. You'll find your footing again."

Would she? Or would the questions she prayed about multiply in number? Why was she malflowed? Why had she met Emmey and become her guardian, only to lose her? Yes, she'd known the time would come, but the part of her that had quietly hoped they'd somehow be able to stay together was now weeping.

Sophia pulled open her drawer and fished out two handkerchiefs. She handed one to Maddy and used the other one to dab at the corners of her eyes. "I know how terribly difficult this will be for you." Her normally strong voice quavered.

They stood at the same time and embraced. Her throat thick with tears, Maddy couldn't speak. She closed her eyes and gave Sophia a squeeze, then fled the study, knowing Sophia would understand. In the stairwell, she started to descend the stone steps, intending to hurry to the chapel, but then turned around and went to her chambers. She wanted to shut herself away, so she wouldn't have to smile, or bob to a mistress, or say "hello" to anyone.

But when she burst into her chambers and closed the door with relief, the sight of Lillian sitting in front of the fire surprised her. She'd assumed Lillian had gone to her laboratory.

Lillian slowly rose. Maddy's throat constricted at the redness around Lillian's eyes. With a cry, she went to her. They clung to each other in front of the fire, lost in their grief and pain.

~

EMMEY SAT UNDERNEATH THE oak tree near the catacombs, gazing at the sisters striding along the nearby paths, but not registering who they were. Bloody Order and its rules. Why couldn't she continue to tend her little garden, watch Lillian in her laboratory, carry things for Maddy, scribe with Mistress Averill, and bow her head in the chapel during prayers? What was so dire about turning fourteen? She deeply respected the Order, but the rule that said she couldn't stay because she wouldn't take the robe, even though she was marked by Salbine and had lived here for six years . . . that rule was stupid.

Of course, she hadn't breathed a word about being marked by Salbine, because the moment she did, Maddy and Lillian would try to convince her to become a novice when she turned sixteen.

Well, Maddy might not, because Emmey wasn't called to the Order, and even though Emmey knew Maddy would love for her to stay, Salbine came first in Maddy's life. Emmey had learned about her priorities during the long months they'd spent in the cell, and those priorities hadn't changed since then.

Lillian wouldn't have any qualms about telling Emmey to stay. Emmey didn't believe she'd be strong enough to resist her desire to be here with Maddy and Lillian and all the sisters she loved, to be able to scribe and stand in the library gazing at all the books in awe, to tend her garden and fill baskets with herbs for Lillian, to touch the sculpture of Lina every time she walked past it in the chapel's vestibule, to inwardly rejoice every time the chapel bells pealed . . . She could go on, because she loved it here. If only Salbine had called her.

Maddy and Lillian had been so sad when they'd told her she'd go to live with the Bennetts. Oh, they'd tried not to show it. Lillian hadn't shed a tear, but during the conversation she'd blustered about their chambers, polishing her carvings. Maddy's voice had shaken, but otherwise she'd kept her composure. Emmey had sat on her hands and managed to appear unfazed, not wanting to make it more difficult. Not that she could have said anything, with her chest and throat so tight that she could hardly breathe.

So here she was, feeling sorry for herself, and for them. They'd be disappointed if they knew. They'd been subdued last night, but today it was business as usual. Lillian was working in her laboratory. Maddy was meeting with the novices. Not wanting to disappoint them, even though they didn't know she was wasting her time moping, Emmey stood and brushed off her robe. She'd water her garden and try to forget for an hour.

She'd only taken a few steps when a Hedgerow sister strode past, one of the same two who'd gone into the trees the first day they'd arrived. Emmey squinted up the path and spotted the second sister hurrying after the first one. Not wanting to draw attention, she darted behind the oak tree and watched the second sister stride past, then followed her. She could guess where they were going. Sure enough, she rounded the curve in the path in time to see the second sister duck into the trees. Was this how sisters lay together at Hedgerow? Outside, in the trees?

Shaking her head, she walked to the garden shed to fetch a bucket, but on the way, she decided to plant seeds first, wanting to feel soil between her fingers and be alone for a while. Intending to also harvest herbs for Lillian, she collected an empty basket. The bucket could wait.

An hour later, she lifted her face to let the afternoon sun warm her cheeks. Tending her garden usually had a soothing effect. When she was gone, her plants and flowers would continue to sprout, grow, bloom, and die. But nothing could calm her today. Believing she could distract herself from thinking about leaving Maddy and Lillian had been foolish. Perhaps she should have shown interest in a trade that would have her occasionally invited inside the towers, but Sophia was right. Emmey would resent not being able to live with the two women she loved, and she'd resent her work too.

The basket was full, and she was working herself into a state. She wiped her dirty hands on the smock she wore. She'd take the herbs to Lillian's laboratory so she could see how Lillian was faring and spend some time with her, perhaps help her prepare an ointment or tincture. That was another thing Emmey wouldn't mind doing. Alchemy. Lillian had already taught her a few recipes, though Emmey wasn't allowed in the laboratory unless Lillian was there. She could have swiped the key. She knew where it was. But there were things she wouldn't do to Maddy and Lillian, however tempting they might be.

After pushing to her feet and picking up the basket, she shielded her eyes with her right hand and headed to the catacombs. A warm breeze tickled her cheeks. As she approached the road leading to the monastery's gate, she spotted someone striding down it, carrying a bulging sack.

Malcom noticed her at about the same time and stopped walking. "Morning, Miss Emmey," he shouted, waving.

"Morning, Malcolm. What's in the sack?"

"What?"

Emmey opened her mouth to repeat the question. It hung open, a sense of familiarity washing over her. She'd done this before. Stood in this very spot, carrying a basket of herbs, shouting at Malcolm. A horse—

The basket slipped from her hand. She ran toward him. "Get off the road!" she shouted.

He cupped his hand to his ear.

"Get off the road!" she shouted again, motioning for him to move. Then she pointed up the road.

He turned—and dove away. A horse pulling a wagon galloped past. Emmey held her breath, then let it out with a whoosh when Malcolm sat up on the other side of the road. She raced over to him and fell to her knees. "Are you all right?" she shouted.

"It's a good thing you saw the wagon, Miss Emmey. I didn't hear it."

Emmey couldn't reply. She could only stare, and tremble, and try to hold it in. But she couldn't and burst into tears.

"Don't cry." Malcolm awkwardly patted her shoulder. "I'm all right. You saw to that."

She wasn't crying for him. She was crying for Maddy.

11

A VERILL STOPPED SCRIBING when Mistress Olivia and Sister Clara's voices broke her concentration. They were outside her cubbyhole, but their voices sounded louder than usual. She bent her head again and scribed a *b*, but then Sister Clara spoke a name that caught Averill's attention.

" . . . almost run over."

"Is he all right?" Mistress Olivia asked, shock hushing her voice.

"Apparently Emmey saved his life by warning him just in time. I heard Master Thomas say he's not sure what spooked the horse. One of the stable boys had only just hitched it to the wagon when it suddenly bolted. I dread to think what would have happened if Emmey hadn't been there. Malcolm's almost deaf. He wouldn't have heard anything until it was too late."

Averill stopped listening and set her quill down with trembling fingers. Scribing would be impossible at the moment. She wiped the ink off her fingers with a rag and stood, wanting to pace.

Mistress Olivia walked in. "Did you hear that? A runaway horse almost ran someone down on the gate road." The mistress waited expectantly. Her eyes grew concerned. "Are you feeling unwell, Mistress? You look pale."

"No, no, I'm fine."

"I'll fetch you some water."

Mistress Olivia left without waiting for Averill to respond. For once, Averill was glad to see her go. She sank into the chair in front of her desk. It had come true! Emmey's dream about Malcolm had come true. That meant . . .

Averill wanted to weep. She lifted a book from her desk and opened it to where she'd placed a bookmark.

There may come a time when a foreteller will recount a dream in which she saw herself. According to the historical record, this happens to approximately eighty-five percent of all foretellers. The mirror dream, as it is known, is a harbinger of death. Those same foretellers will eventually fall into a deep slumber from which they never awake, normally within a month of having the mirror dream. They pass into Salbine's realm within a few days of closing their eyes for the last time. The remaining fifteen percent cease to dream future events at some point in their lives. There is no way to determine whether a foreteller will have the mirror dream. Here is the list of the unfortunates who had the dream and left our realm for Salbine's shortly thereafter.

She scanned the names, counting them as she went. While foretelling wasn't as rare as the malflowed condition, it certainly wasn't common. *Merrin* was noted next to one of the names, with a date over seven centuries in the past. The most recent date was over three centuries ago. Curious. Up to then, a name had been added every thirty years or so.

She flipped back to the title page. The book had been scribed sixty-seven years ago, a few years before Averill was born. She recognized the script. Mistress Carmine, the second to last head librarian. It must have been a routine scribing, not done for any purpose other than to preserve this book of research by a sister at the Swancross monastery.

Averill closed the book and gazed at nothing in particular. Would she have to add Emmey's name to the list of unfortunates? Averill loved books, but she wanted to toss this one into the fire and forget she'd ever read it.

~

ALMOST RUNNING, EMMEY HURRIED through the library and stopped outside Mistress Averill's office. The mistress was spending more time than usual in her little cubbyhole, as she called it. Once she'd finished helping the visiting sisters scribe their books, she'd be out in the library most of the time, helping the novices improve their reading and letters, and occasionally copying the odd book she wanted to preserve. Resentment stirred within Emmey. The Hedgerow sisters *would* have to come when her remaining time with Mistress Averill was running out. Mistress Olivia was in there with her now. The two mistresses were scribing side by side, almost touching each other. Had Mistress Averill told Mistress Olivia that she liked her in that way?

Emmey cleared her throat. Both mistresses looked over their shoulders and greeted her. She bobbed to them. "Mistresses."

Mistress Olivia set down her quill. "I think I'll stretch my legs," she said, demonstrating she was a quick learner. "It must almost be time for supper. Shall we scribe a bit more after we've eaten?"

"Yes, let's," Mistress Averill said. "I don't normally like scribing by candlelight alone, but I wouldn't mind half an hour before evening prayers."

"Then I'll see you later." Mistress Olivia smiled at Emmey as she passed her.

Emmey waited until the mistress was out of earshot. "Perhaps you should go walk with her. I'm sure she'd appreciate it."

"I thought you wanted to talk to me."

"I do, but I think you'd rather talk to Mistress Olivia."

"Why?"

"Because you like being with her."

"I like being with you too."

"Not in the same way."

"What do you mean, not in the same—" Mistress Averill's face flushed. "Sit down," she said, pointing to an empty chair.

Emmey did as she was told. "I'm here because it happened. It bloody-well happened."

Mistress Averill raised a finger. "Language."

"I'm sorry," Emmey murmured, even though she wasn't. Lillian said *bloody* all the time, and nobody said, "Language," to her. Rules again. Bloody rules. "I'm just excited, because it happened, just like in my dream."

Mistress Averill's reaction disappointed her. "Yes, I heard," she said mildly.

But had the mistress realized the significance of what she'd heard? "My dream came true."

"I know." The mistress's voice dropped, and she seemed to talk to herself for a moment. "But there's always a detail or two that are off. Malcolm was almost run down by a horse and wagon. You only saw a horse in your dream. There was a fire at the market, but Sister Maddy wasn't burned. You saw her burn." Mistress Averill frowned in thought.

"You can't say my dreams are just coincidence now. I know every detail wasn't right, but close enough. So have you found out anything? About my dreams."

"Ah." Mistress Averill stood and fussed with a stack of books on her desk, her back to Emmey. "Not yet. Nothing you don't already know anyway."

"Nothing?"

"No."

"But you still have more books to read, don't you?"

"Yes."

The mistress was being terse today. Emmey kicked herself for embarrassing her and wished she could see her face. She should have kept her observation to herself.

The mistress dropped her hands to her sides. "Have you ever seen yourself in your dreams?"

"Myself?"

Mistress Averill faced her and stood awkwardly. "Have you ever talked to yourself in your dreams?"

"In my dreams, I'm there, witnessing whatever's happening."

"But you haven't seen yourself."

"No."

Mistress Averill's shoulders sagged, as if all the air had been let out of her chest.

"Why are you asking? Did the books say something about seeing myself?"

"Oh, I read an account of a dream, you see. I thought it was interesting that the dreamer saw herself. If you ever see yourself, I want you to tell me."

"I don't think I will. I've never seen myself in a dream. Other people, yes, but not myself."

"I doubt you will too. But let me know if you do."

"I will." Emmey hesitated. "You look tired."

Mistress Averill rubbed the back of her neck. "I'm scribing more hours than usual. I'm helping the visiting sisters as much as I can."

"Aren't Sister Clara and Sister Elouise helping?"

"They are, but the book Mistress Olivia and I are scribing is a difficult one. Small script, you see, and the scribe's letters weren't well formed."

"You must confer quite a bit with Mistress Olivia."

"She asks for my opinion quite often. She's a scribe, but not a librarian. She's well read, but I can quickly put my finger on other references when we need them."

"I'd imagine you're more than happy to offer your expertise to her."

"Of course."

Emmey bit her tongue. She wished nothing but happiness for Mistress Averill. Next time she had one of those realistic dreams, she wanted it to be about when she was older, sitting here with the mistress, eating an apple, and scribing. She wouldn't mind one bit if that dream came true.

~

MADDY ALMOST DROPPED HER tea when Emmey bounded into their chambers. She quickly set her cup on the table. "I heard what happened. Are you all right?"

"It was Malcolm who almost got run over."

"I heard you saved him."

"I just shouted at him to get off the road."

"Still, if you hadn't been there."

"But I was." Emmey plunked into the chair across from Maddy and rested her elbows on the table. "Can I ask you something?"

"Of course you can."

"I'm not sure how to ask this." Emmey scratched her nose. "So, I saw two sisters go into the trees."

After a moment, Maddy said, "You saw two sisters go into the trees . . ."

"I thought they were lost, so I followed them. I was going to help them. But then I saw what they were doing and left right away."

"What were they doing?"

"Kissing." Emmey swallowed. "They were going to do more than kiss, though." She lifted her hands. "But I left. As soon as I knew why they'd gone into the trees, I left. They didn't see me."

Maddy was dying to ask, but then answered her own question. "You thought they were lost, so it must have been two of the visiting sisters." Probably Sisters Felicia and Lorelle, but it could have been Mistress Olivia, Mistress Margery, or Sister Cecily, too.

"I was wondering . . . " Emmey squared her shoulders. "I was wondering if that's normal."

"What?"

"Doing it outside."

Maddy almost laughed but caught herself in time. She lifted her cup and sipped her tea. "It's normal." And risky. "Where were they, exactly?"

"Off the path to the training stables. They were in the trees, where nobody could see them." Emmey scratched her nose again. "I saw them again today, going into the trees."

"I thought you were talking about today."

"No, the first time I saw them was on the first day they were here. Then I saw them again and couldn't believe it."

Maddy wanted to chuckle at Emmey's scandalized tone.

"I don't know why they don't go to their chambers."

"Perhaps they prefer the outdoors." Maddy didn't feel the same, not while on monastery grounds anyway. It would be different if she was travelling and she and Lillian had privacy.

Emmey gave her a coy look. "Have you and Lillian ever . . ."

"That's mine and Lillian's business," Maddy said firmly. They never had, not outdoors. They'd travelled with Emmey from Garryglen, making intimacy difficult. That didn't mean they'd limited themselves to their bedchamber, though. It was quite cozy in front of the fire in Lillian's laboratory, once they'd covered the stone floor with a fur.

"What about the time of day? Is that normal? Doing it in the middle of the day?"

"It can happen anytime."

Emmey opened her mouth, then closed it. Once again, Maddy wanted to ask, but she held her tongue. "There are a couple of books in the library I can recommend, if you like."

"About lying together?"

"Yes. Decent ones, not the ones Mistress Averill keeps locked away. You haven't read those books, have you?"

"No. I didn't even know she had any locked away."

She shouldn't have mentioned them. She only knew about them because Sophia had mentioned them once in passing. "There are a few in the general collection. We had to read two of them when we were novices."

Emmey's eyes widened. "You read books about lying together as part of your studies?"

"Yes, but the ones we had to read wouldn't be suitable for you. You'll want the ones for girls not marked by Salbine. I can ask Mistress Averill to set them aside for you."

Emmey stared at her. The silence stretched out. "If you don't want me to tell her they're for you, I'll tell them they're for me." Though what reason Maddy would provide for wanting them, she didn't know. Mistress Averill would see right through her.

"I think it would be a good idea," Maddy said when Emmey continued to stare. "You might marry in a couple of years." Maddy hoped not. But Emmey *would* eventually marry, and have children, and spend her days darning socks, cooking and cleaning, wiping noses, and supporting her husband in his pursuits. If Emmey was lucky, she'd have a business with her him, because

Maddy suspected she'd be bored, otherwise. "I don't know how much you already know about men and women lying together. There's not much point asking me about it. I could tell you the basics, but nothing more. And the books talk about herbs you can use to help you control when you have babes, and with cravings when you're pregnant." Now she was babbling. "I really do think you should read them."

Emmey appeared pained. She was probably embarrassed, but Maddy would be remiss if she didn't try to educate her about sex. She should have done it earlier. "Will you read them?"

Emmey slowly exhaled. "All right."

"Do you want me to ask Mistress Averill—"

"I'll do it."

"Good." Maddy gave her a reassuring smile. "Is there anything else you want to ask me?"

"No." Emmey pushed back her chair. "I'll go fetch more water, so there's enough for when Lillian wants tea."

Maddy frowned at Emmey's lacklustre tone and sombre expression. She'd been excited when she'd bounded into their chambers. Maddy had thought their conversation had gone quite well, but it had dampened Emmey's mood. She shouldn't have mentioned marrying and getting pregnant. Too much, too soon. However, Emmey might not wait until she was married to lie with a man, or to get pregnant. She'd had her first bleed a few months ago. Still, no man inside the walls would dare lie with her. If decency didn't stop him, the certainty of being incinerated by Lillian would.

Once outside the walls, though, Emmey could quickly fall in lust with a stable hand or some other boy, and who knew if they'd be able to restrain themselves. Maddy wouldn't be there to advise Emmey. She wouldn't be at Emmey's wedding, or waiting for news while she was in labour, or hold Emmey's first babe in her arms. She'd be here, behind the monastery's walls, and despite the void Emmey would leave, the effort it would take to live each day until the pain of losing her became bearable, and her inability to not wonder how Emmey was doing, Maddy wouldn't have it any other way. Her place was here. If only Emmey belonged here too.

~

MADDY OPENED THE DOOR to the study room in the library where they'd left the material about malflowed sisters from the other monasteries. She plunked into a chair and waited for Lillian to sit next to her. "It'll be the same old dry passages," she murmured, reaching for the pile they'd left at the corner of the table.

Half an hour later, she wanted to say, "See? I was right." But what purpose would it serve? "Are you finished?" she asked Lillian.

"I think so. Disappointing, I must say. There were a few passages I hadn't read before, but they didn't contain anything new."

Maddy needed to go to Heath, but she wouldn't bring it up here, in case there was going to be an argument. "Let's go tell Mistress Averill."

They found her talking to one of the visiting scribes. Based on the scribe's age and hair colour, it must be Sister Cecily. Maddy wondered if she'd been one of the sisters Emmey had followed into the trees.

When Mistress Averill had finished her conversation, Maddy bobbed to her. "Mistress."

"Have you met Sister Cecily?" Mistress Averill asked.

"No, we haven't."

"Sister Cecily, this is Mistress Lillian and Sister Maddy."

Sister Cecily bobbed to Lillian. "Thank you for your advice," she said to Mistress Averill. "I'll scribe the word *over*." She bustled away.

Maddy didn't understand Emmey's love of scribing. She had an abundance of patience with folk but would quickly grow surly if she had to spend her days laboriously copying documents and doing research just to decide if she should scribe an *a* or a *b*.

"We've finished reading the material from the other monasteries," Lillian said.

Maddy tried not to look disappointed. "You were right. Quite dry, I'm afraid, and nothing we didn't already know, albeit expressed differently at times."

"Ah." Mistress Averill moistened her lips. "But you're still interested in researching your condition."

"Of course."

"Then I have a surprise for you. With the abbess's blessing, I wrote to Heath. I wrote that I understood there was too much material for them to copy and send, but could they give us a taste, perhaps a few pages from the malflowed sister's journals. That's what you want, correct? Not more dry passages?"

Hope rising within her, Maddy enthusiastically nodded.

"Their head scribe was quite accommodating. They sent what I asked for."

"Why are you only telling us now?" Lillian bellowed, earning a stern look from Mistress Averill. Someone hissed "Shh!" behind them.

"Because I wanted you to get through the other material first, or you might never have read it and missed something."

Maddy would have read it, but the mistress was right. She would have wanted the material from Heath first and wished the mistress would stop talking and give it to her, which was terribly uncharitable.

As if Mistress Averill had read Maddy's mind, she motioned for them to follow her. When she pulled a leather scroll holder from one of her desk drawers, Maddy had to stop herself from snatching it from the mistress's hand. "Thank you." She felt as if she held a bag of gold. "When did you receive it?"

"I wrote a few months after you returned with Emmey, when we received material from Hedgerow, as it happens. I thought, why don't we ask Heath for something? The abbess agreed. When it arrived, I thought it best to wait until you approached me about reading the material you knew we'd received from the other monasteries. You were occupied with Emmey, you see, and learning how to do things with your one hand. I didn't want to interrupt."

Maddy couldn't fault her. The thought of doing any research had fallen to the wayside as she took care of Emmey, a more demanding undertaking when Emmey was eight than it was now. And yes, she'd also been determined to do as much as she could by herself. Frustration had often won the day, but she'd persevered. She'd decided to leave Heath for another time and hadn't expected to view any of the malflowed sister's writings until she'd stood in Heath's library. "You were very kind to think of me," she said to Mistress Averill. "You didn't have to take it upon yourself to write to Heath."

"Nonsense. Putting quill to parchment is something I do." Her eyes moved to the holder in Maddy's hand. "I think you'll be more satisfied with what's there. Use the same study room. I want the material to remain within the library. Once you've read it, I'll bind it. If there's anything you want us to scribe so you can have it in your chambers, do let me know."

Maddy's face must have conveyed her surprise at the unusual offer, because Mistress Averill added, "I know this material is of great personal value to you, Sister."

"Thank you." Maddy couldn't wait to get to the study room. As soon as Lillian swung the door shut behind them, Maddy plopped into her usual chair and set the holder in front of her. She was almost afraid to look at its contents.

"Well, go on," Lillian said.

"Do you mind if I read it all? You can see from there, right?"

Lillian fumbled in her robe pocket for her spectacles and popped them onto her nose, making Maddy smile. Silly woman. It must be tedious, taking her spectacles off every time she left their chambers, or a study room, or her laboratory. She looked fine in them. Quite sophisticated, actually.

Holding her breath, Maddy undid the holder's leather string and unrolled the parchment it contained. Five sheets. She read the top one.

Mistress Averill,

I've enclosed four pages of Sister Lavinia's— Tears sprang to Maddy's eyes. She had a name. *Sister Lavinia.* Long dead, but suddenly Maddy didn't feel so alone in her malflowness. She dabbed at her eyes with her fingertip. Lillian rubbed Maddy's back and didn't rush her. Had Sister Lavinia had a Lillian? Maddy hoped so. She continued to read.

. . . Sister Lavinia's journals. Believe me when I tell you that four pages is a drop in a lake when it comes to Sister Lavinia's writings. The sister entered the Order when she was sixteen and departed for Salbine's realm when she was eighty-eight. She wasn't a scribe, but

she loved to write and kept meticulous journals, filling at least two journals every year of her time in the Order except her last.

Maddy did a quick calculation in her head. If she'd died at eighty-eight and entered the Order at sixteen, that meant she'd left behind over 140 journals! And the letter said at least two a year. There could be more for some years. No wonder Heath had said there was too much material to copy, and that was only the sister's journals. Perhaps there was even more material, though it would probably be copies of what Maddy had already read, and terribly dry.

"She must have spent all her time scribbling in her journals," Lillian said.

Maddy's eyes strayed to the next line in the letter. "Not all her time."

Having said that, her journals became slimmer as she aged, and the number of entries dropped dramatically after she turned eighty. Her eyesight was failing, and she had more difficulty writing her letters—and we have more difficulty reading them.

Sister Lavinia was a talented embroiderer and seamstress. She mended many sisters' robes for them, and some of her handiwork still hangs on our monastery's walls. She didn't have much time for people. She preferred to write in her journals, recording not only her days, but her musings about life.

Did those musings include her thoughts about her condition?

It would have taken me ages to read all her journals, so I copied several passages at random. My apologies to Sister Maddy if none of them offer her any insight into her condition, but do tell her that she is welcome here any time and should expect to spend at least six months here if she wants to read everything. I look forward to meeting her; in fact, it will be quite exciting to meet a malflowed sister. We all know of Sister Lavinia, but she passed to Salbine's realm so long ago. Sister Maddy might be able to shed light on passages in Sister Lavinia's journals that we don't understand. Two centuries ago, one of our scholars studied the journals and listed passages that made no sense to her. I have included one of them in the enclosed material.

Yours in Salbine,
Mistress Alexandra

Senior Scribe, Heath

Lillian nudged Maddy. "See? She assumed the sister passed to Salbine's realm. She didn't see the condition as a punishment."

But what had Sister Lavinia thought? And even though the sister had passed when she was eighty-eight, she hadn't died a mistress. Maddy was now an adept, along with everyone who'd lived in the Initiates Tower with her. Sophia had said she'd served Salbine as well as the other initiates, and nobody had protested. Still, Maddy couldn't see herself a mistress, a title that was bestowed because a sister was highly skilled with the elements. She wouldn't mind. Many sisters died adepts. But she couldn't even strive for the title, couldn't spend extra time in the training rooms, or study technique here in the library. Her skill with the elements would never improve. It was non-existent.

Eager to read Sister Lavinia's writings, Maddy moved Mistress Alexandra's letter aside. Another quick calculation told her that Sister Lavinia had been nineteen when she'd written the first journal entry on the parchment. Since she'd entered the Order at sixteen, the entry would have been written around the time she would train.

Shattered. Faith and hope struggling, almost gone. Didn't understand, because the candle burned easily. But not the straw. Wouldn't come. And then it did. Inside. Pain was excruciating. Gave M. Alice a fright. Then told the source would never be my source. Wonder what they told the first one, how she figured it out. No existing history for her. A. Hester not sure what to do with me now. Neither am I. But A. Hester says there will be a way forward. Not sure I believe her. Chapel feels like a tomb now. Because I'm dead. Inside. Crying. Inside. Angry. Inside. Questioning. Inside. Calm. Outside. One word constantly on my lips and in my thoughts. Why.

Maddy wished she could reach through time and hug Sister Lavinia. She knew all too well what Sister Lavinia was feeling when she wrote this entry. She understood—utterly and completely. What she wouldn't give to have someone else in her shoes to commiserate with! She'd have to settle for touching her fingertips to the parchment, even though it was a copy. Were the original journals still in

Heath's library, or had they turned to dust? Would Maddy be able to touch a book Sister Lavinia had held and poured herself into?

"I recognize you in that," Lillian said.

Maddy did too, but something nagged at her. "She never was able to draw the elements. She died malflowed. I'm sure Mistress Alexandra would have mentioned if that wasn't the case."

Lillian's brow furrowed. "You find that surprising?"

"I'd wondered if she'd found a way to draw. Maybe she'd prayed enough, or uncovered the reason for it, or . . . I don't know."

Lillian squeezed her and kissed her cheek. "I've always assumed it was a lifelong condition."

"Because you don't think I did anything wrong. Anything I can put right."

"No, I don't. Only Salbine knows why you're malflowed, but I'm certain it's not a punishment. Otherwise we'd all be malflowed, Maddy. Every single one of us."

Then why her? Yes, the same word that had dogged Sister Lavinia also haunted Maddy. Why? She heaved a sigh and moved on to the next passage, which wasn't about being malflowed per se, but about Sister Lavinia's renewed interest in embroidery, which she'd discovered when the abbess asked her to embroider a tapestry—by herself—while her fellow initiates were training. Sister Lavinia's sour attitude toward the project had transformed to one of joy. Maddy could relate to this too. It wasn't as if her every waking thought was about her condition, and she'd discovered joy in loving Lillian, caring for Emmey, helping folk, and, of course, communing with Salbine.

She continued to read. Except for the last passage on the last page, the passages were a recounting of whatever Sister Lavinia had done that day, written in the same style as the first passage Maddy had read. The sister mentioned her condition in passing but wasn't focused on it. Maddy wished Mistress Alexandra had included more passages from the time when the sister had first discovered her condition, but she understood that the mistress had selected a single passage from several journals.

The very last entry was preceded by a note from Mistress Alexandra.

This is the entry I mentioned in my letter. We don't know what it means. One school of thought believes that Sister Lavinia was able to draw the elements again. The other school believes the malflowed condition is permanent and Sister Lavinia must have been describing something else. It's unfortunate that Sister Lavinia wasn't clearer, but she wrote her journals for herself, not for those of us who would study them later. Unfortunately, Mistress Matilda didn't leave anything behind that would illuminate Sister Lavinia's entry, and we don't have any references to the event in our collection. You must appreciate that Sister Lavinia left us almost six centuries ago, and many of the documents from that time haven't survived, especially since a fire 350 years ago destroyed part of our collection. If Sister Maddy can shed any light on this, we would appreciate her thoughts.

Maddy's eyes quickly moved down the page.

It didn't hurt. Don't know who was more surprised, me or M. Matilda. We were both shaking, but when M. Matilda had recovered, shouting. Lots of shouting. Sisters came from other training rooms to see. Couldn't blame her. Shouldn't have done it. Stupid, really. But it didn't hurt. Only Salbine knows why.

Maddy read the entry again, then stared at the words, willing them to convey more meaning than what was on the page. *It didn't hurt.* Had Sister Lavinia managed to draw the elements without falling to her knees in pain, her head swimming, and retching up her last meal? She'd obviously been in a training room, and whatever had happened had surprised Mistress Matilda. A malflowed sister drawing an element would definitely be a surprise.

She turned to Lillian. "Do you think she could have done it? Drawn the elements?"

Lillian pursed her lips. "I don't know. Why would the mistress shout if the sister managed to draw?"

"Because she'd tried, even though she knew it was dangerous for her? That's why Sister Lavinia said she'd been stupid. Because she tried."

Maddy read the entry's date again and calculated how old Sister

Lavinia would have been. Almost eighty. *Only Salbine knows why.* Why what? Why Sister Lavinia was suddenly able to draw the elements again? Maddy wanted to scream. She was going to Heath. As soon as she was certain Emmey had adjusted to life outside the monastery, she was going.

"It's possible they scribed the entry wrong," Lillian said. "Sister Lavinia wrote it when her letters weren't as good as they used to be."

The sister's age would also explain why she hadn't elaborated about what she meant in later entries. She hadn't been writing many. "She took the time to write this entry, which means whatever happened was significant to her."

Lillian grimaced.

"What?"

"I don't want you to get your hopes up."

"I'm not." Not really. "I'd never dare try to draw again. There's a good possibility it would kill me. I have too much to live for."

"I'm glad to hear you say that."

"I want to go to Heath, though." There, she'd said it, but that was all she'd say for now. She'd planted the seed.

"I'd be surprised if you didn't want to go. But we still have Emmey, and I'm sure you'll want to remain close to her until she marries."

Yes—and no. It could be years before Emmey married, though she'd probably have a husband in under five. Maddy didn't want to wait that long. Once Emmey was settled and had made friends, Maddy would set out for Heath again. Emmey would understand. They could write to each other.

"I'll ask Mistress Averill to copy the last entry. No, I'll ask her to copy everything. This will be all I have of her until Heath." When Maddy was in Heath's library, she would open the very first journal Sister Lavinia had written and read every single entry until she reached the last entry in the last journal. Sister Lavinia might have written something that only another malflowed sister would understand, something that would tell Maddy why the sister had tried to draw the elements again, and how she'd managed to do it.

Maddy and Lillian returned to Mistress Averill, who readily

agreed to have a scribe make a copy of everything for Maddy. It would have to wait until the Hedgerow scribes had gone, but Maddy didn't mind. She'd memorized Sister Lavinia's cryptic entry and would turn it over in her mind, scrutinizing every word for a clue, not that she expected to find one. The entry wasn't long, and its meaning seemed obvious to her. For some reason, Sister Lavinia had tried to draw the elements when she was almost eighty and had succeeded. Perhaps she'd decided that if doing so killed her, it didn't matter at her age. But what had prompted her to try?

On their way out of the library, they ran into Sophia. Maddy was bursting to tell her about the entry she'd just read, but she bobbed along with Lillian and waited for Sophia to speak first. "I'm glad I've run into you. I was going to come see you later."

"Why?" Lillian said.

"The Bennetts are coming to meet Emmey in a few days. They'll meet in one of the study rooms. I'll let you know the time when I have it." Sophia gazed at Maddy. "I thought you and Emmey could meet them together, so Emmey doesn't have to do it alone. Then you'll leave and let them start to get to know each other."

Maddy's excitement fizzled. She'd tell Sophia about the entry another time. "I'll do that." And hate every minute of it.

"I know this will make it more real, and how difficult it will be to let her go."

She was starting to get tired of everyone telling her she'd be devastated about Emmey, as if she didn't know. "I'll be all right. Eventually."

Sophia gulped and patted Maddy's arm. "We'll all lean on each other."

Her words made Maddy feel guilty. She wouldn't be the only one missing Emmey.

12

EMMEY CLIMBED TO THE top floor of the Novices Tower and took a moment to catch her breath. She'd start here and work her way down to the bottom floor, but she didn't expect to find it—the chamber in her dream, the one filled with flames that Maddy calmly walked into. During her first year here, Emmey had explored every inch of all the towers. She hadn't been inside all the chambers, but she'd walked every hall, and none of them dead ended at a chamber. But she had to doublecheck, satisfy herself that Maddy wouldn't die here at the monastery because she strolled into a burning chamber as if she were strolling along the path to the stables.

As she'd expected, she didn't come across a dead end on the eighth and seventh floors. On the sixth floor, humming from the washroom caught her attention. She'd recognize that voice any-where. Sister Dolores. Since it was coming from the washroom, she must be inside, bathing.

Emmey stopped short, not wanting to alert Sister Dolores to her presence, or to accidentally glimpse her without her shift and robe on. She'd seen sisters naked more times than she could count, but they weren't Sister Dolores. Seeing the sister naked would be embarrassing, because Emmey would want to look at her, really look, and she was certain the sister wouldn't appreciate that sort of attention. But Emmey needed to continue down the hall, even though she was certain that when she turned the corner up ahead, the hall would lead to yet another corner, because the Novices Tower was square shaped with a square hall, and two of the square's corners had stairwells leading off them.

If the washroom here was the same as the ones in the Mistresses Tower, the washtub would be behind a curtain. Emmey took a breath and resumed walking. Her heart pounding in her ears, she quickened her pace as she passed the washroom's open door, and slowly exhaled as Sister Dolores's humming faded behind her. The sister probably hadn't heard her because she was soaking in the washtub with a book in her hand. Emmey had been in the library once when Sister Dolores had come in red-faced and told Mistress Averill that she'd dropped a book she'd borrowed into the tub.

"Blot up as much water as you can and then stand it up and fan out all its pages," Mistress Averill had said, her terseness the only sign that she was upset. After Sister Dolores had left, the mistress had tutted and shaken her head at Emmey. "It's probably ruined. Honestly, I wish sisters would be more careful with the books and scrolls they borrow. Every one is a treasure, Emmey. Every one." Emmey knew Mistress Averill was referring to the books and scrolls, and not to sisters.

"Fortunately, the one Sister Dolores borrowed isn't rare," Mistress Averill had continued. "I shall add her to the list of sisters who are not to remove rare items from the library without my express permission."

Emmey had been dying to ask who else was on the list, but she hadn't wanted to upset the mistress further.

Reaching the corner, she turned it and nodded her head. Sure enough, the hall led to another corner with a stairwell leading off it, the same one Emmey had used to descend to this floor. She was back to where she'd started. She went down to the fifth floor, then the fourth. Ten minutes later, she left the Novices Tower, satisfied that it didn't contain the burning chamber.

Unless there was a building on monastery grounds that Emmey had never seen or entered, the chamber in her dream didn't exist as it was in her dream. Which meant nothing, because her dreams always got a few details wrong.

Her hands clenched. Maybe the dream didn't mean anything. No, it was one of *those* dreams, the ones that felt as real as everything did when she was awake, and that kept repeating itself. But did it mean Maddy would die? Next time Emmey dreamed it, she'd pay more attention, force herself to look at Maddy burning in that chamber, rather than turning away and whimpering. Emmey had stopped Malcolm from being trampled. She'd do everything she could to stop Maddy from burning to death somewhere here, where she felt the safest.

~

MADDY SAT IN A study room, the blank parchment on the table taunting her. Given how many letters she'd already written for Emmey, she'd considered not contributing to the tome the community was putting together for her. But what would Emmey think if there wasn't a page from her, especially since Lillian had written one? Maddy had read Lillian's so many times, she'd memorized it.

Things will certainly be different when you're gone. Suddenly everything will still be where I left it. I'll be able to eat in peace without having to answer a hundred questions. The water in the kettle – enough for one more cup of tea – won't mysteriously disappear.

But you won't visit me in my laboratory, either. Or greet me when I return from early morning prayers. Or make me laugh when I don't feel like it. Or teach me how to be more patient (a lost cause, but you do try!).

I'll miss you, my little mite. Be well. Be you.
Love, Lillian.

Short, but that Lillian had written it at all, private Lillian who worked so hard to not let anyone see the gentle woman Maddy loved, was a testament to how much she loved Emmey.

Maddy stared at the blank parchment again, afraid that whatever she wrote would come across as too maudlin or sentimental.

How was she supposed to sum up years of love, pride, aggravation, laughter, and exasperation in one page? She balled her fist in frustration, then slapped the parchment back on the pile on the table and pushed back her chair. She'd try again another time, though the deadline for contributions was quickly approaching, along with what would be one of the darkest days of her life.

~

LILLIAN LOWERED HERSELF into her chair in front of the roaring fire and rotated the wooden carving block she held. She hadn't carried the leather case that contained her carving tools over to the chair. She carved on the table, and she liked to feel the rough wood and ponder what animal she'd create before she began, though her usual excitement was tempered. Emmey wouldn't be here to see the wood slowly reveal its secrets and to confer with Maddy about where to display the finished carving, a task that Lillian had willingly relinquished to them.

She glanced at Maddy, who was sitting to her right. Emmey sat in her usual chair at Maddy's other side.

"So you think she drew the elements, then?" Emmey was saying, her face alight with curiosity.

"That's what it sounds like to me," Maddy said. "She was almost eighty. She might have tried because she felt ready to pass to Salbine's realm, and so she was willing to risk it."

Emmey chewed her lip. "Did she find out she was malflowed the same way you did?"

"I would think so."

"How? You've never told me how."

Lillian glanced at Maddy. Normally they didn't discuss anything related to training with those outside the Order. Emmey was inside the monastery, but she wasn't a sister. But what harm would it do? "I was Maddy's tutor."

"I know that part!"

"When Maddy began her training, I asked her to light a candle. That's how fire training usually begins."

"It can take a lesson or two just to do that," Maddy added. "I couldn't do it at all. Well, I could, but barely. I managed it a few times, but the flame always looked like it was about to go out, as if the candle was sitting outside in the wind." Maddy's voice was level, but Lillian wanted to take her hand.

"And that's how you knew? Because the flame was weak?"

"No. One night, I tried to draw and thought I was on fire."

The blood drained from Emmey's face.

"It's all right," Maddy quickly said. "I wasn't actually on fire, but I thought I was."

Lillian picked up the story. "She ran around the training room, shouting, 'I'm on fire! I'm on fire!' I didn't know what to do. I could see she wasn't, but she was flailing around as if she was."

Her face ashen, Emmey left her chair so she could kneel in front of Maddy and lay her head in Maddy's lap, something she hadn't done in a while. Her hands trembled.

"She wasn't on fire," Lillian repeated, wanting to reassure her.

"I was in a lot of pain, though. I collapsed, and when I woke up, Sophia told me I was malflowed and what it meant." Maddy sighed. "She said I should never try to draw again, but I did, at my trial. You know the rest. That's when I ended up at the prison. With you."

They sat silently for a while, the crackling of the fire the only sound. Were Maddy and Emmey thinking about their time trapped together in a small cell, Maddy hoping that someone would come for her? Lillian eventually had, just in time to save her. Once again, she thanked Salbine that they'd ridden for the prison that day rather than waiting for the next, or Maddy might not be sitting here right now, a thought that curdled Lillian's stomach.

"What would happen if someone who's marked by Salbine but isn't in the Order tried to draw the elements?" Emmey asked.

Lillian shifted in her chair. "Salbine wouldn't permit her to draw to any substantial degree and would likely strike her down."

"You believe that?"

"I do. It would be impertinent to draw without Salbine's blessing. Salbine would not be pleased with anyone who tried."

Emmey lifted her head and gazed at Maddy. "She didn't do

anything to you. You can't draw, but She didn't do anything to you when you tried. That means She wasn't upset with you."

"You're a scholar of Salbine's mind now, are you?" Maddy said, her tone light.

"I'm just saying She didn't do anything to you, like Lillian says She would."

"No, She didn't, and don't ask me why not, because I don't know." Maddy absently stroked Emmey's hair. "I wish I did."

"I think it's because She loves you and She's not upset with you."

"I think that too," Lillian said.

Maddy smiled, but her eyes remained distant.

~

CARRYING A BASKET OF chamomile, Emmey wound her way through the catacomb's narrow passageways, lost in thought. Maddy and Lillian's recounting of how Maddy had discovered she was malflowed reminded Emmey of her dream, the part when Maddy was at the market, dancing in flames and shouting that she was on fire. But how could that be? Had Emmey heard the story before? She didn't think so, but she wasn't sure. Perhaps she'd asked Maddy while they were in prison, or soon after arriving at the monastery, and had forgotten, just as Mistress Averill believed she'd forgotten about what had happened to Eddie. But then the dream about Malcolm had come true.

Were her dreams about Maddy predicting the future, or echoes of the past? Maddy hadn't died at the market, so she might not die in a burning chamber. It could be symbolism, as Sophia had suggested, or perhaps there would be a fire at the monastery, but nobody would be hurt. Perhaps the part about Maddy was wrong and was truly a dream and nothing more.

She was so lost in her thoughts that when she arrived at Lillian's laboratory, she couldn't remember how she got there. The route was etched in her memory. She could do it blindfolded, not that she'd want to.

Lillian looked up from a scroll she was reading and peered at

Emmey through her spectacles. Emmey remembered when she'd gotten them. "I look like a bloody owl!" Lillian had said, making Emmey giggle. Lillian only wore them when she read, and only in the presence of Maddy, Sophia, Elizabeth, and Emmey. That was one of the ways Emmey knew Lillian truly loved her. She wore her spectacles around her.

Lillian eyed the basket. "I was just thinking I need more chamomile."

Emmey plunked it onto the table. "I told Maddy I'd bring you some and that we'll meet her outside the chapel for evening prayers."

"We will, will we?" Lillian set the scroll down and pulled the basket closer to her. "Do you want to help me sort out the best ones?"

"I've already done it."

"Have you?"

"I know how to do it."

"I know you do."

When Emmey had first arrived at the monastery, she'd been forbidden from entering Lillian's laboratory. But Maddy had sometimes brought Emmey with her when she needed to speak to Lillian, and Emmey had instinctively known to be on her best behaviour, to not knock over jars or dip her fingers into any mixtures Lillian was preparing. She always stayed near Maddy, holding her hand. But she couldn't resist asking questions, questions that initially exasperated Lillian, until one day, Lillian threw up her hands and said, "If I let you have a look, will you be quiet?"

She moved Maddy's chair nearer to the table and lifted Emmey onto it, and let her watch as she ground an herb and distilled it. After that, Lillian always let Emmey watch, and when Emmey turned ten, Lillian allowed her to come to the laboratory without Maddy. She wasn't allowed to touch anything or to be there alone. She had strict instructions to leave if she found the laboratory empty.

For once, Emmey had obeyed, not wanting to be banished from the laboratory. Eventually Lillian had let her try her hand at preparing herbs and flowers and distilling them, and mixing tinctures and poultices. But in a queer twist, she'd discovered that she enjoyed growing herbs and flowers more than working with them.

She'd initially read books about gardening because she wanted to be useful to Lillian. She hadn't expected to enjoy it, that nurturing a seed and watching it grow would raise her spirits almost as much as scribing did. Tame, Sophia had said. Not to Emmey. And she delighted in coming to the laboratory with a full basket.

She moved the chair Maddy usually used next to Lillian and sat on it. "I need to say something to you."

Lillian's eyes sharpened. "What?"

Emmey lifted the scroll Lillian had been reading and stared at it without registering the letters. "You *will* make sure Maddy's all right after I'm gone?"

"Do you really need to ask me that?"

"No, but it makes me feel better that I've said it."

"You bloody-well know I'll make sure she's all right. It doesn't mean she won't be sad, though. She will be. Terribly sad. But she knows you can't stay."

She could, if she opened her mouth and admitted that she believed she was marked and she'd take the robe. But she'd be doing it for Maddy and Lillian, not Salbine. They didn't know it, but she was leaving because she respected everything the Order stood for. She would leave because she loved them, Maddy and Lillian and Sophia and Elizabeth and Averill and Rose and Nora and Abigail and Grace—even bloody Gwendolyn. She couldn't—wouldn't—take the robe without Salbine's blessing. To her utter disappointment, she didn't have it.

She would have to leave Merrin, eventually. Seeing the monastery up on the hill . . . no. One heartbreak at a time. She'd work for the Bennetts for a year or two, then go. In the beginning, she'd meet Maddy in the market, but it would hurt, and Emmey would eventually miss one meeting, then more, until she disappeared—after leaving a note in the petition box at the gate. She wouldn't want anyone to worry, but she'd be firm.

Lillian nudged her. "You're certainly quiet today, and you're taking an awfully long time to read that scroll."

Emmey dropped the parchment to the table and blinked at Lillian. She'd probably never see her again when she left the monastery.

Seeing Lillian for the last time in only a couple of weeks . . . she couldn't wrap her head around it. She averted her gaze, not wanting Lillian to see the despair in her eyes. "Give me something to do, something mindless," she said.

Lillian didn't protest or ask why. She plunked a bowl filled with petals in front of Emmey. "Purple ones to the left. White ones to the right."

Fighting tears, Emmey sorted them. Lillian worked silently next to her, and when Emmey finished sorting the petals, Lillian moved the bowl away and put another one in front of her. Emmey's heart swelled with love at the same time her throat constricted, making it difficult for her to swallow. Love could hurt, a lesson she wished she'd never learned.

~

AS EMMEY WALKED WITH Lillian to the chapel, she wanted to take her hand, but she hadn't done so for quite a long time now. She was older, old enough to be thrown out the gates. No, that wasn't fair. Bloody rules were bloody rules, and she was in a foul mood. Even the sight of the chapel up ahead didn't make her feel better. Once inside, the feel of the bench underneath her, the sense of community with those gathered, the stained glass, the songs they'd sing, the prayers she'd say silently, and in unison with those she loved . . . they'd lift her spirits. If only she didn't have to leave. If only she was called to the Order.

Maddy stood outside the chapel, speaking to three of the Hedgerow sisters. Emmey's shoulders hunched. She'd have to face the two sisters she'd seen going into the trees and do her best to not appear embarrassed. If not for Maddy being there, she'd skirt around them and duck into the chapel.

"There you are." Maddy beckoned for Emmey and Lillian to join her. "Have you met these sisters from Hedgerow?"

"Only Sister Cecily," Lillian said as Emmey shook her head. Maddy wasn't blushing or anything. Didn't she remember their conversation?

"This is Mistress Lillian," Maddy said.

The three sisters bobbed in unison. "Pleased to meet you, Mistress," one said. One of the other sisters murmured her agreement.

"This is Emmey."

"Hello," the talkative one said. The other two smiled at her. Keeping her eyes on the sister who hadn't gone into the trees, Emmey smiled back.

Maddy gestured to the sister closest to Emmey. "This is Sister Cecily. This is Sister Felicia, and this is Sister Lorelle, Sister Felicia's consort."

Emmey froze. Time slowed. Her surroundings distorted. No, that wasn't right. It couldn't be right.

" . . . go inside," one of the Hedgerow sisters said. The three sisters filed into the chapel. Maddy and Lillian went inside as well.

Emmey numbly fell into step behind them. She absently touched the sculpture of Lina as she passed it and didn't gaze at her favourite stained glass window as she put one foot in front of the other and somehow found herself sitting next to Maddy near the front of the chapel.

She elbowed Maddy in the ribs, wanting to speak to her before Maddy sank to her knees to pray. "I've already forgotten the sisters' names. Is the one with the brown hair Sister Lorelle?"

Maddy twisted to look behind her. "Do you see where they're sitting?"

Emmey turned to look. "Yes."

"The one sitting on the left with the reddish-brown hair. That's Sister Lorelle. In the middle is her consort, Sister Felicia. The blonde one on the right is Sister Cecily."

"Sister Cecily is the one sitting next to Mistress Olivia?"

"Yes."

Her mind racing, Emmey faced the front of the chapel and sank to her knees. She must have misunderstood what being consorts meant. The two sisters who'd kissed and unbuttoned each other's robes weren't Sister Felicia and Sister Lorelle. They were Sister Felicia and Sister Cecily.

13

AVERILL RAISED HER HEAD when familiar footsteps approached her cubbyhole. Emmey bobbed and hovered in the doorway. "Mistress Olivia isn't here?"

"She's taking a break, probably strolling the gardens."

Emmey came closer and shoved her hands into her robe's pockets. "I need a book about consorts."

"Consorts? What do you want to know about them?"

"Uh, what they can and can't do. With each other."

"Perhaps you should talk to Sister Maddy."

"I already know about that!" Emmey shrieked. She lowered her voice. "I'm interested in the rules."

"Rules."

"Can they do things with other sisters who aren't their consort? Intimate . . . things."

Averill pretended not to notice Emmey's scarlet face. "If you're asking what I think you're asking, no, they can't. Well, they can, but they're not supposed to."

"That's what I thought."

"I can give you a book about the history and obligations of consorts."

"Yes, please."

Averill slid off her stool and led Emmey to the fourth floor.

"Here you are," she said, taking a tome from a shelf and handing it to her. "Do you mind me asking why you're wondering about this?"

"It's because of a conversation I had with Maddy."

"Maddy?" Averill echoed, her voice higher than usual.

"It's not what you're thinking."

"I wasn't thinking anything, but do go on."

"Maddy talked to me about," Emmey's voice dropped to a whisper, "lying together, and it got me thinking about other things. Actually, she told me to come see you to get a book about men and women lying together."

"I see." Something nagged at Averill. She tapped her chin and tried to bring it to the surface.

"Do you have a book, or what?" Emmey snapped.

"Manners, Emmey."

"I'm sorry."

Averill shook herself and walked to another shelf. As she pondered which book would be appropriate for someone Emmey's age, it suddenly hit her. If Emmey was a foreteller, she must be marked by Salbine. Averill gave her a sidelong glance. "You said Sister Maddy told you to ask for a book about men and women lying together?"

"She said it would be good for me to read one."

"You didn't tell her you wanted one."

Emmey shook her head.

She obviously hadn't told Sister Maddy she was marked by Salbine, perhaps because she hadn't realized it yet. It wasn't Averill's place to tell Emmey or anyone else, but that didn't mean she couldn't help. "You know I believe in a well-rounded education, so I'm thinking it might be good for you to read a book about women lying with each other. Do you think that would make sense?"

"You mean a book for girls marked by Salbine?"

"Yes."

"Maddy said a book for girls not marked by Salbine would be more suitable for me."

"I understand, but that doesn't mean you can't read other books too. Would you like me to find one for girls marked by Salbine?"

Emmey hesitated. "I suppose I should read one. After all, look at where I am."

"Indeed."

"When I tell people I lived here, they might expect me to know certain things. They might even ask me for advice."

Averill bit back a laugh. "You have a point, there." She slid a tome from the shelf. "Here's one for girls not marked by Salbine."

Emmey clutched it and the book about consorts to her chest. Averill walked to her left and pulled out another tome. "And here's one for girls marked by Salbine." She wasn't surprised when Emmey tucked it between the other two books. "Now, if you have any questions, you can ask me or Sister Maddy."

"Not Mistress Lillian?" Emmey said.

They both chuckled.

When they returned to Averill's cubbyhole, Mistress Olivia was dipping her quill into ink. "Oh, good morning," she said brightly.

Averill beamed at her. The mistress was a delightful scribing companion. Skilled and studious, and she loved to talk about books. Averill would miss her when she left for Hedgerow. She'd miss the girl staring at her too, the one with a smirk on her face. "Is there anything else?" she asked, a bit more harshly than she'd intended.

Emmey didn't appear perturbed. With a glint in her eye, she curtseyed to both mistresses. "I'll leave you to your scribing."

"She's a lovely girl," Mistress Olivia said when Emmey had gone. "I was quite surprised when I first saw her here, but she fits in quite nicely."

Yes, she did, and if she was marked by Salbine, she could take the robe. Did Emmey know she was marked? If she expressed interest in joining the Order, surely Sophia would allow her to remain here until she was old enough to become a novice. It would be a shame for Emmey to leave and realize afterwards. She could return, of course, but she'd have to wait until she turned sixteen. Better not to leave at all.

Averill certainly wouldn't tell Emmey she was marked. For one thing, her suspicion could be wrong, though she doubted it. For another thing, it wasn't her place to rush Emmey into discovering something she hadn't done yet herself. Averill would add another prayer to the ones she already said for Emmey. She'd pray that when Emmey read the book for girls marked by Salbine, she'd understand, and the tome Averill would bind of all the sisters' memories would become a present that welcomed Emmey into the Order, rather than a parting memento of the six short years she'd spent here.

~

MADDY RESTED HER HEAD on Lillian's chest, basking in the afterglow of lying with her. She hadn't been in the mood, not at first. When Lillian's hands had begun exploring, Maddy's first impulse had been to gently brush them aside. But then her body had responded, and she'd met Lillian's challenge, and as she lay listening to Lillian's beating heart, she reminded herself that this was where it had begun. With Lillian, just the two of them. And this is where it would soon be. Just her and Lillian, but with the shared memories and experiences of caring for Emmey. As she had many times before, she silently thanked Sophia for assigning Lillian as her tutor. Sophia insisted it had been happenstance, so Maddy also thanked Salbine, who took with Her left hand and gave with Her right.

A thump came from Emmey's bedchamber. Then a door creaked open, and a chair slid across stone. Maddy lifted her head. "Do you think she's had another bad dream? I didn't hear her cry out."

"Whatever it is, it's taken her out of bed."

Which was unusual. "I'd better go see what's wrong."

Lillian didn't protest. As Maddy swung her legs off the bed, Lillian lit one of the kerosene lamps, which cast enough light for Maddy to find her way to the bowl of water on the chest of drawers next to the bed. The ice-cold water she splashed onto her face made her suck in her breath. After wiping her face dry, she grabbed the blanket hanging over a chair and wrapped it around her shoulders, knowing the sitting room hearth would be cold.

She couldn't hold the blanket and carry a lamp, so she opened the bedchamber door and waited for her eyes to adjust to the gloom, the only light the burning lamp from the table. It cast an orange glow on Emmey's face, who sat staring at the lamp, her shoulders hunched. She looked up when Maddy approached the table. "Oh, no, I didn't mean to wake you up."

Maddy pulled out the chair opposite her and quickly grabbed the blanket to prevent it from slipping from her shoulders, not because she cared if Emmey saw her naked, but because it was bloody cold. "Are you all right?"

Emmey blew out a sigh. "I can't sleep. I keep going over it in my mind, wondering what to do, whether to say anything or not."

"Can you talk to me about it?"

"If I think it's best that we not tell anyone, will you promise not to?"

Maddy thought for a moment. "I might disagree with you."

Emmey cocked her head. "The whole reason I can't sleep is because I can't decide. I suppose if you think we should tell, then we should."

"What would we tell?"

When Emmey leaned forward, Maddy did too. "Do you remember me telling you about the sisters going into the trees? When you introduced me to the three sisters outside the chapel yesterday, two of them were there."

Maddy's guess had been right, then. "Sister Felicia and Sister Lorelle," she stated.

"No. Sister Felicia and Sister Cecily. That's who went into the trees."

It took a second for Maddy to grasp the implications. "Are you sure?" she breathed. "Absolutely sure."

"That's why I asked you to point them out to me again. I wanted to be sure."

Troubled, Maddy leaned back in her chair.

"I asked Mistress Averill for a book about consorts because I thought maybe I had it wrong, that consorts can lie with anyone."

"We can't," Maddy murmured absently, still not quite believing what Emmey had told her. "Did you tell Mistress Averill what you'd seen?"

"No."

"Good. Don't breathe a word to anyone. We'll go see Sophia tomorrow, after breakfast."

"So you think we should tell?"

"Yes, I do." Betraying the vows made to one's consort was completely disrespectful to the consort, the Order, and above all, Salbine. "Sophia needs to know."

"What do you think she'll do?"

"I don't know."

"Has it ever happened before?"

Not to Maddy's knowledge, but if Sophia had ever had to deal with a sister who'd strayed, the matter would remain confidential. "I don't think so."

Emmey's face was solemn. "I wish I hadn't seen them."

"But you did." Maddy paused. "Why would you think to keep it a secret?"

"I don't like getting people into trouble."

"Even when they're disrespecting Salbine?"

Emmey's head dropped. "I know. I think I would have told. I couldn't get to sleep because I kept thinking about it. I wanted to tell," she said more firmly.

"You needed time to work up to it. I can understand that."

Emmey lifted her head. "And you'll be with me when I tell Sophia?"

"Of course I will."

Emmey's mouth turned up at the corners.

"Do you think you can sleep now?" The chill in the room was seeping into Maddy's bones, despite the blanket. She wondered at Emmey, who didn't have a blanket and wasn't shivering. "You should get back into bed, get under the covers."

Emmey suddenly leaped to her feet and wrapped her arms around Maddy. "Thank you. I don't know what I'll do without you."

Maddy squeezed her eyes shut. "You'll find your way," she whispered.

Emmey grabbed the lamp and padded away. Maddy waited until Emmey's bedchamber door had closed, then followed the light of the kerosene lamp burning in her bedchamber until she was standing next to the bed again. She draped the blanket over the chair and doused the lamp.

"What was wrong?" Lillian murmured, making Maddy jump.

She climbed into bed and snuggled against Lillian's warm body. "I'll tell you in the morning." There was no reason for both of them to lie awake thinking about consorts who break their vows.

14

Wanting to pace, Sophia drummed her fingers on her desk and waited for the sister she'd sent Barnabus to fetch. She would have gone herself, but this was a conversation that must take place behind a closed door. When Maddy and Emmey had come to her study, Sophia had been delighted to see them—until Emmey had stammered out what she'd witnessed. Now Sophia had to sort through the mess with sisters she didn't know.

Mistress Margery strode into the room and bobbed. "You wanted to see me."

The faint scent of ale reached Sophia's nose. The first time the Hedgerow sisters had entered her study, she hadn't been sure, but that wasn't the case anymore. She'd leave the mistress's excessive taste for ale to Hedgerow's abbess. Was Hedgerow completely in disarray, or were the sisters visiting Merrin the worst it had to offer? "Please shut the door."

The mistress did so. Sophia was tempted to make her stand, but Sisters Felicia and Cecily's dalliance wasn't the mistress's fault. She gestured toward a chair.

Mistress Margery sat down and waited.

"I've called you here as a courtesy." And to find out what the mistress knew before she summoned Sister Felicia. "You're Hedgerow's head scribe, so you're the leader of your little group." Sophia clasped her hands on her desk. "It has come to my attention that Sister Felicia is sexually involved with Sister Cecily."

Mistress Margery blinked at her but didn't react otherwise.

"You don't seem surprised. If you knew, why didn't you bring it to my attention?" Sophia's voice was rising. She gulped down air and consciously calmed herself.

"I didn't know. I'm not surprised because we had an incident a few years back, with Sister Felicia."

"A similar incident?"

"Unfortunately, yes."

Sophia's knuckles whitened. "What happened?"

"As you can imagine, I don't like to talk about this. It doesn't reflect well on any of us."

"Try."

The mistress's shoulders sagged. "We—not me, personally, but the abbess—found out that Sister Felicia had become enamored with a novice. Someone caught them kissing, apparently. The girl hadn't taken her vows yet, so we put her outside the gates."

Sophia waited for more, but the mistress needed encouragement. "How did Sister Felicia explain herself?"

"I wasn't there, but I heard she was very apologetic and regretted her terrible lapse in judgement."

"Did Sister Lorelle know about it?"

"I believe so."

"How did you find out?"

"The abbess called the mistresses together to find out if any of us had noticed anything, and to remind us to keep our eyes open for that sort of thing. As far as I know, it hasn't happened again, with anyone. Sister Felicia did promise that she'd never do it again."

"Well, it's happened again, and this time, it's gone beyond kissing. More than once."

The mistress's eyes widened. "Do you mind me asking how you found out?"

"From a trustworthy source. Now, based on what you've said, I gather that your abbess gave Sister Felicia another chance." Sophia wanted to shout at Hedgerow's abbess for being optimistic, an irrational urge, but her inclination, all the same.

"But you won't be?"

"We can see there's a pattern now." Sophia paused. "Is that why you're so hard on Sister Felicia?"

The mistress hesitated. "Not all of us were pleased with the abbess's handling of the situation."

"You didn't notice anything between them on your journey."

"No, but I'm not their favourite person, and when I travel to scribe, I scribe."

"What about as you travelled?"

Mistress Margery barked a laugh. "Nothing happened on the road. The tents are too close together, and we'd go looking for anyone who went off to do her business and was gone for too long. And we'd certainly notice if two sisters were taking a while."

"Then it must have started at Hedgerow."

"You think so?"

"I doubt they suddenly decided to lie with each other here." Especially since Emmey had first seen them on the day the sisters had arrived.

"What are you going to do?" Mistress Margery asked. "I'll abide by whatever you decide, of course."

Sophia wanted to snort. She'd bloody-well better! "I'll start by speaking to Sister Felicia."

"Only Sister Felicia?"

"Yes." She was the one with a consort. Sophia wanted to rub her temples. "Please tell her I'd like to see her."

"Is that all?" Mistress Margery asked, after a moment.

"Yes." Sophia raised a finger. "Not a word to anyone else, do you understand?"

Mistress Margery bustled from the study.

While she waited for Sister Felicia, Sophia thought about whether she'd have handled the sister's first indiscretion in the same manner. The abbess had done right by ejecting the novice. It was too bad she'd been unable to eject Sister Felicia. It wouldn't be an option for Sophia, either. The woman was an adept. She had to remain in a monastery. Unfortunately, whichever abbess had agreed to allow Sister Felicia and Sister Lorelle to pledge had erred. There were a handful of sisters Sophia would refuse based on their pattern of behaviour, but for all she knew, Sister Felicia hadn't struggled with remaining in a relationship for long, or hopped from bed to bed, before she'd pledged.

Sister Felicia hovered in the study doorway. "Come in and shut the door," Sophia said.

The sister did so, curtseyed, and stood awkwardly.

"I'll be blunt. What's going on between you and Sister Cecily?"

Shock froze Sister Felicia's face. She recovered quickly. "What do you mean?"

"Don't take me for a fool, Sister. I know you're lying together. I want you to explain to me why you've betrayed your bond with Sister Lorelle."

Sister Felicia shifted her weight. "I didn't mean for it to happen."

Sophia wanted to roll her eyes. "You just found yourself lying with her?"

"It didn't happen like that."

"How did it happen, then?"

"We fell in love." Sister Felicia raised her chin. "Cecily isn't a passing interest."

"Is Sister Lorelle?" Sophia shouted. "Because you kneeled in front of Salbine and pledged to honour her as your consort for the rest of your life."

The sister stared at her feet. "I know."

"That's all you have to say? That you know?" The air hung heavy between them. "Do you love Sister Lorelle?" Sophia asked, lowering her voice to its normal level.

Sister Felicia raised her head. "I don't know. I'm very fond of her. But I don't know if I love her. To be honest, I'm not sure I've loved her for a few years now."

"Since you kissed some novice?"

The sister's face tightened, but she didn't reply.

"So now you believe your true love is Sister Cecily."

"She is!"

"You believed that of Sister Lorelle."

"I . . ." Sister Felicia's nostrils flared. "We pledged too young."

"But you pledged. You can't change that."

"I want to be released. I've asked Lorelle to agree to it before, but she refused."

"When did you ask?"

Sister Felicia finally appeared contrite. "After the novice. Lorelle said we'd get past it. We never did. It's never been the same."

"Don't you dare tell me that's why you're carrying on with Sister Cecily."

"Cecily is my true love."

Again, Sophia wanted to roll her eyes. Yesterday, Lorelle. Today, Cecily. Tomorrow, who knew? Sophia wouldn't judge—if Sister Felicia wasn't a consort.

"I don't like carrying on behind Lorelle's back. But she refused to release me."

"So it's her fault? You knew what you were agreeing to—in front of Salbine—when you pledged to her."

"Our love burned out, or at least it did for me. I tried to remain true to her, but I failed. I asked to be released. She refused."

"How long have you been carrying on with Sister Cecily?"

Sister Felicia clasped her hands behind her back. "Two years."

Sophia wanted to gape. Two years? And nobody had noticed? Or had they, and they were turning a blind eye. What about Sister Lorelle?

"Having to give Cecily up and stay with Lorelle will put me into an unbearable situation."

Sophia was trying, really trying, to muster some sympathy for Sister Felicia's plight, but the woman had pledged. Still, Sophia didn't have a heart of stone. The question was how to move forward. Clearly Sister Felicia was no longer in love with Sister Lorelle and wouldn't settle for a loving friendship with her consort, the path most sisters walked when they found themselves in the same situation. Not that many did. Love could be rekindled. Most sisters were wise enough to fan the dying flames, but two pairs of hands had to hold the fan. One alone wouldn't do it.

"Does Sister Lorelle know about you and Sister Cecily?" she asked.

"I don't think so."

"It's time you told her."

"Today?"

"Yes, today. Tell her Mistress Margery will understand if she doesn't feel like scribing for the next few days."

"Mistress Margery knows? Is she the one who told you about Cecily?"

"That's none of your affair. Now, tell Sister Lorelle you need to speak to her in your chambers." Sophia lifted a finger. "And don't tell Sister Cecily about this conversation before you speak to Sister Lorelle. Concern yourself with your consort."

"And then what?"

"You will wait until I call for you again, and you will restrain yourself from lying with or doing anything else with Sister Cecily. I'll speak to Sister Lorelle in a couple of days." After the sister's initial shock had passed, assuming she *was* shocked.

Sister Felicia frowned but wisely kept her mouth shut.

"That's all."

The sister whirled and marched from the room. Sophia slowly exhaled. She wasn't looking forward to her conversation with Sister Lorelle, but she wore the abbess's cassock. Lately, it weighed a ton.

~

EMMEY FORCED THE SCOWL off her face when she and Maddy approached the study room where the Bennetts were waiting to meet her. She already hated them, which wasn't fair. They weren't the ones taking her away from Maddy and Lillian, not really. It was those rules. Bloody rules. Bloody, bloody, bloody rules.

When they reached the door, she looked up at Maddy. "Be polite," Maddy murmured, but she didn't smile. Emmey wanted to hug her, but she'd cry, and Maddy would probably cry, and that would make it impossible to walk into the study room with kindly expressions and dry eyes. When she lived with the Bennetts, she'd have to cry into her pillow and make sure to wash her face every morning before she saw anyone.

Maddy knocked at the door and swung it open. Emmey followed her into the room. A couple in their mid to late forties sat at the table. There wasn't anything remarkable about them. They'd put on their best clothes. Mrs. Bennett had even worn a hat, one she quickly snatched off her head as she and her husband rose to their feet and stared awkwardly at Maddy. They hadn't been around sisters much, then. It didn't matter. Emmey wasn't about to share any of her precious memories with them. She'd hold those close to her heart.

"You must be the Bennetts," Maddy said. "I'm Sister Maddy, and this is Emmey. Welcome to the monastery."

Emmey did as she'd been told to do and bobbed to them, not that she thought they deserved it. The Bennetts exchanged approving glances. Mr. Bennett bowed. Mrs. Bennett performed a respectable curtsey. Suddenly both pairs of eyes were on Emmey. Blood rushed to her face. What did they think of her? She wasn't in one of her usual plain robes. The seamstresses had sewn her a dress, a dark blue one that Maddy said accentuated her eyes.

She supposed she should say something to the Bennetts, who were still staring at her. "Pleased to meet you," she mumbled.

"Why don't you all sit down?" Maddy suggested.

Emmey pulled out a chair across from where the Bennetts had sat. Fortunately they retook the same seats.

Maddy remained standing. "I won't stay. I just wanted to introduce you and then leave you to get to know each other a bit."

Mrs. Bennett twisted to look at Maddy. "Are you the sister who's been responsible for her while she's stayed here?"

Emmey lowered her head.

"Yes," Maddy said.

"I'm sure you'll be glad to have her out of your hair."

Silence. *Don't look. Don't look!* Emmey gripped the idiotic blue dress and balled it in her hands.

"I will notice her absence daily." Maddy's voice was even. "Emmey can show you to the gate when you're ready to leave."

A lump in her throat, Emmey listened to the door thud shut. She wanted to race after Maddy, loop her arm through hers, tell her about something interesting she'd seen that day, laugh with her, eat with her, learn from her, stay with her, love her to pieces and take care of her.

Instead, she steeled herself and lifted her head. "I've been looking forward to meeting you. Thank you so much for agreeing to let me work for you." Because it was what Maddy would want her to do.

~

AFTER TAKING THE BENNETTS to the gate, Emmey strode up the monastery's gate road, wanting to rip her stupid dress off. Just wearing the bloody thing made her stick out like a sore thumb. Worse, she felt like an outsider, like she didn't belong here. She'd never felt like that in a robe because she'd looked like everyone else, not like a visitor. Well, she'd better get used to not belonging here. How long would it take everyone to forget her? Days? Weeks? Maddy and Lillian and Sophia and Elizabeth and Averill—Mistress Averill—would always remember her, but in a distant, fond way. That girl they'd taken care of all those years ago.

Her hands clenched. She wanted to be here with them in the flesh, not in their memories. If only she felt called to the Order. If only she believed taking the robe was what she was meant to do. She could stay! She could tell the Bennetts to stick their bloody farm up their arses. Not that she would. They were being kind, and Maddy had taught her to be better than that. Lillian would tell them to stick their bloody farm up their arses, a thought that made Emmey chuckle, despite her mood.

"Emmey!"

Almost at the entrance to the Mistresses Tower, Emmey would have pretended she hadn't heard and kept on walking—if it had been anyone else.

She swung around. Sister Dolores caught up to her. "You look nice today."

Normally a compliment from Sister Dolores would have Emmey

touching the sun, but not after meeting with the Bennetts, and not in this stupid dress. "Thank you," she said. Maddy's influence again!

"When I saw you, I didn't realize it was you at first. I thought, 'Who's that girl in the dress?' I'm used to seeing you in a robe."

"I just met with Mr. and Mrs. Bennett. The ones I'm going to live with."

"Oh." Sister Dolores's eyes were sympathetic. She lightly touched Emmey's arm. "That must have been difficult for you."

No, no, not now! She couldn't tear up now. She bit her lip, forgetting for a moment about acting sophisticated when Sister Dolores was around.

"It won't be the same without you here, scurrying around and scribing and planting herbs. I'll miss seeing you at morning and evening prayers."

Sister Dolores would miss her? A smile tugged at Emmey's lips.

"I'm surprised you're leaving."

"I'll be fourteen soon."

"Yes, but I'm surprised the abbess isn't letting you stay. I haven't been privy to the conversations and I would never question the abbess's judgment, but I would have thought she'd let you stay until you were old enough to become a novice."

"A novice?" Emmey squeaked. "But I'm not called to service."

Sister Dolores frowned. "You're already a sister in everything but name. Becoming a novice would merely formalize what already is." Her hand went to her throat. "But forgive me if I've misunderstood."

"Th-that's all right. I hadn't thought, well, I didn't realize, um . . ."

Sister Dolores patted her shoulder. "I'll let you get on."

"Yes, thank you." Thank you? She wanted the ground to swallow her up.

Somehow she managed to mumble good-bye. As she watched Sister Dolores stroll away, a thought struck her. The sister knew she was marked by Salbine, but how? Emmey hadn't told anyone.

She would miss Sister Dolores, but not anywhere near as much as she'd miss Maddy and Lillian and the other sisters she was close to. Her feelings for Sister Dolores were a passing fancy that would fade over time. She was young, not stupid. She'd witnessed enough relationship drama during her six years here, especially between novices and initiates, that she knew how quickly intense feelings flared and fizzled. Sister Dolores would eventually fall in love with a sister and take her as a consort. By then, she would have forgotten that a girl named Emmey used to live at the monastery, and to Emmey, Sister Dolores would be a distant memory.

That wouldn't be true when Emmey thought about Mistress Averill, who came to mind now because of her feelings for Mistress Olivia. Emmey couldn't recall the mistress feeling that way about anyone. She had a vague memory of Maddy saying that Mistress Averill's consort had gone to Salbine not long before Maddy had entered the Order. Perhaps she was ready to love someone else. Just because Emmey was miserable didn't mean everyone had to be. Mistress Olivia would leave soon, and Mistress Averill might regret not having told the mistress about her feelings. A plan hatched in Emmey's mind. She was still here, could still do something nice for the mistress.

As she climbed the steps in the Mistresses Tower and strode along the hall to her chambers, she kept her mind off the Bennetts and her impending departure by thinking about how she could help Mistress Averill along. But when she walked into her chambers hoping Maddy was there, and discovered that she wasn't, the still and empty sitting room pierced her defences. Soon her life would always be like this.

She went into Maddy and Lillian's bedchamber, collapsed to the floor, and wept.

~

LILLIAN STRODE UP THE chapel's central aisle, wincing at the hunched figure sitting near the front. She wasn't any good at this, but she'd try. She sat next to Maddy but didn't take her hand. Maddy's head was bowed and her eyes closed. Lillian was prepared to wait silently for hours, if necessary, but Maddy raised her head. Her red-rimmed eyes made Lillian wince again. "I thought I might find you here."

"Why would I be here?" Maddy said softly. "Because I should be stronger than this. I should honour my vows. I should care about Salbine above everything else."

"You shouldn't love those around you? When a sister's consort passes into Salbine's realm, she shouldn't grieve?"

"I was supposed to leave it all behind. No children. No distractions."

Lillian snorted. "Of course there are distractions. When we entered the Order, we didn't die, Maddy. We still have our interests. We still want to learn. We don't sit in the chapel from morning to night, praying. We drink cider and gossip and sometimes get angry with each other, and if we weren't meant to love, we wouldn't take consorts. You couldn't have left Emmey behind. It isn't who you are."

"You wanted us to leave her."

Lillian shifted on the bench. "Yes, well, it's a good thing you don't always listen to me."

Maddy raised her brows.

"I know you're going to feel terrible for a while, perhaps a long while. I see it already. But you'll do what you always do. Muck in. Help folk. You can't not help folk. It's the reason Emmey's here. I'll let you mope around for a bit, but then I'll keep reminding you of who you are. You saved Emmey. Now she'll go on with her life without us." Lillian swallowed. "I'll miss her too. I wish she could stay too. But she can't, so we have to let her go and wish her well and one day, we'll realize we've thought about her and laughed, not cried."

When Maddy's hand covered hers, she grasped it and held onto Maddy's fingers. "It won't be easy. But somehow, we'll muddle through to the other side."

Maddy laid her head on Lillian's shoulder. "Thank you for not trying to buck me up with empty words."

"If you want someone to tell you it will be all right for you to wallow, you'll have to find someone else to talk to."

"I don't want anyone else. I need you." Maddy paused. "After Emmey's gone, I want to go to Heath."

Lillian straightened, causing Maddy to lift her head. "I thought you'd wait a few years."

"No. As soon as I'm confident Emmey will be all right, I want to go."

"I thought you'd moved past it enough—being malflowed—that it wouldn't be so urgent." She'd hoped Maddy would give up on the idea, though she supposed that was foolish, especially now that Maddy had received a taste of the material at Heath.

"It doesn't bother me as much as it used to, but you read Sister Lavinia's entry," Maddy said, echoing Lillian's thoughts. "There must be something in her journals that will help me understand, and now that I think she managed to draw again, I have to read everything. I have to find out how. I wish Sister Lavinia was still alive. She would understand how I feel more than anyone else can."

So that was it. Irritation and irrational jealousy tightened Lillian's jaw, but she quashed the foolishness. As much as she'd love to be everything to Maddy, she wasn't, and when it came to being malflowed, she had no experience with it. Drawing the elements and sensing others who did the same was as second nature to her as breathing. She had more trouble not snapping at novices and initiates and reading without her spectacles. Drawing fire? She could probably do it in her sleep. She had no idea how it would feel to reach for the elemental source and not find it, or worse, not even sense it.

"I suppose I can understand that," she said to Maddy. "But I hope you still don't think Salbine is punishing you for something you did."

"It hurt when I tried to draw, Lillian. If I'd kept trying, it would have killed me."

"Because the elements won't flow through you. They get trapped. That's why you were in pain, and why cutting the flow stopped the pain. It allowed the elements to dissipate. To try to draw again and again would damage your insides." She chuckled when Maddy gave her a pointed look. "I do think about it occasionally, but only about the nature of the condition. I never question whether you're being punished. I only think about that when you bring it up."

"I've already told Sophia I want to travel to Heath again."

"You're not going alone, not like last time." Lillian cast her mind back. The memory of all those days on a horse, of her sore bottom and inner thighs, having to listen to inane townsfolk, sleeping rough and in smelly inns . . . now *she* felt like weeping. "I suppose I'll go with you," she muttered.

"Really?"

"I won't pretend I want to go. You know me, I'd rather stay here. But you're not going alone."

"Because of what happened last time?"

"That too, but only partly. I'll go because I couldn't bear to be parted from you for so long."

If Lillian hadn't already decided to travel with Maddy to Heath, Maddy's smile would have changed her mind. She'd do anything to see that smile. Then Maddy leaned over and kissed her. Lillian kissed her back, not worrying about who else might be in the chapel. It wasn't fair, wasn't fair at all, that she was so blessed and Maddy was malflowed. She would never pretend to know Salbine's mind. She drew conclusions based on her five senses. But she would also never doubt that Salbine had marked her and watched over her, that her ability to hurl fire and make rain fall and churn earth and blow thieves off their feet came from the goddess she respected and adored. She didn't pray as fervently as everyone else and hadn't felt the Order call to her like a siren, but in her own way, she was as dedicated to Salbine as every other sister in a robe.

"I wonder if Emmey's finished meeting with them," Maddy murmured. "I should go see how she is, but I'm not ready yet." She laid her head on Lillian's shoulder again. "Will you sit with me for a bit?"

"With pleasure." Lillian wrapped her arm around Maddy's shoulders and drew her close.

15

THE NEXT DAY, EMMEY returned to her chambers when she knew they'd be empty. Lillian was where she usually was, and Maddy was helping at the clinic. Last night, she and Maddy had talked about her meeting with the Bennetts, which had felt like it had taken hours and had been very polite, but awkward. Mr. and Mrs. Bennett seemed nice. They'd told her about her bedchamber and how she'd grow herbs and help with the harvest. They'd asked her about her interests and what she liked to eat. They'd said she'd be allowed to go to the market to see Maddy. She should have been grateful and tried to get to know them, but instead she'd spent every moment resisting the urge to bolt from the study room.

At least she wouldn't spend her remaining days here wearing a silly dress. She was back in one of the comfortable robes she'd worn ever since she'd turned twelve, when Sophia had said it was time for her to stop wearing dresses. Her robes weren't Salbine robes, which had tinier buttons and were usually made of softer or silkier cloth. They were also cut differently, with their flared sleeves and lower collars. But they were more like Emmey's robes than dresses were. At the Bennetts, she'd have to wear dresses and work clothes again, which would feel strange and constantly remind her that she wasn't at the monastery anymore.

But enough about the bloody Bennetts. It was time to help

Mistress Averill, something that felt even more urgent to Emmey now. She went to the desk that stood near the door to Maddy and Lillian's bedchamber and rummaged around in a drawer for a small piece of parchment, one on which she could write a short note and then fold it to conceal the words. Ah, perfect. She'd found a piece that would suit her needs.

She sat at the desk, dipped a quill into ink, and carefully wrote *Mistress Olivia. I would enjoy it very much if you would have supper with me in my chambers. Let's discuss it next time we scribe together. Mistress Averill.*

Emmey read the words she'd written and shook her head. She'd scribed enough times with Mistress Averill to imitate her script, but a couple of the letters in her first attempt weren't quite right, especially the *m*'s. She fished another piece of parchment from the drawer and tried again.

Four attempts later, a grin split her face as she admired her handiwork. Mistress Averill just needed a little encouragement and would be delighted when Mistress Olivia showed her the note. She'd know she hadn't written it, but hopefully would have the sense to keep it to herself.

Emmey imagined the two mistresses smiling at each other from ear to ear, sharing supper in the mistress's chambers, and then ... she didn't want to think about it, especially since she'd read most of the book Mistress Averill had given her, the one for girls marked by Salbine. It contained quite a few illustrations, ones that made her furtively look over her shoulder just thinking about them, even though she was by herself and the book was in her bedchamber. Mistress Averill and Mistress Olivia? Not what she wanted to think about. The important thing was that Mistress Averill wouldn't regret not saying anything to Mistress Olivia before she left for Hedgerow. The mistress deserved a little happiness. She'd always been kind to Emmey, and this is what friends did for each other.

Emmey folded the parchment over once and slipped it into her robe's pocket. After throwing her earlier attempts at imitating Mistress Averill's script into the fire and waiting until she was sure the parchment had been reduced to ash, she went in search of Mistress

Olivia. Given the time, she was probably in the music room. Emmey had noticed that the mistress spent fifteen or twenty minutes every afternoon practicing on the harpsichord. She hung around outside, and when the mistress emerged from the Community Tower, Emmey hurried after her. "Mistress Olivia!"

The mistress glanced over her shoulder. "Oh, hello, Emmey."

Emmey bobbed to her. "Mistress Averill wanted me to give this to you."

"Oh?" The mistress took the parchment from Emmey, her eyes burning with curiosity. "Thank you."

Emmey walked away as quickly as she could without being accused of running. It was only when she was safely back in her chambers that she realized it didn't make sense that Mistress Averill would give her a note to give to Mistress Olivia. After all, the two women spent most of every day together, their heads down, scribing. Why would Mistress Averill write a note and send Emmey to Mistress Olivia with it?

It wouldn't matter—unless Mistress Olivia figured out the note wasn't from Mistress Averill and quietly disposed of it. Emmey wanted to stamp her feet. She'd have to keep an eye on the mistresses. If they didn't have supper together, she'd come up with another plan. This matchmaking business could turn out to be more complicated than she'd expected, but if it worked, it would be worth it.

~

AVERILL LIFTED HER HEAD and smiled when Mistress Olivia sat on the stool next to her. "Good afternoon, Mistress."

"Good afternoon."

Averill expected Mistress Olivia to pick up her quill, but the mistress pulled a piece of parchment from her robe's pocket and offered it to her. "Someone gave me this."

Intrigued, Averill took the parchment and unfolded it. *Mistress Olivia. I would enjoy it very much if you would have supper with me in my chambers. Let's discuss it next time we scribe together. Mistress Averill.*

Heat scorched the back of Averill's neck and spread to her cheeks and ears. She gripped the parchment and searched for something to say. "I didn't write this," she blurted, then wanted to kick herself.

"I know," Mistress Olivia said.

Averill forced herself to look at her. The mistress's eyes were kind, not mocking, but Averill didn't feel any less mortified. "Who gave it to you?" she asked, suspecting the answer.

"Young Emmey."

"I see. I'm sorry you were put into this awkward position."

"It's not your fault." Mistress Olivia paused. "I don't think we need to mention this to the abbess, do we?" It was more a statement than a question.

"No, I'll speak to Emmey." She wanted to shake her and hug her, the foolish, impetuous, lovely girl.

With as much dignity as she could muster, Averill folded the parchment and slipped it into her robe's pocket. She wouldn't pick up her quill again, not just yet. She didn't trust herself to not flub the first letter she scribed. "She did quite a good job. The letters look very much like mine. How did you know I didn't write it?"

"We see each other every day. You'd have no need to write to me. If you wanted to have supper with me in your chambers, all you'd have to do is ask me." The mistress's eyes held Averill's for what felt like an eternity. Then she picked up her quill and dipped it into the inkpot.

Averill blinked at her, then picked up her own quill, but took her time dabbing it into the ink.

~

SOPHIA WALKED NEXT TO Barnabus as he escorted her to Sisters Felicia and Lorelle's chambers on the fifth floor of the Mistresses Tower. "Thank you," she murmured when Barnabus stopped outside a door. After he'd gone, she pressed her ear against the door and listened. All was quiet. No wailing or hysterics, but then Sister Felicia had told Sister Lorelle about Sister Cecily the day before yesterday.

Sister Lorelle should have cried herself dry by now. Sophia rapped on the door.

Rustling inside, then the door creaked open. "Abbess." Sister Lorelle curtseyed. She was robed, but the top two buttons were undone, and if Sophia didn't already know what was wrong, she would have asked. The woman's hair was unkempt, and she'd obviously been weeping.

"Do you mind if I come in?"

"Not at all." Sister Lorelle moved aside to let Sophia pass, then swung the door shut. "I'm sorry I haven't been scribing. Felicia said Mistress Margery wasn't expecting me."

"That's quite all right. I'm not here because you haven't been scribing. I thought we should have a chat."

"About Felicia and Cecily? About Felicia not loving me anymore? About why I'm the only sister between here and Hedgerow whose consort can't keep her robe on when she's outside?"

Oh, dear. Sophia moved to the square table and pulled out a chair. "She's told you everything, then." She motioned for Sister Lorelle to sit down.

The sister sat across from her. "I'm sorry. I don't mean to be disrespectful."

"I don't expect you to stand on ceremony when you're so distressed."

"I do," Sister Lorelle said, raising Sophia's appraisal of her. The sister pulled a handkerchief from her robe's pocket and dabbed at her eyes. "Maybe I should have released her last time, but I thought we could put it behind us."

"She says things were never the same."

"I thought they were. I'd forgiven her. But this time is ten times worse, not only because it's gone as far as it has, and for as long, but because Cecily is my best friend."

Sophia quickly masked her surprise. Mistress Margery hadn't mentioned that important detail.

"I've lost both of them now. Both of them." Sister Lorelle dabbed at her eyes again. "I don't know how I'm ever going to trust anyone."

"You're thinking of releasing her?"

"May I stand up, please?"

"Of course."

Sister Lorelle rose and went to the window. "If I release her, she'll never be able to take a consort again."

"Would that bother you?"

"I'd feel like I'd done something to her, even though it's the other way around."

"Yes, it is. And if I may, I doubt Sister Felicia will mind very much that she can't take a consort." In practical terms, it would mean she wasn't bound to one woman for life, and she couldn't share chambers with anyone. Sophia doubted Sister Felicia would care. "Of course, I don't know her well."

Sister Lorelle gazed out the window, the sun silhouetting her face. "I'd have to sit by and watch them carry on with each other, because I doubt they'll give me a second thought. At least now, they have to hide it."

"But is that what you really want? To know Sister Felicia will carry on with someone else? To know that she's only paying you attention out of obligation?"

"No, it's not what I want! I want her to love me and care for me and tell me I'm the most beautiful woman in the world to her. But I'm not going to get that, am I?" She swallowed. "Begging your pardon. I don't know what you must think of me. I pledged to her."

"I see someone who's been betrayed by her consort and is struggling to come to terms with what's happened."

Sister Lorelle returned to the table but remained standing. "You're very kind. Others won't be. Felicia and Cecily are popular. I'm quiet. I spend most of my time scribing."

"I'm not sure their popularity will win the day this time. They've both disrespected Salbine and betrayed you."

"Still, I'm sure there will be talk. And in a few months when everyone's gotten used to the idea, they'll treat them like a happy couple right in front of my face. I don't know how I'll withstand the humiliation."

"I'm sure the abbess and others will support you."

"This is going to sound uncharitable, but I don't care. Some things are difficult to bear no matter what support you have."

Sophia didn't disagree. "Refusing to release Sister Felicia isn't the answer. The decision is yours, but do think through the implications of both sides. If you don't release her, will you be able to trust her again? Will she be able to give up Sister Cecily?" Or resist temptation. It wasn't a question of if Sister Felicia would stray again, but when. "If you do release her, you'll go through a very bleak time, but you'll come through to the other side. And you'll be able to take another consort in the future, if you wish."

"I'm not sure I'd want to. I can't even imagine it right now. I still love her, you see. I'm such a stupid woman, because I still love her." Sister Lorelle's face crumpled. Tears splattered onto the table.

Sophia rose and slipped her arm around Sister Lorelle's shoulders. "I'm so sorry you're having to deal with this, and somewhere that isn't home."

"I doubt it would be any easier at Hedgerow," Sister Lorelle sniffled. When she lifted her handkerchief and blew her nose, Sophia let her go. Sister Lorelle stuffed the handkerchief into her pocket and held on to the back of a chair for support. "Would it be possible to arrange separate chambers for me?" she whispered.

"Does that mean you're going to release Sister Felicia?"

Sister Lorelle's lips pressed together. She lowered her head and nodded.

"This will be small solace to you, but I believe you're making the right decision."

"What do I have to do? I've never—I mean . . . " The sister gulped.

Sophia would prefer that the abbess at Hedgerow deal with it, but she wouldn't make Sister Lorelle wait, because Sister Felicia and Sister Cecily certainly wouldn't, the selfish cows. "I'll draw up the appropriate document that you and Sister Felicia will have to sign. You'll also have to declare that your bond is broken in the chapel. Usually you'd do it in front of the entire community, but this isn't your community. I'll ask a few sisters to attend, along with Mistress Margery and Mistress Olivia.

Sister Lorelle lifted her head. "What about Cecily? Will she have to be there?"

"I think we can leave her out." And Sophia would make it clear to Sisters Felicia and Cecily that they were not to sleep in each other's chambers or publicly express affection while here at Merrin. If they had any decency, she wouldn't have to tell them, but she wasn't sure they did and would be glad to see the back of them. She had no quarrel with sisters who preferred to keep their relationships casual. They usually had the good sense not to pledge to anyone, and if they didn't, their abbess usually prevented them from pledging. "Shall we meet in my study tomorrow afternoon at two o'clock to sign the document? We can proceed to the chapel from there."

"Tomorrow afternoon," Sister Lorelle echoed flatly. "Almost fifteen years gone, just like that."

"Not gone. You lived those years. They're part of you."

"I'll try to remember that."

"Try to get some air," Sophia said, even though she'd be surprised if Sister Lorelle did. If she were in her shoes, she'd want to shut herself away and weep too. "Would you like me to ask Sister Felicia to come see you?"

Sister Lorelle thought for a moment, then shook her head. "Would you tell her?"

"If you wish."

"I'm only asking because I'm afraid of what I'll say."

And perhaps back out? "I understand." Sophia pulled the chamber door's iron ring. "I'll arrange chambers for you right away. I'll send Master Barnabus when they're ready. You might want to pack your things."

"I'll do that. Thank you."

Sophia left the chambers, feeling ever so sorry for her. The sister was right. She'd have to return to Hedgerow, watch her former consort and best friend carry on with each other, and somehow not feel humiliated and small. Would she ever be able to trust and take another consort? Sophia hoped she would, and that her next consort would cherish their bond, not squander it.

16

EMMEY FILLED A BUCKET with water from the well nearest to the tomato garden she was tending. She'd only taken a few steps back to the tomatoes when she stopped. Someone was marching toward her. Mistress Averill. She never came to see Emmey in the gardens. Oh, Mistress Olivia must have shown her the note and Mistress Averill had gone along with it and wanted to thank Emmey for her help. Emmey wanted to drop the bucket of water and clap her hands in delight. Then she saw Mistress Averill's face, noted the stiffness of her shoulders and the downward turn of her mouth, and she wanted to drop the bucket for another reason. She could run faster without it. She lowered the bucket to the ground. Mistress Averill fished a folded parchment from her pocket. "You know what this is."

There was no point denying it. Emmey bobbed to her. "I wanted to help."

"By embarrassing me? By making me feel like a fool?"

"No! You like Mistress Olivia and she's leaving soon. I wanted to give you a little nudge, that's all."

The mistress huffed. "I am perfectly capable of carrying on my own affairs."

"But you weren't going to ask to see Mistress Olivia outside your office. You were going to let her leave without saying anything."

"What if I was? That would be my choice. My business, Emmey. It wasn't your place to interfere. You put Mistress Olivia and me into a terribly awkward position. You embarrassed us both."

"I'm sorry." Emmey smiled coyly. "But you're having supper with her in your chambers, right?"

"No, I am not having supper with her."

Emmey couldn't believe it. "Why not? You like her, and she likes you. I can see it in the way you look at each other. So why wouldn't you—"

"Have you not heard a word I've said? I don't have to explain myself to you. It wasn't your place to interfere. Next time you see Mistress Olivia, you will apologize to her. Do you understand?"

The mistress's eyes blazed. Emmey could swear she was shaking. She'd never seen her so upset and didn't understand why Mistress Averill was so distressed about it. All right, she'd embarrassed the mistresses, but surely they understood she'd had good intentions.

"Do you understand?" Mistress Averill snapped.

"Yes. And I'm sorry. I didn't think it would upset you so much."

"Most people don't like others meddling in their affairs without invitation, something you'd do well to remember." Mistress Averill went to hand Emmey the forged note, then snatched it back. "I'll throw it into the next fire I pass," she muttered.

Emmey wanted to let it go, she really did, but she couldn't let Mistress Averill walk away without one last try. "Mistress, I know you're upset, and I obviously misjudged how you and Mistress Olivia would react, but that doesn't change that you like each other, so why don't you ask her to have supper with you, or go with her when she strolls the grounds?"

The mistress scowled. "Because I don't want to. And don't ask me why, because it's not your affair. When you're older, you'll understand that just because something seems obvious to you, doesn't mean it is, and that people know what's best for themselves. You think you know what's best for me, but you don't. I know you meant well, but I'm asking you to respect my wishes now and let the matter drop. Will you do that for me, please? I don't want our remaining time together to be awkward."

"I don't, either." But she still didn't understand why Mistress Averill didn't want to spend time alone with Mistress Olivia, time when they'd relax and drink cider and do something other than scribe. Was it because Mistress Olivia was leaving and so Mistress Averill didn't want to get any closer to her? No, if that were the reason, why wouldn't the mistress just say it?

"I'll let you get back to your gardening," Mistress Averill said.

Emmey did her best to appear contrite. "I am sorry."

"I know you are. Just don't do anything like that again, all right?"

"I won't." She'd do what the mistress wanted and never raise the subject with her or Mistress Olivia again, even though she thought the mistress should have seized the opportunity she'd been given. When Emmey was older, Mistress Averill had said. Unfortunately, she wouldn't be able to tell the mistress when she finally understood. The mistress would be behind monastery walls, and Emmey would not.

~

MADDY CLUNG TO LILLIAN's hand as Sisters Lorelle and Felicia kneeled at the front of the chapel and declared that their consort bond was broken and irreparable. This had never happened since she'd arrived at the Merrin monastery's gate. Lillian and Sophia could recall it happening once, to two elderly sisters who'd gone to Salbine before Maddy had entered the Order. Neither had strayed, though. They'd pledged late and had discovered they were too set in their ways to accommodate one another. Their loud arguments had disrupted the Adepts Tower, the dining hall, and other public areas, and one or the other was always so upset that she couldn't perform her duties. "Perhaps Abbess Margaret shouldn't have allowed them to pledge, but she was probably delighted that they'd found love so late in life," Sophia had said when she'd told Maddy about it.

Along with Maddy and Lillian, Sophia had invited Elizabeth, Rose, Nora, Abigail, Mistress Olivia, Mistress Margery, Mistress Phyllis, Mistress Bertha, and Sister Elouise to witness the sad event. A good mix of those with consorts and those without. Sister Cecily had been told to stay away and to make herself scarce until tomorrow. She was probably in her chambers, grinning from ear to ear. Maddy agreed with Sophia. The sister had better cherish her time with Sister Felicia, because she would eventually be replaced, especially now that Sister Felicia didn't have a consort bond restraining her.

Before coming to the chapel, the assembled sisters had crowded into Sophia's study and witnessed the two sisters signing a document that stated their union was over. Sister Felicia hadn't hesitated. To her credit, neither had Sister Lorelle, even though it wasn't what she wanted.

Thinking about this service had kept Maddy up last night. After one toss, turn, and kick too many, Lillian had rolled over and asked her if anything was wrong. "Sorry," she'd mumbled, struggling to understand how things had gone wrong between the two sisters kneeling in front of Sophia. Maddy would never carry on with another woman. She didn't even want to consider it hypothetically. She'd pledged to Lillian. Whenever they'd hit a rough patch, they'd worked through it. Almost six years in, Maddy had learned that when she was irritated with Lillian to the point of wondering whether she should have pledged to her, her disenchantment never lasted. Her hurt feelings passed. She loved Lillian and they were both committed to muddling through life together, but Maddy assumed Sister Felicia had loved Sister Lorelle. What had gone wrong?

Sophia lifted her hands from the two sisters' heads and motioned for them to rise. When they turned to face the small gathering, Maddy wanted to rush to Sister Lorelle and hug her. The woman needed a handkerchief and obviously hadn't been sleeping. She gave Lillian a sidelong glance, and almost smiled when she caught Lillian doing the same thing. She hoped the same thoughts were running through Lillian's mind that were running through hers: that she couldn't imagine her love for Lillian dying, that she would never hurt Lillian so deeply, and that Lillian would never be so unkind to her. But Sister Lorelle had trusted Sister Felicia too. "Still loves her," Sophia had told them when she'd asked them to attend the service.

"It is done," Sophia said. "You are no longer consorts, but be kind to each other. You loved each other once."

Maddy wasn't surprised when Sister Lorelle fled down the chapel's centre aisle, her footsteps muffled by the green carpet that ran along it. Sister Felicia also left straightaway, composed, but sombre.

Everyone else silently filed from the chapel behind Sophia and Elizabeth. The two mistresses from Hedgerow strode away. When Sophia and Elizabeth stopped walking, Maddy and Lillian joined them. "Do you think Sister Lorelle can sit with you at meals?" Sophia asked Maddy. "I doubt she'll want to sit with the other Hedgerow sisters, not with Sister Felicia and Sister Cecily there."

"They should be the ones to move," Lillian said.

"Perhaps, but I doubt they will. And perhaps Sister Lorelle won't want to sit with anyone, but I'd like to tell her she'd be welcome to join you."

"Of course," Maddy said. "I'll go see her tomorrow before breakfast and invite her to go to the dining hall with me."

Sophia patted Maddy's arm. "I'd give her a few days, unless you see her out and about before then." She sighed. "I hope the day improves. Oh, well, duty calls. Salbine be with you."

"And with you," Maddy and Lillian murmured. As Sophia and Elizabeth walked away, Elizabeth wrapped her arm around Sophia's shoulders and squeezed her.

"She's dealing with a lot lately," Lillian said.

"I hope she knows we don't blame her for Emmey. We knew the rules from the outset."

"I'm sure she doesn't, but I wouldn't be surprised if it still weighs on her."

Maddy made a mental note. When Emmey was gone, she and Lillian would invite Sophia and Elizabeth to their chambers. They lived across the hall from each other, but except for their monthly suppers, they rarely visited one another, which seemed odd now. They saw each other every day at evening prayers and often chatted in Sophia's study, but soon that wouldn't be enough.

She was about to voice her thoughts to Lillian when Rose joined them. Maddy glanced around and noticed that everyone else had left.

"Mistress." Rose bobbed to Lillian, something she hadn't done in private for years. She shifted her attention to Maddy. "Ready to go to the kitchen?"

"Yes, let's go. I need to remind myself that everything isn't all doom and gloom."

She pecked Lillian on the cheek and fell into step with Rose. They didn't speak much as Maddy collected nuts one of the cooks had put aside for her and strolled to a copse on the western grounds that was popular with the squirrels. She handed some nuts to Rose.

"They won't come for me," Rose said.

"They might." She pulled a nut from her pocket and crouched. It didn't take long for one of the squirrels to dart over to her and pluck the nut from her fingers. "I wish I could tell them apart."

Still as a statue, Rose didn't respond. A squirrel was tentatively approaching her. She squealed in delight when it took her nut and scurried away, frightening the poor thing. It hung on to its nut, though.

When Maddy's pocket and Rose's hand were empty, they stood gazing into the trees for a moment, lost in their own thoughts.

"How are you feeling about Emmey?" Rose finally said. "It must be terribly difficult for you."

Maddy wanted to hug herself. It was becoming harder to answer this question without dissolving into a puddle. "I'll try not to cry on your shoulder too much when she leaves, but I might not be able to help it. She's going to the Bennetts. They're good folk. She'll be able to garden." Maddy swallowed the lump that had risen in her throat. "Of course, I'd much rather she gardens where she always does," she said, her voice strangled.

Rose's forehead puckered. "We'll all be upset, but you and Lillian will feel it the most. We'll all be here for you."

Maddy managed a small smile. "I'm so grateful you and I arrived here almost together."

Rose beamed at her in return. "How is Lillian doing?"

"Putting on a brave face as much as she can. She won't weep on everyone's shoulders, just mine and the abbess's."

"We'll support her however we can without making it obvious."

"She'll shut herself away in our chambers or spend all her time in the laboratory, not just most of it."

"She might not. She'll know you're upset, and if there's one thing I've learned about Lillian, she does her best to be there for you."

And Maddy loved her for it. "Usually she's not as upset as I am, or at all, but this time will be different." She'd try to be with Lillian as much as she'd tolerate it, especially given Lillian's confession that she'd wondered if she'd be enough after Emmey was gone. Maddy wouldn't betray her trust by telling Rose about that conversation. She changed the subject. "I've told the abbess I'd like to go to Heath again."

"Really?"

"Lillian said she'll go with me."

"I wouldn't expect otherwise," Rose said, making Maddy smile again, this time an almost genuine smile. When she'd told her friends that she'd pledge to Lillian, they'd all congratulated her and had never given her the impression that they thought her mad, even though they must have wondered. Lillian was eighteen years older than Maddy, and she wasn't exactly sociable, especially with initiates, which they'd all been at the time.

All right, Gwendolyn had gotten in a few barbs, but she felt it was her duty to poke at anything Maddy said or did. But she'd never actually done anything to back up her words. She hadn't gone to Sophia and told her she shouldn't allow Maddy to pledge to Lillian, hadn't refused to attend their pledge ceremony, hadn't said anything snide in Lillian's presence, though the latter was probably Gwendolyn protecting herself. That was all it was with Gwendolyn. Words. Maddy had given up on wondering why Gwendolyn always needed to belittle everyone and everything. She was quite pleasant to be around when she forgot she was supposed to be a miserable cow.

"I'd like to go too," Rose said.

Surprise raised Maddy's voice. "What, to Heath?"

"Yes."

"What about Nora?"

"Nora wants to come too." Rose shifted her weight. "We've talked about it, if we'd go with you. We thought that maybe you'd want to try the journey again, after Emmey was gone."

Maddy wanted to hug her—platonically! The only people who knew her better than Rose were Lillian and Emmey. In some areas, she and Rose were more kindred spirits than she and Lillian, but that was natural. Nobody, including Lillian, could be everything to her.

"It's not because you're malflowed and we'd worry," Rose quickly added. "With Lillian along, there will be no need to worry about that. We'd just like to go, assuming the notion doesn't upset Lillian too much."

"It won't." Lillian was still very much a loner, but she'd accepted that Maddy wasn't and wanted to spend time with her friends. So Lillian had tried, and she'd grown more relaxed around Rose in particular, and by extension Nora as well. When Maddy told her they'd like to come to Heath, Lillian would grumble and roll her eyes, but she'd agree.

"Still, I'll talk to her about it, if you don't mind."

"To Lillian?"

Rose nodded. "It will be a long journey. I want to be sure she won't resent our presence."

"I'm sure she won't, but if you feel the need to ask her, please do. I'd love to have both of you along."

She wished Emmey could travel with them. She'd frequently think of her during the first part of the journey, especially when they passed through Garryglen. If she could skirt around the town, she would, but it was on the most direct route to Heath and going around it would add days to their journey. Would anyone remember the sister—or imposter—who'd passed through, been dragged before the magistrate, condemned to Dunmurk Prison, and left to rot? Perhaps it would do her good to walk through the town again, with Lillian and her dear friends, and her head held high.

The chapel bells struck half past three. "We should go back," Maddy was starting to feel idle. Rose looped her arm through Maddy's, and they strolled together.

When they reached the courtyard, Rose pulled Maddy to a stop.

"How do I get to Lillian's laboratory? When I pluck up the courage, that's where she'll probably be."

Maddy chuckled. "She won't bite your head off."

"I know, but she might not like me and Nora elbowing our way into your journey."

"That journey is still a ways off, and I doubt she'll mind. She'll appreciate you asking how she feels about it." She ignored Rose's dubious expression and gave her directions to the laboratory. "Will you remember them?"

"I think so." Rose paused. "I've tried not to think about it, to ponder other things, but I can't help it."

Maddy was instantly intrigued. "What?"

"The service we just attended. What a tragedy! I don't like to speak ill of others . . ."

"But you will anyway?"

Rose gave Maddy's arm a playful slap. "I was just going to say that those sisters from Hedgerow have been nothing but trouble."

"Sister Lorelle didn't cause any trouble, and the two mistresses are all right."

"Mistress Olivia seems upstanding, but I'm not so sure about Mistress Margery."

Because she often stank of ale, but Maddy was too polite to say it out loud, and so was Rose. The mistress didn't stumble around with a bottle in her hand, but it was difficult not to notice how many ciders she drank with her supper, how her voice grew louder as the day wore on, and how she occasionally dozed off in a study room. Emmey had noticed her snoring at a writing podium in the library. Sophia would never stand for such behaviour and would ensure a sister who couldn't do without ale had no access to it. But Mistress Margery was a visitor, and so Sophia was doing her best to ignore it and probably talking Elizabeth's ear off about it.

"She's loud and sometimes says inappropriate things," Rose said primly. "And she should have put a stop to Sister Felicia's antics."

"I doubt she knew."

"What are you two talking about?"

They whirled. Gwendolyn strolled up to them, a book tucked

under her arm. "Returning this to the library." She smirked at Maddy. "Finished feeding the squirrels?"

"Yes." Maddy wondered what was coming.

"The only way I like a squirrel is with a mug of cider and a nice thick slice of bread."

Maddy rolled her eyes. "You'll have to do better than that."

"Yes, not up to your usual standard," Rose, who merely tolerated Gwendolyn, said with a sniff.

"What are the three of you doing standing around, gabbing?" a voice bellowed.

Maddy wanted to groan. The very mistress she and Rose had just gossiped about was bearing down on them.

Mistress Margery's hands went to her hips. "We don't allow this at Hedgerow, you know."

Rose pulled her arm from Maddy's so they could both bob a curtsey along with Gwendolyn.

"At least you know how to do that. Ooh, I don't know. Things are very lax here. Very lax. Take you." She jutted her chin toward them.

It took Maddy a moment to realize the mistress's chin was directed at her.

"There you are an adept, even though you can't draw an element to save your life. You should be a novice, or not here at all."

Shock made Maddy's mouth drop open. Next to her, Rose stiffened. Maddy went to put a calming hand on her arm, but Rose was past the point of restraint.

"How rude!" Rose spat.

Now it was Mistress Margery's mouth dropping open.

"How dare you usurp Salbine's authority by deciding who deserves to be here and who doesn't?"

"It's all right," Maddy murmured.

"No, it isn't. Sister Maddy has every right to be here. Nobody here has any doubt that she was called to take the robe. Ask any sister here and they'll tell you the same. So please, keep your inane comments to yourself. They do you no credit."

"Don't speak to me like that," Mistress Margery snapped. "I belonged to the Order before you could walk. You're exactly what

I mean, a sister who doesn't respect her betters." She wagged a finger. "Lax, I tell you. This impertinence wouldn't be permitted at Hedgerow."

"But drinking oneself silly is?" Gwendolyn drawled.

Mistress Margery's eyes focused on her. "I beg your pardon."

"I'm merely asking if stinking of ale at this time of day is commonplace at Hedgerow, or if it's only you? And I can assure you that all the consorts here will be in their own beds tonight, and when they're not with their consorts, they keep their robes on and their hands to themselves. I've heard you do things differently at Hedgerow."

Mistress Margery's mouth moved, but nothing came out. She took a step back, then finally found her voice. "You—you impertinent swine!" she sputtered. She jabbed her finger at nobody in particular. "The abbess shall hear about this, I assure you!" She stomped past them.

Maddy met Gwendolyn's eyes, then Rose's.

Rose swallowed. "I had to say something." She didn't sound as if she regretted it, but it might have been the first time she'd ever spoken back to a mistress. Maddy couldn't recall her ever doing it before.

"Thank you," she said sincerely. "Both of you."

"She should mind her own business," Gwendolyn said, appearing unfazed. "Especially given that she does stink of ale." She strode toward the library without saying good-bye.

"Don't take any notice of what the mistress said," Rose said to Maddy.

"I won't." Mistress Margery hadn't said anything Maddy hadn't thought herself at one time or another. What Rose had said was true. None of the sisters here had ever suggested she didn't belong. The mistress's words had shocked her precisely because nobody had ever voiced such thoughts to her face. This was her home. She'd come to accept the truth of it. Still, the mistress's words had stung, because Maddy was different, and she didn't understand why. That was the piece that eluded her. Why? Why had Salbine called her and then denied her?

"Do you think she'll speak to the abbess?" Rose said.

Maddy could see the apprehension in her eyes. "She might."

"I don't regret what I said."

But perhaps wished she hadn't said it? "You're a good friend, you know. The best."

Rose grinned. "Wait until I tell Nora! She won't believe it."

They looped arms again and decided to embroider together until supper.

17

EMMEY'S FINGERS GRAZED THE stone wall as she trailed behind Maddy. "Not this bloody dream again!" a voice—her voice—shouted in her head. Tugging on Maddy's robe would be pointless. She never turned around. It was as if Emmey wasn't there.

In the glow cast by the flickering torches lining the hall, something skittered across the stone floor. Emmey bit back a scream. The dank air clogged her nostrils and thickened her throat.

Maddy turned a corner. Emmey felt compelled to do the same. Up ahead, flames flickered beyond the single doorway at the end of the hall. As usual, Emmey was sure they were in one of the towers, but she knew none of them housed a hall that ended at a chamber. She'd checked.

The roar of the flames deafened her. Heat didn't wash over her, but she was still wary. The fire could burn her and she was powerless to stop it.

Maddy wheeled around in front of the doorway. "We're here. I'll go first."

Emmey couldn't help herself. She grabbed Maddy's sleeve and held on to it. "No!"

"Don't be silly," Maddy said, in the emotionless voice she never used in real life. "The fire doesn't hurt."

"Yes, it does!" Even though she knew she was dreaming, Emmey's stomach lurched when Maddy scowled at her. She hated irritating her.

"I'm going in. You'll see it's safe."

Emmey tightened her grip on Maddy's sleeve, but as she had many times before, Maddy pulled her sleeve free and stepped through the doorway and into the fire.

Emmey's hands clenched. Her mouth opened in horror. She could see Maddy standing in the fire and turned away, ready to clap her hands over her ears. But Maddy didn't scream. Her flesh didn't melt. Her robe didn't burn. This wasn't the way the dream usually went. Maddy usually screamed, and Emmey woke up, sweating and shaking.

Maddy beckoned to Emmey. "Come join me."

Emmey gulped. "No."

She should run, but she never could. Some invisible force held her here. Maddy grabbed Emmey's wrist. "Come. In."

"No!"

Maddy pulled. Emmey resisted. A tug of war ensued. Emmey inched toward the flames, pulling away with all her strength, but Maddy was stronger, her grip like a vise. Emmey's fingertips almost touched the flames, but the unnatural fire wasn't giving off any heat. She clenched her teeth and tried to yank her hand free. Maddy grinned at her through the flames and pulled harder.

It's a dream. Wake up! She drew back, trying to protect her head and torso. Her fingertips touched flame, then she was ablaze, scorching pain ripping through her and—

"Open your eyes, girl," a voice snapped.

That didn't sound like Maddy. Emmey realized she was gulping down cool fresh air and that she lay on soft ground, and not on hard stone. She opened her eyes and blinked into the sun. Birds twittered. The scent of apple chased away the dankness in her nostrils. Chamomile.

She propped herself up on one elbow and surveyed her surroundings. She was lying in a chamomile field on monastery grounds, but no sisters were strolling along the nearby path. She was alone, except for a robed woman standing several paces away from her.

"What's going on?" Her voice sounded small, fearful.

"Get up."

The woman's voice conveyed authority. Emmey scrambled to her feet and would have met the woman's eyes, except the hood of her robe somehow hid her face, even though Emmey was looking directly at her.

"I thought it was time we spoke, face to face." The woman laughed. Emmey didn't understand what was so funny, but then the woman drew back her hood. The air around her shimmered. She . . . transformed. Emmey's eyes widened. Her jaw dropped. She hugged herself, digging her fingers into her arms.

The hooded woman without a face was no more. In her place stood a girl who exuded confidence and power. Her long blonde hair was pinned up in a bun, and she wore clothes made of the finest silk. Her face . . .

Emmey's stomach roiled. She was staring at herself. She said the first words that popped into her mind. "I'm dreaming."

The girl's—her—eyes bored into her. "Are you sure?"

"I've had this dream before, a variation of it, but you're not usually in it. Who are you? What are you doing here?" *Why do you look like me?*

"Are you sure this is a dream?"

"Pretty sure."

A smile tugged at her double's lips. "Listen to me, girl. Don't ignore me when I speak to you."

"I'm not ignoring you."

"Yes, you are. I'm speaking to you as loudly as I can, but you aren't listening. I don't know why you're being so obtuse, but you are."

"This is the first time you're talking to me."

The woman frowned. "I'm constantly speaking to you, girl. You need to listen."

Bewildered, Emmey didn't know what to say. Then she shook herself and chuckled. "This is weird. I'm talking to myself. Except I'm me, and you're not real. You're just someone in my dream."

"Am I?" Her double smirked. "I suppose you won't mind another visit to the tower again with Maddy."

Emmey's fingers grazed the stone wall as she trailed behind Maddy. No. No, no, no. *I'm not going. I'm not bloody going!* But she couldn't turn around, couldn't sneak or race away from Maddy, who stepped into the flaming room and gripped Emmey's wrist.

"Don't do this, Maddy. I can't take any more. Don't do this!"

With a sense of futility, she tried to pull away from Maddy. This time, Maddy gripped Emmey's other wrist too. "Come inside," she said. "Come to me, Emmey."

Maddy pulled. Emmey resisted. A tug of war ensued. Emmey inched toward the flames, pulling away with all her strength, but Maddy was stronger.

Emmey's fingertips touched flame. She clenched her teeth, tried to yank her hand free. Maddy's jaw set, and her pull strengthened. The fire engulfed Emmey's left arm. "Stop it!" she shouted. "You're hurting me. Please, Maddy." A sob escaped her throat.

She drew back, trying to protect her head and torso, but that only meant her feet edged toward the fire quicker. Her toes erupted in flame. Wisps of smoke rose from the tops of her feet; the noxious smell of burning flesh clogged her nose. Agonizing pain ripped through her. She flailed around, the stench of her melting flesh choking her and cutting off her screams.

Maddy smiled her sickly dream smile. "See? I told you it wouldn't hurt."

Then something gripped her, squeezed her, pressed her burning, blackened arms against her sides. She pushed through the pain, struggled against it . . .

Emmey!

Emmey fought to free her arms, kicked wildly . . .

Emmey, wake up!

She knew that voice, a concerned voice, a loving voice. Not the flat, emotionless voice she loathed. She pushed through the pain and ran toward it.

Wake up, Emmey. Wake up!

She opened her eyes, felt the nightshirt balled in her hands and the warmth of loving arms around her. Her cheeks were wet. She drew back. Maddy anxiously gazed into her eyes. Lillian hovered behind her, holding a burning lamp.

Emmey collapsed against Maddy and sobbed into her chest.

"It's all right," Maddy murmured. "You were having a bad dream." Her arms slipped around Emmey. Despite missing part of one arm, Maddy gave the best hugs. Emmey trembled against her, her sobs subsiding.

The bed sagged further. Emmey lifted her head from Maddy's chest and gave Lillian, who'd perched on the edge of the bed, a wan smile.

"That must have been some dream," Lillian said.

What could Emmey tell them? It hadn't been real. She wasn't burned. She was here, in her bedchamber, safe. She didn't want to tell Maddy that in her dream, she was afraid of her, that Maddy smiled as she listened to her screams and watched flames consume her. "Someone drew fire and burned me," she whispered, being deliberately vague.

"It was only a dream," Maddy said.

But it had felt so real.

"Do you want some water?"

"No, I think I can sleep now," she said, even though she wouldn't mind them staying a bit longer. She wanted to be at the library first thing in the morning. Mistress Averill had asked whether Emmey had ever seen herself in a dream. It couldn't be a coincidence that Emmey had now dreamed such a dream. The mistress must know something and would chuckle when Emmey described the sophisticated girl in the robe. Emmey was sure of it.

~

"IT HAPPENED!" EMMEY ANNOUNCED, without bothering to knock. She knew Mistress Averill wasn't scribing. She'd lingered near the entrance to the library until the mistress had arrived, then waited a few minutes and rushed to her office.

Mistress Averill placed the quill she'd just picked up back into the inkpot and smiled at Emmey. "What happened?"

She bobbed a quick curtsey. "I saw myself in a dream."

The mistress's smile faltered, then broadened again. "That must have been strange."

"It was. I'll tell you all about it." Emmey plunked into a chair. "I wouldn't mind an apple." She'd eaten her porridge quickly and not asked for seconds.

The mistress went to her desk drawer. She took longer than usual to select an apple, her back to Emmey the whole time. Finally she turned around and handed Emmey not only an apple, but a sugar pill.

Emmey eagerly gulped down the treat and murmured a thank you. "It was the same dream, about Maddy, but this time she dragged me into the burning chamber and I was in pain. Real pain. But then I was on the monastery grounds, lying in one of the chamomile fields. A woman who didn't have a face—"

Mistress Averill sat on her stool and peered down at Emmey. "No face?"

"She had a hood on, and even though I looked right at her, I couldn't see a face. But then she removed her hood." Emmey rested the apple on her lap so she could mime drawing a hood away from her face. "And it was me! Well, not me exactly. The other me's hair was in a bun, and she was dressed in silk, and she carried herself differently, all hoity-toity like. And she talked down to me."

Mistress Averill swallowed. "What did she say?"

"That she kept talking to me but I wasn't listening to her. I said she wasn't real, and she said," Emmey dropped her voice an octave, "You won't mind another visit to the tower with Maddy again." She returned to using her normal voice. "And suddenly I was back with Maddy, being dragged toward flames again, except this time I knew how much it would hurt. But then I woke up and Maddy and Lillian were in my bedchamber."

"I see."

"So. Tell me."

"Tell you what?"

"What it means! You asked me if I'd ever seen myself in a dream, and I said no, and you said to tell you if I did. Well, I have. What does it mean?"

Emmey crunched on a bite of apple while she waited for the mistress to enlighten her. Mistress Averill scratched her nose. Her eyes briefly met Emmey's. Emmey was about to prompt her again, when she finally spoke. "I don't think it means anything. I only asked because I found a book that's a bit like a community journal, you see. The sisters all recorded their dreams for a month, and a number of them mentioned seeing themselves in their dreams." The mistress shrugged. "I was just curious to know if you'd ever seen yourself, since you have such an active dream life."

"Active dream life." Emmey giggled. "So it doesn't mean anything, then."

"No."

"Have you found anything that sounds like the dreams I'm having."

"No."

"Oh, well." She bit into her apple again and studied the mistress as she chewed. Mistress Averill's face was drawn, pale. There were shadows under her eyes. "You're working too hard," she said to her.

Mistress Averill gave a curt shake of her head. "I'm scribing a bit more than usual, that's all."

"Helping Mistress Olivia?" Emmey couldn't keep the glee out of her voice. She sighed when the mistress gave her a warning look. "I suppose I should go. Off to the garden." She leaped to her feet.

Mistress Averill rose. "Do you mind if I give you a hug? Come here."

Emmey went to her without hesitation, still clutching the apple. The mistress held her tight. Emmey could only hug her back with one arm, receiving a taste of how Maddy must feel.

"I'll miss you very much," Mistress Averill said. "You've been— you are—a delightful girl."

Tears sprang to Emmey's eyes. "I'll miss you too."

When they parted, Emmey was surprised to see the mistress brushing away tears. "I'll be in Merrin. I might see you occasionally."

"I dearly hope so, Emmey. I really do."

With a lump in her throat, Emmey gave her a quick wave and bounded from the office. She raced down the steps to the first floor and burst from the tower and onto the path, her chest heaving. By the time she reached the chapel for morning prayers, she'd calmed down, but she'd held back tears the entire way.

She entered the chapel with dread hanging over her like a wet woolen blanket. If it had been that difficult to part with Mistress Averill—and she hadn't actually left the monastery yet—how would she be able to bear parting with Maddy and Lillian?

~

SOPHIA WANTED TO PACE as she waited for the two sisters she'd summoned to arrive at her study. This wasn't like her! No matter what she was facing, she usually remained calm, serene. Lately, every little thing made her want to rub her forehead and rest her head on her desk and weep. She needed to spend more time in the chapel.

A tentative knock at the door made her straighten. She beckoned for Sister Rose to enter. Sister Gwendolyn walked in behind her. The two sisters bobbed.

Sophia studied the women. Sister Rose smoothed her robe and fidgeted, avoiding Sophia's eyes. Sister Gwendolyn appeared relaxed but kept blinking.

"Do you know why you're here?"

Sister Rose glanced at Sister Gwendolyn. "We can guess," Sister Gwendolyn said. "Mistress Margery?"

"Correct. Sister Rose, I don't usually see you in my study under these circumstances."

Sister Rose had the good sense to appear stricken.

"Sister Gwendolyn, I'm wondering if I should get you your own chair, you're in here so frequently."

Sister Gwendolyn raised a finger. "That's not quite—"

Sophia quirked a brow.

"True," Sister Gwendolyn finished. She cleared her throat and folded her hands together in front of her.

"Mistress Margery was quite upset about the way you spoke to her. Insolent was her word. I asked her what was said, but she declined to tell me. She said she didn't want to repeat your cruel words. Would one of you enlighten me, please?"

Once again, Sister Rose deferred to Sister Gwendolyn, who gave her an exasperated look in return. "She was rude to Sister Maddy," Sister Gwendolyn said.

Sophia masked her surprise. The mistress hadn't mentioned Maddy at all. "How?"

Sister Rose answered her. "She said Sister Maddy shouldn't be an adept because she can't draw the elements."

"Along with how lax things are here," Sister Gwendolyn added. "Imagine, her telling us how lax things are."

Sophia shared Sister Gwendolyn's indignation, but mistresses needed to be respected. "What did you say to her?"

The two sisters hesitated. "I said she was rude," Sister Rose said. "I said Maddy—Sister Maddy—has every right to be an adept and that every sister here would agree with me. I wasn't rude to the mistress. I spoke back. No, I spoke up." Her chin came up too.

Sophia approved.

"I might have said her comments were inane, though."

"That sounds rude to me."

"I suppose it was." Sister Rose's shoulders sagged.

Sophia shifted her attention to Sister Gwendolyn.

"I was a bit blunter," the sister said. "I . . . " She cleared her throat again. "I mentioned her love of ale."

Oh, dear. Sophia wanted to pull off her spectacles and wipe her brow.

"And I implied that she shouldn't be pointing out how lax things are when Hedgerow consorts can't keep their robes on with other sisters."

Sophia stared at her. "Anything else? Did you insult her looks, or her parents?"

Sister Gwendolyn shook her head.

"So you defended Sister Maddy, then?"

"Yes, I did."

"I'm a bit surprised. You like to tease her." Sophia wanted to say torment her, but Maddy had told her she could handle Gwendolyn and had asked her to stay out of it.

"Well, she's *our* sister, isn't she? If anyone's going to tease her, we are. She knows we're only joking."

Sophia didn't quite agree with Sister Gwendolyn's explanation, but for Maddy's sake, she'd let it go. "How did Sister Maddy respond to Mistress Margery?"

"She didn't say anything. She just stood there."

"She did the right thing. I know the mistress can be trying and the Hedgerow sisters have brought drama with them, but they're our guests. The way to counter any opinions Mistress Margery holds about us is by example, not with insults. Having two sisters turn on her only supported her assertion."

Good, now Sister Gwendolyn's shoulders were sagging too, though if Sister Rose's sagged any further, they'd be touching the floor. "I want both of you to apologize to the mistress by the end of today. You'll also spend an hour in the library refreshing yourselves about how to properly respect a mistress."

"Yes, Abbess," both sisters murmured.

"Mistress Averill will let me know when you've completed your hour."

Sister Rose raised her hand.

"Yes, Sister."

"Do we have to apologize to Mistress Margery first, or can we go to the library now?"

Sophia almost smiled. "You can go to the library any time. Do so before the end of the week."

"Thank you."

"Now, the Hedgerow sisters aren't here for much longer. Put up with them. No more mouthing off."

"Yes, Abbess."

"Return to your duties."

They left her study. Sophia leaned back in her chair and rubbed her temples. Next time she received a letter informing her that sisters from another monastery would rest their heads under Merrin's roof, she'd be tempted to throw the missive into the fire. She'd pray for the time until the Hedgerow sisters departed to pass quickly, but Emmey would leave soon too.

18

Sophia paused outside the closed door to the training room, then rapped on it loudly. She waited, knowing not to enter until Elizabeth opened the door. Walking into a training room unannounced could result in dire injury, or worse.

The door swung open. Surprise flickered across Elizabeth's face. "I wasn't expecting it to be you."

"I hope you're not disappointed," Sophia snapped, then she winced and brushed past Elizabeth. "I'm sorry. I'm here precisely because of my mood."

Elizabeth shut the door and drew Sophia into a hug. "What's wrong?"

Sophia leaned into Elizabeth and closed her eyes. "I'm not myself, lately. I feel cynical, and impatient, and irritated. I can't seem to find the bright spots, no matter how hard I try. It goes beyond my usually worrisome nature. I feel down, not worried."

"We're all feeling a bit down right now."

She opened her eyes and lifted her head. "I wish there was a way Emmey could stay. I feel like everyone wants me to figure out how."

"That's not true. We all understand why she can't." Elizabeth drew back to meet Sophia's eyes, but still held her. "Let's say you decided to let her stay longer. How long? Until she turns sixteen? Eighteen? Twenty-one? Twenty-five?"

"I know. She's not marked. She's not taking the robe. She'd have to go sometime."

"Yes, and while it's going to be heart wrenching for everyone, the agreement you made with the duke said fourteen. And honestly, I think it will be better for her. She'll need time to adjust to the outside, and the younger she is, the better chance she'll have."

"Are you just saying that?"

Elizabeth gave her an indulgent look. "No. I mean it."

"I suppose you're right." Sophia rested her head on Elizabeth's shoulder. "Emmey leaving is colouring everything, of course, but there's also more going on than usual. The trouble with the Hedgerow sisters. Maddy wanting to go to Heath again, meaning we'll lose her and Lillian for a time, and other sisters too, because I won't allow just the two of them to go, not after what happened last time. And last time, we didn't know Maddy very well. We knew Lillian cared for her, but we didn't love her, not like we do now. Half of our little family will be gone."

"It'll just be the two of us for a while." Elizabeth's voice suddenly lacked vigour.

Sophia tightened her arms around her. "I didn't mean to upset you."

"I was already upset. I'm just hiding it better than you are, and I'm not the abbess. I only have my own problems to deal with, and those are small because you carry so much on your shoulders. But you're only human, Sophia. I'd be worried if you weren't feeling down. It wouldn't be natural."

"I don't like being surly with everyone."

"I doubt you're letting it show as much as you think you are, and it helps everyone to see that you're affected by Emmey leaving too. Otherwise everyone would question their own reactions to it, along with their dedication to Salbine. They shouldn't, because what they're feeling is natural."

"Perhaps you're the one who should be wearing the abbess's cassock right now."

Elizabeth snorted. "I'd be a terrible abbess. I don't have your patience. I'm an excellent abbess's consort, though."

Sophia pressed her palm against Elizabeth's cheek. "I couldn't agree with you more."

"How long has it been since you've drawn the elements?"

"Why?"

"I find drawing quite therapeutic. What do you think I'm doing here?"

"When Sister Amelia said you were in one of the training rooms, I did wonder," Sophia admitted.

"I've been spending more time in here than usual. Works wonders for my mood. I think it'll do you some good too."

"You think so?"

"I do."

Elizabeth let Sophia go. A moment later, Sophia sensed fire swirling around her. A pile of straw burst into flame, then the flames abruptly died.

"Come on," Elizabeth said. "Your turn."

Sophia stepped farther away from Elizabeth and reached for the elemental source. Fire raced through her. Flames leaped from the straw again, Sophia's spirits rising along with them. She exhaled slowly and stopped drawing. Smoke rose from the straw, but the fire was gone.

"You're right, that did make me feel a bit better," she said to Elizabeth.

"Stay with me, then." Elizabeth pointed at a candle in a tall candlestick. "Pretend that's Sister Felicia."

Sophia frowned. "That's a bit childish, don't you think?"

"It might be childish, but don't tell me you won't relish setting it alight now."

Sophia gave her a sly look. The wick burst into flame, followed by the wicks of the three candles closest to it.

Elizabeth grinned. "Show off."

Sophia jutted her chin toward an extra-high pile of straw. "That will do better as Sister Felicia." It burst into flame. She cackled and stopped drawing, then set the straw alight again.

Elizabeth clapped, then another pile of straw burst into flame.

Sophia raised her brows in appreciation and stopped drawing, so she could make her pile of straw burn again. She was enjoying herself and would suggest to Elizabeth that they do it again soon. An excellent abbess's consort, indeed. Once again, Sophia thanked Abbess Margaret for her wisdom. She couldn't imagine her life without Elizabeth at her side, one of the reasons Sister Felicia's cavalier attitude toward her former consort had infuriated Sophia so much. She needed to regain her equilibrium so she could return to keeping a watchful eye on those in her community, especially after Emmey had gone. Everyone would be off-kilter for a bit. They might have to draw up a schedule for the training rooms.

~

AVERILL WANTED TO THROW down her quill when she dabbed too much ink onto the parchment. "What a bloody mess," she muttered, then she remembered she wasn't alone. "I do apologize," she said to Mistress Olivia, who did her work so quietly and diligently that Averill sometimes forgot she was there. "A momentary lapse."

Mistress Olivia's quill stilled. She set it down. "If you don't mind me making an observation, your heart doesn't seem to be in it today. Is something on your mind?"

Someone. Poor Emmey. Cheerful, mischievous, playful Emmey, who didn't know . . . didn't know she wasn't long for this realm. And what about Sister Maddy and Mistress Lillian? They expected to part, but not because Emmey was . . . Averill's eyes welled with tears. She buried her head in her hands.

"Oh, I'm so sorry." Mistress Olivia's stool scraped across the stone floor. She fluttered around Averill. "I didn't mean to upset you. Whatever is the matter? Do tell me. Sharing a burden with another usually helps."

She shouldn't. She should keep it to herself. But the knowledge was crushing her, pressing on her chest and dulling every moment. "There's a book—"

Sister Clara knocked on the open door and bobbed. "Excuse

me, Mistress Olivia, but I was wondering which book you'd like me to start on next? I'd ask Mistress Margery, but she stepped out to get some air."

Averill ducked her head and pretended to study the text she was scribing.

"Give me a minute, and I'll come out and see where we are," Mistress Olivia said.

"All right." Sister Clara's departing footsteps grew fainter.

Mistress Olivia fished a handkerchief from the pocket of her robe and handed it to Averill.

"Thank you." Averill managed a smile, and Mistress Olivia returned it. The mistress was pleasing in her own way. Not a beauty by anyone's standards, with a nose that was too wide, scars marring her cheeks, and jagged lines radiating from the corners of her eyes and mouth. Oh, but those eyes! They were so bright and curious. And that mind, and the mistress's love of books!

"Let's meet somewhere more private later so you can tell me what's upsetting you," Mistress Olivia said. "Somewhere we won't be interrupted. Have supper with me in my chambers. Shall we say, five o'clock?"

Averill wiped her eyes. "All right," she heard herself say. She immediately wanted to take it back. But the mistress's smile had broadened. Averill didn't want to make that smile go away, and she wanted to have supper with the mistress. She was sure Mistress Olivia didn't mean for the supper to be anything but innocent. Averill was sitting here blubbering like a babe. The mistress knew something was bothering her.

"I'll go see to Sister Clara." Mistress Olivia bustled from the office.

Averill gave her eyes another wipe and tried to rally herself but couldn't part the dark clouds. Soon all life would be gone from this library. No more Mistress Olivia, and no more Emmey asking for apples and being cheeky. *Please, Salbine, let Emmey be gone because she's with the Bennetts in Merrin, and not because she's cold and silent in the catacombs.*

EMMEY GAZED OUT ONE of the windows on the top floor of the Mistresses Tower, watching sisters stroll across the courtyard but not registering who they were. Not long ago, she'd sat at the table in Sophia and Elizabeth's chambers, feeling loved, accepting gifts, tasting cider for the first time and wanting to spit the bitter liquid out. Sophia had chuckled and said they should try a sweeter cider next time. Then they'd remembered there wouldn't be a next time.

Fourteen. She was bloody fourteen. She could swear that a girl who'd lived nearby to her when she was around six had married at fourteen. So had another girl on the next road over. No, she'd been thirteen. Another reason to thank Salbine for landing in that cell at Dunmurk Prison, even though Emmey had been bored out of her wits until Maddy had arrived. If she was still with her ma today, she'd probably be married—or dead. Ma would have sold her for coin and never looked back, and she wouldn't have waited until Emmey was fourteen, or thirteen, for that matter. *Ma.* Cassy—that had been her name—didn't deserve to be called that anymore. Two other women did, and Emmey could hear one of them climbing the steps to this floor, her footsteps so familiar. She turned toward the stairwell.

"There you are. My first guess was right." Maddy slipped her arm around Emmey's shoulders. "I wish your birthday was a happier occasion. I've struggled with what's best for you. To show my sorrow or appear strong. I chose the latter. Now I'm wondering if that was right. I wouldn't want you to think I won't miss you."

"I know you'll miss me, but not half as much as I'll miss you."

"I'm not sure about that." Maddy smiled down at her. "You'll be all right. You're one of the most resilient people I've ever known. You showed it in spades when you were in prison. You were an inspiration to me. I wondered how you did it, remained energetic and happy."

Emmey wanted to laugh and cry. "Because of you, silly. Before you came, I sat and sat and sat and counted the hours between meals, when I'd get to see someone and say a word to them. The day you came was the best day of my life."

She felt Maddy's chuckle. "That will change when you get married and start having babes."

No, it wouldn't, because neither of those events would happen for her. She leaned into Maddy, fighting the urge to tell her that she was marked. But she knew what would happen. Maddy's face would light up. She'd say, "That's wonderful! You can stay!" And Emmey would have to open her mouth and tell her, wipe the happiness from her face and cringe at the bewilderment that replaced it.

On the other hand, it would be the perfect opportunity to talk to her about how to tell if one was called to service. Emmey had pondered the topic ever since she'd spoken to Sister Dolores after meeting with the Bennetts. Was she a sister in all but name? How could she distinguish her love for everyone here, and her affinity for monastery life, from being called to service? Did they feel the same, or should she be feeling something she wasn't if she was truly called?

She wanted to talk to Maddy about the questions dogging her, but the moment she told her she was marked, she'd never be able to take it back. She couldn't risk it—hurting her. Maddy would never let it show. She'd answer Emmey honestly. Because of her faith, she'd understand why Emmey wasn't racing to take the robe, but she'd be hurt. She was human, and she'd suffered enough losses already. She still wondered why she was malflowed and didn't need another loss to wonder about. If Emmey wasn't marked, it would all be so simple. There would be no questions. But she was, and she was trying to do the right thing, for everyone. She was fourteen, after all. She wasn't a girl anymore. She could be married. She could already have a babe. It would be easier for everyone if they believed she'd had no choice but to leave.

She slipped her arm around Maddy's waist. "You coming into that cell was the best thing that ever happened to me. I know you can't say the same, and you don't need to. I doubt I'd be alive now if you hadn't come. I'm going to miss you all so much, but I'll know I'm loved, which I never knew before."

Maddy let out a shuddering breath. "Yes, you are loved, dearly loved. That will never change. A day won't go by when I won't think of you many times."

Emmey rested her head on Maddy's shoulder and gazed out the window again, feeling loved, feeling blessed.

~

AVERILL FORCED DOWN THE last bit of stew with relief and moved her bowl aside. She'd gamely held her end of the conversation with Mistress Olivia, though the mistress had done most of the talking and probably regretted inviting Averill here. Normally Averill would glance around the sitting room with curiosity, to see if there was anything that would tell her more about the mistress. Was she neat or disorganized? Had she brought any cushions or ornaments with her that would hint at her inner world. Most importantly, what books were on the shelves? There were books. Averill had spotted them as soon as she'd stepped over the threshold from the hall, her eyes drawn to them like iron to a magnet.

But her mind was in too much turmoil to satisfy her curiosity. She couldn't get the image of Emmey out of her head, Emmey with her eyes closed, never to open them again.

"Would you like more milk?" Mistress Olivia asked.

"No, thank you. I still have some left."

The mistress topped up her mug and eyed the book Averill had placed on a corner of the table, out of harm's way.

Averill managed a smile. "I've bookmarked a passage."

Taking her words as permission, Mistress Olivia snatched up the book and opened it to the place Averill had marked. Her eyes quickly moved down the page. Averill fingered the handkerchief in her pocket, hoping she wouldn't need it.

The mistress lifted her head, her face questioning.

"It's Emmey, you see. She's been having dreams that partially come true. The essential details are correct. And recently . . ." Averill gulped down air. She took out the handkerchief and wrung it underneath the table. "Recently she had a mirror dream. She spoke to herself."

"Salbine preserve us," Mistress Olivia breathed. "Are you sure? About the other dreams?"

"She foresaw Malcolm almost being run over by the horse and wagon. In her dream, he died. But in reality, she was able to warn him in time. And she foretold the fire at the market. In separate dreams, mind you. She's also having a recurring dream about Sister Maddy." Averill hesitated, not sure she wanted to say it out loud. "She dies horribly in the dream. Sister Maddy."

Mistress Olivia swallowed and carefully set the book down. "Sister Maddy is the one who cares for Emmey. The one with," the mistress waved two fingers over her left arm, "one hand? The one with the older consort?"

"Mistress Lillian." Averill remembered her skepticism about Lillian and Sister Maddy's relationship. If she was honest, she'd looked down her nose at it and expected them to part within a few months. Until Lillian had ridden through the gates and not returned for ages. Nobody, including Averill, had questioned the depth of Lillian's love after that, and Sister Maddy clearly loved her back. One of life's mysteries.

"What can I do?" she said to Mistress Olivia. "I can't stop Emmey . . . I can't stop it from happening. I don't see what telling Sister Maddy and Mistress Lillian would do except upset them, because they can't do anything. The knowledge would utterly shatter them. The abbess has enough to deal with right now, and she wouldn't be able to do anything, either. I have to keep it to myself, you see. But I can't stop thinking about it. Every morning I wonder if Emmey's awake. Every time I hear someone approaching, I wonder if they'll give me bad news."

The mistress clasped her hands on the table. "You've told me now."

"You'll be gone soon."

"But you still won't be alone. You'll know I know. I'll pray for you and Emmey at every opportunity. And we can speak of this whenever you feel the need."

"You can't tell anyone."

"I won't. I promise."

When the mistress sipped her milk, Averill took the opportunity to quickly wipe her eyes and stuff the handkerchief back into her pocket.

"Emmey must be marked by Salbine," Mistress Olivia stated.

"I came to that conclusion too. She hasn't said anything."

"Perhaps she doesn't know. She's only thirteen, isn't she?"

"Just turned fourteen. Today, in fact. I think she knows, though, or at least has an inkling."

Mistress Olivia gazed at her with piercing eyes. "Why would Salbine give these dreams, only to take the dreamers to her realm? Did you see the ages of some of those sisters? One was only seventeen."

"And most only dreamed of banal events. Few of the dreams had any significance."

"The book chronicles their dreams?"

"Yes. Emmey's dream about Malcolm had more significance than most of them. Her dream about the market fire didn't influence events. Her dream about Sister Maddy . . . " A flood of tears threatened. Averill gripped her half-empty mug. "I don't pretend to understand Salbine's ways. Look at Sister Maddy. Utterly devoted to Salbine, yet she can't draw."

Mistress Olivia's eyes widened. "Oh, yes. I remember hearing about a malflowed sister, years ago. I'd forgotten she was here, and I don't think I ever knew her name."

"Now you do. Sister Maddy. Malflowed, and if that wasn't enough, Salbine will take Emmey. And if Emmey's dream comes true—" Averill's constricting throat cut off her words.

Mistress Olivia took Averill's free hand. The kind gesture further threatened Averill's composure, but she mastered herself and clung to the lifeline the mistress offered. "Don't mind me. It helps to talk about it."

"I can understand why you're so upset. Anyone can see you're fond of Emmey, and you seem to have a high regard for Sister Maddy."

Averill nodded. "She's already had so much taken from her. She already wonders whether Salbine loves her. And now . . . "

Mistress Olivia's warm fingers tightened around Averill's. Averill met the mistress's eyes, curious, kind eyes that hinted at the depth of the mistress's mind. She could lose herself in those eyes and felt perfectly comfortable pouring out her heart to the mistress, as if she'd done it many times before. It had been so long since she'd—

She snatched her hand from the mistress's and leaped to her feet. "I don't appreciate what you're doing," she snapped.

Mistress Olivia's brow furrowed.

"Clearly I'm upset, and you're taking advantage."

"What?"

"Was that the plan? Invite me here, wait until I'm sobbing into my handkerchief, and then offer your support? What was the next step? Hugging me? Unbuttoning my robe?"

The mistress's brows shot up. She stood and stared at Averill.

"You must think me stupid. I'm not that gullible."

"No! I—"

"I'll be glad to see the back of you and everyone who came with you. You can't leave soon enough." Averill glared at the mistress, then whirled and fled from her chambers.

It wasn't until she was back in her own chambers and stood shaking just inside the sitting room that she realized she'd left the book behind. She sank into the nearest chair, shouting at herself, not because of the book, but because of her boorishness, the mortification on Mistress Olivia's face, and the tears glistening in her eyes.

Why, oh why, had Averill agreed to meet with the mistress in her chambers? If she hadn't been so upset . . . if Sister Clara hadn't interrupted . . . Averill had vowed to not meet with the mistress alone. Because it was only ever going to lead to exactly where it had. To tears.

The chapel bells pealed half past six. It would soon be time for evening prayers. Averill rarely missed the service, but she would tonight. She couldn't face the mistress, not now. Would Mistress Olivia attend the service? Averill cursed herself for wondering. She went to the wardrobe in her bedchamber and searched for the robe that was too small for her. She hadn't felt it in a while, hadn't fingered the broadcloth and breathed in the scent she wasn't sure lingered with it, or was only etched in her memory, the memory that taunted her at the worst times with images she wished she could forget, of the woman she would always remember.

19

Sophia waited until mistress margery had settled into one of the guest chairs, then offered her tea. The mistress shook her head.

"Did Sisters Rose and Gwendolyn speak to you?" Sophia asked.

"Yes, they did. Thank you for handling the matter so swiftly."

"You're welcome. Now, what can I do for you?"

"I'll be quick. I don't think Sister Felicia and Sister Lorelle will be able to bear living in the same monastery. Sister Lorelle still doesn't want to leave her chambers. I saw her yesterday, and I don't see how she'll ever grow used to seeing the two sisters together. So I have a proposal. I've already run it past Sister Cecily and Sister Felicia."

Sister Felicia. Sophia wouldn't mind never hearing her name again, or Sister Cecily's. Fortunately, they were having the good sense to stay out of her and everyone else's way, only coming out of their chambers—their separate chambers—to eat, scribe, and use the privy. The next time Sophia's eyes settled on them, she wanted it to be at the gates, when she was bidding them good-bye. "What's your proposal?"

"They remain here and become part of your community."

"No," Sophia said flatly.

The mistress's face fell. "But they can't coexist with Sister Lorelle."

"I understand. But I don't want them here. I know that sounds uncharitable, but I don't. I've seen enough to know that those two, particularly Sister Felicia, will only mean more drama in the coming years. They're Hedgerow's problem, not Merrin's. It started there, and it will finish there."

Mistress Margery grunted.

"I would, however, be willing to accept Sister Lorelle into our community, if she's amenable to the notion."

"Ah." The mistress slowly nodded. "I suppose that would do."

"Do you want to put it to her, or do you want me to do it?"

"I'll do it."

Sophia leaned forward. "After what happened between Sister Felicia and the novice, I'm surprised a closer eye wasn't kept on her. Two years, Mistress. That's how long they were carrying on."

"They were very discreet, I can assure you. I didn't notice anything, and I work with Sister Cecily daily."

Should she say it? Sophia couldn't help herself. "Perhaps it's not my place, but I *have* noticed you enjoy your ale."

The mistress straightened. "What are you suggesting?"

"That your mind wasn't clear enough to notice."

"Are you suggesting I'm a drunk?"

"Mistress, I can smell ale now."

"Because it's on me."

"What do you mean?"

"I rub it on my skin. Not ale exactly, but an ale-based tincture."

"Whatever for?"

"I have pimples . . . in areas you can't see."

Sophia blinked at her. "And you think rubbing this tincture on them helps? To smell so strongly, it must be composed of ninety-nine percent ale."

"Someone suggested it to me. A woman in Hedgerow's market."

"Is it helping?"

"Not really," the mistress mumbled.

"Then why do you keep doing it?"

"Habit, I suppose."

Sophia wanted to bury her head in her hands. "Go see one of the adepts who work at the Monday clinic. I'm sure she'll be able to suggest something that others can't smell." And that might actually work. "You could also talk to Mistress Lillian or Mistress Dorothy."

"I don't like telling others. It's a private matter."

"You'll be leaving soon, and I assure you that anyone you talk to about your physical woes will keep it to themselves." Sophia paused. "You're sometimes caught napping."

"I'll admit to being guilty of that. I should go to my chambers for an hour every afternoon, but I usually just put my head down wherever I am. They're used to it at Hedgerow."

"I see. Well, I can't fault you for that. But you do enjoy your ale."

"Perhaps I've tippled a bit too much at times. I don't usually enjoy cider so much, and I didn't realize my behaviour was upsetting others. But this journey has tried me more than I'd expected. I'll try to limit myself to milk until I'm back in my chambers for the evening." Mistress Margery bit her lip. "You must think Hedgerow is a mess."

The thought had crossed Sophia's mind more than once.

"It's not. You've seen the worst we have to offer in Sister Felicia and Sister Cecily. Look to Mistress Olivia and Sister Lorelle if you want to see what most of us are made of. I'll include myself in that group too, despite everyone thinking I can't hold my ale."

"I do apologize, but you can understand why everyone is jumping to that conclusion."

"I'm not used to having to explain myself. I'm usually around sisters who know my ways."

"You must be looking forward to going home."

"Yes. No offense meant to Merrin, but I've been wanting to go home for months. This is the last time I'll volunteer for one of these journeys. I'm getting too old. I want my own bed."

Sophia found herself warming to the woman, a reminder that she shouldn't be so hasty to judge. "When you supped with me and my consort, you mentioned your Joan. I wouldn't mind hearing more about her."

"And I wouldn't mind telling you about her, but can I do it another time? I have to get back. We're down two scribes today."

"Two scribes?"

"Sister Lorelle and Mistress Averill."

"Mistress Averill isn't scribing today?" Now that Sophia thought about it, she didn't recall seeing Averill at this morning's service and wasn't sure if she'd been at last night's.

"She isn't feeling well, according to Sister Clara. She went to check up on her when the mistress wasn't at her podium at her usual time."

"I'll have to go see how she is." Concern snaking through her, Sophia wanted to go see Averill immediately, but she couldn't ignore everyone and everything else. "If you're falling behind, you could ask Emmey to help you."

"You mean the girl?"

"Yes, the girl. She's a competent scribe. If you give her a page to do, she'll scribe it." Sophia could tell from Mistress Margery's dubious expression that she wouldn't be speaking to Emmey, which perhaps was just as well. Emmey's scribing days were over. "Is there anything else?"

"No, I just wanted to make my proposal. I'll see Sister Lorelle this afternoon."

"Thank you."

As soon as the mistress had left the study, Sophia pushed back her chair and headed for Averill's chambers.

~

LILLIAN PULLED OFF HER spectacles and shoved them into her robe's pocket when footsteps she didn't recognize echoed in the passageway outside her laboratory. Lighter than Maddy's, too slow for Emmey's, quicker than Sophia's. She fussed with the ginger she'd been about to cut, not wanting to appear curious.

Rose stumbled into the laboratory, swiping at her hair. "Those passageways need a good clean," she wailed. "My hair's full of cobwebs."

An exaggeration. Lillian could see only one. Rose batted it away. "What can I do for you, Rose?" she asked, wondering if Rose needed a tincture or other medicinal aid.

Rose stood just inside the doorway and folded her hands in front of her. "I want to talk to you about Heath."

Lillian crossed her arms.

"When you and Maddy go to Heath, Nora and I want to go with you. We know you're quite capable of protecting Maddy. More than capable. That's not why we want to go. We just want to be there for her. Not that you won't be there for her, but after what happened last time, and with Emmey leaving, and . . . " She trailed off.

"Are you asking my permission?"

"I suppose so. I've already mentioned it to Maddy, but I said I'd talk to you about it. We don't want to, uh . . . "

"Get in the way?"

Rose's faced screwed up. "Not quite. But we don't want to become a bother. To you. It will be a long time away. Months."

Lillian didn't need reminding. She dropped her arms to her sides. "I think it would be a good idea for you and Nora to come along."

Rose's eyes widened. "You do? I mean, that's good."

"As long as you don't go putting foolish notions into Maddy's head."

"Such as?" Rose said, frowning.

"That she'll be able to draw again."

"She doesn't believe that."

"She believes it's possible. Something she read in the material from Heath."

Rose gasped. "She's read material from Heath?"

Maybe Lillian shouldn't have said anything, but she was certain Maddy would eventually tell Rose. The two friends had few secrets between them. "It included excerpts from the malflowed sister's journal. One of them is a bit cryptic. Maddy's interpretation is that the sister drew the elements again, without feeling any pain."

"Is that your interpretation as well?"

"Maddy could be right, but she could equally be wrong. If we arrive at Heath and she discovers the sister never drew again, she'll be shattered. She'll be even more devastated if there's nothing at Heath to help her practically or spiritually. If that happens, she'll need all of us to remind her that she belongs in a robe." If only

Sophia and Elizabeth could go too. Lillian didn't want to leave them for so long again, but if Maddy didn't go to Heath, she'd always wonder. Lillian couldn't deny her the journey and fervently hoped that Heath's library held an answer that would put Maddy's wonderings to rest, once and for all.

"That's why we want to go," Rose said. "To be there for her."

"Then you'll be most welcome."

Rose smiled. "Wonderful! I look forward to travelling together."

Lillian hoped her answering smile appeared genuine.

"Of course, we'll need the abbess's permission when the time comes."

"I expect you'll receive it."

Rose turned to go, then swung around. "Lillian."

"What?"

"Perhaps we can all go down to the river for a quiet afternoon. In a few weeks' time."

Lillian's first impulse was to be non-committal. She didn't mind Rose and Nora's company, but in small doses, which went for everyone except Maddy, Emmey, Sophia, and Elizabeth. If she didn't truly believe that Maddy would do better on the journey to Heath with her friends around her, she would have told Rose to stay in Merrin.

But Maddy was different. Maddy enjoyed being with folk, and she'd soon need her friends more than ever. Lillian would agree to the outing. For Maddy. "Perhaps we should."

Rose's face lit up. "I'll talk to Maddy about it, then. I'll see you at evening prayers."

"See you then."

Lillian listened to Rose's receding footsteps, then pulled out her spectacles and popped them back onto her nose. Long gone were the days when she only had to think of herself, her needs, her desire to mix with folk as little as possible. But she had Maddy, and she wouldn't want it any other way.

~

SOPHIA WAITED AT THE door to Averill's chambers, then swung

it open when she heard a muffled invitation to enter. In the dull light, she could see Averill sitting at the table, a blanket around her slumped shoulders. She shut the door and went to the nearest window. "Do you mind if I open the shutters? It's a glorious day today."

"Go ahead," Averill mumbled.

Sophia unhitched the latch and swung the shutters aside. Sunlight streamed into the room. Averill stood and bobbed, the blanket almost slipping off her shoulders. Underneath, she wore only her shift, and she hadn't brushed her hair since rising. She didn't appear ill, though. Her eyes were clear, and she wasn't coughing or sniffling. If Averill wasn't feeling well, she was ill in spirit. "Do you mind if I sit down?"

Averill gestured toward the only other chair at the table. The hearth was cold, and the chill air gave Sophia goosebumps, but she didn't want to ask. First things first. She sank into the chair and sat on her hands, to warm them. "Mistress Margery mentioned that you weren't at the library today, that you're not feeling well."

"No." Averill pulled the blanket tighter.

"You weren't at prayers this morning, either. I thought I'd come make sure you're all right."

"Do you want a cup of tea?"

"No, I'm fine, thank you. Do you want one?" Sophia glanced hopefully at the hearth.

Averill shook her head. "Do you know if Mistress Olivia is scribing today?"

Ah, a hint. "I believe she is."

"Have you seen her?"

"No. Why?"

Averill shrugged. "I was just wondering how she is."

"Why? Was she not feeling well yesterday?"

Averill's shoulders hunched more than Sophia had thought possible. "I might as well tell you, because you won't leave me alone unless I do."

Sophia chuckled. "We've been friends for a long time. That's why I'm here."

"Oh, tosh. You'd be here even if I was a novice you barely knew. But I appreciate the sentiment."

"Then stop asking me questions and tell me what's going on."

Averill gave Sophia a pointed look, but her eyes were dull. "I had supper with Mistress Olivia in her chambers last night."

"Oh?"

"Not that type of supper. Well, not really. I think, well, I'm not sure now, but perhaps—"

"Start at the beginning, Averill."

Averill drew a deep breath and slowly exhaled. "We had a pleasant supper together. Afterwards, we discussed Emmey . . . leaving, and I became upset, and Mistress Olivia took my hand and held it. She was only trying to offer comfort, I'm sure, but—" Averill shot up from her chair and paced. "It all came rushing back, Sophia. Because I felt so comfortable with her, and holding her hand felt natural, and I remembered how long it had been, and it all came rushing back."

Averill didn't have to explain what had come rushing back. Sophia would never forget the hysterical screaming that had made her rush to her chamber door and yank it open, her heart thudding in her chest. Averill had been running up the hall without a stitch of clothing on her, waving her arms, shouting for help, sobs wracking her body. Mistress Dorothy had wrapped her arms around her, Mistress Edith had covered her with a blanket, and Sophia had rushed to her and taken her hand, not understanding what had happened, but needing to do something. Abbess Margaret had arrived at some point, her face ashen. The rest of the morning was a blur, but Sophia would never forget the shock that had taken her breath away when she'd understood what had happened.

Her eyes felt moist. She dabbed her tears away with her fingertip. "What did you do?" she asked, guessing that Averill must have done something that was now making her avoid Mistress Olivia.

Averill stopped pacing. "I treated the mistress badly. I said she was trying to take advantage of me and ran away."

"You were frightened."

"That's no excuse."

"Don't be so hard on yourself. You said yourself this is the first time you've felt comfortable enough to forget."

"That's just it. I forgot. Until I remembered." Averill's eyes were dry but anguished. "I don't know if I'll ever be able to relax with anyone again. To feel carefree, to not wonder—no, expect—it all to end horribly."

"You forgot for a second. That's a good sign."

"But then I remembered and was rude to the mistress. I said I'd be glad to see the back of her."

Sophia winced. "Oh, dear."

"She must think terribly of me."

"You won't know what she thinks unless you speak to her."

Averill grimaced. "I don't know how I can face her."

"You'll have to do it sometime. You're our head scribe. You can't hide in your chambers until they've left for Hedgerow, and I don't think you should." Sophia paused. "How much do you like Mistress Olivia?"

Averill was silent for a moment. "Time passes quickly when we're together. I enjoy her company." She snorted. "Contrary to what I shouted at her, I wish she wasn't leaving us soon. Does that answer your question?"

"It does."

"Perhaps I allowed myself to relax because she *is* leaving."

"You're overthinking it. But yes, she's leaving soon. That doesn't mean you can't enjoy her company while she's still here."

"I doubt she'll want to see me when she's not forced to."

"That might be true. But if you care for her, you won't let her go back to Hedgerow without offering her some explanation for your behaviour. Whether you tell her what happened or skirt around it is up to you. But you'll have to tell her something."

Averill shuffled back to the chair but remained standing. "I know. She needs to know it wasn't her fault, that I behaved badly and didn't mean a word I said. I'll understand if she never wants to spend another minute with me outside the library. It would be for the best."

Sophia disagreed with Averill on that point, but apart from

encouraging her to speak to Mistress Olivia, something that needed to be done for both their sakes, she wouldn't interfere. "Why don't you go to the library after lunch? If anyone asks, you can say you had a headache that went away. Except for Mistress Olivia, of course."

"I'll speak to her as soon as I arrive." Averill brushed a stray hair away from her face. "I don't know what I'll tell her."

"You'll know when you speak to her."

"I hope so." Averill muttered something under her breath, then tapped the table with her left hand. "I know you're busy, but would you like a cup of tea now? I'll robe while the kettle's boiling."

"I'd love a cup. I'm not meeting with anyone this morning." Sophia moved to the fire, but Averill motioned for her to stop.

"Let me do it."

Sophia didn't protest. She wouldn't mind someone making her a cup for a change. Averill crouched to top up the kettle and light the fire. Sophia gratefully moved closer to the flames to warm her hands.

Averill straightened. "I was a right cow to her, Sophia," she murmured. "I hope she can forgive me."

Not knowing Mistress Olivia, Sophia didn't want to respond with a platitude. "If she's the woman you believe her to be, she'll understand."

Averill nodded, but doubt pinched her mouth.

20

Emmey folded one of her newer shifts and placed it into the travel bag Lillian had carried into her bedchamber a few days ago. The bloody thing had drawn her attention every time she'd come into the chamber, to the point that she'd avoided coming in here except at bedtime. But she couldn't delay packing it any longer. In five days, she'd sling the bag onto her back, trudge through the gates, and hear them figuratively clang shut and lock behind her. The sun would go in that day. It would never come out again.

"You should take at least three shifts," Maddy said from where she was sitting on the bed.

She'd wanted to help, but Emmey had waved her away. Maddy wouldn't be able to fold anything, but that wasn't why Emmey had told her to sit down. She was fourteen. Old enough to leave childhood behind and do everything on her own.

She turned back to her armoire, and after adding two more shifts to the bag, eyed her robes. She'd have no use for them in a week, a thought that frightened and saddened her. When she left her bedchamber for the last time, she'd leave them folded at the end of her bed and walk out the gates wearing a plain work dress. She'd considered taking one of the robes with her as a remembrance, but there was no point when looking at it would make her clench it in her hands, bury her face in it, weep for the family she'd lost, the library she could visit no more, the chapel she'd never pray in again, the garden someone else would tend.

Maddy shifted position, making the bed creak. "Take two pretty dresses, just in case you need them."

Emmey nodded. Maddy must be wondering why she was standing like a statue, rather than selecting the next item she'd take with her. She pulled one of the dresses the seamstresses had sewn, a new one she hadn't worn anywhere, from the armoire. But when she was in the middle of folding it, she suddenly wanted to rip it to pieces and throw the shredded cloth out the window. Despite telling herself—shouting at herself—to be strong and push through and do what she had no choice but to do, she couldn't keep it in any longer. Sister Dolores's words haunted her as much as her nightmare about Maddy did. Emmey kept questioning herself, going around and around in circles and poking holes in her answers. If she didn't ask, she'd always wonder.

She placed the dress into the bag and forced her gaze to Maddy. She'd ask about her, rather than talk about herself, and hopefully prevent Maddy from asking whether she was marked. "How did you know you were called to be here?"

"You're full of questions lately. Getting them all out of the way before you go?" Maddy's tone was light, but the air was heavy with sorrow.

"How did you know?" Emmey's lower lip trembled. She bit it.

"I felt a palpable longing to be here, in a monastery. It was the first thing I thought of in the morning and the last thing on my mind when I fell asleep at night."

"But why? You lived on a farm. What would make you think to leave your parents and come here when you could have stayed? You told me once you enjoyed living on a farm."

"I did."

"Then why? Why would you even think of it?"

"We're going back a few years now." Maddy smoothed her robe. "Let's see. There was a lay chapel in the closest village. I'd go there with my ma and pa."

"They were religious, then."

"Not really. But everyone always paid their respects when they were in the village. We went every month." Her eyes grew distant. "I loved the chapel. It wasn't as large or exquisite as the one we have here, but I loved the silence, the hushed feeling of it, the sacredness. It was always the first place I'd go when we got to the village. Ma and Pa would go to the market. I'd go to the chapel."

"Why? You said they weren't religious, so why would you rush to the chapel?"

"It was different. Beautiful. You have to remember I spent most of my time in fields and barns, with cows, pigs, and crops. There's a kind of beauty in that, but a natural beauty, not one crafted with man's hands as an offering to a goddess." Maddy waited, then continued when Emmey didn't say anything. "Usually there weren't many in the chapel, and they'd all be on a bench, heads down. But one day, when I skipped inside, there were four women there in colourful robes."

"Sisters."

"Yes. They were passing through our little village. I don't remember seeing any defenders, but they must have been there. I couldn't take my eyes off those women in the robes."

"How old were you?"

Maddy pursed her lips. "Ten, I think. I didn't know I was marked by Salbine, not then. The sisters were talking to folk in the chapel. I was too shy to approach them, but one of them spotted me and came over. Sister Ava. I wish I'd asked which monastery she was from, but I didn't. I didn't say much of anything, really. She asked my name and if I lived in the village and why I'd come to the chapel."

"What did you say?"

"I think I said because I liked the pretty windows."

"That's what you said?"

"My wits were frozen. But she wasn't offended. She said she loved the windows too. Then she asked me if I knew what the tapestry at the front was about and I said no, and she beckoned me over to it and explained it to me. It was about Salbine searing the mark onto those She'd chosen, the ones—"

Without thinking, Emmey jumped in. "—She claimed for herself, though few are marked, fewer are summoned, and even fewer answer the call, for they must leave behind what they know and give all to Salbine, and in return, receive the blessings of Her anointed, with no promise of Her gaze. Thus is the covenant between Salbine and those who fall into Her loving and indifferent embrace."

Maddy raised her brows. "Very good."

Emmey frowned. "I've never understood that last part. Loving and indifferent."

"When we studied Salbine's Covenant in our basic theology class, Sister Garnet said we're never to feel as if we're important to Salbine, that we have to get the notion out of our heads that She called us because we're special to Her, that She needs us and can't do without us. She marked us and bestows Her gifts. Beyond that, nobody knows whether She pays us any mind. We like to think She does, but nobody can say."

"But the covenant doesn't mention the gifts. It says blessings. You being malflowed . . . " Emmey wanted to stamp her feet. She'd love to discuss the covenant and how blessings could mean anything, but she had a more pressing concern. "Continue your story. About the sister."

Maddy crossed her legs and leaned forward. "She explained the covenant to me, and I remember wondering if Salbine had chosen me. I asked what it meant, and the sister explained it to me, and I remember feeling disappointed because the sister said that most girls weren't marked. Anyway, I don't remember what else we talked about, but what it meant to be marked stuck in my mind."

"So when you realized you were marked, you knew you wanted to take the robe."

"I wish I could say it was that easy, but it wasn't. I knew I was marked when I was fourteen. Your age."

Emmey held her breath, then relaxed when Maddy continued her story.

"I asked one of the women who cared for the lay chapel what I'd have to do to join the Order, and she said I had to be sixteen. So I waited, and life carried on. Even though I felt the Order was where I was meant to be, it warred with leaving my parents, leaving the farm. I'm the only one of their five children to survive long enough to take my first steps. And I loved them very much. I knew they'd be terribly disappointed. And so my sixteenth birthday came and went, and I was still on the farm, and then my eighteenth birthday arrived, and I was in love."

Emmey gasped. "You were?"

"And then it was even more difficult to tear myself away, even though I felt as if Salbine Herself was following me around, telling me to get my arse to a monastery."

"What was her name, the woman you loved?"

"Joanna."

"Does Lillian know?"

Maddy chuckled. "Of course she does. It was a long time ago." Her gaze sharpened. "Lillian's not the first woman I've loved, and I'm not the first woman Lillian's loved."

Emmey wanted to gape. She couldn't imagine Lillian with anyone else, or Maddy, for that matter. And she'd never considered that Maddy, and Lillian, of all people, had loved others before they'd found each other. Every time she thought she'd figured everything out, new information came along that proved her wrong. She couldn't wait until she was an adult and wouldn't have to worry about that anymore.

"I talked to Joanna about the Order. Endlessly. She told me to shut up about it several times. She wasn't called. It would have been easy if she was. I tried to ignore my longing to be here, but in the end, I couldn't. I told her I had to enter the Order. I told my parents. I almost went back on it because there were so many tears. My parents tried to be supportive, but I could see they didn't understand. Joanna was angry."

"But you left them."

"I did."

"How did you get here?"

"My parents gave me the coin they'd saved for me in case I married. When I told them I was marked by Salbine, they continued to save for me." Maddy's voice dropped. "They'd planned to give it to me if I ever left the farm, though they thought I'd leave to make a home with someone, and someone I couldn't marry, so I thought that was wonderful of them. I'd dearly love to see them again, but Heath is in the opposite direction to the farm."

"You left them, Joanna, the farm you loved. You must have felt pulled here."

"I did."

Emmey didn't feel any longing to be here, but why would she? She was already here, with everyone she loved, and doing everything she loved. When she thought of leaving . . . that was when she felt she belonged here. That was when she wanted to weep. That was when she wondered how she'd live outside the Order, how she'd ever be able to make sense of her life again. She wanted to slap herself. It seemed so obvious now. "What keeps you here?"

Maddy's brow furrowed. "That's a strange question. Are you asking me because I'm malflowed?"

"No. But some novices leave. They must have felt called in the beginning. So I'm wondering if other sisters would leave, if they could. Do they cling to their vows when they need to?"

"I can only answer for myself. It's not my vows. I'd be miserable if that's all that kept me here."

"Lillian."

"She's not keeping me here, either. I learned that when I was away. I'm here because I want to be here, because this is where I belong. My family is here. There's a reason we call each other sister."

"Lillian didn't feel called, though."

Maddy smiled ruefully. "There was a time when Lillian not feeling called irritated me, but I don't feel that way anymore. I'll tell you something I wouldn't say to Lillian." She wagged a finger at Emmey. "And don't you say anything, either."

Emmey pressed her lips together and patted her mouth.

"I've come to believe that every woman in the Salbine Order has been called, whether she realizes it or not. Perhaps Lillian and Sophia are sisters because Sophia's call to service meant they'd both enter the Order, even though Lillian didn't feel called. Salbine's call to Lillian took the form of Lillian's desire to remain with Sophia."

"She might not have been able to distinguish one from the other," Emmey said excitedly. "Her longing to be with Sophia with her longing to be here. They would have felt like the same thing."

"I'm only speculating."

Still.

"Every sister was drawn here for a reason, and all had at least two years to decide whether they wanted to stay. There's no doubt in my mind that those who did belong here."

"Including you?"

Maddy hesitated a beat. "Including me."

Emmey wanted to hug her. She wanted to take that smidgen of hesitation away. She wanted to read every single word sisters had written about Salbine's Covenant to see if any of them had argued convincingly that "blessings of her anointed" meant the gifts of the elements, but she doubted she'd find anything. How could anyone know for sure? She'd look, though, and would love to counter any such arguments.

I'll look. To do so, she'd have to be here, at the monastery. Where she belonged. *You're a sister in all but name. Will confirm what already is.* Would she fold her robes at the end of her bed, or eventually replace them with proper Salbine ones? She wanted to tell Maddy so badly, to kneel before her and take her hand and say, "I'm marked, and I'm called to be here. I'm falling into that indifferent but loving embrace." But she wanted to think about it a bit more, to be sure. She'd assumed the thought of leaving made her want to cry and throw up and rage at everyone and everything around her because she'd miss her family—her smaller family within the larger one, but she belonged to that larger family too.

The chapel, stained glass, hard benches, study rooms, library, prayers, Lina's sculpture, Lillian's laboratory, herbs, communal meals with the sisters she loved, bobbing, the whisper of her quill on parchment and the caress of words recorded through the centuries by the hands of those who'd fallen, fallen into that loving and indifferent embrace that Emmey now wanted to run toward. How could she not have seen?

Using her foot, she nudged the travel bag away from her. "I'm not packing anything else."

"You need more than one dress."

"I do, but I'm not packing anything else today."

"I know it's hard," Maddy said softly. "But you have to face it."

"I am facing it." Emmey felt more at peace than she had in ages. "But not right now. Let's go outside and stroll around the gardens together. We haven't done anything like that lately. It's all been doom and gloom and we spend all our time thinking about when we'll be apart, when we should be together right now." She grabbed Maddy's hand. "So, come on. Come outside."

"It looks like I have no choice." Maddy didn't sound stern, and her mouth turned up at the corners, and Emmey wanted to tell her what she'd come to realize, but not until she'd slept on it, just in case. Once she said it out loud, there would be no going back. She had to be sure.

~

AVERILL PAUSED OUTSIDE THE library to collect herself, something she couldn't remember ever having to do. Then she strode inside, hoping she appeared as if she didn't have a care in the world.

Sister Clara lifted her head as Mistress Averill passed her podium. The sister's face lit up, but she didn't leap off her stool and bob. It would be impractical for scribes to have to set down their quills and curtsey every time a mistress or the abbess came into the library. "Are you feeling better, Mistress?"

"I am, thank you," Averill said, wondering if Mistress Olivia could hear them. She continued to her cubbyhole, took a deep breath, and stepped inside. Mistress Olivia was hunched over her podium, her quill scratching along parchment. "Good afternoon," Averill said stiffly.

"Good afternoon," the mistress said. Her head didn't come up.

"I—"

Mistress Olivia lifted her free hand, a gesture every scribe understood. *Wait until I reach the end of the word or line.* Averill wanted to wring her hands. Perhaps the mistress would make her stand here until she'd reached the end of the parchment. But then Mistress Olivia set down her quill and wiped the ink from her fingers.

"May I speak with you?" Averill quickly said. "We can take a stroll in one of the gardens."

Mistress Olivia slid off her stool and met Averill's eyes. Her eyes were unreadable, but Averill wilted at the sight of her downturned mouth and tight face. She'd already chided herself umpteen times for her behaviour last night, but once more wouldn't hurt. If only she hadn't panicked. If only she hadn't spoken without thinking first. If only fear hadn't translated into rudeness. Oh, how she hated feeling discombobulated in one of her favourite places, but it was her own fault.

"Lead the way," Mistress Olivia said.

Relieved, Averill walked as casually as she could from the library, trusting Mistress Olivia to follow her. Outside, they walked side by side. Averill could sense the tension and wanted to shove her hands into her robe's pockets, but she'd come prepared, just in case. Several handkerchiefs were stuffed in her right pocket, and another two were in her left, for good measure. She still hadn't decided what to tell the mistress about the reason she'd behaved so badly, or more accurately, how much to tell her. And she'd admitted to herself that should the mistress make it clear that their nascent friendship was over, she'd find an empty study room and have a little cry.

They reached the southern gardens. Averill surveyed the area and strode to an empty bench under a tree some distance off the path. She sat down, hoping the mistress would do the same and not tower over her. The bench creaked when Mistress Olivia sat next to her, albeit leaving quite the gap between them.

"I'm sorry," they both said at the same time. If the air wasn't so fraught, Averill would have laughed.

Mistress Olivia gazed out at the garden. "I wasn't trying to take advantage of you. I was . . . well, I thought you regarded me better than that. I would never take advantage of anyone's distress."

"No, no, it's not your place to apologize. It's mine. I behaved badly for reasons that had nothing to do with you. You were only being kind, and I felt so comfortable with you, and I . . . " She couldn't bring herself to tell her, to pour it all out and relive it. "It frightened me. I haven't felt the way I do with you for a long time." Averill swallowed. "I said some terrible things, all of which are untrue. I'll miss you very much when you leave."

The mistress didn't look at her, but her shoulders relaxed. "To be honest, I'd hoped we'd spend some time alone, just the two of us. I'd be lying if I said something more than friendship between us hadn't crossed my mind, despite me leaving. There are always letters. We both enjoy writing."

"Indeed, we do," Averill said, sadness welling within her.

"But I never would have abused your vulnerability. When I took your hand, I was offering you support. I wasn't expecting anything more."

"I know. I am sorry."

"I'm not here for much longer. Can we try again?"

Averill wanted to, with a ferocity that surprised her. But to what end? Even if the mistress wasn't leaving, Averill wasn't sure she'd be capable of letting herself enjoy any affection Mistress Olivia might express. "I don't know."

Mistress Olivia twisted toward her. "Can you tell me why? You've said you feel comfortable with me, and if I've interpreted your words correctly, that you can envision more than friendship between us. I'm usually not this forward, but I don't want us to squander what could be. I suppose it's because we have so little time to figure it out."

Averill pulled a handkerchief from her pocket. She'd have to tell her. She wanted to tell her. For now, the handkerchief was out so she could hold on to it.

"Did someone hurt you and you can't trust anyone now?"

"I wish it were that, I truly do." Averill held the handkerchief by its ends and stretched the cloth until it was taut. "This is very difficult for me." She stopped, so she could moisten her suddenly dry throat. "I had a consort. Elena. She went to Salbine about ten years ago."

"I'm sorry," Mistress Olivia murmured.

Now for the difficult part. "We were well matched and quite content. She was only fifty-one when she left us. We . . ." She cleared her throat. "We had supper in our chambers that night. We didn't do that very often, and we especially didn't skip evening prayers, but we were celebrating twenty years together, so we allowed ourselves the indulgence. It felt a bit conspiratorial, even though what we were doing was completely innocent." The tears she'd expected welled in her eyes, and her constricting throat was beginning to strangle her words, making her hoarse. "We reminisced about the last twenty years, talked about the next twenty, and drank cider. We were quite tipsy by the time we went to bed. We didn't go to sleep right away." She hoped that was enough for Mistress Olivia to understand that they'd lain together.

Averill wiped her eyes, a futile gesture, as more tears would come. "We fell asleep warm and happy and optimistic and looking forward to many more years together. When I woke up the next morning . . ." The inevitable tidal wave washed over her as the memory rushed back. She held her handkerchief against her mouth to stop herself from wailing, but that allowed her tears to roll freely down her cheeks.

Mistress Olivia slid closer to her. When she lightly placed her hand on Averill's arm, Averill didn't shake it off, but the tears came faster. She pulled another handkerchief from her pocket. "The sun was out that morning," she managed to say. "I remember rolling over and saying something to Elena, and when she didn't reply, I thought she was still asleep. So I threw my arm over her . . ." She couldn't finish. The horror of it was as real now as it had been that morning. It crushed her heart, curdled her stomach, made her want to cry out at the unfairness of it. But all she could do was weep.

She didn't protest when she felt Mistress Olivia's arms around her shoulders, and she was exceedingly grateful when the mistress said the words she couldn't say. "You discovered she'd gone to Salbine," she said quietly.

Averill nodded. When she'd wrapped her arm around Elena and pressed into her bare back, she'd wondered why Elena felt so cold, especially since the blanket was drawn up to her shoulders. She wasn't sure what had made her realize that Elena was gone. Her memory was patchy after that. Yanking open the door. Screaming, irrationally, for help. A blanket around her shoulders and sisters gathered around her. The certainty that she'd never know joy again, and the days and nights spent going over every second of their last evening together, searching for signs that it would be Elena's last night in this realm. Hanging over it all, the guilt that she'd never completely shaken. "I like to think she fell asleep as happy as I was and feeling loved. It doesn't help, but I like to think it."

Mistress Olivia's arm tightened. "Anything I say will sound trite, so I'm not going to say anything."

Her words saddened Averill, because she appreciated them so much. She dropped wet handkerchiefs one and two onto her lap and pulled out handkerchief number three. "We don't know what happened. We could only speculate. Her heart or a brain seizure, perhaps. I like to think it was peaceful." After all, she hadn't woken up. She'd lain next to her, for who knew how long, oblivious. Had Elena cried out? Had she realized in her last seconds? Had she lain there unable to move until her lights had dimmed? Questions that had taunted Averill late into every night for the longest time. If not for her sisters and her vows to Salbine, she would have drunk herself silly to still the accusing questions and the frustration of never knowing the answers. But her sisters hadn't allowed her to take a single step down that path. They hadn't forbidden her to touch cider and ale, or from doing anything else destructive in an effort to numb her pain. They'd simply loved her.

At some point that morning, Averill had gone back into her chambers to see Elena. Her dear, beloved consort had appeared as if she were sleeping, her eyes closed, her hands tucked under her chin. For a second, Averill had expected Elena to open her eyes and murmur, "Good morning, Av," as she had every morning since the first night they'd shared a bed. But it wasn't to be. Averill had stroked her hair, and kissed her one last time, and told her she loved her, and prayed for her, and wondered how she'd ever be able to smile or laugh or read or scribe or appreciate the warmth of the sun on her face or the splatter of raindrops on her head and cheeks as she hurried from one tower to another. Time didn't heal all wounds, but it did lessen the pain.

"Life does go on," she said, not wanting Mistress Olivia to think she sat in her chambers a weepy mess when she wasn't in the library. And it was time she explained how this related to her awful behaviour toward the mistress. "Elena would want life to go on for me. She did love me and wouldn't have wanted to see me give up on life and love. I would have wanted the same for her, if the shoe had been on the other foot. She'd be calling me an arse for the way I behaved to you and telling me to enjoy your company while you're here." A fresh set of tears threatened.

"What's holding you back?" Mistress Olivia asked.

"This will sound silly, but I can't think of being with anyone without imagining them dead in my bed. I can't see how I'll ever manage it. I'll be a nervous wreck. Not that I assumed for a second we'd end up in anyone's bed," she quickly added. "Just a flirtatious chat can make my mind jump right to the end, and brings everything back for me, and frightens me." Not caring how shrivelled and red her eyes must look, she turned to Mistress Olivia. "I reacted so badly when you were comforting me because I could see us together, and then it all came back, and I ruined it all."

"You didn't ruin it. I'll admit you upset me, but I knew there must be something behind it. Your manner changed so abruptly. This will sound arrogant, but I didn't believe you when you said you'd be glad when we were all gone."

"I didn't mean it. Well, I won't mind when Sister Cecily and Sister Felicia are gone. The sight of them makes me angry." And she didn't want to think about them right now. "I *would* like to see you again. I just don't know how to do it . . . get close to anyone in that way."

"Slowly, which doesn't help us very much, does it? Still, I enjoy your company, and I'd like to spend time with you while I can. Perhaps we can do it with no expectations. I'm not saying I won't want to take your hand or comfort you again, but since I won't be here much longer . . . "

Not long enough for Averill to overcome her fear, or to push through it. She understood that. But now her letters to the mistress would be of a more personal nature rather than from one scribe to another, and perhaps sometime in the future, they'd find themselves at the same monastery again for a time. "I'll do my best not to behave like I did last night."

"No. I mean, I don't want you to shout at me like you did, but if you feel frightened, tell me. I don't want you keeping it in."

Oh, how Averill would love to close her eyes and lean into her and not jump to that horrible place, the morning that was seared into her memory. She told herself she wasn't honouring Elena by remembering her so. She did think of the wonderful times too. She'd been able to do so, eventually. But she couldn't escape that terrible morning, or the guilt that asked her how she could have slept soundly as her beloved consort left this realm.

Mistress Olivia squeezed Averill's shoulders. "This might sound terribly insensitive, but you survived. You came through to the other side, not the same as you were before it happened, but you do have hope. You still love your books and your scribing. What happened was horrible beyond imagining, but it didn't rob you of your heart, your soul. You're stronger for it, though I'm sure you wish Elena was still with you."

"I've said the same things to myself many times." She wished she could say it helped, but it didn't. But again, she appreciated the mistress's words. Hedgerow was fortunate to have her. Averill would miss her immensely and hoped the mistress enjoyed reading and scribing letters as much as she did books. "Now that I've explained my boorish behaviour, is it all right if we talk about something else?"

"Of course."

"Would you like to meet in the library after evening prayers tomorrow night?" Averill couldn't face it tonight, despite feeling as if one weight was off her shoulders, at least. "I have some books I'd like to show you."

"I'd be delighted. Speaking of books, you left the one with information about foretellers in my chambers. I'll bring it to the library with me tomorrow."

"Thank you."

"How are you feeling about Emmey? We didn't finish our conversation."

"To be honest, I haven't thought about her situation since last night. I've been too preoccupied with how I behaved toward you."

"We've cleared the air about that now," Olivia said briskly. "I was thinking that we should continue searching for more information about foretellers."

A lump formed in Averill's throat. "You'd want to do that?"

"I believe in being armed with knowledge. Did you pull all the tomes and scrolls you could think of?"

"Everything in the catalogue, though I haven't had time to skim them all."

"I'll help you skim, if you'll let me."

"I'd like that." Averill blew her nose. "We should go back before they all start looking for us." She collected her handkerchiefs and stuffed them into her pocket. When Mistress Olivia lifted her arm from her shoulders, Averill missed the warmth—her warmth.

The mistress stood and smoothed her robe. "Don't be offended, but you might want to go to your chambers and wash your face before you go to the library, or people will gossip."

"I'm not offended. I appreciate you telling me." She rose, then groaned. "You'll have to go back to your chambers as well," she said, wincing at the dampness on Mistress Olivia's left shoulder that was too obvious for anyone to miss. It would eventually dry, but not in time.

"We can stroll to the Mistresses Tower together, then."

As they walked, Averill felt both comfortable and embarrassed. Comfortable because she trusted the mistress and felt close to her, and embarrassed because of that emotional intimacy. She'd bared her soul, told the mistress about the worst time in her life, wept on her shoulder. "You're very kind, Mistress," she murmured.

"Can we dispense with the mistress when we're alone? I think we're at that point."

Averill managed a smile. "I think we are too." Somehow, the sun broke through. But as usual, the cursed memory quickly chased it away, the memory of her warm arm encircling a cold, stiff body, her realization that the intelligent and laughing bright brown eyes that had met hers only hours earlier were now dull and lifeless and would never laugh again.

21

MADDY PLUNKED HER PORRIDGE on the table and sat down in her habitual spot between Emmey and Rose. She poured herself some milk and ate her porridge, waiting for a lull in the conversation. "I'm bringing Sister Lorelle down for breakfast tomorrow," she said when the usual topics of conversation at breakfast—the weather, plans for the day, and any interesting gossip—had exhausted themselves. "She's very fragile at the moment, so do be gentle."

Everyone gazed at Gwendolyn. "Why are you all looking at me?" she snapped, provoking much eye rolling. "I think it's good that she's coming down tomorrow. I was beginning to think she'd spend all her days locked in her chamber, never to be seen again. How long has it been?"

"She broke her consort bond," Rose said. "I can understand why she hasn't wanted to face anyone."

"I heard she's staying here, that she's not going back to Hedgerow."

Now everyone looked to Maddy, but not because they knew of Lillian's relationship to Sophia. Well, Rose and Nora knew, but nobody else. They were staring at her because she'd said she was bringing Sister Lorelle. "She is. She doesn't want to have to see Sister Felicia and Sister Cecily every day."

"I can't say I blame her," Nora said.

"You must worry about your consort sometimes," Gwendolyn said.

It took Maddy a moment to realize Gwendolyn was talking to her. "Why?" she asked, curiosity getting the better of her.

"You don't go to prayers together, except for in the evening, but you don't have to speak to each other, do you? You don't eat breakfast together. She shuts herself away in the catacombs. It must be awful, having a consort who doesn't want to be with you. Or is it that you don't want to be with her?"

Maddy tuned her out. She was used to Gwendolyn's abrasive form of teasing; it rolled right off her back. And she certainly wasn't going to explain how she and Lillian spent plenty of time together every evening, and how their daytime schedules suited them just fine, with their divergent interests. Emmey usually had the good sense to ignore Gwendolyn too, but not this morning.

"I don't see you with anyone," Emmey said.

"I've yet to meet someone who can hold my attention for more than five minutes."

Voices erupted around Gwendolyn. "Oh, Salbine preserve us."

"It's more like you don't hold anyone's attention for more than five minutes."

"Nobody can get past your big head."

Maddy chuckled but didn't contribute. Also used to everyone ribbing her, Gwendolyn didn't react, and she was in fine form this morning. Her porridge remained untouched, the wooden spoon still sitting next to her bowl. "You will be kind to Sister Lorelle, won't you?" Maddy said to her.

"Don't worry, I will. It's no fun teasing someone who's already upset."

"Do you think she'll eat with us all the time?" Grace asked.

Maddy swallowed a mouthful of porridge. "She needs our support. I don't know her well, but she's been polite every time I've spoken to her."

"Let's hope she's not boring," Gwendolyn grumbled, finally picking up her spoon.

Emmey's bowl was empty. "I'll see you at prayers," she said, then she left before Maddy had a chance to respond. Emmey's mood had changed recently, in a way Maddy didn't understand. She seemed, not happy, but not down, either. With only a few days left until her departure, perhaps she'd accepted it. Maddy hated to admit it, but she was disappointed, and surprised, that Emmey was already putting her time here behind her. Maddy was going through the motions. Three days. Three days and the place next to her on the bench would be empty.

~

HER ANTICIPATION BUILDING, AVERILL ushered Olivia into her cubbyhole. They hadn't sat together at evening prayers, but they'd met outside the chapel and walked in companionable silence to the library. Averill felt refreshed today. She'd barely slept the night she'd shouted at Olivia. After clearing the air yesterday afternoon, she'd managed a good night's sleep and had spent a delightful day scribing next to Olivia, stealing the occasional look at her, and finding herself smiling every time the mistress—Olivia—smiled in return. Smitten had crossed her mind, and smitten she was. If only they had more time.

She lit a torch the conventional way and handed it to Olivia, then pulled her desk key from her pocket and unlocked one of the drawers. The burning torch illuminated the drawer's contents when Olivia leaned over to see what Averill was doing.

"I'm looking for a key." Averill moved a stack of parchment aside and fished underneath the few stray pieces left behind. "Ah, there we are." She pulled out the key and held it up.

"A key under lock and key. I'm intrigued." Olivia bounced on her heels. "Where are we going?"

"To the fifth floor, I'm afraid."

"It's only three flights."

"True." Eager to show Olivia the treasures few ever saw, Averill bustled from her cubbyhole. "It's where we keep the books we've decided aren't for sisters to read," she explained as they climbed the wide staircase to the fifth floor. "I'm sure your library has a locked room or two."

"I wouldn't know if it did. Mistress Margery might."

"No rumours flying around about forbidden books?"

"Not in my hearing."

Come to think of it, there weren't any at Merrin, either, but why would there be? Averill had inherited the key from the last head scribe, who always doubled as the head librarian. "Only the abbess knows about it, in case you leave this realm before you retire your post," Mistress Winnifred had whispered. Sadly, the mistress had gone to Salbine a mere two years later.

"Ah, here we are." Averill stopped outside a wooden door, inserted the iron key into the lock, and turned it with a *click*. She pushed the door open. The square chamber wasn't very large and contained only two shelves. Olivia followed her inside and stood a safe distance away from the tomes, not wanting to set them on fire.

Averill jutted her chin toward the empty sconce on the wall. "You can put that in there."

"Should we shut the door?" Olivia asked, sliding the torch into the sconce.

"I never do, not that I come in here very often. I've come here twice, once out of curiosity after I received the key, and once due to an inquiry from Redworth." She surveyed the shelves and slid out a book. "One of the original copies of The Salbine Doctrine, thought to have been scribed by one of Lina's followers."

Olivia's eyes glowed. She carefully accepted the book from Averill. "I'm afraid to open it." But she went ahead and did so anyway. The ink on the parchment was faded but still legible. "It's quite something, isn't it, to think my hands are holding the same book held by a sister who actually sat in Lina's presence."

Averill grinned at the awe in Olivia's voice. "Perhaps Lina herself held it."

Olivia swallowed and gently ran her hand along the tattered cover.

"We have numerous copies of it, of course, but I've never compared them against this one. I should." She accepted the book from

Olivia and carefully placed it back in its place. "This shelf contains rare and sacred books. This one," her eyes moved to the lower shelf, "contains the forbidden books I mentioned earlier."

"Such as?"

Averill tapped her chin as she surveyed the books on the lower shelf, then she pulled one out. "I think you'll understand why this one is in here."

Olivia took it from her and opened to the first page, then flipped to the next. "Dear me." She frowned. "You'd have to be missing a few joints to twist yourself into this position, wouldn't you?"

Averill moved to her side and examined the sketch of two women in what could only be described as an anatomically impossible sexual position. "I certainly couldn't twist my body that way now."

"You mean you could do it when you were younger?"

Her face flushed. "No, I was just . . . " Averill trailed off when Olivia snickered. She was being teased. "Emmey asked me for books about men and women lying together. I added one for girls marked by Salbine because I'm fairly certain she is."

"I hope you didn't give her this one. The poor thing would pull something trying to figure out if this is possible." Olivia turned the page. "And this. That looks painful, actually. Who drew these?" She went back to the first page in the tome.

"I didn't give her this one. This is the only copy here, perhaps the only copy in existence."

"No wonder it's in here. In addition to being what can only be described as someone's sexual fantasies, anyone who tried to follow it likely injured themselves," Olivia said, making Averill laugh.

After they'd tittered over a few of the other sketches, Averill returned the book to the shelf. "Now this one." She pulled out a slim volume. "This one you might have heard of. It's a treatise by Sister Richolda."

Olivia gasped. "You don't mean . . . "

Averill nodded.

"The one that makes the argument," Olivia lowered her voice, "that Salbine is insane."

"The very one."

Olivia's mouth formed an 'o'. She reached for the book. At the same time her fingers touched it, the burning torch suddenly hissed and brightened.

Averill and Olivia jumped. They stared at each other.

"You don't think . . . " Olivia murmured.

Averill swallowed. "I'm sure it was just a breeze."

Olivia waved the book away as if it were a poisonous snake. "Put it back."

Her heart pounding, Averill shoved the book back onto the shelf. She hurried after Olivia, who'd already pulled the torch from the sconce and was halfway out the chamber. "Hold it steady," Averill hissed as she fumbled to lock the door.

They hurried away, almost tripping over their robes as they raced down the stairs and back to Averill's cubbyhole, their footsteps echoing loudly in Averill's ears. "It feels like the key is burning a hole in my pocket," she wailed. She rushed to her desk, threw the key into the drawer, and quickly locked it away.

They didn't speak until they'd left the library and had almost reached the Mistresses Tower. "I still have the torch," Olivia said, making them both burst into relieved laughter.

"I feel so foolish," Averill said. "Of course it was just a breeze. The torch isn't burning with elemental fire."

"Even if it was, how silly of us to scurry away like frightened children." Olivia doused the torch in a bucket of water sitting outside the entrance to the Mistresses Tower for that very purpose.

"As far as I know, Sister Richolda lived into her nineties," Averill said. "If her treatise had angered Salbine, surely she would have left this realm at an earlier age."

Olivia nodded her thanks as she passed through the door Averill held open for her. "And the treatise wouldn't have survived. Have you read it?"

"No, I haven't. I'm not sure I want to."

"It likely doesn't say anything we haven't all thought ourselves at times. Who hasn't questioned our goddess's wisdom?"

"That's true." Averill's mind immediately went to Elena, and Emmey as well. If Emmey's fate was to be that of the other foretellers who'd had the mirror dream, Averill wouldn't understand Salbine at all.

"Here we are," Olivia said, confusing Averill for a second. Lost in her thoughts, she'd absently followed Olivia and now stood outside her chambers.

"Do you want to come in and have a cider with me?" Olivia lightly touched Averill's arm. "Just a cider, nothing more. I understand you need time."

Time they didn't have, much to Averill's regret, but she had to be ready. If she pushed herself, it would result in disaster and spoil what had been an enjoyable evening so far. "I'd like a cider."

Pleasure lit up Olivia's face, much to Averill's delight. She followed her inside, then bumped into her when Olivia abruptly stopped and turned around. Averill couldn't stop herself from reaching for Olivia's face and running her fingers along the marks on her cheeks.

"Pox," Olivia said. "I'm fortunate I survived, though it left its mark." She gave Averill a wry smile. "Don't say it adds character. I've heard that line one time too many."

"I was going to say that you're quite lovely in my eyes, and I'm enjoying myself tonight. I wish you weren't leaving. A selfish thing for me to say, considering the circumstances, but I wish you weren't."

Olivia caressed Averill's cheek. "Do you think you can manage a kiss?"

Averill tentatively touched her lips to Olivia's, then applied more pressure and lost herself . . . until Elena's face flashed into her mind, Elena with her stiff hands tucked under her lifeless chin.

Wanting to cry out in frustration, she pulled back and anxiously searched Olivia's eyes. "I'm sorry. It's not that I don't want to."

Olivia squeezed Averill's hand. "One day you'll kiss without thinking about her," she said softly, without a hint of resentment or impatience.

"I hope so." Averill felt guilty, even though she truly believed with all her heart that Elena would want her to live. Not forget. But to live!

Olivia squeezed Averill's hand again and let it go. "Shall we have that cider?"

"Yes," Averill emphatically said. She wanted nothing more, except to have more time with Olivia.

～

THE NEXT DAY, EMMEY bounded into her chambers and plunked into a chair in front of the cold hearth. Maddy and Lillian didn't know it yet, but they were about to get a wonderful surprise—well, she hoped they'd think it wonderful. She'd been bursting to tell them yesterday but had decided to wait until today, when they were down at the river enjoying the picnic lunch Maddy had suggested. "Our last chance to lunch down at the river together," she'd said, her voice quavering. Emmey would begin by telling them she was marked by Salbine, and after they'd calmed down about that first bit of news, she'd make them even happier by telling them she wanted to take the robe.

Speaking of robes, she'd dirtied hers while planting seeds in her garden, and there was soil underneath her fingernails too. Knowing she'd be chilly after she'd washed her hands and changed, she lit the fire. A few minutes later, with clean hands and wearing a fresh robe, she plunked into the chair again and waited for Maddy and Lillian to arrive. Maddy should be finished with the petitions soon, and Lillian would come when her stomach grumbled or the chapel bells struck noon, though she couldn't hear them in the catacombs. Despite that, Lillian had an uncanny knack for knowing the time. She must have a timepiece hidden somewhere in the laboratory, though she denied it every time Emmey asked her.

Emmey had woken early this morning, and now the warmth from the fire was making her sleepy. She yawned into her hand and stared into the flames, struggling to keep her eyes open.

～

MADDY'S FEET FELT LIKE they weighed a ton as she climbed the stairs to the second floor and strode along the hall to her chambers. She was looking forward to the picnic lunch with Lillian and Emmey. But it would be the last time they'd stroll to the river together and bask in the sun, telling stories, laughing, and dozing. She felt numb and suspected she'd feel that way until Emmey walked through the gates. For once, she didn't try to push through the defences rising to protect her. She didn't want to waste her remaining time with Emmey crying. There would be plenty of time for that later.

Wondering whether Emmey was inside, Maddy opened the door to their chambers. Emmey was in front of the fire, sitting twisted away from Maddy. "Are you ready for our lunch, then?" she said with as much cheerfulness as she could muster.

Emmey didn't reply. She must have dozed off. Maddy rounded the chairs and stood in front of her. "Come on, sleepyhead. Time to wake up." She frowned. "Emmey?" Maddy's hand trembled. She shook Emmey's shoulder. "Emmey. Emmey!"

She shook Emmey harder. "Emmey! Wake up. Wake up!" Her heart in her mouth, she pressed her hand against Emmey's chest and sagged with relief when she felt her beating heart. But . . .

Maddy raced from her chambers, rounded the corner in the hall and waved her arms at Barnabus, who was striding toward her from Sophia's study. "There's something wrong with Emmey!" she cried. "I can't wake her up. Tell the abbess to come. Please!"

She whirled and ran back to her chambers, hoping with every fibre of her being that she'd find Emmey awake, wondering what all the fuss was about. Maddy would feel silly and ruffle her hair and then hug her tighter than she ever had before. But when she reached her, Emmey hadn't moved. Her eyes were still closed, her body slightly twisted to her left.

Tears in her eyes, Maddy crouched and took Emmey's hand. "I'm here," she said. "Please, oh Salbine, please, open Emmey's eyes."

The clink of armour announced Barnabus's arrival. Sophia put her hand on Maddy's shoulder and examined Emmey.

"She won't wake up," Maddy said flatly. "I don't know what's wrong with her."

"Barnabus, fetch Mistress Lillian, please." Sophia's voice was hushed.

Barnabus's boots rang on the stone floor as he hurried away.

Sophia kneeled next to Maddy. "Did you find her like this?"

"Yes," she managed to say. Now that Sophia was here, she couldn't hold it in any longer. She lowered her head and brought Emmey's hand to her cheek. "Please, not Emmey. Please, Salbine, no. Not Emmey." Her tears watered Emmey's fingers.

"She's been having dreams," Sophia said.

"She always wakes up." Though last time Emmey had cried out, it had taken longer for her to open her eyes, caught in the grip of her nightmare. Was that what was happening now? Was she dreaming a dream so powerful that she was trapped inside it? Maddy studied Emmey's face. She appeared peaceful, but why wouldn't she wake up? What was she seeing? Was she dreaming, or . . . dying? Maddy tightened her grip on Emmey's hand. *Please, Salbine. Please don't take her from me. Please.*

22

EMMEY WOKE UP AND waited for her eyes to adjust to the gloom. Her bed felt awfully hard. Then her fingers touched stone, and she bolted upright. No, it couldn't be. She was in her cell, in Dunmurk Prison, except it didn't stink, and nobody was moaning, and a quick look around told her Maddy wasn't here.

Footsteps approached, then a door creaked open. Emmey scrambled to her feet. A man strode in. She peered at him. The governor? But he was older. His temples were gray, his once youthful face sagged, and his wife obviously fed him well.

He met her eyes. "Are you finished, Sister? Sister Maddy is waiting for you."

Sister? Emmey looked down at herself, at the Salbine robe that flowed to the stone floor. But her hands weren't marked. A novice, then.

"I'll take you back to the office."

Hoping she *would* find Maddy there, she followed him, her mind racing. This had to be a dream, but if it was, it was the most realistic dream she'd ever had. But what else could it be? The last thing she remembered was sitting in front of the fire. She must have fallen asleep. So, a dream, but this one was new.

The governor led her along a dank passageway and through a wide doorway. The guards swung a thick iron door shut behind them. The next doorway led to a cramped office. Maddy sat on a chair in front of a desk, drinking tea. She smiled at Emmey, but something wasn't right. Her hands. Two of them. She was holding the cup to her lips with her right hand and the saucer on her lap with her left. Definitely a dream, then. Hands didn't grow back.

"I thought it was much smaller than I remembered it. What did you think?" Maddy asked brightly.

"Uh, yes, I suppose. What are we doing here?"

"We're on our way to Heath."

"You mean, I'm going with you."

Maddy laughed. "Of course you're going with me. If you don't go with me, how will I know what to do?"

"What do you mean?"

"Fire!" someone yelled.

Suddenly Emmey was in the passageway again, but this time smoke billowed up it, making her cough. Her eyes stung.

"Hold my hand and don't let go," Maddy said. "No matter what happens, do not let go of my hand."

Oh, no. Not here. Maddy grabbed Emmey's hand and pulled her down the passageway. A bell clanged somewhere far away. Shadows loomed up ahead, then two men materialized, blocking their way. One held a flaming piece of wood and swung it at Emmey.

"No, Maddy, don't!" Emmey shouted, then her mouth opened in horror when Maddy grabbed the flaming end of the wood and held on to it. But her hand didn't burn.

Maddy turned to Emmey, a ghoulish smile on her face. "See? It doesn't hurt." Then her arm burst into flame, and her chest, and her other arm, and—

Emmey averted her eyes and tried to pull her hand from Maddy's, but Maddy's grip was strong.

"It doesn't hurt," Maddy said calmly. "It really doesn't hurt. See?"

Pain ripped up Emmey's arm. She screamed and tried to yank her hand away, but Maddy wouldn't let go.

"What's wrong with you?" Maddy shouted. "It doesn't hurt."

Burning flesh—her burning flesh—made Emmey gag. She sank to her knees, tried to pat out the flames with her free hand, but the fire consumed her, its roar drowning out her agonized screams. Her lips burned, her nose, her eyes. She descended into darkness.

~

AVERILL LIFTED HER HEAD when Sophia strode into her cubbyhole, then set down her quill when she saw how bewildered Sophia appeared. It took a lot to faze her. "What's wrong?" She slid off her stool, not wanting to converse over her shoulder. Olivia did the same.

Sophia glanced at Olivia. "It's Emmey. There's something wrong with her. She won't wake up."

Dread almost drove Averill to her knees. She wanted to look at Olivia, but they were standing next to each other. Turning to her would be too obvious.

"Can you think of anything that might help? Anything you've read?"

"Would you mind giving the abbess and me a moment?" Averill said to Olivia.

"Of course." Olivia gave Averill's hand a quick squeeze and shut the door behind her.

"I do have a book." Averill went to her desk and picked up the book Olivia had returned to her. "You know Emmey's been having dreams, dreams she says feel different from normal dreams, for lack of a better way to express it."

"Yes."

"She asked me to do some research, because some of her dreams have come true."

Sophia stared at her. "Are you sure?"

"She dreamed about Malcolm being run over before he almost was. She dreamed about a fire at the market. Not all the details are correct, but close enough. So she asked me to investigate, and I did, and I found this." She opened the book to where she'd placed the bookmark and handed it to Sophia.

She waited while Sophia read the text about foretellers, mirror dreams . . . and how those who've had the mirror dream soon fall asleep for the last time.

"She had the mirror dream a couple of weeks ago," Averill said quietly. "Mistress Olivia and I searched the library for tomes that would contradict or shed light on what you've read, but we couldn't find anything."

Sophia set the book down and placed both her palms on the desk for support, her back to Averill. "Why didn't you tell me?"

Averill winced at the sorrow in Sophia's voice. "I struggled with whether I should."

"I sat in your chambers not long ago, and you didn't tell me."

"I know. Let me tell you my reasoning. I thought telling you would steal away any pleasure you'd have in Emmey's company until . . . until this happened. I thought it would be better for you to enjoy being with her, because there's nothing you can do, nothing any of us can do."

"We can pray."

"And we will. Fervently. But you haven't had it hanging over your heads."

"You've had it hanging over yours."

"Yes."

Sophia slowly turned to face Averill. Her eyes were moist. Averill was torn between abandoning all protocol and hugging her, and remaining a respectful distance away. That horrible morning came back to her, how her sisters had rallied around her, made sure she was warm, fed, supported. She went to Sophia and embraced her. "I did what I thought was best," she murmured. "Have a good cry. It's only me and you here."

Sophia laid her head on Averill's shoulder, clung to her, and wept. "She's only fourteen," she sobbed. "Why would Salbine take her? Why?"

Averill wished she knew the answer. "I remember what Mistress Bella said, may Salbine bless her in Her realm. It was during one of the first novice classes I took. One of the other novices said she was going to pray to Salbine that her pimples go away, and Mistress Bella laughed and laughed and said if you want a goddess who cares about you, who coddles you and cares about your concerns, you should walk out the gates right now, because Salbine isn't for you.

She has no time for petty concerns, and mark my words, all your concerns, your very lives, are petty to Her. We lost half the novices that year." She patted Sophia's back. "I like to think it's not true, but I've yet to see any evidence to the contrary."

"But you stayed."

"You know as well as I do that we're blessed here, that we have more and learn more than just about anyone else. And I do so relish feeling the raw power of the elements flowing through me."

Sophia stepped back and accepted the handkerchief Averill offered her. "I believe Salbine does care," she said, wiping her eyes. "I don't believe we're wasting our time in the chapel."

Averill had given great thought to that after Elena died. "I've wondered if what's important to us isn't important to Her, if She has her own priorities that we'll never understand. But I can't deny that She takes notice of us. She marks us. She bestows the gifts. We go to Her realm along with others who love Her, but She draws us closer to Her. Perhaps being in Her presence is a reward beyond imagining. Perhaps that's why She wouldn't think it cruel to take a fourteen-year-old away from our realm and into Hers."

"Emmey hasn't left us yet. I'll admit that after reading that text, I'm not terribly hopeful, but I do believe in prayer."

"Will you tell the others about foretellers and the fate of those who have the mirror dream?"

Sophia shook her head. "I don't want to take away their hope. I want their prayers to be optimistic, heartfelt. Not angry, like mine will be." She met Averill's eyes. "I understand why you didn't tell me. Don't tell anyone else."

"I won't, and I'm sure Mistress Olivia will know not to say anything."

"You sorted things out with her?"

"Yes."

"Good." But Sophia didn't smile. "I should go back. I left a very sombre chamber."

"I'll go to the chapel and gather as many sisters as I can along the way."

Sophia wearily nodded. "We can't avoid word spreading, and if many sisters raise their voices to Salbine, perhaps She'll hear and listen." But her defeated tone betrayed her words. "Thank you, Averill." At the door, Sophia paused to straighten the shawl she always wore. She squared her shoulders and left.

Averill waited a moment, then left her cubbyhole to search for Olivia. She didn't have to look very hard. Olivia leaped up from one of the writing podiums and rushed to her. "It's happened, then?"

"Unfortunately." She felt strangely calm, perhaps because she'd cried herself out over reliving Elena's death and wouldn't entertain Emmey's until it happened. "Let's go to the chapel and take as many sisters as we can with us." After what she'd just said to Sophia, she felt like a fool, but given the choice between believing her prayers would be futile and believing they would be heard, why not go with the latter option?

Averill motioned for Sister Clara and Mistress Margery to join her and gathered many more sisters as she and Olivia walked to the chapel to pray—beg—for Emmey's life.

23

THE GLOW FROM A single burning lamp cast a yellowish light on Emmey's pale cheeks. Kneeling next to Emmey's bed, Maddy clutched her hand, wishing she could also hold Lillian's. After Sophia had gone to see Mistress Averill, Jonathan had carried Emmey to her bed. When Sophia had returned with no information that would help them to understand what had happened to Emmey, Maddy's spirits had plunged, and Sophia's red eyes had unsettled her. By then, Elizabeth had joined them, and as she'd reached for Sophia, Lillian had raced into the room, her chest rising and falling from exertion. She'd felt Emmey's forehead, then drawn Emmey against her chest and sobbed into her hair. Maddy's composure had crumbled and she'd wept into Lillian's shoulder, still holding Emmey's hand.

Almost ten hours later, Emmey hadn't stirred, hadn't moved, hadn't rolled over, sighed, cried out—oh, how Maddy would love to hear her cry out in terror, just this once. She'd dreaded Emmey leaving for the Bennetts, but now she'd give anything to see Emmey walk through the gates with her bag slung over her shoulder, so she could garden, marry, live! *Please, Salbine, let her live.* Maddy did not want to say the Prayer of Deliverance to Salbine's realm for Emmey, not tonight, not ever. *Don't even think it.* Emmey was alive. The chapel was packed with sisters on their knees, praying.

According to Sophia, everyone had jumped at the opportunity to draw up a schedule that would ensure the chapel would be full, day and night. Sophia and Elizabeth were in the chapel now. Even the Hedgerow sisters were taking their turns.

"Do you think she knows I love her?" Lillian whispered.

Maddy turned to her. "Of course she does."

"Because I've shouted at her sometimes."

"Only when she deserved it." Maddy tried to smile but failed, and she wished she had two bloody hands. She settled for giving Lillian a gentle nudge with her elbow, then returned her attention to Emmey's pale face. "I've dreaded her leaving so much, and now I could kick myself for not enjoying the time I had with her over these past few weeks. It's not right. She was healthy. Absolutely fine. I'm supposed to go first."

"It doesn't always work that way."

"It should, especially since she spent all that time stuck in that prison cell. She was owed more time, Lillian. Owed."

Lillian slipped her arm around Maddy's shoulders. "She's asleep, not gone."

"But there must be something wrong with her. She can't wake up. That's never a good sign." Maddy knew of several cases of people falling unconscious and never waking up again, or they did wake up but didn't have their full wits about them anymore. "We assumed she fell asleep, but it's more likely she fell unconscious."

"She's too young for a brain seizure."

"Well, something happened," Maddy snapped. Then she sighed and leaned into Lillian. "I'm sorry."

"Don't be. I feel like smashing everything in this chamber to pieces, and everything in the sitting room for good measure. If we lose her like this . . . " Lillian slowly shook her head.

They both jumped when someone tapped on the open bedchamber door. Rose tiptoed into the room, with Nora right behind her. Nora peered at Emmey and frowned. "The abbess sent us," she whispered. "She wants you both to get some sleep."

Maddy shook her head. "I can't. I need to be here."

"You'll only be next door."

"If she wakes up . . . "

"We'll be here, and after us, Mistress Averill is coming. You won't be much use to her if she does wake up and you're too exhausted to keep your eyes open."

Why was she arguing? Emmey wasn't going to wake up. Her life would slip away, her breathing slowing until her chest stilled. A burst of anger clenched her hand. She quickly let go of Emmey's and silently apologized.

Lillian tightened her grip on Maddy's shoulders and lifted Maddy with her as she rose. "If there's any change at all, come get us," she said to Rose and Nora. "I don't care if we're asleep. Shake us awake. All right?"

"We will, promise," Rose said.

Maddy glanced over her shoulder as Lillian steered her from the bedchamber. She doubted she'd sleep. She'd pray that she'd wake tomorrow and find Emmey sitting at the table, that Emmey would call her a slowpoke and tell her to hurry up or they'd be late for breakfast. But as Maddy lay next to Lillian, she raged at Salbine, questioning Her. *If you wanted Emmey so young, why did you bring us together? Why?*

Maddy listened, but as usual, there was only silence.

~

BRIGHT LIGHT WARMED EMMEY'S eyelids. The scent of chamomile wafted into her nose. Cool earth caressed her. She opened her eyes and sat up. Sisters strode by on the nearby path, but she didn't recognize them, and the stone building in the distance wasn't Merrin's monastery.

"It's Heath's monastery," said a voice to her left.

Emmey wanted to scream. She knew that voice and forced herself to turn and look. Her double sat against a tree, holding an apple. "Not you again."

"Watch your tongue, girl!"

Her double—double-Emmey, she decided to call her—bit into the apple and took her time chewing it. She swallowed and threw the apple away. It thudded onto the ground several feet away from her.

"Was there a worm in it?" Emmey asked.

"Don't waste my time. Many hearts stopped beating so you and I could speak. So listen to me, now that you are listening."

Emmey heaved an exasperated sigh.

"Heath." Double-Emmey swept her arm toward the monastery. "Make sure you come here."

"I just dreamed I was on my way here with Maddy."

"Telling you twice is better than telling you once."

"I'm not stupid," Emmey snapped.

"I didn't say you were, girl."

"My name's Emmey."

"You haven't claimed your name yet. To me, you're girl."

"I'm calling you Double-Emmey."

Double-Emmey snorted. "Are you blind, girl?"

Emmey frowned and folded her arms. "Why do I keep having these dreams?" she said aloud, but to herself. "And why do you keep—"

"Hush, girl, I'm listening."

"To what?"

"The voices."

Emmey strained to listen but couldn't hear anything. "What voices?"

"The ones calling out to me. The ones asking for help. I'm waiting."

"What for?"

"The perfect time."

"To do what?"

"Do you ever shut up, girl?"

"Maddy says I'm curious. It reminds her of Lillian."

"Perhaps I should satisfy that curiosity. I'm waiting for the perfect time to answer a prayer."

To answer a—Emmey blinked at Double-Emmey. No, it couldn't be. She was dreaming. This was all a dream, everything in it conjured from her own mind. Maddy, the prison, Heath, chamomile, eating apples in Mistress Averill's office, Salbine robes . . . her mind was conjuring it from what she already knew. She hadn't been to Heath, but she could imagine what another monastery would look like. No, she was dreaming. This was a dream.

"Not so talkative now, are you, girl?"

Emmey could only stare. On the minuscule chance that it was true . . . "Can I ask you a question?"

"Didn't I just say I'm listening to others?"

"I'm sure you can do that and talk to me."

Double-Emmey's mouth twitched. "Are you now? All right. What's your question?"

"Why is Maddy malflowed?"

Double-Emmey cocked her head. "Out of all the questions you could ask me, that's the one you choose? It's not your question to ask."

"Maddy's asked that question quite a bit, but she never gets an answer."

"Maddy will get the answer when she needs it."

Emmey opened her mouth to argue that Maddy had needed the answer for quite some time, but she'd only be arguing with herself. She wouldn't tell Mistress Averill about this dream. It was too stupid for words.

~

NUMB WITH DREAD AND defeat and sorrow, Maddy lifted her head and checked for any sign that Emmey was stirring, that her life wasn't slipping away. But there was none. Over a day now. She'd hardly slept last night and had returned to Emmey's bedchamber soon after Sophia and Elizabeth had taken over from Mistress Averill. Rose and Nora had returned after taking a nap, and so all four women were with Maddy and Lillian now, on their knees, their prayers meant for the lips of a goddess who might not have ears. A terrible notion, and one Maddy immediately chided herself for.

But she was weary, so weary, of praying, of asking, of begging, and in return, receiving nothing but stony silence.

Up until now, she'd always picked herself up, trudged and then strode on, still questioning, still asking, but accepting. But if Emmey died, Maddy would have to somehow push herself to her feet, brush off her robe, put one foot in front of the other, enter the chapel, and lift her voice in prayer and song, without resentment, without rage, without seeing Salbine not as a goddess who'd chosen her, but as one who hated her, hated her so much that She'd taken her hand, taken Emmey, denied her the gifts.

Lost in her thoughts when she should be praying, she sucked in her breath when she sensed someone hovering over her. "We've brought you some soup," Abigail said. Grace stood beside her. "It's on the table."

"Thank you." She wouldn't be able to eat, but she appreciated the gesture. "Why don't you all go have some?" she said to Sophia, Elizabeth, Rose, and Nora. "And you," she murmured to Lillian, who was leaning into her, the pain etched on her face deepening Maddy's agony. "I'll have some later."

Nobody moved. "We're going back to the chapel." Abigail placed her hand on her heart. "Salbine be with you."

No sooner were they gone when Mistress Averill crept into the chamber. "Any change?"

"No," Sophia said.

"I'll join you, if you don't mind."

The mistress's robe rustled as she kneeled. Maddy bowed her head and pressed her hand against her chest. *Salbine, return Emmey to us. Please, return Emmey to us. Whatever I've done, don't punish Emmey for it. Return her to us. Please, return her to us.*

24

Emmey plucked the petals off another chamomile flower and tossed the stem aside. This had to be one of the most boring dreams she'd ever had, though between this one and seeing Maddy on fire, or angry Maddy, or indifferent Maddy, or having her own body going up in flames, she'd take this dream.

She glanced at Double-Emmey, who still sat against the tree trunk, her eyes closed. "Still listening for that perfect time? Why don't you just answer whatever prayer you're waiting for and get it over with?"

Double-Emmey's eyes remained closed. "I'm waiting for the right moment, girl, so they'll know I answered the prayer."

"Everyone knows when their prayers are answered."

"Do they? Did you realize your prayer had been answered, the one you endlessly shouted while you wasted away in that wretched cell?"

"I didn't pray back then. I wish I had."

"Not all prayers are spoken, girl. You prayed with your heart. You cried out so loudly for me to save you that you gave me a headache."

Emmey giggled, then grew serious when she thought back to her time in Dunmurk Prison. Her days spent there had all blurred into one, until the day her cell door had creaked open and a woman had hurtled into the cell and fallen to her side. Emmey's throat constricted at the memory. The Miss. Her Miss. The one who'd saved her.

"The one I knew would save you, girl. Do you see what I mean about prayer? Most of the time, I answer a prayer, and the fortunate one thinks about how lucky she was, or how everything just happened to work out. Of course, when things aren't working out, *then* she invokes my name and blames it on me."

Once again, Emmey studied Double-Emmey. No, she was dreaming. Dreaming! But she felt compelled to reply. "I don't believe Maddy's malflowed because she was meant to leave Merrin and get dragged in front of that stupid magistrate and end up in my cell. That would be arrogant."

"What do you believe?"

"That whatever happened to Maddy was going to happen and had nothing to do with me. Perhaps I did pray with my heart, but long before I ended up in that cell. I prayed for someone to rescue me from stealing, and from grubbing around in rubbish for something to eat. I prayed for someone to love me." Tears prickled at Emmey's eyelashes. "And yes, I believe Salbine answered my prayer, but not by being so horrible to Maddy. I believe Salbine made sure I was in that cell when Maddy ended up in that cell, on her own journey, just like I was on mine. Salbine made sure we met, so we'd help each other, because we did, because Salbine made sure we were there for each other. Though the one thing I wonder about is why Maddy had to be there at all. If she wasn't malflowed, she would never have been there. She wouldn't have lost her hand protecting me. But you can't answer that, can you? Because this is all a dream and I don't know the answer. I can't dream what I don't know."

"But you dreamed about Malcolm being run over. You dreamed about a fire in the market. You dreamed about going to Heath, the only thing you'll remember about this supposed dream of yours." Double-Emmey opened her eyes and lifted a finger. "Ah. I sense the time approaching." She beckoned to Emmey. "Come to me, girl. Come closer."

Emmey hesitated, then scrambled to her feet and walked over to her double.

"Crouch girl. Look me in the eye."

Emmey did so. Double-Emmey grabbed Emmey's face and drew it so close that their noses touched. Love—and fear—stirred within her.

"Continue on your road, girl. You have already decided to claim your name. When we meet again, I will use it. As for your beloved Maddy, she deserves something for being so steadfast, so I have been waiting to answer her prayer, one I intended to answer anyway, and one I want her to be almost certain I heard."

Emmey's eyes widened. "You're going to give her the elements?"

Double-Emmey's fingers dug into Emmey's cheeks. "Is that what you think she's crying out for? Oh, girl, you underestimate the depth and power of the love those you call family have for you. It's for them as well that I answer this prayer, those gathered with her, because they'll need something to cling to through dark times."

"But—"

Double-Emmey's lips touched her forehead. "Be well, girl."

Emmey's surroundings shimmered. Then she grimaced and squeezed her eyes shut and clapped her hands over her ears. She could hear them. Voices. Mistress Averill, Rose, Nora, Sophia, Elizabeth, Lillian, Barnabus, Jonathan . . . and Maddy, whose voice was the loudest.

Return her to us. Please, return her to us.

~

MADDY'S KNEES AND SHOULDERS were sore and her back ached. The chapel bells had already announced eleven o'clock in the evening. She'd managed a bit of soup and some water for supper, had forced it down. Apart from taking a privy break, she'd remained next to Emmey, begging Salbine to return her. But she was losing hope, and she could sense those praying with her were also tiring.

Return her to us. Please, Salbine, return her to us.

She raised her head, but Emmey lay still. "She's going to die, isn't she?" When Lillian didn't answer, Maddy elbowed her. "Isn't she?"

"She's still with us."

"But for how long? She hasn't taken any food or water since yesterday at breakfast. How much longer can she survive?" Her voice was rising, but she was weary, and angry, and frustrated.

"We're all tired and hungry," Sophia said. "We should try to get some sleep and come back in the morning."

"Sisters will be praying in the chapel all night," Rose added.

"Why?" Maddy wanted to cry. Their prayers were falling on deaf ears. Her nails dug into her palm. She now understood why Lillian had said she wanted to smash everything in their chambers.

Lillian, whose sorrow was evident in the set of her shoulders, the anguish on her face, and her silence, slowly got to her feet. When had the fight gone out of her? Had her prayers turned to wishing Emmey a peaceful journey to Salbine's realm? Was Maddy the only one still hoping that Emmey would open her eyes?

She turned around, searched the faces of Sophia, Elizabeth, Rose, Nora, and Mistress Averill. She wanted to cry. These were her friends, her family. They all loved Emmey. They wanted her to survive. Even Barnabus and Jonathan were here, down on one knee, their heads bowed.

When Lillian grasped Maddy's arm and lifted her, Maddy shook her off, even though the others were also rising. "No!" She took Emmey's hand. "I need to be here." Tears rolled down her cheeks. "Please, Emmey, come back to us. Salbine, please. I've never wanted anything more, Salbine, please. Please hear us. Please, Salbine. I've never wanted anything more than to see Emmey open her eyes and sit up. Please—"

Emmey's eyes snapped open. She inhaled loudly and bolted upright.

Maddy's mouth dropped open. For a moment, she thought she was hallucinating.

"Salbine preserve us!" Rose breathed.

"Salbine be praised." Sophia, her voice filled with awe. The others joined in—even Lillian.

"Salbine has spoken."

"Salbine has answered our prayer."

Emmey's eyes settled on Maddy first, then she eyed Lillian and the others. "What's going on?" she said slowly. "Why is everyone in my bedchamber?"

Maddy leaped to her feet and embraced Emmey, holding her so tight that Emmey gasped. "I love you so much. Thank you, Salbine, Praise be to Salbine." She drew back, still not quite believing it. Emmey's eyes were open and bright, her cheeks had colour, her bewildered expression brought a smile to Maddy's face, the first one since she'd discovered Emmey asleep in front of the fire. "You've been asleep for quite some time."

"What do you mean?" Emmey squeaked.

"You fell asleep yesterday, just before lunch. It's almost midnight now. You've been asleep for over thirty hours."

Emmey's shocked face made Maddy smile again.

"Get her some soup," Lillian said to nobody in particular. She nudged Maddy aside and hugged Emmey. "I don't say this very often, but I do love you, my little mite."

Emmey squeezed her back. "I love you too."

Maddy's eyes blurred with happy tears for once. Salbine had answered her prayer! It couldn't have been coincidence. Well, she *had* been praying for the same thing repeatedly since yesterday afternoon, so Emmey waking up when she had could be coincidental. No, she'd not only woken, she'd sat up. Maddy had said she'd give anything for Emmey to open her eyes and sit up, and that was exactly what had happened. It had to be Salbine. She must have heard Maddy's prayer. She must have listened, and heard, and granted Maddy's heartfelt wish. Maddy was certain of it. Almost certain.

~

"SO WE WERE AT the prison again, and Arthur was older, and I still had my right hand," Maddy said, perched on the edge of Emmey's bed.

Emmey accepted another mug of milk from Lillian. She could get used to this, being waited on hand and foot while she lounged in bed, though not in the middle of the night. The others had left about an hour ago. Maddy and Lillian were both shattered, but they were also too keyed up to sleep, and so here they sat at past one in the morning, chatting.

"Then we were suddenly in one of the passages." Emmey gulped down some of the milk. She'd decided to tell them about the part of her dream when Maddy had grabbed the flaming wood. The time for keeping secrets about her dreams was over, in case she fell asleep for a long time again. They couldn't help her if they didn't know, and it must have been difficult for Mistress Averill to stay silent on the subject. From the conversation before everyone had gone, Emmey had gathered Mistress Averill hadn't told them about her "Maddy dreams."

"You won't like this part," she said to Maddy. "The passage was filled with smoke. Two men came toward us, one—"

"With a makeshift torch?" Maddy grimaced.

"Yes. And you grabbed it with your right hand, but something weird happened. And it's something that's happened a lot when I dream about you." Emmey paused. "You went on fire, but you didn't burn. You kept saying it didn't hurt."

They straightened and looked at each other. Lillian spoke first. "What did you say?"

"I said she went on fire, but she didn't burn."

"No, after that."

"She said she didn't hurt."

Maddy's eyes widened. "That's what Sister Lavinia wrote."

Lillian patted Maddy's leg. "You said you've had this dream a lot?"

"About Maddy burning? Yes. In one of them, she screamed and kept shouting that she was on fire. But lately, you stand in fire, you grab fire—you go on fire! And you keep telling me it doesn't hurt. But it hurts me. You always spread the fire to me, and it hurts." She bit her lip. "I don't like you in those fire dreams. You always want to hurt me."

"I'm not sure she does," Lillian murmured.

Emmey voiced the question that was plain on Maddy's face. "What do you mean?"

Lillian answered with a curt shake of her head. "We'll talk about this tomorrow. Carry on, Emmey."

"There's not much else to tell. After you set me on fire, Maddy..."
She gave Maddy a pointed look. "I was in a chamomile field outside
a monastery, which has happened before. And she was there. My
double. I've seen her in a dream before."

"Your double?" Maddy said.

"A more sophisticated me. She has a bun in her hair, and she
doesn't sound like me. Calls me girl. She was sitting eating an apple.
And then..." Emmey tried to remember, sure there'd been more,
but if her dream had stretched out longer, she'd forgotten it. Her
double had been eating an apple, and suddenly Emmey had been
sitting up in her bedchamber, wondering why everyone was holding
their hands to their mouths or hugging, or staring at her as if she
had three heads. "I think that's when I woke up."

"And thanks be to Salbine you did." Maddy swallowed. "You gave
us an awful fright. When I couldn't wake you up." Her eyes closed.

Emmey rubbed Maddy's arm. "I did wake up." Just in time to
go to the bloody Bennetts. She was supposed to be leaving today.
Supposed to be. "I have something—well, a few things—to tell you."
She drew a deep breath. "I'm going to Heath with you."

They both frowned. "It's a nice thought," Maddy said. "A very
nice one. I'd love nothing more. But I doubt the Bennetts will let
you go with us. We'll be away for months, and as much as it hurts
me to say this, we're not supposed to have much contact. You know
I have to focus on my service here, especially after Salbine answered
our prayers and brought you back to us. I'm fairly certain She did."

Emmey had the feeling Salbine had too, though she wasn't sure
why. "I haven't told you everything about my dreams, the realistic
ones that wake me up in the night. Parts of them usually come true.
I talked to Mistress Averill about it, and she's researching it for me."

"It sounds like everyone knows about these dreams except us,"
Lillian bellowed.

"I didn't want to tell Maddy about what was happening to her
in the dreams. Because in the early ones, you died." Emmey's voice
dropped. "You died."

"You were only dreaming," Maddy said softly.

"Still. And in the more recent ones, you were hurting me. I didn't want to tell you."

"So you told Mistress Averill."

Emmey nodded. "Talk to her, because I don't want to spend time telling you now, because I have other things to tell you." She looked for somewhere to put her milk. Lillian took the mug from her and held it. "You have to put it down. I don't want you to spill any when you hear what I have to say."

They glanced at each other, their brows etched with worry. Emmey wasn't very good at this, but she'd only have to tell them the once. She waited until Lillian had set the mug on top of the armoire and sat on the bed again, then took Maddy's hand and one of Lillian's. "In my dream, when we were at the prison, I was in a Salbine robe," she said solemnly.

She'd expected them to smile or at least appear pleased, but they continued to gaze at her. She needed to be clearer, spell it out for them. "I was in a Salbine robe because I'm marked by Salbine and I took the robe," she said slowly.

All right, now she was beginning to wonder if fatigue had addled their wits, because they continued to stare.

"I'm marked," she shrieked. That woke them up. They both jumped.

"Are you sure?" Maddy said.

"Of course I'm sure."

"How do you know?"

Emmey tutted. "I didn't think I'd have to explain it to you. How did you know?"

"Well, I . . . " Maddy met Lillian's eyes, then focused on Emmey. "Is it someone we know, someone here?"

"Perhaps."

They raised their brows at each other, but they didn't ask, and she wouldn't have told them. "You're not involved with anyone, are you?" Maddy asked faintly.

"No. I just like her in that way. It'll pass. She's too old for me. But it's clear to me I'm marked."

"We could test you and make sure," Lillian said. "Not me.

Someone else. I mean, I could, but it would be better if someone else did it."

"Why?"

"Because she'd be extremely biased. Because we would be—are—absolutely delighted," Maddy said. "Not that it would have mattered if you weren't. It wouldn't change how much we love you. But now you can take the robe, if that's what you truly want to do."

"It is," Emmey said firmly.

"Are you saying that because you want to serve, or because you want to stay?"

Emmey squeezed Maddy's hand. "I've asked myself that since I realized I was marked. Not explicitly, though. I kept telling myself I wasn't called and that made me sad, because I love it here. But I came to realize that I couldn't see I was called because I'm already here. I had assumed I desperately wanted to stay because of you two. And that's still true. But it's not all of it." She was about to tell them what Sister Dolores had said that had helped her to see it, but she was worried she might blush, and then they'd know. "This is where I should be. I want to scribe. I want to pray with everyone in the chapel. I have a research project I want to do."

Maddy's face lit up. "A research project?" For a moment, Emmey thought she was going to chuckle, but she didn't. "About what?"

"I'll tell you if I'm allowed to do it, and I hope I'll be able to, now that I'll be here." She grinned at the thought. "I can't imagine myself outside the Order. I couldn't imagine leaving you two, and I still can't, but it's the Order too."

"You certainly left it to the last minute." Lillian's tone was light.

"I wanted to be sure. Because I respect the Order, and you, and most of all, Salbine." Emmey's voice quavered. "I would never wear a Salbine robe if I didn't think I belonged in one."

Maddy's face shone. "I woke this morning in utter despair and now I feel as if my heart will burst."

"Do you think Sophia will let me stay until I turn sixteen and can become a novice?"

"She'd bloody-well better," Lillian muttered.

"I don't see why not." Maddy lifted Emmey's hand and gently

shook it. "But don't tell her. Ask her. Respectfully. She's always been your abbess, but now that means so much more."

With a lump in her throat, Emmey could only nod.

"This has been a day I'll never forget." Maddy let go of Emmey's hand and pulled her into a hug. "Who would have thought we'd be here when I landed in that cell?" she murmured.

Not able to speak, Emmey could only hug her back. She hadn't understood at the time how fortunate she'd been that Maddy had ended up in her cell. Only later, when she was older, had she come to believe that Salbine had brought them together, something she thanked Her for every time she sank to her knees.

She drew back. "You're tired." She looked past Maddy. "So are you," she said to Lillian. "Go to bed. I'll be fine. I probably won't sleep, but I'll be fine."

Maddy bit her lip. "I'll be anxious every time you go to sleep now."

"I woke up. I don't know what happened, but I woke up."

"So you did. All right, then. I'll try to get some sleep. I want to be at morning prayers tomorrow, to thank Salbine for what She did."

"Me too."

"I'll go to morning prayers too," Lillian said. "I doubt many will be there for the early morning service."

"Why?" Emmey asked.

Maddy tapped Emmey's nose. "Because sisters prayed day and night for you. The chapel was always full, no matter the hour."

Emmey didn't know what to say, because there was nothing she could say that would express how humbled she felt.

"Good night." Maddy ruffled Emmey's hair. Lillian echoed Maddy's words.

They left the door open. Emmey didn't get up to close it. They needed to sleep, and if leaving the door open would help them, so be it. She lay back, clasped her hands behind her head, and stared into the dull light cast by the burning lamp. She'd been asleep for a day and a half, and all she could remember was that short dream at the prison, and then seeing her double again. Surely there must be more. She reviewed her dream, saw her double leaning against

the tree trunk eating an apple, and then nothing. No, a whisper . . .
go to Heath, girl, and claim your name. *Claim your name.*

She suddenly understood her message to herself. Her double
must represent her inner wisdom, the part of her that knew what
was buried deep inside. She would claim her name. She'd take the
first step tomorrow.

~

THE MOMENT MADDY LEFT Emmey's bedchamber, she wanted to
rush back to her and sit next to the bed, in case Emmey fell asleep.
She summoned all her willpower to resist the urge. Emmey would
have to sleep sometime, and Maddy would have to trust that she'd
wake up, as she had countless mornings before. Still, she felt unsettled as she disrobed, despite her happiness that Emmey was marked
and would join the Order. "Quite the day," she said to Lillian after
she'd slid under the blanket and pressed into her. "Marked and
called. I should have suspected, but I didn't see it."

"She didn't want us to know until she was ready."

"It sounds like she didn't know until recently that she wanted to
take the robe." Emmey, in a Salbine robe. The notion felt so natural.
"Oh, what were you thinking when she told us about her dream,
the part about me not burning? You said you'd tell me tomorrow,
but you can tell me now."

"No," Lillian said flatly.

"Why not?"

Silence, then, "Because I don't want to ruin your mood. Not that
it should, but it probably will. If I'm right."

Maddy wanted to shake it out of her, but her eyelids were heavy,
and she was still digesting Emmey's declarations. "Tomorrow, then,"
she murmured, already dropping off.

25

A VERILL WATCHED SISTER MADDY and Lillian's faces as they read the passage about foretellers and the list of those sisters who'd fallen asleep and slumbered their way into Salbine's realm.

Lillian lifted her head. "When did you find this?"

Averill shifted her weight. "A few weeks ago." She raised her hand. "And before you shout at me for not telling you, I didn't see what good it would do. I wanted you to enjoy your remaining time with Emmey, not fret every minute of every day."

"She woke up." The tone of Sister Maddy's voice matched her awed expression. "Salbine answered our prayer."

Averill remembered her shock when Emmey had bolted upright, at almost the exact moment Sister Maddy had prayed that she would. All right, Sister Maddy had probably been praying for the same thing day and night, so any time Emmey sat up would have occurred at the same moment Sister Maddy prayed for it to happen. Or was Averill overthinking it and being overly skeptical? She couldn't deny that Emmey had woken from a too-long slumber, and if the tome Lillian held was accurate and complete, Emmey had been the only . . . what? Emmey wasn't a sister, though she was clearly marked by Salbine, and if she was a foreteller, she belonged here, at the monastery. Averill was sure of it.

But was it up to her to voice her thoughts, to see Sophia and urge her to keep Emmey here? Emmey had never said anything about taking the robe. And Averill had kept one too many secrets lately. "Has Emmey talked to you about, er, anything about herself? Perhaps this isn't my place, but I do believe she's a foreteller, and I'd be surprised if Salbine took such an interest in a girl who isn't marked."

They smiled, surprising Averill. "She's marked," Sister Maddy said.

Oh, so she had told them.

"She wants to take the robe."

Averill wanted to do a cartwheel. "That's wonderful news! I suppose the Bennetts will be disappointed, but Salbine claimed her long before they did."

"She's with the abbess now, asking if she can stay here until she's old enough to become a novice."

"Surely the abbess will agree." Especially since she already knew Emmey was a foreteller. Emmey's place was here.

"She mentioned wanting to do a research project," Lillian said. "Do you know anything about it?"

"No, I don't. She hasn't said anything about it to me."

Lillian snapped the book shut and handed it back to Averill. "You believe she's a foreteller?"

"I do." She told them about all the dreams Emmey had recounted to her and how they'd come true, albeit not exactly as Emmey had dreamed them.

"She dreamed that she was with me on my way to Heath," Sister Maddy said. "She says that means she has to go with me."

"That would be allowing the dream to affect the future, which is different than a dream predicting the future."

"She's seen the past too." Lillian turned to Sister Maddy. "I don't think you ever told her you were running around the training room shouting that you were on fire."

"No, I didn't. She was young then. I didn't want to frighten her. I didn't go into any detail about how I knew I was malflowed except to say that it hurt when I drew." She paused. "You still have to tell me something."

"And I will."

"I haven't found anything that mentions seeing the past." Averill tapped her chin. "I'll keep looking. And I'll write to the other monasteries, see if they have anything about foretellers that we don't have. Our copy of this tome might not be the most recent."

"You'll have to add Emmey's name now."

"Yes, and that she woke up." And Emmey would have two projects, unless her proposed project matched the one Averill would have for her. "I'll want her to record everything she remembers about her dreams, and to write them down from now on."

"She's had two mirror dreams now," Sister Maddy said.

"It's possible the other sisters did too. It says they fell into their final slumber soon after having it but didn't say they only had it once. Oh, I hope the other monasteries have more material. Now we have two unique sisters here, or we soon will."

"Are we causing problems for you, Mistress?" Sister Maddy said, her eyes bright.

"You're certainly making things interesting."

"When the abbess came to see you, when Maddy couldn't wake Emmey up, did you tell her about the book and your suspicion that Emmey is a foreteller?" Lillian asked.

Averill didn't hesitate. "No. I didn't tell her for the same reason I didn't tell you. I didn't see the point in alarming you when there was nothing you could do."

Olivia appeared in the doorway behind the two sisters and hovered there. Averill couldn't help smiling, which made Sister Maddy glance over her shoulder. "We won't keep you," the sister said, making Averill wonder if Emmey had told them anything about Olivia. "Please keep us informed if you find anything." Sister Maddy paused. "We're not angry, or at least I'm not. I understand why you didn't tell us. Thank you for being so good with Emmey." If Lillian was angry with Averill, she held her tongue.

"Emmey is most welcome here. In fact, if she's staying, I want to claim her for the library. She has the makings of a good little scribe." She'd want to properly train Emmey, round out the lessons about scribing that Emmey had already received.

They said good-bye. As soon as they'd gone, Olivia came into the cubbyhole. "It all worked out, then."

Yes, when it came to Emmey, it had all worked out.

~

SOPHIA LEANED BACK IN her chair and studied Emmey, who'd refused the offer of a chair and stood tall, with her arms straight at her sides. "You are marked by Salbine and you wish to take the robe," she repeated, in case she'd heard what she wanted to hear, rather than what Emmey had said.

"Yes."

"And you're sure."

"I wish everyone wouldn't keep asking me that."

"Everyone meaning Maddy and Lillian?"

Emmey hesitated, then nodded, making Sophia smile. "You can test me. We can go to a training room right now."

There was no need for that. They took women who showed up at the gates to a training room for two reasons. First, so they wouldn't be revealed as liars in front of others, if it came to that, and second, to impart the impression that the elements were to be drawn under controlled conditions because to do otherwise would be dangerous. But Sophia could test Emmey right here, right now.

"You're fourteen, which is enough to know your own mind, but still young. If you enter the Order, you'll be dedicating your life to it. That's a long time."

"Yes, I'm fourteen, but if I'm old enough to be put outside the gates to make my own way, I'm old enough to know I want to take the robe." Emmey's eyes dared Sophia to disagree.

Sophia didn't. She could see Emmey's determination and knew of her dedication to the services she already performed in Salbine's name. She squared her shoulders, drew the faintest wisp of air, and directed it toward Emmey.

Emmey's eyes widened and she clamped her hands to her chest. "I think my heart just fluttered," she said, her voice tinged with alarm.

The air Sophia had drawn returned to her. She savoured its

caress for a moment, then cut the flow. "Are you sure you want to take the robe? You don't want to stay because you'll miss Maddy and Lillian?"

"And you, and Elizabeth, and Rose and Nora, and Mistress Averill, and I could go on and name every sister here, and I would miss all of you, but that's not why I want to take the robe. Salbine has called me to serve. I didn't realize it because I was already here, but I do now."

"How?" Sophia asked, genuinely curious.

"Because I respect and adore Salbine. I pray to Her daily, and I couldn't imagine being anywhere else. I've tried, and I can't. I thought it was because of Maddy and Lillian and everyone, but that's not the only reason I want to cry every time I think of leaving. It's not being able to pray with you. It's not being able to scribe and run my fingers along all the spines in the library, and touch the sculpture of Lina, and grow herbs, not just for Lillian, but for everyone she makes tinctures and poultices for. I already feel like I live and breathe this monastery and everything it stands for. I belong here, Sophia. I really do. So please, take me to a training room and test me and tell me I can stay until I'm old enough to become a novice."

Sophia pulled off her spectacles and cleaned the lenses with a rag she pulled from her drawer. "I've already tested you."

"When?"

"When you felt a fluttering inside you." Sophia slipped her spectacles back on. "I drew air and directed it through you, and it returned to me. Which means you *are* marked by Salbine. If you weren't, the element wouldn't have flowed through you. It would have dissipated."

Emmey gasped. "I passed. You have to let me stay now."

"I don't. I could tell you it would be good for you to experience the outside world for a couple of years, and then return to us. But I won't," she said quickly, when Emmey appeared as if she was going to sink to her knees and beg. "Of course you can stay. You've already experienced how harsh the world can be, and it wouldn't make sense to turn you out now, especially when you might be a foreteller."

"A what?"

"Mistress Averill didn't tell you?"

"Tell me what?"

Sophia had assumed Averill had told Emmey but kept it from Maddy and Lillian. "You should speak to her about what she found out about your dreams, and don't be angry with her because she didn't tell you. She thought it would frighten you and ruin your last days with all of us."

"Why would it do that?"

"Because sisters who've had the same types of dreams as you and seen themselves in a dream, like you have, fall asleep one day and never wake up. Except you did. You woke up."

Emmey moistened her lips. "You mean, you all thought I was going to go to Salbine when I wouldn't wake up?"

"Yes, but not for the same reasons. Those of us who knew thought Salbine was taking you as She has other foretellers. Maddy and Lillian didn't know, but the longer you slept, the less likely it was you'd ever wake. Mistress Averill didn't tell them for the same reason she didn't tell you." Sophia hurried on when Emmey appeared troubled. "But you woke up, Emmey. Salbine returned you to us. She answered our prayers, I'm sure of it. Maddy prayed for you to wake up and sit up, and you did. It was quite shocking, actually, to witness a prayer answered in front of my eyes. It humbled me greatly, made me realize that my own prayers had grown rote, and that my belief in Salbine's ability to answer them had perhaps waned. But no longer. I have what happened to you, and Salbine's intervention, to forever remind me of Her wisdom and diligence."

"I might fall asleep another time and not wake up."

"I don't believe you will. I believe if Salbine wanted to take you that way, she would have. For some reason, She chose to return you, the first time it's happened, to our knowledge. So I sincerely believe you belong here, and I will welcome you into the Order with open arms."

"Thank you, Sophia." Emmey bobbed, evoking yet another smile from Sophia. Goodness, it felt so wonderful to genuinely smile, to feel invigorated and renewed.

"You'll have to move to the Novices Tower when you turn sixteen."

"I won't mind. It won't be the same as moving completely away. Will I still be able to sit with Maddy and Lillian in the chapel?"

"Of course. But we can talk about all that later, because there will be a later for you with all of us now, won't there?" Sophia couldn't resist anymore. She rose, rounded her desk, and hugged Emmey tightly. "I'm very pleased, Emmey."

"Me too."

They drew back and beamed at each other.

"I need to tell you something about the dream I had when you were all praying for me."

Sophia dropped into one of the guest chairs and motioned for Emmey to take the other one.

Emmey sat down and met Sophia's eyes. "I have to go to Heath with Maddy. In my dream, and it was one of those dreams, I was in a Salbine robe, and I was at the prison with Maddy. The governor was older. It was the future, I'm sure of it. Maddy had both her hands, but there's always something that tells me I'm dreaming, because honestly, if there wasn't, it's so real, I wouldn't know."

Sophia tilted her head. "You want me to send you with Maddy because of your dream."

"Yes!"

"It would be a self-fulfilling prediction."

"My dreams have already influenced what I do. When I saw Malcolm that day, if I hadn't dreamed about the horse, I wouldn't have waved him off the path. I only saw the horse coming because I knew to look, otherwise I would have waved hello and watched him get trampled. What would be the point of having these dreams if they don't change anything?"

"I see your point." Though the passages Averill had shown her said that most of the dreams foretellers had were about future events that didn't really matter. "What about your dreams about Maddy?"

"The ones when she burns and dies? I know what that one was about now. I know what she meant when she said I wasn't listening. But she hasn't died in the last few. She's stood in fire and said it doesn't hurt. Lillian might know what it means but she didn't want to talk about it last night."

Sophia would ask Lillian later. "I'll keep an open mind about Heath. If Maddy actually goes—"

"She will."

"If she does, we'll discuss it then."

"All right, now let's talk about my research project."

Sophia wanted to chuckle.

"I want to examine the part of Salbine's Covenant that mentions blessings. I want to know what's meant by that."

"The elements."

"Maddy didn't get them. It must mean more than that."

Sophia was momentarily nonplussed, which didn't happen very often. "I think you'll find that it's universally interpreted as the elements."

"I'd like to read those interpretations and anything else I can get my hands on about the Covenant. This could be a long project."

No doubt. "I suspect scribing will become your primary area of study. Is that what you'd want."

"Yes," Emmey said firmly and without hesitation.

"I don't have any objection to you studying whatever you like when you're not needed elsewhere. In fact, I'd encourage it, and I'm sure Mistress Averill will too."

Emmey leaped to her feet and threw her arms around Sophia's neck. "Can I go now? I want to tell Maddy and Lillian I can stay."

"Of course you can." Sophia rose and gazed into Emmey's bright eyes, warmth suddenly welling inside her. "Speaking not as your abbess, but as your . . . " She trailed off.

"Aunt," Emmey prompted.

Oh dear, now she wanted to weep—with happiness. "Yes, your aunt. I am so very pleased you'll be staying. I'm especially looking forward to our next supper now. It was going to be quite a dreary affair without you."

"I'm looking forward to it too." Emmey's eyes glinted. "I would have run away from the Bennetts, you know."

Sophia tutted. "No, you wouldn't have. Now go, before I change my mind about letting you stay."

Emmey grinned and swung the door open.

"Oh!" Mistress Olivia stood outside and grinned sheepishly. "I was just about to knock. How are you feeling today, Emmey?"

"Very well, thank you." Emmey bobbed to her, then hitched up her robe and strode from the study.

Mistress Olivia bobbed to Sophia. "May I speak with you, Abbess?"

"Of course." Sophia gestured for the mistress to sit down and returned to her own chair. After the mistress had gone, she'd find Elizabeth and suggest a stroll around the gardens. She might even suggest they have a quiet lunch and spend the afternoon reading in their chambers, or sewing, or whatever else came to mind. After the stress and worry over Emmey, and now the joy and optimism that made her feel like singing, she didn't want to be cooped up in her study all day. An afternoon off in who knew how many days would only be a small indulgence.

She clasped her hands on her desk. "What can I do for you, Mistress?"

Mistress Olivia cleared her throat. "I've come to request that I be allowed to join the Merrin community. To stay here, rather than return to Hedgerow."

Ah. Sophia hadn't expected this, but at the same time, the mistress's words weren't a complete surprise. "Don't you like it at Hedgerow?" she asked, even though she suspected it wasn't the reason behind Mistress Olivia's request.

"Hedgerow is a wonderful monastery. It's been my home for many years, and I have friends there. But I'll miss Mistress Averill. I thought letters would be enough, but I've grown quite fond of her." Blood dotted the mistress's cheeks, colouring the scars on them. "I'd like the opportunity to stay and—I know it will take time to grow closer . . . I can be patient, but I'd like to be here, not writing to her. I—" Her voice choked off.

Sophia's forehead creased with sympathy. "Breathe, Mistress."

Mistress Olivia gulped down air. "I've given this considerable thought."

"Am I correct in assuming you've never taken a consort?" The mistress hadn't mentioned one when they'd discussed consorts over supper soon after the sisters had arrived.

"No, I haven't."

"Given recent events, I have to ask why."

The mistress straightened. "It's not because I want to be available to flit from sister to sister, I can assure you. I've always hoped to take a consort, but reciprocal feelings, to the extent that we both wanted to pledge, has never happened for me. I asked once and was turned down, and I was asked once and turned the asker down. But this time . . . " Her face brightened. "I'd like the opportunity for my friendship with Mistress Averill to grow, and for once, I'd prefer not to be writing letters."

"I doubt your abbess will be very pleased. Five sisters left Hedgerow, and only three return because Merrin gobbled the rest up."

"She won't be, but on the other hand, Hedgerow is bursting at the seams. We're close to the intersection of three major trade routes. Some of the initiates and novices are having to double up. It's different here. You're tucked away behind Merrin."

Only one trade route passed by Merrin's gate, and there were empty chambers in all the towers. Not many, but Sophia couldn't remember sisters ever having to share. "Have you spoken to Mistress Margery about this?"

"I have. She said she'd be sorry to lose me, but she understands. You can speak with her, if you like. She told me to tell you that."

There was no need. Sophia didn't believe Mistress Olivia would tell her such an easily refutable lie, especially when dishonesty would not endear her to the woman who'd decide whether she could stay. Quite the contrary. Sophia would murmur her regrets and send her packing. No, the mistress was telling her the truth. Still, Sophia was protective of Averill's heart, which had suffered one cruel shock too many. "I'm willing to extend your stay for six months, to give you the opportunity to see whether Merrin will suit you. During that time, you'll serve as if you're a permanent member of our community. However, if you change your mind about staying here because Merrin isn't what you hoped it would be, you can leave at any time with my blessing. If it's everything you hope it to be, then in six months, we'll formally welcome you to our community. Would that be acceptable?"

The mistress nodded. "Thank you."

Sophia would have to add more to the letter she'd already started to Hedgerow's abbess about why Sister Lorelle had stayed behind. Mistress Margery would no doubt recount the sordid affair to her, but Sophia owed her an explanation in her own words, especially now that two sisters would remain behind. "Mistress Averill will be pleased for two reasons. She'll gain a scribe as well. That will be two new scribes for her." She answered the mistress's unspoken question. "Emmey is staying. She's marked, and she intends to take the robe."

"That's delightful. Mistress Averill is very fond of her."

"We all are. Now, is there anything else?"

"No." Mistress Olivia rose.

"I'll let you tell Mistress Averill that you'll be staying." Sophia imagined the surprise and happiness on Averill's face.

"Thank you, Abbess. Salbine be with you."

"And with you."

Sophia waited until she could no longer hear Mistress Olivia's receding footsteps, then pushed back her chair, doused the fire, and shut her study door behind her, not intending to open it again until tomorrow morning. It was a glorious day. She couldn't wait to find Elizabeth.

26

Her cheeks hurting, Maddy kissed the top of Emmey's head and tried to stop smiling, but she couldn't. "I knew she'd let you stay. It would be silly to make you leave just for the sake of it."

"She thinks I'm a foreteller. She told me to speak to Mistress Averill."

Maddy caught Lillian's eye, then moved aside, dragging Emmey with her, so Mistress Phyllis would have enough room to pass them in the hall just outside their chambers. They both bobbed to her. The mistress stopped and stooped, her hands pressed to her legs.

"Did I just hear you're staying?" she said to Emmey.

"Yes, I am."

"That's excellent news. You're taking the robe, I assume?"

Emmey's brow furrowed. "How did you know?"

"Because the Order fits you like a glove," the mistress said.

"But you didn't know I'm marked by Salbine."

The mistress's eyes danced. "I had a feeling. Anyway, I must dash. I have a class to teach. I just wanted to tell you how happy I am for you." She straightened. "All of you," she said, briefly meeting Lillian's eyes, and then Maddy's. "See you later."

They murmured good-bye. Maddy put her hand on her hip. "All right, out with it," she said to Lillian. "What do you think Emmey's dream means?"

"Let's go to a training room."

"A training room?" Maddy's mind raced. Had Lillian figured out how she could draw the elements?

"Can I come too?" Emmey piped up.

Lillian was already at the stairwell. "Yes, yes, come. You can help me demonstrate. Assuming I'm correct."

Maddy and Emmey raised their brows at each other and caught up to Lillian. Several minutes later, Lillian knocked on a closed training room door, listened, and then entered it. Maddy and Emmey followed her in.

"I'll train here soon," Emmey said. "Which will be a bit strange, because all the time I've been thinking about why I belong here, drawing the elements hasn't been on the list."

Maddy wondered if it was because of her. Emmey spent most of her time with a sister who couldn't draw the elements to save her life.

"That's not unusual," Lillian said. "I wasn't thinking about drawing when I came, either."

"Nor I." Maddy had longed to be here for other reasons, though once she'd arrived and began her education, she and the other novices had eagerly awaited their day in the training rooms.

Lillian closed the door. "Let's get started, shall we?" She held her hand toward Emmey. "Give me your hand."

Emmey hesitated, then grasped Lillian's hand. A moment later, she yelped, yanked her hand away, and shook it. "What did you do that for?"

"I wanted to demonstrate what happens when I draw enough fire to heat your hand, but not enough to burn it."

"We could have guessed what happens," Emmey said indignantly, making Maddy chuckle.

Her mirth quickly died when Lillian gestured for her hand. "I've only got the one, so do be careful." Even though she knew Lillian wouldn't burn her hand, her mouth felt dry.

Lillian took her hand. Maddy braced herself and waited. "Well, go on."

"Hush," Lillian snapped.

One minute went by, then two. A bead of perspiration trickled down Lillian's left temple and onto her cheek. Emmey skirted around them so she was behind Lillian and lifted her hands in a questioning gesture.

Lillian finally let go of Maddy's hand and quickly examined her palm. "Look."

Maddy frowned down at her palm. "I don't see anything."

"Exactly. I've been drawing fire against it for the last five minutes, and your skin isn't even the slightest bit red."

Maddy frowned and peered at her palm again.

"I did to you what I did to Emmey. Drew just enough to make you feel it, but not enough to burn you. When you didn't react, I increased the intensity. Your palm should be burned."

"But it isn't, and I didn't feel anything."

Emmey gasped. "It didn't hurt. It doesn't hurt. Salbine preserve us."

Confused, Maddy looked to Lillian.

"The elements can't hurt you," Lillian said. "Don't ask me why, but if I were to hurl a fireball at you, you wouldn't feel it."

Maddy snorted. "I find that hard to believe."

"Stand over there." Lillian pointed to a spot on the other side of the room.

"You're not going to do it," Maddy shrieked. "What if you're wrong?"

"I'm going to draw water. The worst that'll happen is you'll get soaked."

Maddy glared at her, then went to where Lillian had indicated. She tried to stand casually, but her shoulders and back felt stiff. "Go on, then."

Emmey stood next to Lillian, her hands folded under her chin. Water streamed from Lillian's fingertips. Maddy braced herself, expecting the water to hit her face, plaster her hair to her head, and make her robe soggy.

Only the latter happened.

The water raced toward her and . . . seemed to part in front of her eyes. She looked down at her robe. Sure enough, water was deepening its purple, but Maddy didn't feel any dampness. The water must be penetrating through to her shift, but her chest and stomach felt dry, and so did her face and hair. "Stop drawing!"

The moment water stopped striking her, she pulled off her robe and shift. "I'm dry," she said, patting herself. The same couldn't be said of the crumpled robe and shift on the floor. "I don't understand."

"The elements can't touch you," Lillian said briskly.

"You mean I'm so closed to them now that they can't even stand to be near me? I'd probably fail the Test of Salbine now!"

"That's been true since we found out you're malflowed."

"That makes me feel better."

Lillian picked up Maddy's soggy clothes and handed them to her. Wincing, Maddy struggled to get back into them, but it was more difficult to dress when her clothes were drenched. She didn't protest when Lillian helped pull her shift over her body. Lillian stepped back so that Emmey could help with the robe.

"So that's why you were standing in fire and saying it wouldn't hurt," Emmey said.

"But I feel the warmth from the fire in our chambers and everywhere else."

"Natural fire," Lillian pointed out. "You're only immune if the source is elemental. I think that's what Sister Lavinia discovered. I think she entered a training room without knocking and was hit with fire or water or air, and it didn't hurt her."

"You think the mistress shouted at her because she'd been reckless?" Maddy said.

"I'm sure it frightened her too. Imagine a sister walking into the training room just as you unleashed something in that direction. You'd have to be very quick to cut the flow in time. I doubt anyone could do it. The mistress would also have been angry with herself, I would think. We know to direct the elements away from the door, but it's easy to forget. Sisters know they could be taking their lives in their hands if they don't knock."

Maddy hadn't gotten that far with her training. She'd still been stuck on lighting a wick so that it burned strongly and brightly. "What about when you shielded us in town?"

"You were close to me, close enough that you didn't touch the shield. If you had, it would have dissipated. Remember that. If someone is ever shielding you, make sure you stay close to her. Wrap your arms around her waist, if you have to. Otherwise you could destroy the shield."

"Oh, so now I can hamper others too." Maddy threw up her hand. "What does it change? I'm still malflowed. Well, now I won't skip to Heath expecting to discover how to draw the elements, but other than that, it doesn't change anything."

"But you'll still want to go?"

"She has to go," Emmey said.

"And I still want to. I'd still like to understand why." Though as soon as she said it, she realized Heath likely wouldn't hold the answer. *Only Salbine knows why.* Unless Sister Lavinia had discovered the reason during her remaining few years of life, she'd been as much in the dark as Maddy was. Still . . . "I'd like to read Sister Lavinia's reflections, and anything she wrote about how she saw her place in the Order, and how she related to Salbine, I suppose."

"I wonder why you're immune to the elements, a question that Sister Lavinia's journals won't answer," Lillian said. "What possible purpose does it serve? A sister would never draw against another sister."

"Another mystery."

Lillian went to hug her, then eyed Maddy's wet robe and dropped her arms. "You sure you're not upset?"

"Like I said, it doesn't change anything. And I can't deny that Salbine has answered my prayers recently." She shot Emmey a quick smile, though guilt snaked through her. They'd think she meant her prayers for Emmey to wake up, but long before then, in her weaker moments, she'd prayed that Emmey would be able to stay at the monastery, even though she knew it was wrong. "If you'd performed your little experiment after Emmey had walked through the gates, I wouldn't be as calm about it. But honestly, it doesn't matter. I've learned to count my blessings, not dwell on what I don't have and can't do." Though as she said the words, bitterness bloomed within her. She quashed it, not wanting it to mar a wonderful day. After her joy over Emmey staying and taking the robe had tempered, she'd think about why she was malflowed and immune to the elements. Her resentment and bitterness would stir, and they'd linger until she prayed and reminded herself of all the good in her life. But not today.

"Let's go tell Rose and Nora you're staying," she said to Emmey. "And Grace. And Abigail."

As they left the training room, Emmey continued to name sisters. Maddy reached for Lillian's hand, wondering if Emmey would name them all. Every one of them could or would draw the elements, but not her. The elements couldn't even touch her. Quite a useless trait to have, but lucky her. She had it!

No, she had Lillian, and Emmey, and Sophia, Elizabeth, Rose, Nora, a warm bed, a roof, plenty to eat, her left hand, a community of interesting and well-educated women, and a goddess who she believed loved her. She would not be bitter. Not today.

~

AVERILL CLIMBED THE STAIRS to the fifth floor of the Mistresses Tower, wishing her mood would lift with each step. She'd hardly been able to muster a smile this afternoon, even though the news that Emmey would stay and take the robe had brightened her mood. The Hedgerow sisters would depart tomorrow. While Averill would look forward to scribing with Emmey again, Olivia's absence would be palpable. Averill had expected Olivia to also feel sad about her imminent departure, but Olivia had been cheerful all afternoon, and her mood hadn't seemed forced. Several times, Averill had caught Olivia smiling to herself. Stinging, she'd quickly looked away. She understood that Olivia would want to return to her own chambers and community, but she couldn't help but feel slighted.

At least Olivia had invited her to share a cider tonight, just the two of them. Averill would try not to sound sentimental. She'd only known the woman for a month, but she'd shared her worst experience with her, kissed her, and allowed herself to imagine more, even though the prospect frightened her. But Olivia seemed happy to be leaving, and Averill wouldn't make things terribly awkward by going on and on about how much she'd be missed. She'd certainly express the sentiment, but she wouldn't gush.

She knocked on Olivia's door and forced a smile when Olivia opened it. Inside, a chest sat on the floor, almost filled with folded clothing. Averill tore her eyes away from it, wanting to search Olivia's face for any sign that she was distressed about leaving. Her dismay deepened when Olivia beamed at her.

"Oh, I'm so glad to see you," Olivia said. "I've been waiting for this all afternoon."

"It's good to see you too," Averill said, taken aback by Olivia's effusive mood. "I see you've almost finished packing," she said stiffly.

"Yes, but I'm not going very far." Olivia's eyes shone. "Only two floors down."

Averill wasn't sure she'd heard correctly. "Two floors down?"

"Mmm. Into the empty chambers next to Mistress Clarissa. It will be nice not having to climb five flights of stairs."

Averill could only stare.

Olivia laughed and took Averill's face in her hands. "I'm staying, Averill. The abbess has agreed to extend my time here by six months, to give me the opportunity to see if I'd like to become a permanent part of the community."

"Six months," Averill repeated stupidly, her mind a whirl and her heart racing.

"To see if, how did the abbess put it? To see if things go as I hope they do."

"You asked to stay?"

"Letters aren't going to be enough, and let's face it, if I were to leave, we'd probably never see each other again." Olivia's voice dipped. "Letters would be painful, to read your delightful words knowing I'd never lay my eyes on your ever so pleasing face. So I thought, pluck up your courage, Olivia, and go see the abbess. I'll miss my friends, but we can write." She waited for Averill to say something, then frowned. "Are you all right? I hope I haven't misunderstood and you'd prefer that I leave tomorrow."

Averill's legs felt like jelly. Fear begged her to shout, "Yes, you've misunderstood, you imbecile!" and then bolt from the chambers and hide until Olivia was gone. But she stood fast, determined to not retreat this time, but to push through. To try. She lifted her trembling hands and gripped Olivia's to bolster her courage. "The last thing I want is for you to leave tomorrow."

"Then it's settled." Olivia pressed her lips to Averill's.

Averill kissed her back, but then . . . she wanted to curse!

Perhaps sensing Averill's discomfort, Olivia abandoned the kiss and touched her forehead to Averill's. "You'll find I'm a very patient woman, especially when I'm extremely motivated by the reward. And we're not in a rush, are we? We have all the time in the world now." She let Averill's face go and plucked a robe from over the back of a nearby chair. "Let me pack this and close the chest, and then we'll have a celebratory cider, and then, if you don't mind doing a defender's work, we'll carry the chest down to my new chambers. How does that sound?"

Lovely. Absolutely lovely.

27

THE NEXT AFTERNOON, SOPHIA had just returned to her study after bidding the three departing Hedgerow sisters good-bye when someone tapped at her open door. Averill hovered in the doorway. "Come in, Mistress." Sophia had wondered when Averill would speak to her about Olivia.

Averill shut the door behind her and bobbed, then accepted the guest chair Sophia gestured toward. "Thank you for letting Mistress Olivia stay," she said. "I lay awake half the night fretting about it, but I'd feel much worse today if she'd ridden through the gates."

"She seems a decent sort, and willing to go at your pace. I gather you told her about Elena."

"I felt I owed it to her."

"I'm hopeful for the two of you."

Averill's mouth turned up at the corners. "If she's as patient as she says she is, I am too."

Sophia expected her to leave, but Averill crossed her legs and leaned back in the chair. "With that out of the way, I want to talk to you about Emmey."

"Emmey?"

"I've spoken to a few other sisters, and we think we should accept her as a novice now, rather than waiting until she's sixteen. I said I'd speak to you about it." Averill lifted her hand. "Hear me out."

Still digesting Averill's words, Sophia intended to do just that.

"She's already here, and she's already ahead of the novices she'd join in two years. She can read. She can write." Averill checked off the points on her fingers. "She's already completed about two thirds of the lessons the novices do. She's almost an initiate, when you think about it. She's also a foreteller."

Sophia found her tongue. "And fourteen. Only fourteen." If she could have brought Lillian here when she was fourteen, they would have set out for the monastery two years earlier than they had.

"We're not proposing that she be an initiate right now. She does have that one-third of lessons to complete, but she can start them now."

"And live in the Novices Tower?"

"Well, that's the thing. I spoke to a few of the novices, the newer ones who aren't moving up to initiates yet, about whether they'd feel resentful if Emmey remained with Sister Maddy and Mistress Lillian but took some classes with them, and they said they'd prefer it. Not because they don't like Emmey, but because she's fourteen and if she lived in the Novices Tower, they'd worry that they'd have to temper some of their conversations about what sixteen- and seventeen-year-old girls talk about a lot. They'd also feel obligated to invite her to gatherings where she might not feel comfortable. They don't want Emmey to feel left out because they can't talk about certain things in the hallways, and so they have to socialize in their chambers without her."

Sophia nodded. "I can see their point."

"Mistress Lillian's name came up a few times, in the context of the novices inadvertently saying or doing something that upsets Emmey, and it getting back to the mistress. They're worried that they'd find themselves hopping around in agony because the mistress burned the soles of their feet. It will be a brave sister who takes Emmey on as a consort, let me tell you."

"Oh, dear. Let's hope Sister Maddy can exert some influence when the situation arises. But we're getting ahead of ourselves. Is it wise to ask Emmey to commit to the Order at fourteen?"

"She'd still have time to change her mind before she's marked and takes her vows, more time than most novices get if we decide she'll wait until she's eighteen to become an initiate. And that would make sense. She'd be the same age as the other initiates then."

"But what's the rush? Why don't we just wait until she's sixteen, and have her become a novice and live in the Novices Tower at that time?"

"Because she's already a novice in everything but name. I want to formalize her training as a scribe. I want her to record her dreams, and she has a research project she wants to do."

"Salbine's Covenant," Sophia murmured.

"Yes, and she'll need to learn proper research techniques. Sister Clara has said she'd be willing to teach Emmey the basics."

"I see. Emmey will certainly be busy."

"She'll need structure if she's to accomplish it all. Right now, she does whatever she pleases. We could make her adhere to a schedule, but would it be fair when she's not a sister? She deserves to be one now, with the robe, and with proper duties."

Sophia leaned forward. "Are you sure you're representing others? I'm hearing a lot of I's in your arguments."

"It was actually something Mistress Ivy said over lunch. She was saying Emmey knows more about some areas than the initiates do, and Mistress Phyllis jumped in and said Emmey would be welcome in her upcoming basic history class, and the conversation took off from there. Before we knew it, Sister Rose was there, and Sister Gwendolyn, and Mistress Edith, and Sister Garnet, and others too. We were all wondering why she couldn't become a novice now. Yes, she's fourteen, but if we wait until she's eighteen to move her up to initiate, she'll have four years to change her mind. But she won't. Mark my words, she won't."

Sophia believed Emmey wouldn't, either. She'd seen the certainty in Emmey's eyes that this was not only where she belonged, but where she wanted to be. And she was a foreteller, the only one on record who'd woken from a long slumber. If Emmey were to ask to leave, Sophia would do everything she could to persuade her to stay, and it would have nothing to do with how much she loved her.

"If you agree, I'll want her to spend most of her day in the library, learning how to become the cracker of a scribe I know she'll be. That will leave her time for one novice class a quarter. She'll have completed them all by the time she's ready to take her vows and train."

Emmey drawing the elements. The thought pleased Sophia immensely. "There's a problem with your proposal. If Maddy decides to go to Heath, Emmey insists that she must go with her. She says she saw it in one of her foretelling dreams."

"Only adepts are permitted to travel."

"Do you believe her foretelling dreams come from Salbine?"

Averill gave Sophia a withering look. "Where else would they come from?"

"Where else, indeed. If there's even a smidgen of a chance they do come from Salbine, and I agree with you that it's likely much more than a smidgen, Emmey goes to Heath."

Averill grunted. "A year away won't put her behind, because she's already ahead. She can always double up on her novice lessons and pull back on the scribing until she's on schedule to become an initiate when she's eighteen. Normally I wouldn't begin training a sister to scribe until she's finished her training with the elements. As I said, Emmey's already way ahead. Her research will be her own activity, not her primary duty."

Sophia largely agreed with Averill's arguments, but she didn't want to make this decision in haste. "Let me think about it and talk to some of the sisters you mentioned."

"That's all we can ask. Of course, we'll accept whatever you decide." Averill rose. "Thank you again for Mistress Olivia."

"Be kind to yourself, Averill. And be kind to Mistress Olivia when you can't be kind to yourself. You know my door is always open, if you need to talk."

"As is mine."

Sophia stared after Averill after she'd left. Her relationships with her sisters—her family—brought her great joy. If Emmey hadn't been marked, if she hadn't wanted to take the robe, she would have been forced to walk away from the relationships she'd forged here, from sisters who loved and cherished her. Sophia would have had no other choice but to push her out the gates, and the deed would have cast a long shadow, one that might have stayed with her until she left this realm. Fortunately Salbine had lifted the burden from her shoulders. Salbine had acted quite a lot lately. Sophia fervently believed it to be so.

She pushed back her chair, not to find Elizabeth this time, but to go to the chapel and thank her goddess.

~

MADDY SAT IN FRONT of the chapel, holding Lillian's warm hand and eagerly anticipating her first glimpse of Emmey. The morning prayer service had gone on longer than usual, and the chapel was packed, with sisters who normally attended early morning prayers here as well. Sister Lorelle had already been welcomed into the Merrin monastery, and so had Mistress Olivia, though that part of the service had been shorter than the part for Sister Lorelle. The mistress hadn't committed to this community yet. The rumour was that she'd remained behind because she wanted to stay for Mistress Averill. Sophia would know, but Sophia kept her own counsel on most matters, though she probably talked things over with Elizabeth.

The rumour explained why Emmey had invited Mistress Olivia to join her as she performed her first duty as a Salbine sister, which would take place immediately after the service. Because there would only be room for a handful of sisters, Maddy had wondered why Emmey had asked that Mistress Olivia be included, until the rumour had reached her ears. Then she'd understood.

She straightened when Sophia strode back into the sanctuary from one of the two chambers located behind it. Maddy craned her neck and saw Emmey. Her mind flashed back to the day she'd been thrown into a stinking cell and found herself in the presence of a filthy, smelly brown-haired girl—or so she'd thought. She'd never once thought she would sit in this chapel and see that same girl with her lovely blonde hair follow the abbess into the sanctuary in a Salbine robe. Tears sprang to her eyes. She squeezed Lillian's hand and risked a look at her. Lillian's glistening eyes made her heart swell. Was it all right that she was busting at the seams with pride? This was all Salbine's work, but Maddy couldn't help it.

Whispers and exclamations rose behind her. An unusual occurrence during a solemn occasion such as accepting a novice, but these were unusual circumstances. They were accepting someone they already knew and loved. She risked a glance behind her, then wished she hadn't when she spotted Rose dabbing at her eyes with a handkerchief, bringing on a fresh set of tears in her own. Her throat tight, she drank in the sight of Emmey in her robe, a deep blue one with a red collar and sleeves. "Blue for Lillian, and red for you," Emmey had said when she'd explained her choices. Emmey was more like Lillian in that she preferred plain clothing. Maddy had accepted the dash of red for what it was: a great gift to her. One she'd cherish.

She felt a hand on her right arm. "She looks so grown up," Elizabeth whispered hoarsely. "I usually don't sniffle at these things, but . . . " She cleared her throat.

"I know," Maddy whispered, wanting to pat Elizabeth's back.

While she still had the chance, she caught Emmey's eye and briefly let go of Lillian's hand so she could place her hand over her heart and nod. Emmey returned her nod, then faced Sophia. "It is time," Sophia intoned.

Emmey kneeled on the cushion that had been placed there for that purpose and pressed her palms together in front of her, but she didn't lower her head. She gazed up at Sophia.

"You now wear the robe." Sophia said.

"I do," Emmey said, loudly enough for those occupying the benches in the back to hear.

"Tell me what it means."

"Salbine has seared her mark upon me, because She has claimed me for Herself. Though few are marked, fewer are summoned, and even fewer answer the call, for they must leave behind what they know and give all to Salbine, and in return, receive the blessings of Her anointed, with no promise of Her gaze. Thus is the covenant between Salbine and those who fall into Her loving and indifferent embrace."

"Have you fallen into her embrace?"

"I have."

"When you are eighteen, I will ask you again. Until then, perform your duties, respect the others Salbine holds in Her arms, and pray daily for Salbine to not let you go."

"I will."

"Then rise and join your sisters."

She didn't have to go very far. In another departure from the way this part of a service usually went, sisters leaped to their feet and surged forward to greet Emmey. Maddy stayed where she was, knowing Emmey would find her and Lillian, and content to listen to the excited chatter around her. *Salbine, I thank you for throwing me into that cell and bringing Emmey to us. To me.* Would her life have been better if Salbine had granted her the elements, if she'd never left for Heath and still had her right hand? She couldn't say. All she knew for sure was that sitting here waiting for Emmey, she felt loved, and blessed, and couldn't imagine her life being any different.

"The robe suits her," Lillian said.

"How could we have missed it?" Maddy replied.

"What?"

"Emmey being marked. Emmey wanting to take the robe. We're the closest to her."

"That's precisely why," Elizabeth said. "We're the closest to her. We still saw the little girl who arrived clutching your hand. Other sisters could see the woman she's becoming."

That wasn't quite true. Maddy had known full well that Emmey was growing up and would walk out the gates. She'd told herself a story about how Emmey would meet some merchant or fall in love with a farmhand and forget the sisters on the hill, because the knowledge that Emmey was marked but had chosen to leave anyway would have been too much for Maddy to bear. And so it had been right under her nose, but she hadn't seen it, or had unconsciously refused to acknowledge it. Emmey had said something similar when she'd explained how she'd realized Salbine was calling her. But it didn't matter now. It had worked out exactly as it was supposed to, and Maddy couldn't be happier.

She stood when Emmey came toward them, hugged her tightly and wanted to pinch herself. Then she drew back and examined her. Strange. Though she'd never imagined Emmey in a Salbine robe and was seeing her up close in one for the first time, it was difficult to imagine her wearing anything else. "I don't know what to say." She drew Emmey to her for another quick embrace and held her at arm's length again. "I can't express how happy this makes me, not only that you're where you're meant to be, but that you're still with me and Lillian. I probably shouldn't say that now, when you've just taken the robe."

"I don't see why you shouldn't," Emmey said. "I doubt Salbine would be angry because we love each other and would have hated to be parted. Just because I love you and Lillian and would have hated every minute without you doesn't mean I love Salbine any less." She lifted her chin. "I bet I could find an argument in the library that says so."

"Not just a scribe, but a scholar too," Lillian muttered, but she was smiling. "Come here, little mite."

Maddy blinked away her tears and waited for them to part. Emmey hugged Elizabeth, then sat between her and Maddy. Everyone else also returned to their places.

"Thank you for enthusiastically welcoming our newest novice," Sophia said, making everyone laugh.

Maddy only half listened as Sophia closed the service. She kept glancing at Emmey, still marvelling at how it had all turned out. Emmey, a Salbine sister. May Salbine be praised!

~

EMMEY FOLLOWED MISTRESS AVERILL into her office and waited for her invited guests to file in behind her. The mistress swept her arm toward Emmey's habitual stool. "Shall we?"

She slid onto the stool and waited for Mistress Averill to place the parchment in front of her, the parchment that contained the title of the book of poems she'd scribed, along with Sister Annora, the poet's name. But the title page wasn't complete.

"Tomorrow you'll watch me bind the book," Mistress Averill said. "Your first lesson in book binding."

Emmey couldn't wait.

"I've already added your tome to the library, so we're all set."

Her tome. Sophia had presented it to her yesterday. Emmey had read the first two pages—from Rose and Nora—and had shut the book, not wanting to stand at the front of the chapel today with red, puffy eyes. She'd savour it, read a page a day, which would be all she could bear, in a good way. Because she was staying, there were blank pages at the end of the book, so both herself and her sisters could add more about her over time.

Mistress Averill coughed. "Whenever you're ready."

Emmey took a moment to close her eyes and pray. *Thank you Salbine. Thank you for bringing me here. Your will be done.* She opened her eyes and glanced over her shoulder at those behind her. Maddy, Lillian, Sophia, Elizabeth, Rose, Nora, Mistress Averill, and yes, Mistress Olivia, who Emmey knew would become someone special. She'd also invited Sisters Grace, Abigail, and Gwendolyn. She'd eaten more meals with them than she could count and had great affection for all three of them. If she'd been brave enough, she would have asked for Sister Dolores, but her courage had failed her, and now, sitting here and seeing the shining faces and eyes of those she dearly loved, she realized Sister Dolores would have been out of place. Emmey would always love her as a sister, but those other feelings would pass, unlike the love and bond she shared with those gathered here.

She turned back to the writing podium, lifted a quill and dipped it in ink, and bent over the parchment. Certain that she was meant to be here, in this chamber with her sisters, from the moment she was born, she scribed the words she was sure she'd write many more times in the years to come: *Scribed by Sister Emmey, of the Merrin monastery.*

Other Books by Sarah Ettritch

Thank you for reading *Salbine's Embrace.*

Books set in the Salbine world

The Salbine Sisters
Playing With Fire
Rose and Nora
(to get *Playing With Fire*, sign up for Sarah's email list at
sarahettritch.com/salbine)

The Rymellan Series

Disobedience Means Death
Shattered Lives
The Triad
Identity Crisis

The Deiform Fellowship Series

The Atheist
The Cult
Unseen Bonds
Scarred Souls

The Daros Chronicles

Pawns and Puzzles
Fate or Folly

Other Titles

Threaded Through Time
The Missing Comatose Woman

Their Last Hope
The Voice in My Head
The Perfect Christmas Gift

Thanks for reading!